The Spirit Hunter

William Wolfe

The Spirit Hunter

William Wolfe

The Spirit Hunter

ISBN: 978-1-7750856-0-7

Printed in the United States of America
Published simultaneously in Canada by

INFINITY  PRESS

First Edition

www.williamwolfeauthor.com

William Wolfe

The Spirit Hunter

Author's Note

This book is based on some true events and some writer's embellishment and certain persons' names have been changed in order to protect their privacy. In some descriptions of events changes have been made to better describe the event and dialogue has been altered to make it easier to understand, and specifically the court dialogue has been altered however the sources are identified in the acknowledgements section.

Search for and find your Spirit and when you do embrace it, use it, copy it, live with it, and succeed in life while being it.

For Celia,
our Children,
and the Grandchildren.....
dream always, follow your dreams,
and make your dreams reality.

William Wolfe

ACKNOWLEDGMENTS

I am indebted to those who wrote before me.

To Ian Fleming, who experienced and then wrote about the life of a Secret Agent, licensed to kill, who brought James Bond to life, and then created a multi-million dollar franchise , which still lives to this day. As a teenager I could not put down his novels, sometimes reading through the night, in order to absorb every exciting moment as I moved from chapter to chapter.

Thanks to Arthur Lismer of the famous Group of Seven who wrote with his pencil and paint creating real life images as he reported on a fire or accident before cameras recorded such events. Who taught us art history and how to select colors and apply paint on canvas and record history.

To John Grisham who using his experience as a working lawyer continues to narrate complex fascinating stories with tight plots, neat twists and memorable characters.

To Bill who in St. Petersburg, Florida gave us a personal tour of the Salvador Dali Museum, and described in intricate detail the paintings and drawings that from afar looked strange and out of place but up close one could see wondrous figures and scenes that only someone as knowledgeable as Bill could pull out of the Dali mindset.

I am not now an Ian Fleming or a John Grisham and this is my first novel , but I always thought of myself as a good storyteller and teacher, and I have attempted to paint pictures with words and bring action to life so that you the reader can see the story, the characters, the scenery before you as if you were right there. Enjoy the read and may your Spirit be with you!

THE SPIRIT HUNTER

The great blue heron sits hunched and forlorn at the edge of the marsh, the gusts of raw wind periodically ruffling feathers on its head.

Occasionally, it would lean forward and dabble in the water like an old man on a park bench poking in a pool with his sun-bleached cane.

Only when a hawk flapped and glided across the valley would the heron cock its head to check on the other's flight.

The turkey vulture drifts down from further north, soaring along the ridges and sweeping down over the lowlands. Its circling flight seems effortless, its search for a carrion meal endless.

On two-toned wings of black and gray, the turkey vulture tips and glides above the blazed landscape, an unhurried migrant travelling only by the outward weather conditions or by some *inner seasonal clock. The Canada goose courses across the heavens, a single animated body in a large pulsating flock. Down it comes from the nesting grounds on the Hudson Bay lowlands to the tidal flats of the James Bay estuaries. Here on Scugog Lake it gathers friends and strength for the next leg of its journey.*

Art Briggs-Jude, Correspondent
The Scugog Tribune

ONE

"He rides without a helmet because he rides without a head". said Elayne Christofaro, Port Perry's chief librarian, part-time psychic, card reader and fortune teller.

"A modern day Ichabod Crane on a Harley instead of a horse."

Elayne knew this story well, as she had repeated it for several years, always to an interested audience of between thirty and fifty fascinated souls. As she continued on about the local legend the sun was slowly disappearing behind the town of Port Perry. Shadows of the town's buildings stretched out over Lake Scugog as Halloween Eve's black darkness was replacing the daylight. A full ivory white moon sat over the ridge to the east. A mirror image lay in the lake, like a huge underwater light protecting its' territory. Quiet eerie time when day changes into night. Forbidding cold black replaces warm white.

The faithful were gathering near the water's edge. They would soon witness the unfolding of one of the mysteries of their world. Fathers and mothers were setting up their beach chairs, laying down blankets. Families were jockeying for the best place to observe what was to come.

The temperature was balmy for the last day of October in the north east. Light jackets and sweaters were all that were required to keep the night chill at bay.

Mayor Kay Aldred rested on the stone pedestal of the statue of the founder of Port Perry. She watched with anticipation of an event that she had witnessed many times before She knew everyone who was there. Twenty-one years as Mayor of the town. Kay Aldred had become a mother to all. She had protected her beloved little town and it's children. like a mother hen protects her chicks. She was determined that nothing would harm them, nothing. Suddenly the sound of a four cylinder engine with too many miles on it to be alive disturbed Kay's rest.

Cory Littlehorn downshifted from fourth to second and eased up on the clutch. His ten year old nicely preserved Honda civic convertible grunted and cursed as it hiccupped over the hill onto main street. Cory's Boston Red Sock's Baseball hat was perched down on top of his jet-black hair, and his police-style mirror sunglasses sat on his little hook nose perhaps an imitation of the state troopers that he frequently had seen on his travels to Ithaca and back. Cornell University windbreaker and khaki shorts, with a mustard stain near the brown leather belted waist, dirty sneakers, and a start of a two day beard on his weathered face, with the weight of his mission on his shoulders.

It had been a long run-almost six hours, two cheeseburgers, two fries, three cokes, a chocolate bar, and a quart of oil from Ithaca. The little Honda that could almost eased by the faithful when Cory picked out Elayne standing by the children's swing set.

Elayne Christofaro could always be picked out from a crowd. She always wore red and always dressed weird. From the day she was born she was weird-out of place; or at least out of this place! She had spent some time in Hawaii and rumor was she had got married there to some local but something happened that she does not talk about.

Now there she was, twenty-six weird years of age. Everyone in town thought she was a bit touched.She believed in the hereafter, in Ghosts, and Goblins and such. There was only one reason people sort of respected her, she had scored the highest twice on the school I.Q. exams and rumor was that her I.Q. was Mensa level.

And to top it off she was a knockout, a real beauty. Red hair now, of course. Slim, trim five foot seven beauty. Long suntanned legs covered from the mid thigh up by a red and white sleeveless polka dot dress that covered a slim body that was only fed vegetarian style foods. A tanned face that only a Hollywood Model could have, decorated with dangling earrings and topped off by a white enormous brimmed hat. She controlled everything and everyone around her.

Elayne jumped out into the street right into the Honda's path. Cory jammed on the brakes, forgot the clutch, and the civic lurched forward, inhaled, and stalled.

"Elayne, are you crazy?" he yelled out in astonishment. Elayne ignored his outburst with a very calm question."Cory, I thought you were immersed in your law books at Ithaca, and couldn't make it up this year?" Elayne stated, wondering why he was there.

"I promised my Grandfather I'd be here". "Well, as long as you're here take me to Ghost Road" she implored."

"You know I don't like going there on Halloween", he said.

Elayne knew what button to push. She put her hands in her armpits and moved her elbows up and down imitating a bird trying to fly.

"Come on. What are you Chicken?Buc,Buc,Buc" One chicken and three Buc, Bucs and Cory Littlehorn, with the short fuse, shrugged

"Ok, Ok, Get in".

The passenger side door squealed as Elayne opened it, pushed aside the discarded fast food bag and empty coke cans, and slid onto the cracked seat. The interior of the car smelled like a workout room at school after twenty kids had lifted weights , sweated and stunk up the place.

Elayne had known Cory since she was a child and as a teenager had dated him several times, even though he was an "Island Indian". She couldn't resist his good looks-his dark black hair, cleft chin, and muscular build.

Besides his Grandfather was Chief and he would someday be chief, so it was like, dating royalty. Cory raced the civic onto the causeway, up the hill past George's bait shop and left onto Island Road.

"Cory. Take it easy. You'll end up in a ditch beside the road, and me with you." Elayne yelled out. She had to yell as the wind whipped by them, with the top down, words were hard to hear.

Cory noticed that Harold Bains had already cleared his field and had the bundles ready for storage. The Scugog Island General Store was already closed for the evening, and up in the distance on the right sat the unfinished steel frame of the Great Blue Heron Casino, in this twilight looking like the skeleton of a monstrous dinosaur whale-like, beached, dead and available to be destroyed by nature's wind and fury.

"Stop right here. Here where Ghost Road meets Island Road. This is the spot, on this side, the south side. He never crosses over to the south side".

Cory parked the civic on the gravel edge and awaited what was to come. His heart started to race as fear and apprehension took over. He always feared what he knew would come, and what he didn't know was coming. He was brought up with Spirits and Ghosts and such and he feared them-and his heart started beating fast at what was to come.

Goosebumps first appeared on Viola Poole's arms. She ran her hand over her head of close cropped hair and her fingers formed a curve over her eyebrows. The makeshift binoculars and squinting convinced her that she had spotted the light. Still her education and professionalism held her voice back until she was positive, and then Viola Poole, Port Perry's assistant chief Librarian finally yelled out with conviction.

"There. There it is! See? A white light across the lake, a few feet above the level of the road."

The faithful saw the light and watched as it dipped lower and then higher, always moving. A dim dull light for several seconds, and then astonishingly a bright iridescent white light for several more. The light danced, weaved and bobbed as it moved from north to south along the far shore. Kay Aldred and others of the faithful had seen the light each year.

The legend of the light began around the late 1970s,but some say it has been around much longer. Despite her many sightings, the mayor remained baffled by the light.

"There is something to it but I don't know what it is," she whispered to Viola."Sometimes you see the light and sometimes you don't. It's something you have to see to believe."

On Island Road Cory could barely make out a ball of yellowish/white light floating eerily across the night sky. The basketball sized sphere was several hundred feet away. It was heading in their direction. The light was getting brighter as it approached. It looked exactly like the headlight of a motorcycle.

"Come on Elayne, it's getting awfully close!" Cory said nervously. "Don't worry yourself it never crosses the road" She reassured him. Cory hoped Elayne was right. The light was blinding as it crossed the intersection of Island Road and Ghost Road, and that recurring vision of the bag in the scooter basket and the nightmares it had brought to Cory flashed before his eyes; and he recalled a story that his aunt had told him well.

Two

Cory remembered his Great Aunt Sara's story as if it were told to him yesterday and not almost fifteen years ago when he was just a teen, and rumors and innuendo were still to this day swirling around and through his people, the" Mississauga" like a puzzle to be solved. And everyone said Aunt Sara was talking crazy talk. And most of the time it sounded like crazy talk. She mixed languages, sometimes in the white man's words; sometimes in the Mississauga words; sometimes in words nobody understood.

The problem is that sometimes those mixed up words went round and round in Cory's head like it was someone there beside her talking crazy talk.

"You are not the one. You are not the one. The one is out there. It is not you. You are not the one." She kept repeating over and over. Most of us ignored her, so she told me the storey.

" The Mississauga knew the drill. The squaws squatted, and the Warriors worried with the Elders deep in thought. The question was: Would their future Chief arrive today, on this frigid day in February? or would a war of who should be Chief break out? Josephine , the Eldest of the squaws pondered.

The grey smoke spiraling up from the medical centre gave them no clue. Seven hours had passed since the future Chief's mother was rushed into the centre and the word had passed through the village that today could be the day.

The sun was just appearing over Simha's Mountain to the East when the future Chief's mother eased into the bed in the centre. She was attended to by three experienced midwifes all being Mississauga; and they did their best to help ease her pain as the hours slowly moved on.

After Eight hours with no future Chief appearing two tribal elders paid a visit as tradition dictated.

"You understand that if you do not produce a future Chief, then being the leader of our tribe will be disputed? stated Amok Kinshu, one of the elders."And if that creation is not your first born the council will reject him?"Amok added.

"Please leave her alone!" demanded Elsa, the youngest of the midwives. "Yes. Get out! She knows. She knows. Go on, Get out!" echoed Josephine. Amok, as the Elders were leaving repeated" First born, a boy, First born".

Twelve hours more had now passed and the smoke was still grey. The sun had moved out over the lake and was just starting to disappear behind the town's grey/white buildings on water street. The bright red scooter barely made a sound as it was driven past the church and the single pump gas station at the corner of Purdy's Trail.

Whoever was driving this little red scooter was very careful to keep it as quiet as possible as it came to a stop on the right side of the medical centre next to the very tall Cedar trees.

In fact the scooter putt-putted not even breaking the quiet of the cold dark February night. You had to be within 20 feet to hear the putt-putt and the night quiet was not being disturbed.

The centre was raised about three feet above ground and sat on cinder blocks to guard against any spring flooding that might occur. Suddenly near the middle of the centre a ladder dropped down to the ground and a dark figure appeared with a small sports bag like the type to carry tennis racquets or such.

The crawl under the centre building was difficult but the bag was passed to the scooter driver as if gold or drugs or something valuable was being let go. The bag was securely in the scooter basket and the driver sulked off using a path between the cedars it seemed so as not to be heard or seen, and so he wasn't.

The hour hand on the one hundred year old clock on the city hall tower had just struck eleven and it was close to one hour since the scooter's escape when the tribe discovered the joyous news.

The smoke had turned white. The future Chief had arrived.

Amok and the other elders returned to the centre to verify and participate in the celebrations.

"He has his father's look" said one.

"No, his nose and ears tell us he is of his mother's heritage" insisted another. "No matter" confirmed Amok. "He is first born of a First born of a Chief". "So he is our future Chief. No matter what he looks like. Let the other tribes know!"

The Red scooter made it through the cold , damp February night and the driver was careful with his valuable package that sat in his basket.

12,020 miles showed on his speedometer and he had remembered to look at his speedometer at the medical centre and noticed he had just hit twelve thousand so as the numbers clicked over to 12,020 he pulled up to the house with the double front French style doors , the gold leaf trim on the doors at the end of the circular driveway that even tonight contained three exotic cars including a Bentley and Mercedes.

The transaction was swift without any words being passed between the driver and the brown skinned rather diminutive woman who answered the door. The package in the basket was exchanged for an envelope that was too fat to just contain a letter. The driver verified its' contents and sped off into the

February night satisfied with a task well done and hoped that the package would be taken care of and that the secret of its' contents would never be revealed. He avoided the Bentley and had to maneuver around the Mercedes.

Great Aunt Sarah's secret would not be revealed as long as everyone dismissed her talk as crazy talk.

There was an usual smell lingering in the air outside , that of the aroma of something sweet and piney, with hints of citrus, lemon and spice. The thoughts of Christmas swirled around the head of the scooter driver, although it was dead of winter in February. Bright green buds ,with frost generously sprinkled over them and coated in light orange hair, rich with trichomes, lined the circular driveway like little gnomes guarding a sacred path to the wizard's castle. In fact twenty or so real garden gnomes with red pointy hats interspersed with the bright green buds, and the driver chuckled as he passed each one for he noticed their faces, although bearded resembled the master of the house.

Little signs were propped up against each one, and the driver smiled as he passed, and read 'Squinty, Itchy, Gassy, Saggy, Cranky, Gimpy and Snoozy', obviously a reference to Disneys' Snow White and the Seven Dwarfs, of course taking a little literary license by changing the names. There were two empty spaces along the row of gnomes, probably some locals stole two, and sent photos of the two to the owner , holding them hostage, as a practical joke, which had become popular to do. The driver had thoughts of taking one himself, but decided against it, as they were quite large, almost 2 feet high.

Yes, Great Aunt Sarah's secret would not be revealed as long as everyone dismissed her talk as crazy talk.

Three

Cory could hear Elayne prodding him "Cory, Cory wake up!" "Cory, wake up! It's gone. The Ghost Rider is gone" She shouted. And she was right.

The blinding headlight had flickered and disappeared into the darkness as mysteriously as it had appeared. Fog lingered filling the air with a pungent, sulphur-smelling odor reminiscent of manure or pulp mills, or like dead fish or sewer water. Cory's eyes stung while the smell stuck around.

" It's gone", sighed Cory, his heart beating a thousand times per second. "Sorry, Elayne. I guess the stress caused me to black out, and I was thinking about something else"."A red scooter and a mysterious package. My Aunt Sara and crazy talk; and Cory certainly would not be the one to reveal anything but her words" Search and Hunt for the Spirit" was deeply embedded in his brain, and he could't shake it's possible importance for his future.

"It was him," Elayne stated ignoring Cory's explanation. We've just had an encounter with Scugog Island's headless ghost rider."

"You know what Elayne? I don't believe in that crap, and to tell you the truth, I don't want to."

"Then what was it?"queried Elayne."

"I don't know, maybe the reflections of car headlights coming from West Quarter line Road."Answered Cory. "Listen Elayne. I'm probably the only real red blooded Ojibway Indian to not believe in Myths & Spirits, Ghosts included. Ya sure I'm proud of my heritage, but I still have nightmares from the stories my father told me as a child. Stories of The Great Spirit, the Vision, Gitche Manitou, and all that.

And you know my father was drunk most of the time so I couldn't tell if his stories were passed down through the generations or made up in a drunken stupor."

"Cory, you're father died in his forties, right?"

"Ya, drank himself to death. Liver disease. No Ojibway medicine man could save him. Anyway Elayne the reason I'm here is my grandfather is close to death himself and I promised him I would see him." "What happened to your mother?"

"Drowned in a freak accident. I was five years old. My Grandfather brought me up". Cory explained.

"How old is he?"She asked."

"Eighty-Seven" stated Cory."And you know he wanted to finish that Blue Heron Casino before he died. It doesn't look like he will do that. Look at it". Cory pointed to the blue metal skeletal hulk on the horizon.

"It's been ten years since construction was halted.

My people, The Mississauga had hope. They had hope that the Casino would generate profits that could help them sustain their lives, educate their children, buy land, build better lives. My grandfather, the Chief gave them that hope, but hope died when construction shut down. Now The Great Blue Heron Casino is a rusting blue metal skeleton of steel wasting away in a sea of weeds and cow dung. What a pity. What a waste."

"Cory, you're right. You're 100% right. Come on let's get out of here. I have an extra bed at my place if you need it."

"What do you mean extra bed? You have that huge bed with only you to take up all that space."

Elayne thought for a moment and said "Let's go and we will see when we get there."

"Promises, Promises" Cory exclaimed.

Cory always liked Elayne. They had dated a few times as teenagers, but she was rarely around town as she had been sent out of town to attend private school. Cory had dated a few girls but had an inferiority complex thinking he never had a chance because there existed underlying racism in that town and boys of color were just playthings to the white girls. He in turn didn't want to date any Native Girls so he was stuck in a real no man's land. Cory yearned for affection as his alcoholic father never showed any towards him; and his mother although affectionate, died when he was just five years old.

His Grandfather took him under his wing but acted like he was a General in the Army and Cory was an enlisted man. Tough, strict, no laughter in the house. Always being trained and groomed to take over as Chief someday. One day when Cory was twelve his Grandfather set up a bed of charcoal, poured kerosene over and lit the charcoal, and after thirty minutes when the charcoal was on fire, Grandfather duplicated Tony Robbins 'fire walk' and the method of training the mind to believe the hot coals would not burn the bottoms of the feet and forced Cory to run across the hot coals. Cory's feet were burned badly and he kept running until he reached the lake, where he immediately jumped in to cool off his burning feet. An experiment gone wrong, but his Grandfather believed this had made Cory into a man, a warrior , a Chief, and that by running over the burning coals evil spirits would be driven away.

There it was just like he remembered, a neat white country cottage set back about 100 yards from the road. The kind of country cottage where you knew you would find flowerpots on the wind sills, calico curtains held apart with little ribbons, flowered tea cups sitting on the mantle over the fireplace as if in a museum of 19th century porcelain, glassware and pottery. The standard living room, dining room and kitchen downstairs and the three bedrooms upstairs, all decorated with floral wallpaper. The standard cat slinking on the couch facing a roaring fireplace. The smell of fresh baked bread coming from the kitchen at the back of the neat country cottage.

Elayne pushed open the door and the animal jumped out and overpowered Cory. A 250 pound St. Bernard can easily push a 170 pound unsuspecting human onto the cold hard ground with a resounding thud. This was no little cat from a country cottage with calico curtains. This was a big slobbering ,bad breath, living animal who lay over Cory like a huge heavy oversized bearskin rug.

"Bernie, get off him right now!"yelled Elayne. Bernie the St. Bernard didn't move.

"Come on Bernie. Get up!"she deplored. Bernie, the lookalike bear skin rug preferred to lie spread out all over Cory.

"Elayne , Will you do something? And what is this Bernie business?" Elayne pulled at Bernie's collar. Elayne pushed playfully into Bernie's ribs. Elayne tugged at Bernie's ear. Elayne tried again-

"Bernie Baby, Please get off of little teeny tiny weenie Corey." Bernie Baby didn't move.
This 250 pounds of slobbering , dripping, bad breath was beginning to get to Cory. Six hours driving up from Ithaca, a headless ghost rider, and now a 250 pound weight sitting on his stomach, chest and face.

The shrill almost eardrum piercing sound coming from the cabin split the twilight into mirror-like broken pieces of glass.

"Bernieeee, suppperrrrrrr" screeched Elayne's Aunt Gloria. The magic words had been spoken. The beast had been tamed. The giant behemoth lifted his head and purred. Seconds later the bovine, bulky hound lumbered off to his feast, called by his master to savor his nightly fare.

Cory, still stunned and exhausted by this event, lay on the ground and whispered" What was that?"

"That was Bernie. Lovable Bernie, my St-Bernard".

"Thanks for warning me! If it wasn't for your aunt I'd still be a welcome mat for Gargantua."

"Oh, come on, it wasn't that bad!"

"Oh yeah! Look who's talking. You were up there while I was down here."

"Ok. Alright. I'm sorry. Let's go in and eat. I'm famished". No calico curtains. No teacups on the mantle. No flower wallpaper here. Cory noticed.

Elayne pushed the heavily-loaded bead curtain aside and immediately upon entering the cottage the burning incense hit Cory's nostrils with a sharp pungent blow. His eyes began to tear and he could barely see the wood table through the haze.

"Hey, could you cut down the smoke a little? It's making my eyes water." "I see enough smoke when I visit my Grandfather in his village".

A mammoth meal , and a content St-Bernard lay sprawled out next to the fireplace. The drive up from Ithaca, a head-on meeting with a headless ghost rider, and a healthy dose of Elayne's great cooking induced Cory to fall dead asleep on the couch in front of the glowing fire. A fire that occasionally sparked as it tried to postpone the inevitable end.

Elayne glanced at the clock on the mantle as she eased Cory's legs onto the couch; covered him with the nearest blanket, and observed that it was ten minutes to midnight. She softly made her way to the bedroom, passing her aunt's room while saying "Goodnight!", and turned into her room. She thought 'What a day! What a day!"

Four

What a party was had last night.

A representative from each of the tribes attended.

Only because it was Cory's twenty first birthday. Each one brought tributes, gifts and salutations.

Only because Cory was a future Chief. Only because he had only five years to go to be officially Chief or if his grandfather 'bit the dust' before. Only because they knew it was like he would be the Godfather of the Tribes so they had to make nice.

And the fortune teller, palm reader, and all around clairvoyant Great Aunt Sarah had predicted a snow storm the next day. Cory was excited. He barely slept all night.

He woke up at 3:00 am shouting "Go Bernie! Go!"He woke up at 5:33 am after having a vision of being lost in a snowstorm. Cory awoke at 6:48 am, ran to the window, pushed the blanket aside that covered the dirt infested window, and shouted "Unbelievable! An unbelievable snow storm!".

He raced to put on his snow suit, mukluks , musher gloves, tuque, and he turned the tuque around so the Boston Bruins Logo was in back not front. He ran past the community center , the birthing unit, the village grocery, and he jogged up the hill past Great Aunt Sarah's shack yelling.

"Thank you! Thank You! Great, Great Aunt Sarah. Thank you for the snow. Thank you for the mukluks. Thank you for"-well , he had no more time for any more thank you. He had arrived, and heard the barking. Bernie was already outside, had finished his business, and was ready to go. Cory untied him and walked him to the shed.

The door creaked open as all shed doors should with the snow falling fast and because snow had fallen all night everything was covered with the thick white powder. Cory could barely see through the darkness in the shed but located the sled.

A sled in a shed. It sounded like a Dr. Seuss book. "A sled in a shed. A sled like no other in a shed. A shed that contained only one sled. Now we will go sledding with the sled in the shed." Thought Cory. "Alright enough Dr. Seuss; He told Bernie".

Cory dragged the sled out and set it up outside the shed. He attached a make-shift harness and buckled in Bernie in front, just like when Santa's helpers arrange the reindeer, or so he imagined.

He pulled out the cushions that Great Aunt Sarah had sewn together for him and his sled and he set them down and punched them playfully a few times to push them in and settle them against the wood railing that acted as a railing around the sides and back of the sled. Cory found the white blanket with green, gold, and red stripes hanging on the wall and put it over the sled and tucked it in as if he was making a bed at the Waldorf-Astoria.

Next he retrieved the bamboo pole that he needed to direct Bernie. Ok. He thought. We are ready to go.

Cory closed the shed door, which creaked and groaned , and fastened the latch. Ok. We are ready to go. He thought again. The snow was coming down in buckets now. Like Cats and Dogs the whites say.

Cory forgot he needed goggles.

Bernie was now lying down with his head on his paws looking up at Cory every so often just to check up on what he was up to. He opened the shed latch, creaked open the door, and looked for goggles and couldn't find any. He rummaged through the picture frames, the old curtains, the skis, the broken chairs and threw into the back old boots, shoes, tennis rackets, lacrosse racquets , lamps, trinkets, and he found Uncle Jimmy-Two-Shoes' horn rimmed black spectacles.

"These will have to do" He exclaimed to Bernie. He slammed the shed door, ran up to Bernie and punched him playfully on the nose.

"Bernie, get up!" He pleaded. "Get up!"

To his surprise Bernie, the behemoth rose, and stood straight on all four legs ready to go into action, so Cory jumped into the sled, fell down on his ass, grabbed the pole and directed Bernie with a "Mush, Mush! Let's go" and a gentle touch with the pole.

Bernie sprang into action. He strained against the straps of the harness, tried to push with his rear legs and tried to move his front legs and the straps creaked and stretched but the sled went nowhere.

Bernie tried again and then decided to lie down admitting defeat. Cory immediately knew what the problem was- A lot of Bernie but not enough to move him and the sled. One dog power was not enough when a sled normally is equipped with nine dogs. He needed to round up more Bernie(s).

"Bernie, stay here! He yelled", and he knew Bernie had no problem with staying put as he was already exhausted from trying to pull a man and a sleigh himself. Cory ran past Great Aunt Sarah's and down the road to the community centre where he spotted two small animals that seemed to resemble dogs, although they could have been wolves for in the early morning dawn light and snow falling he wasn't sure. He didn't care. He grabbed them by the neck and dragged them down to the sleigh. More scrounging through the shed until he could pick out more straps and stuff to use as harnesses which he put around the necks of these two animals.

He knew where he could find some other volunteers. He ran up the road away from the town and found Little Georges' cabin. Twin German Hounds tied up in the back would do just fine. Little

George had brought them up from puppies and they knew him and did not make a fuss. They were already tied with harnesses so he untied them and they walked nicely back down the road with him as if they knew exactly what their future task would be. Little George had named them Hansel and Gretel although right now he didn't have time to determine who was who. That was it. Five dogs and Cory was ready to go. The snow was still falling.

"Let's Go Bernie! Get Up" Cory pushed him with the stick and Bernie stood up while the other four were trying to get all twisted up in the make shift harnesses. Once Bernie got going in the correct direction the other four followed and they were on their way, gliding over the snow like it was butter.

"Yea Bernie Yea!" Cory shouted. "Let's go. Move it. Yea Let's go" He at that time did not know any musher language and he was sure his team of mutts would not understand anyway.

"Go Hansel! Go Gretel!" He yelled.

"Go Little George's Twins." He was excited. They were speeding down the road but up ahead Cory could sense trouble. The road makes an abrupt right turn almost at a 45 degree angle.

"Bernie go right. Bernie go right. Bernie please go right". Bernie went right, unfortunately Hansel, Gretel and the twins didn't.

The four animals plowed into the forest and Bernie got dragged back with them. Cory didn't know Hansel and Gretel were so strong. His sled went over the edge of the road at the curve and became airborne with just enough momentum to lodge in the fork of the tree where it had been split years ago by lightning.

Cory was Ok. He survived. He landed on a pile of snow that cushioned his fall while Uncle Jimmy-Two-Shoes' glasses flew off somewhere into space. The White Blanket dislodged itself and landed on top of Bernie and the sled was ok. What a ride! Thought Cory. The Iditarod itch was firmly in place.

Five

Cory started to scratch the itch.
But the more he scratched the more it itched.
"Cory, what kind of contraption is that?" Elayne seemed puzzled.
"I am determined to be a musher and run dogs and a sled in the Iditarod. This is my test and practice vehicle."
"The Idiotrod? What's that?"
"Not Idiotrod! Iditarod Elayne". Cory corrected her.
"The Iditarod Trail Sled Dog Race that was first run to Nome , Alaska in 1973 and now starts in Anchorage at the corner of 4th and "D"."

"What does Iditarod mean?" She questioned.

"Iditarod is an Ingalik Indian word which means clear water and names the river on which the town of Iditarod was built and also means distant place.

The trail is a network of more than 2,300 miles once used by ancient native hunters, then by Russian explorers and early 20th century gold seekers".

The Alaskan gold rush brought renewed interest in the use of sled dogs as transportation.

Most gold camps were accessible only by dogsled in the winter. Everything that moved during the frozen season moved by dog team, prospectors, trappers, doctors, mail, commerce, trade, and transportation of supplies. If it needed to move in the winter it was moved by sled dogs.

Sled dogs were used to deliver the mail in Alaska during the late 1800s and early 1900s and Malamutes were the favored breed with teams averaging 8 to 10 dogs. Dogs were capable of delivering mail and conditions that would stop boats, trains, and horses. Each team hauled between 500 and 700 pounds of mail.

Recreational mushing came into place to maintain the tradition of dog mushing. The desire for first larger, stronger, load pulling dogs changed to one for faster dogs with high endurance used in racing, which caused the dogs to develop later than they were historically.

In 1925, there was a diphtheria outbreak in

Nome, Alaska and there was not enough serum in Nome to treat the number of people in the area affected by the disease. There was serum in a town 700 miles away and accessible only by dogsled. A dogsled relay was set up by the villages and 20 teams work together to relay the serum to Nome. The serum reached Nome in six days.

The Iditarod trail was established on a path between the two towns. In 1973 the Iditarod was established by Joe Redington Senior and the first race was won by Dick Wilmarth who took three weeks to complete the race. Today's Iditarod is a 1100 mile long endurance sled dog race that usually lasts for 10 to 11 days, weather permitting. The winner of the race receives a prize of US $50,000, and the race ends when the last musher either drops out of the race or crosses the finish line in Nome.

"That's wonderful history, Cory! But how the hell are you going to get proper sled dogs to compete in a race like that?"
Cory could not answer that. He had no idea where he was going to get proper sled dogs as Elaine called them. Of course Bernie, the twins, and any other little mutts that he would find around here would not be suitable. Well maybe Bernie but nobody else. He would need dogs that can race through blizzards, subzero temperatures, survive gale force winds where the wind chill can reach -

100° F. He would need 16 Alaskan Huskies to compete.

Of course he might have an advantage in that the best Alaskan Huskies come from native villages in Alaska and northern Canada, where of course he could contact his cousins who might be able to help him.

"Elayne, Elayne, that's no problem all I need to do is to contact my cousins in northern Canada and I am sure that they will get me the best Alaskan Huskies that will assist me in what is known as the last great race on Earth."

"Cory when do you plan to run this last great race?"

"Elayne I would like to practice this year and run in next year's race which starts on the first Saturday in March with the first checkpoint on fourth Avenue in downtown Anchorage, Alaska. It's a great race and it's an honor just to be allowed to compete. The teams continue through several miles of city streets and city trails before reaching the foothills to the east of Anchorage and the teams pass through several checkpoints and within the first 100 miles the teams travel through "Moose Alley", where in the past several teams have had their chances of continuing stopped by coming up against a Moose."

"Cory I think you're dreaming. How are you going to be able to afford the cost of participating in a race like that? And don't you have to enter some qualification races?"

"Elayne you are absolutely right! There are three smaller races in order to qualify for the Iditarod so I will first train to run those smaller races and I believe that I have it in my blood to win. As far as the cost it is probably between $20-$30,000 which covers the cost of lightweight gear including thousands of booties and quick change runners, special high energy dog foods, dairy care, and breeding costs. The biggest cost is probably the cost of getting the sled and the dogs to the race and also dog food. But I think I can cut costs by having my cousins supply dogs as close as possible to the race start and probably my cousins will contribute to the cost of being in the race."

"Cory I don't like what you're doing. I think that the Iditarod race that you are talking about is dog abuse, whether or not it is also an adventure or a test of human perseverance. I am sure that many dogs have died and have been injured during those races in the past. Pushing dogs beyond their endurance or capabilities is absolutely cruel and I don't want you to do it."

"Elayne I assure you that I will take care of my dogs and that none of them will suffer any hardships and that I guarantee you that I will complete the race and finish in Nome with every dog that I start with even if I have to put any of the tired or exhausted Huskies into the sled with me to finish the race."

"My cousins are Athabascan's and live in the village of Nikolai and I will contact them tomorrow to see if they have any dogs that I can use."

"Cory it seems like a great adventure but is there anything that you might be afraid of that may get in your way during this great adventure?"

"Yes there is one thing that I'm afraid of and that is hallucinations. The greatest hazard in the long stretch covering 10, 11, or 12 days is that there is a tremendous amount of sleep deprivation and many mushers have reported hallucinations. You know, Elayne that I am afraid of ghosts and goblins and spirits and such. I can train for the cold, and I can handle any dogs, and I am not afraid of Moose, or any other wildlife.

I am pretty good at guessing directions and distances and even fire hazards don't worry me. My grandfather the chief and my father trained me well to survive in the wilderness. But as you know ghosts and spirits might arrive from hallucinations and I don't think I would be able to handle that.

And the crazy talk from Great Aunt Sarah comes back to haunt me every so often."

"Gitchie Manito and Ahki created one and your Geesis is not your Neebageesis. The Megis has put forward another. Waynaboozhoo will light the

Three Fires and you will be consumed. You must seek out the spirit and befriend him."

Great Aunt Sarah every few years would screech out those words with a ferocious yell that even every dog within miles could hear; and it was unnerving and not entirely understood. Every time I heard the screech I clutched the woven beadwork around my neck with the Blue Heron design that had been given to me as a child in order to interpret dreams and visions and to protect and guide me.

The Great Blue Heron spirit that dwells in the design would protect me against everything and of course against Great Aunt Sarah's screeching.

But I was afraid.

" Well Cory if there is anything that I can help you with just ask, just ask!" Elayne didn't understand, but she was trying to be helpful.

Six

LAW SCHOOL
Ithaca, New York

The People of the Hills welcomed me with open arms as I brushed aside the blanket hanging over the entrance to the Haudenosaunee longhouse and entered the world of the Onondaga nation. I approached with trepidation the group of men sitting around a blackened pot belly stove that was belching out warmth from a fire within that appeared to be too hot.

It appeared to be too hot however I would guess it was necessary to keep out the autumn chill that existed that day near Ithaca, in the finger lakes area of New York.

"Here, take some ohanda dehkahwhi " one of the men offered.

"Thank You" I accepted, and took a handful of the bright red strawberries. "I thank you for giving me this field of fire".

"We know that you come from our cousins , the Mississauga, and that you are to be chief someday!" "Yes , and I accept your hospitality and your offer to allow me to stay in your longhouse while I complete my studies at Ithaca. I accept your offer to share your corn, beans and squash; and I hope to bring you much sustaining foods in return."

"The only thing we cannot offer you, son of a chief, is clear water to bathe in or to drink from; for as you know our lake , the Onondaga was once clear as glass , but the Whites put their sewage into the lake and created the most polluted lake in America.

The Onondagas were good stewards of the lake for many of the white man's years until the white man came and took control of the lake and all that surrounds the lake. The chemicals of ammonia and phosphorous appear with such high levels because the whites dumped waste with no treatment and no respect of us or nature.

The fish which were once abundant and fed our people disappeared. Toxins are everywhere in the lake. Many years of digging in the earth by the whites to produce soda ash and dumping of byproduct such as chloride, sodium and calcium were dumped every day into the lake. Over at Solvay great waste beds were created which to this day put toxins into our sacred lake.

Yes , my son, the whites destroyed our way of life; and destroyed our people. People who were so gentile. The People of the Hills. The Fire-Keepers. Keepers of the Wampum. The Elder Brothers.

Mercury was poured into the lake by the whites for a long time creating levels of mercury now found in the remaining fish that are at unacceptable levels. Any of our brethren who will attempt to eat those fish will get deathly sick."

"Go seek out the Clan Mother "Cory implored.

The Clan Mother appeared and she looked just like I had imagined , sort of like the Indian version of Mama Cass. She spoke out to me at first in her native tongue and said "welcome to our home you are welcome to stay here as long as you want and partake of our food and hospitality. I was told that you were coming and I prepared a bed for you; come and you will see where you will be resting. I hope that you have a pleasant stay here with us and that your studies at Ithaca are successful.   Come, walk with me, walk with me and I will show you where you will be able to spend your nights"

There was no more of an introduction to her world than this and the simple words that she spoke were very comforting to me as I understood that in my years in attendance at Ithaca I would be comfortable here with my people. So we walked past the longhouse, past three or four cabins that look like they had been there for several years and down a steep cliff with about 10 stairs of stone pushed into the side of the cliff.

Another short jaunt and I could see by the side of the lake a small log cabin with an improvised tent roof covering it. The Clan Mother pushed open the wooden door and as I walked into the cabin I quickly glanced left and right and saw the potbelly stove, the makeshift sink and toilet and the bunk bed to the right.

It was chilly in this cabin because of course the potbelly stove was not on and there was a lot of dust particles floating around in the air as the light shone through musty dirty panes of glass that probably were never cleaned in all the years that this cabin had existed but this was home and I was grateful for it. "Thank you Clan Mother, thank you, really thank you for providing me with such wonderful hospitality and a place to rest. I hope you understand that I will be spending a lot of time at Ithaca and less time here but I really appreciate what you and my cousins here are providing me. Perhaps someday I will be able to repay you."

"Son. Son out of my sister. Future Chief! I am pleased to have you here and enjoy your stay. I know that your studies at Ithaca are very important to all of us and to your people. I will pass the word to let you be, to allow you to concentrate on your studies and to not have any other diversions although I would caution you be careful of those who approach you for even in this little reservation where the white man have put us there will be possible diversions.   Watch out for the elders and those with hair of red for it will be hard for you to resist their demands and should you ever have any problem in deciding what to do please do not hesitate to come forward and ask my advice. Now I leave you so that you can prepare your little cabin to your liking. Come and share soup, corn and venison with us when you are ready." And with that final invitation to share some food the Clan Mother exited and the silence that remained as I stood there looking through the dust yelled out for some noise.

I left the door open on purpose so that some air could get into this cabin and as I exited I breathed in the fresh air coming off of the lake I could tell the difference that the air in the cabin was musty and stale. I made my way up the stone steps past the cabins past the longhouse and retrieved some of my belongings from my vehicle. Back down past the master longhouse past cabins down the stairs and into the cabin and started to clean wash mop sponge down tile up where I would be residing for the next couple of years. What I was trying to figure out was where I would be able to take a shower or bathe because there was no shower or bath in this cabin and I knew that the lake was too polluted to swim in so I went up to the longhouse, went in and inquired.

"Where is it possible to cleanse oneself and remove the dust and dirt that has accumulated these past few days?"
"Here come here,- here in the back of the longhouse we have what you need exactly what you need!" Replied the Elder.

Seven

Cory followed the Elder towards the back of the longhouse and after he moved the curtain aside there it was a great big old fashioned tub on four legs just like you see in the movies or in the Wild West movies.

"To use this tub just take a bucket to the back of the longhouse where the water comes from the pipe and fill the bucket and return with the water to put into the tub. You may have to make several trips and in any way to heat the water is leave in the bucket on the potbelly stove over there!" The elder had pointed to the black potbelly stove where several of the elders were sitting around and now he understood why the potbelly stove was hot all the time probably for situations like this, so because he had traveled quite a distance and because he had worked for a few hours cleaning the dust and dirt in the cabin he decided that now was the time to try out this revolutionary bathing system. He could see the aluminum bucket resting on the floor next to the tub. What he could not understand was that one aluminum bucket and in questioning the elders they confirmed yes they only have one bucket, so the process was pretty slow as you can imagine filling up one aluminum bucket and bringing it to put on the potbelly stove sitting around for 20 min. while the water heated up, bringing it over and pouring it into the tub, going back outside to fill up the bucket bringing it back, putting it on the potbelly stove.

After 15 to 20 minutes the water heated up and while pouring into the tub and running back outside and after repeating this several times Cory began to realize that it was a waste of time because by the time you get the bucket of water, bring it back, put on the stove, getting heated up, bring it into the tub and come back your water starts to cool off in the tub so Cory basically decided well he's going to be taking a bath in water which would be between cold and lukewarm.

Cory managed to bring about 20 buckets of water and fill half the tub and then pulled the curtain back so that he had some place where the elders and/or others would not view everything that was going on and he removed his clothes and got into the tub. He lathered up with the scrub brush and all of a sudden someone had brushed the curtain aside and in his view was this striking heavy set red headed young woman who spoke to him in her native tongue and spoke too quickly so he did not understand. The only thing he didn't understand was that she was standing there well fully clothed while he was in this tub fully unclothed, but there was enough water to cover the parts of his anatomy that needed to be covered, however he was still shocked by her sudden appearance.

"I was sent to help you bathe" she blurted out in her native tongue.

"What?" He questioned.

"The Clan Mother sent me."

Without another word this creature took the lathering brush and started to lather up his back , neck and head. He didn't object. Her hands massaged his neck and shoulders. Her fingers pushed into his skin , head and chest. He was relaxed.

And then he was surprised. She didn't remove any clothing but climbed right into the tub and squatted down right on his legs and without a word started lathering, massaging and applying her fingers over his chest and legs. He started to squirm when she got too close to areas where she should not be, but he was enjoying the work out.

"Turn over!" She ordered as if he was a piece of meat on a bar-b-que. He obliged and the massaging, fingering, and pleasuring continued.

Then she proceeded to phase two.

She grabbed his head, put her knees into his back and pulled his head back until he had to yell out."Hey, What are you doing? This is a bath tub , not a wrestling ring."

"Exercise. Exercise." She responded.

The sound of crackling in his back prompted him to again yell out."Stop! Stop right now!"

She didn't, and pulled his head back more.

He reached out with one hand, managed to grab the high sides of the tub and with the other hand pushed her off his legs and under the water. Who cares about being embarrassed due to his nudity. He had to escape this torture. He jumped out of the tub and grabbed a towel and wrapped it around his waist. The creature was floundering around in the water like a massive whale trying to flip over to breathe.

He reached over and had thoughts of pushing her under the water but instead he yanked her head out of the water by grasping one of her red-haired pony tails and lifting upwards. She took in air like a vacuum cleaner had just turned on.

As soon as he viewed that she was ok he let go and dropped her head back into the tub.

Cory picked up his clothes and quickly exited the room, past the Elders and their stove and out into the Autumn air believing he had just escaped from a potential continuous torture session with a red-headed female Bigfoot.

As he brushed past the Elders he heard in a joking manner " How was your bath with Little Big Red?" and a lot of laughter by most of the group.

"It was wonderful. Just what I needed after a tough long day".

He ran down through the woods to his cabin by

the cliff, pushed open the door, and shut it and fell into the bed while welcoming the creaking noise as he settled under the heavy wool blanket thinking he was safe.

Someone, something pushed open the door with such force it crashed against the wall and dislodged some ceramic cups on a shelf which came crashing down onto the wood floor. The sun was shining behind the creature who filled the doorway so he could only see a form silhouetted against the sun.

Then it came in.

It must have been Little Big Red's bigger brother! Way over six feet tall, huge massive shoulders , same red hair tied back in a pony tail under a bandana wrapped around a giant head at the forehead. This was the legendary Bigfoot, for sure. But what was he doing here! Almost three thousand miles east of the Rockies.

Every step he took shook the cabin and rattled the dishes.

Cory thought he was gonna die at the hands of this beast. Cory was shocked. His little voice sounded like it came from a ventriloquist somewhere else.

"Hi. Welcome. I am Johnny Red Bear Littleworth . You must be our cousin, right?" He inquired.

"Yes I am." Cory answered.

"I am in second year Law Ithaca". He pointed out. And I will show you around!".

"Oh what a relief. I thought you were here to

avenge my treatment of Little Red Bear , who I guess is your sister, cause you look like her; or, she looks like you, or you look like each other".

"Yes she is my sister"

He seemed to admit with reluctance.

"She is a little aggressive however I think she likes you!".

"Liking like that I sort of don't need".

"Ya I know; any way tomorrow you will go with me to Ithaca and I will show you around. OK?"

"Sure. Looking forward to it!" Cory exclaimed. As Johnny Red Bear lumbered out the door he slammed it as if that was the only way he knew how to close a door.

Eight

Johnny Red Bear could not fit in the passenger seat of Cory's little sports car so Johnny Red Bear had to sit on the top of the trunk with his feet on the back seat as if we were celebrating a Super Bowl win and Cory was driving in the parade down main street.

"South on 1-81 and exit at Cortland!" Yelled Johnny.

Cory followed his instructions , and after a few "South, rights, and lefts" they were on Hoy Road and the cool breeze from Cayuga Lake was great.

Cornell Law School was started in 1887 and tuition was $75 a year when Andrew Dickson White wrote that he wanted to educate "not swarms of hastily prepared pettifoggers, but a fair number of well-trained, large-minded, morally-based lawyers in the best sense".

A pettifogger as far as Cory knew was a petty, quibbling, unscrupulous lawyer or a lawyer of inferior status who conducts unimportant cases or a lawyer of little importance , or a lawyer who is a shyster.

Well, a pettifogger certainly won't be me! Cory thought.

Six months of law school and part time Iditarod training was exhausting .The snow was swirling all around, it was a white out, Cory couldn't see Bernie and Cory couldn't see the first five dogs behind him. All he could see were the five dogs directly in front of the sled, just barely could he see anything around him, the snow was covering his goggles and his arms were starting to get cold.

He couldn't remember how long he had been out here but he had to get through this because this was a test. This was a test to see if he has what it takes to get through the Iditarod.

If he couldn't get through this, then what's the use he might as well give up his dream of running in the Iditarod. His sled was caked with snow. Snow was all over the first five dogs. He couldn't see where he was going.

Cory heard that the area around here could sometimes get up to 60 to 70 inches of snow but now all he cared about is to survive this blizzard, and where the hell was big Red?

He was following in the snowmobile and where is he now? Cory could't hear the engine. "This is a blind man driving" He yelled out with desperation.

He thought this snow is getting worse.

"Bernie, Bernie. Where the hell are you Bernie?" Things started to let up a little, he could see more of the dogs upfront. Wow! What's that totem pole doing here? What's Great Aunt Sarah doing here; and why is she yelling now?

"Ahki! Megis! Three Fires!" Fire all around. Great Blue Spirit, help me. Help me! He burst out. What's Grandpa doing here? What's those soldiers doing here? What's that Great Blue Heron doing flying around here? Cory was having hallucinations. He hated this. He gotta get out a here. "Help me! Somebody Please! Help me!" Yelled Cory.

"Cory, Cory!" "Cory, get up. Come on Cory. Get up" Johnny Red Bear had caught up to him and was trying to wake him up. He guessed either the cold, the hallucinations, or just being dead tired knocked him out.

"Where are we? Big Red?" asked Cory.

"We're on Tug Hill Plateau, remember. remember, Tug Hill Plateau? in upstate New York".

"Johnny I swear I saw messengers and spirits in the swirling snow. You know, Johnny, messengers and spirits come to us in many forms and in many ways. They are carriers of wisdom, information and often a sign we need to help us navigate our way forward. They help us to see the hidden treasures in our paths and open our eyes to what is there before us, what lessons and growth are present for us to experience.

When these messengers and spirits appear before me I am afraid, yet I listen and I do my best to stop and listen to what they have to share with me, but I am afraid sometimes to hear what they have to say, and they don't always come in friendly forms; sometimes as beasts or ferocious animals." Cory explained.

"OK Corey, OK! Relax and calm down. Let's get going home. You need rest badly."

The blizzard had died down and he could see Bernie and all the dogs and now it was coming back to him that they were on Tug Hill Plateau, an area of New York State which is renowned for its bountiful snowfall. The location of the region in relation to Lake Ontario often creates ideal conditions for Lake effect snow. Snow that commonly reaches 5 feet or more and it's a great place to practice mushing .

In fact there is so much snow here that the hunting camp that they were staying in has second floor entry doors because so much snow accumulates that the ground-level doors cannot be accessed, and of course the most wonderful benefit is that it's close to his friends and cousins of the Onondaga nation.

"Okay Johnny Red Bear, let's try it once again."

"Oh come on Cory haven't you had enough? You've been out here over five hours already. Leave something for tomorrow."

"No Johnny we have to stay out here another couple of hours.Okay mush! Bernie mush! Let's get going!" and the sled started to move and they were off.

Another three hours of mushing, racing, carting, weight pulling, freighting. Cory had to teach Bernie how to be a lead dog. Cory had to teach the other Huskies, that the Onondaga got for him, to be swing dogs and team dogs and wheel dogs. Cory had to do it, and he was determined to succeed.

Today on Tug Hill Plateau they had two sleds going. Cory was on one with Bernie and the gang and Johnny Red Bear was on another one and they were sliding across the Plateau side-by-side pretending they were competing in the Iditarod.

"Mush Bernie Mush" He kept repeating and Bernie and the gang were really doing a great job. Johnny Red Bear started to fall back into the distance and Cory started to get the hang of it. Soon he would be ready to compete in the tryouts.

He called his cousins, the Athabascan, and Chief George Whiteheart promised him as many Siberian Huskies as he needed when he arrived out West; and the best news was that they had available $25,000 to fund what he would need for food and expenses.

Nine

IDITAROD

"Elayne, Elayne, Can you hear me?" Cory shouted into the payphone.

"Yes Cory. I haven't heard from you in weeks. What's happening?"

"I had to drop the twins as they would never survive a 1000 plus mile race. Bernie and the others were ok and the Athabascans lent me some pros. The 1st small qualifying race was only 100 miles and Bernie and the team performed beautifully and we finished twenty-two which allowed us to continue.

The 2nd qualifying race was mostly up and down several mountains and we finished twenty-fifth. The 3rd race was run in a snowstorm and took seven days to complete but we qualified, and I only lost one dog due to a foot injury.

I learned how to keep a veterinary diary and have it signed by a veterinarian at each checkpoint. I qualified for the Great Big Race! Elayne, I qualified!"

"That's wonderful Cory. When is the race?"

"It's in March".

"But it's October now. What are you doing for the next six months?"

"Training. I've been training all summer. Using wheeled carts."

"What about money?" she queried.

"The Athabascans are great. They raised $60,000 because I promised to give them all the winnings, if I win. And hey I just wanna finish in the race."

"OK Cory but please take care of the dogs. You know I read that a guy named Ramy Brooks was suspended for abusing his sled dogs; and that many dogs have died and been injured during the race. The practice of tethering dogs on short chains in their kennels, at checkpoints and dog drops is highly criticized, and I don't like it. The dogs are

pushed beyond their endurance or capabilities."
Cory be careful. Be very careful. Come back alive
and well and with all the dogs. By the way, How's
Bernie?"

"Bernie's fine. He's made many friends and he
has bulked up, and in great condition. Don't worry
we will all be fine. But Elayne, before you go let me
tell you what happened at Cornell. I was ready to
enroll for my second term at Cornell and I was
ready to study hard but I was not ready for what
happened next.

Johnny Red Bear and I drove right into the
occupation of the Straight Building. I never heard of
the SDS, Students for a Democratic Society. I didn't
know any white students from Delta Upsilon
Fraternity so when we turned onto Campus Road I
had to jam on the brakes to avoid slamming into the
crowd. All white, all student, all yelling

" Give back the Straight or die!"
The Straight referred to Willard Straight Hall, a
student union building on the central campus of
Cornell University, located on Campus Road,
adjacent to the Ho Plaza and the Gannent Health
Center.

Willard Straight Hall was initiated by Willard
Dickerman Straight's widow, Dorothy Straight, as a
memorial to her husband. The building was
intended to lead to "enrichment of the human
contacts of student life" according to Dorothy

Straight , and it was noted by historians that in 1925when the hall was built it was unusual to have a building with no academic purpose. The concept of a "student union" building was a recent invention at that time.

When Willard Straight Hall opened, the main desk was staffed by undergraduate students and the building's policies were set by a student-led Willard Straight Hall Board of Governors. The upper floors of the Straight served as a hotel for Cornell's visitors and guests. The broadcast studios of the WVBR Radio station were in a lower level and the building also housed the University Theatre and almost 50 performances a year were staged there.

As Cornell built more dormitories on the West and North Campus two additional buildings supplemented the Straight to serve students. Just months before I was accepted at Cornell the university judicial system was the center of a controversy in connection with the disciplining of African-American students who had engaged in a protest.

I couldn't have been aware that as I turned onto Campus Road the African-American students were in the middle of occupying the Hall and had demanded amnesty for the accused protesters as well as the establishment of an Africana Studies center. They ejected parents who were visiting for the "Parents Weekend" from the hotel rooms on the upper floors.

The all white crowd of students that I almost drove into were attempting to retake the building by force; and some of the occupying students had firearms. I looked at Johnny Red Bear and I was confused. I didn't know what to do. I had sympathy for the African-American students, for my people had experienced the same poor treatment by the Whites for centuries.

I said to Johnny "We should go join the protesters inside the Straight!". "Are you crazy?"He answered.

Before I could respond a Cornell Administrator, who I learned later was Vice President Steven Muller, was out in front with a bullhorn negotiating; and he successfully convinced the protesting and occupying students to end the occupation.

The students marching out of the Straight carrying rifles and wearing arm bands made the national news and photographs of the students marching out holding rifles was in newspapers and television news reports everywhere.

A foundation of the Africana Studies and Research Center was established.

This was an epic moment in University student life. When the students left the Straight holding rifles after occupying the building they were surrounded by administrators, policemen, students, and many photojournalists. The Associated Press photo taken by Steve Starr won the Pulitzer Prize.

The photographers took pictures of an historic exit that captured a moment in time, a moment of action, excitement, fear and uncertainty. Out of numerous stirring images that were in line for the Pulitzer Prize, the photo taken by Steve Starr and labeled "Guns on Campus" emerged as the winner of the Pulitzer Prize.

In a decade of protests and violence, many spoke out that a student protest was hardly newsworthy as you know because the '60s were packed with assassinations of JFK, MLK, Malcom X, and remember the often violent Civil Rights protests and gatherings, as well as the Vietnam war and it's protests?

The photo of the students leaving the Straight holding guns was chosen by the Pulitzer Prize committee not for its' showing of the protest action but for the extraordinary image of guns on the steps of a student union.

The protest was peaceful, political and was armed nonviolent resistance, however except for intervention and brilliant negotiating by the Cornell Vice President, could have erupted into a violent who knows what may have happened bad situation. This was the first time that campus protesters were openly armed and it foreshadowed future events.

Unfortunately the Pulitzer Prize was a key factor in legitimizing the takeover and was the best depiction of the events that will never be forgotten. Ironically some photographers included a full view of the Welcome Parents sign which pushed the takeover and occupation into the weird zone.

Campus riots were not new as in the same year protests of a similar nature happened at both Harvard and Berkeley; however the only Campus protest involving guns was this one at Cornell.

One of the protesters wore a strap of bullets capable of massacre which contrasted with his white school sweater. That strap of bullets and the rifle he held high was a powerful and terrifying symbol of what it represented and what could happen.

Armed violence had installed itself in a picturesque college campus that might have originated in inner cities and the jungles of Vietnam.

Elayne-" I was in shock. I had never witnessed such an event." A student at Cornell or Harvard looking like a heavily armed soldier in a bullet vest with a rifle that could spew death at any moment and that made me fear the present and the future; anyway, bye for now" "Bye, Cory, take care, and take care of Bernie" pleaded Elayne.

Ten

The time between October and March went very quickly. The 16 dogs that were training with Cory reacted very favorably and Bernie was able to lead them all.

Cory's cousins the Athabascans helped a lot with dog food, sleeping bags, transferring the dogs and the sleds from training sites to resting areas and were almost as enthusiastic as he was. The big race was approaching and the announced date of March 7 was coming in three weeks. He couldn't wait. 52 Mushers were entered this year, of course most from Alaska and a few from the lower states two from Canada and one from Sweden.

Cory's cousins helped him bring the 16 dogs and the sled to Anchorage; and all his dogs were subjected to examination by veterinarians who checked their teeth, eyes, tonsils, heart legs, and joints and look for signs of illegal drugs, and any wounds and pregnancy. Although the dogs would be tracked with microchip implants and color tags.

Thankfully every one of his 16 dogs passed the extensive testing.

They were ready to go. They all lined up on fourth Avenue in downtown Anchorage and the ribbon-cutting ceremony was held. The first musher was off at 10 o'clock and every 2 minutes another musher departed. He was 18th. This is a very exciting time as they took their time going through Anchorage and through several miles of city streets and city trails before reaching the foothills to the east of Anchorage in Chugach State Park and the Chugach Mountains. Then they followed Glenn Highway for 2 to 3 hours until they reached evil River which was 20 miles away when they arrived at the Veterans of Foreign Wars building they checked in on the Star team and returned them to their boxes and drove 30 miles of highway to the restart point.

The race really started the next day at two clock in Fairbanks because the weather was too warm in Anchorage and the trail conditions were poor. The 52 mushers departed every two minutes and all experienced the same thrills as they arrived at the second checkpoint.

The first hundred miles from Willow to the checkpoint to squint had a lot of Moose in the area and it was difficult to move because they cause hazards for a lot of the dog teams. Cory didn't encounter any Moose and his route to squint was easy over flatlands and he didn't miss any markings or flags. He also decided to push through the night as he wanted to arrive at squint before dawn. From Skwentna he followed the Skwentna River into the Alaska Range to finger Lake and now the trail became really difficult as he followed the narrow happy River gorge where children died at the site of the heavy incline. Rainy Pass is part of the historic Iditarod Trail and is the most dangerous checkpoint in the Iditarod.

Back in 1985 a musher named Austin broke his hand and two dogs were injured when his sled went out of control and hit a standard of trees and many others have suffered from this dangerous checkpoint. Cory made it through. After Rainy Pass he continued up the mountain and passed the tree-lined divide of the Alaska Range and then down into the Alaska interior. At this point the elevation of the passes are 2200 feet and the Valley in the mountains is exposed to blizzards. He had a thermometer with him and the temperature was -30°F and the wind was 30 mi./h so the wind shear really stung but he was protected by the heavy bear skins and other materials that his cousins had given to him.

Great aunt Sarah screeching got to him at this point. He couldn't get her out of his mind. The wind was swirling, the snow was blinding again and he could not see Bernie. He yelled out "Bernie, Bernie, where are you? Please Bernie, where are you?"

He had to pull the team over. They all needed a rest. He fed the dogs and ate some chocolate that he had and camped on the trail.

The trail down Dalzell Gorge from the divide, as

he discovered is steep straight and drops 1000 feet in elevation and in just 5 miles. Had no choice, he had to put on the brake almost all the way down because if he didn't he would lose control. There's no traction, the team is hard to control and uses chain for traction, and he had heard that a rookie musher had fallen through an ice bridge into a creek a few years ago. He then followed the Tina River which was treacherous. The next checkpoint is Rohn which is located in the spruce forest with no wind and a poor airstrip. After Rainy Pass it was a great place to take a long break. He knew from talking to other mushers that past this pass is 75 miles to the next checkpoint so he took a full eight hour break and Bernie and the dogs were well rested. From this point in Rohn the trail follows the bend and forks of the Kuskokwim River where freezing water running over a layer of ice is a hazard. After 45 miles away from Rohn the path leaves the river and passes into the farewell burn and Cory had to be very careful going slowly because clumps of grass and sledge and fallen timber can cause severe injuries to the dogs' feet. Nicolai, an Athabasca settlement on the banks of the Kuskokwim River which just happened to be where his cousins were from, is used as a checkpoint and as soon as he arrived there was a big party going on.

The trail then follows the South Fork of the Kuskokwim to the former mining town of McGrath which has a population of about 400 and because it has a good airfield many journalists were present who had flown in to meet the mushers. After McGrath is Takotna and then a ghost town of Ophir is the next checkpoint. He was now running in the middle of the pack about 25th and he was told that about 10 to 12 Mosher's had gone through this checkpoint three days before him. He was very happy to make it this far and very happy to be in the middle of the pack.

A rookie musher named Roger and Cory decided to run together and help each other out. After Ophir Castor the trail divides into a northern and southern route which rejoins at Cal tag. Because this was an even numbered year they used the northern route which first passes through Cripple, which is 3 miles from Anchorage and 609 miles from home. Making it the middle placed, little most used checkpoint. From Cripple the trail passed through a cell at the crossing to Ruby on the Yukon River and Ruby is another former gold rush town which became Athabasca village.

Ruby is on the longest river in Alaska, the Yukon, which is swept by strong winds which can drop the wind chill below minus 100°F. A greater hazard is uniformity of this long stretch suffering from sleep deprivation as many mushers report hallucinations and this was what he was really afraid of. Not only hallucinations but also Great Aunt Sarah's noise in his head. He was afraid, really afraid. This year the route did not pass through the ghost town of Iditarod as it does in odd numbered years.

The trail meets Cal Tag which for hundreds of years has been a gateway between the Athabasca village in the interior and the settlements on the coast of the Bering Sea. The Caltech portage was through a 1000 foot pass down to an intimate town backing onto the Bering Sea. Now the trail passes through the hills to the new village. The route then passes across the frozen North Bay and the markers on the Bay are young spruce trees frozen and mounted through holes in the ice. Through dense West Winds along the shore of Seward Peninsula and through the tiny village as it whips through the white mountain.

Cory like all mountain teams must rest their dogs for at least eight hours before the final sprint. From white mountain to safety is 55 miles and to the home is 22 miles. The last leg is crucial because the lead teams are off within a few hours of each other and in 1991 the race was decided by less than an hour and the closest race in recent history was '97 with the winner and runner-up only one set apart. The official finish line is the red Fox Olson trail monument, known as the barrel burled arch in the home which is a spruce log with two distinct marks similar but not identical to an old arch that lasted until 2001. The new arch has the words of an Iditarod sled dog race.

A Widows' lamp is lit or maintains the arch until the last competitor crosses the finish line. The finish line is based on a kerosene lamp lit in an outsider roadhouse and a good musher can carry goods or mail en route. For this reason possibly its completed setting is referred to as all red lantern on the way to the arch. As each musher passes front Street and down the fence off fifth yard and in the Street stretch the city's fire siren is sounded as each musher hits the two mile mark before the finish line. Cory just wanted to finish the race and Roger and him were into the stretch from white mountain to safety when he learned that they were now running 44th and that eight teams had either quit or been forced out of the race by injuries to their dogs and that they were four days behind the leaders.

Obviously he was not going to win the race but he was happy to just finish and he told Roger that on the final stretch from safety to Nome they would just take it easy and finish the race. Fifteen days and 1100 miles later he finished the race, and crossed into Nome and was welcomed by his cousins. Three of his dogs needed veterinarian care but were not seriously injured and Bernie was in great shape. The biggest surprise was that the rookie of the year award was given to him because he placed best among the rookies.

Bernie would not be famous like 'Andy' in 1982 or 'Goose' in 1991 or April 2010 but then Bernie ran a great race. Roger and Cory celebrated their accomplishment, but now it was time to go back East.

Eleven

Missy Shaw

Fiona could hear the putt- putt- putt of the small engine motorcycle as it approached the semi-circular driveway of her boss's mansion.

She wiped her hands on her purple- with- flower design apron to wipe off the dirt that had stuck to her fingers and hands as she was cleaning the huge flower pots next to the front doors.

The driver did not have to ring the bell as Fiona opened the double glass doors in anticipation of a delivery. There it was!

Something wrapped up in a traditional Bay blanket with the colored stripes.

Fiona gave the driver the envelope stuffed with the cash and closed the doors quickly as the early morning chill was beginning to creep in. The smell of the flowers outside began to permeate the room.

She began to unwrap the package and was shocked at the amount of dense black hair that first appeared; and then the oval shaped face with eyes shut.

Fiona, a native of the Philippines, and one of those ten million Filipino health care workers who work all over the world for sometimes minimum wage, all the while sending back money to support their families had never seen a baby who was only a few hours just born with such a head of hair.

"Who was at the front door?" bellowed the mansion's owner Raeburn Shaw from one of the seven bedrooms on the second floor.

"The delivery!" Fiona responded.

"Well. What does it look like?" Raeburn asked.

"Very nice. Very Nice"

"Bring it up so we can all see."

"OK Mr. Ray."

Climbing up the twenty stairs and shuffling down the hall to Mr. Raeburn's room was effortless for Fiona as even though nearing the age of fifty-five, she kept in good shape and the bundle was very light. In fact, after bearing three children of her own, she was a pro at balancing the bundle while climbing, walking, talking , etc.

"Let's see what we paid for!" Raeburn Shaw very roughly bellowed, as was his style.

Fiona again uncovered the baby's head and face and now noticed the silver necklace with pendant around the baby's neck; and Fiona, because she did not have her glasses with her, could not make out what was on the pendant. It was all a blur to her.

"Mr. Ray. What is that on the pendant?" she inquired. Raeburn Shaw saw the immense bundle of hair, the round face, the closed eyes, and he squinted to try to make out what was on the pendant.

"Fiona, stop moving around. I can't make out what's on the pendant".

"It looks like a dog. No wait I think it is a wolf. Yes definitely a wolf." Raeburn Shaw was positive the image on the pendant was a wolf.

"It's probably some type of symbol that the midwives put around the baby's neck for good luck or be healthy; and look I can make out some symbols underneath the wolf."

"Mr. Ray, those symbols are like little stick figures, right?" Fiona questioned.

"Yes. I don't know what they mean, anyway put the baby in its' room".

Fiona walked down the hall with the bundle and turned left into a room that was all prepared waiting for its' young inhabitant.

Drawings of racing cars on one wall with full color drawings of Batman, Robin, and Superman on the opposite wall. A train set on a table under the window; and a crib with birds and bees hanging above it from the ceiling.

All the walls were painted powder blue, and three mini pajama sets were slumped over a padded flower strewn armchair.

Fiona gingerly put the baby down, removed the Bay blanket and put the baby into one of the mini pajama sets, even though the set tag read age 3-6 months this baby was a whopper and almost filled the set from neck down to toes.

"Only several hours born and looking like six months old already." mumbled Fiona.

Raeburn Shaw and Audrey, his third wife, former Miss Illinois, and runner up in the Miss USA Contest, had anxiously awaited this arrival, and had prepared the baby's room to welcome their newly acquired son.

All decked out in blue, with cartoon characters painted on the walls that already include racing cars, Batman and Robin and Superman .

"Where's Audrey?" Raeburn inquired.

"Comin' back from Church. Mr. Ray" answered Fiona. "Comin' back."

Fiona knew that Ms. Audrey would be very pleased that the baby had arrived , for two years she yearned for the child that she herself could not bear, and the tense atmosphere between her and Raeburn could not last much longer. Raeburn Shaw had no patience.

When Raeburn Shaw wanted something, he did whatever was required to obtain what he wanted, whether whatever was done was legal or not, Raeburn didn't care, as long as the end result was what he had wanted.

After all when Raeburn had moved to this small town he had immediately started to build houses the way he had in the big city, and he acquired the land he wanted quickly, efficiently, with some muscle, or without.

Raeburn Shaw was not liked by the towns people. They had a peaceful , sleepy town and Raeburn moved in and disturbed the peace.

He had some heritage homes torn down , even at the objection of the Mayor and Council, in order to clear the way for his project, and his million dollar homes , which appeared gross, too large, and out of place in the outskirts of the town.

Raeburn bribed council members to vote changes in by-laws in his favor.

Raeburn supported several candidates for political positions in the elections who voted his way; and Homer, don't forget Homer who was suspected to be involved in some suspicious stuff and who was employed by Raeburn Shaw, auspiciously as a gardener /chauffeur.

Strange that Raeburn was a born-again Christian and opposed gambling and Casinos. As soon as he arrived in town he arranged for construction of the Casino that the local Natives were trying to build to be shut down.

It was rumored that he had hired all the construction workers away from construction on the Casino to work on his project-the homes he was building and selling to city folk.

Every time a vote came up at city council concerning the Casino, Raeburn would make sure nothing got approved, and the Casino construction just stopped, leaving a steel skeleton rotting in the sun.

Raeburn didn't care that the Natives were desperate. That they had no income. That they were starving, and that even though the government had allowed them to construct the Casino, they could not because city council would not approve further construction, and the workers had abandoned the site.

The Chief had even hired a lawyer who filed a claim for one hundred million dollars against the town and Raeburn's own lawyers were able to squash the claim.

No Raeburn was not liked by the townspeople and Raeburn was despised by the Natives.

It was hard to believe that someone like Raeburn, who resembled a little Napoleon , could cause so much grief and hardship.

Audrey Shaw hated living on the edge of the small town. She had grown up in Chicago and had entered the Miss Illinois contest when she was nineteen and her talent, besides being beautiful, which is no talent, was playing the piano.
Her parents had noticed she loved music at a young age and had arranged for her to have piano lessons from the age of five, and after she won the Miss Illinois contest she participated in Miss USA which was held in New Orleans.

Raeburn was one of the judges and they met

briefly during the contest. Audrey was first runner-up and Raeburn insisted she go out with him. She resisted but Raeburn persisted and after a few weeks they were married.

She was several inches taller than the diminutive Raeburn but the lure of money and the good life persuaded her to take the plunge. Raeburn treated her like a queen and bought her anything she desired.

Trips around the world and many weeks spent on their yacht in the Caribbean soothed the unhappiness she felt at not being able to have children.

However it was ten years ago when they got married and Audrey never dreamed of having to live in a small town with nothing to do except watch the sun rise and set.

She had pushed Raeburn to adopt a child and now she was driving home , breaking the speed limit to see her new baby. Audrey Shaw pushed the front door open and entered the house with the greatest anticipation of seeing her new baby.

She raced up the stairs , down the hall and turned into the babies' room. She shrieked with delight when she reached over and picked up the little bundle of joy.

"Fiona" she questioned, "Is it a boy or a girl? Fiona actually had never checked and she figured now was the time. Taking the diaper off , both

Fiona and Audrey were shocked to see no appendage.

No little penis. No nothing.
They had ordered and were expecting a boy. It turns out that a girl with a huge hunk of hair was what was delivered.

"Oh Oh Mr. Ray is going to be mad!" exclaimed Fiona.

"No. Fiona! Ray is going to be happy, because I'm happy and you know what? Fiona? I'm going to bring up Missy my way."

"Is that her name? Missy?" asked Fiona.

"Yes!" Audrey stated strongly. "Now Fiona , we have to make sure the breast milk is delivered every four hours. Have you made those arrangements?"

"Yes Ma'am"

"Every four hours?" questioned Audrey again.
"Yes, for sure, Ma'am!"

"OK. Because I watched that British TV documentary called *Bringing Up baby* and I definitely don't want Missy to be brought up using the Benjamin Spock approach; and definitely no sleeping in my bed and no carrying around in a sling during the day. I don't care if South American Indians believed that a bond would develop between the baby and mother, and I don't believe that method will have a positive effect on Missy's development."

I also don't like the Paleolithic lifestyle that Mary

Higgins down the street used when bringing up her monster, Gerry."

"This baby is not going to dictate to me.
Missy will fit into my way of life, not me into hers."

"Now Fiona, put Missy outside to air"

"But Ms. Audrey It's cold outside!"

"Fiona, we have gone over this subject many times before this baby arrived, and we are not going to discuss it again. Put Missy outside to air!"

Audrey Shaw was defiant and ordered Fiona to do what she asked. Fiona couldn't understand the method to be used thinking this could increase the risk of Missy dying.

Audrey continued " And I don't want to see any cuddling or picking up Missy when feeding. You understand?"

"Yes, Ma'am" Fiona answered reluctantly, knowing the approach was wrong.

"A baby doesn't want to be touched all the time- just wants to be left alone to grow" Audrey stated emphatically."Missy is going to grow up and be smart, aggressive, intelligent, self-sufficient, and succeed in this nasty world of ours"

"Yes Ma'am" Fiona repeated.

"Missy will sleep in her own room, and even if crying we will not pick her up, or comfort her, and no unnecessary contact specifically when she wakes during the night. Only milk every four hours. You got that, Fiona?"

One last "Yes Ma'am!" reassured Audrey that her wishes and comments would be followed. Fiona thought that it's unbelievable that a woman coming from a family with so much love would want to bring up her child, even adopted, like that.

MISSY SHAW developed faster than any of the children her age and at age four was writing short stories, singing and writing songs, and had already by age eight skipped a grade and was on the way to skip another.

However she started to have nightmares with not being able to sleep with visions of spirits and such. She thought she was seeing wolves, bears, birds, and all sorts of ghosts and wildlife.

Her mother Audrey's insistence of a certain type of 'bringin' up baby' was starting to have an effect. The answer was to introduce her to Dr. Winterstein who put her on a regiment of drugs including those to calm her down.

Missy was so ahead of her classmates she started to study physics , geometry, and astrophysics.

At the age of twelve she was sent to Cambridge University to spend the summer as an apprentice with Stephen Hawking, after winning a school contest.

More problems developed with Missy having hallucinations and images of physics and other math and astrophysics images filling her head while attempting to sleep. The dosage of the medications she was taking were increased. Back at home she began crying without any reason and depression soon followed. Her mother Audrey's solution was put her in a hospital for six months.

When she was released she returned to school but told her mother "I am not Missy" "Fiona had told me I was adopted and you named me Missy"
Audrey Shaw, shocked, asked "So if you are not Missy, Then who are you?"

"I was Missy, but I left Missy back at the hospital. I have been searching for my Spirit to guide me all my life. I was given this pendant with these symbols which I do not understand, and the symbol of the wolf is deceiving, as it is not my Spirit. I will hunt for my Spirit and when it is found I will tell you who I am."

The girl who said she is not Missy left her mother puzzled, collected the hair coloring that would turn her hair blonde. A bleach , and a coloring and Missy with black curly hair disappeared.

"From now on I am Elayne!" proclaimed the girl."The Torch! The Light. I shall be the Light searching for my Spirit. I will be the Spirit Hunter and when I discover my Spirit, I, the Light will descend upon it and the Spirit will be enlightened just as the sunrise peeking from over the horizon in the new day, and when I find my Spirit you will know and so will I

Twelve

BOSTON

Elayne ran through the Boston Common, past Frog Pond, and up onto Beacon Street towards Charles Street and then past Mt. Vernon turning left onto Longfellow Bridge when suddenly someone must have tripped because the thousands of runners next to her stopped, and of course kept running in place, including the fellow members of her Harvard Women's Running Club.

She was almost on the middle of Longfellow Bridge with a great view of Charles River at 7:58 am in the morning, as detailed by the Sony Digital Clock hanging over the main span.

Jenny Munro, Elayne's great friend at Harvard Business School, and the one who convinced Elayne to start running was beside her, providing encouragement.

"Elayne, did you remember to put Vaseline everywhere?"

"Everywhere?" questioned Elayne.

"Yes. Everywhere. As you run parts of your body, specifically those parts that are protruding, continue to rub against your clothing and start to get chaffed or raw, and it hurts, I tell you, it hurts."

"What parts?"

"Well, breast nipples are one area" replied Jenny.

"Oh dam, I forgot"

"Well as soon as we get off this bridge you better run into one of the "Johnny-on-the-Spots" and grease up"

"You mean those temporary pee cans?"

"Yes those" answered Jenny.

The multitude began to move and of course you have no choice but to move with them, or you may get trampled. The bridge seemed longer than ever as Elayne, Jenny, and the multitude slowly moved across.

As soon as the curve around and down to Memorial Drive was achieved Elayne spotted the dozens of green colored metal boxes with doors that hundreds of runners were trying to get into. The gallons of water that each runner had devoured pre race in order to not get dehydrated had made its' way down the bodies to the exit area, and frankly a ton of people had to pee.

Elayne waiting patiently in line finally got her chance to hop in , removed her T Shirt with the Boston Marathon Logo, removed her sports bra, and began applying Vaseline to her nipples, and put some more under her arms. Quickly dressing she exited the box, however forgot to pee so said "excuse me" and went back in. A quick pee and she was out onto Memorial Drive , Jenny at her side.

It was a great day. The sun was out, and it was not too hot. Elayne had been training for twelve weeks and was prepared to finish. Jenny was already a pro at running as she had run at least ten or more marathons.

Past MIT Sloan School and along the Charles River. Past Harvard Bridge and then Boston University Bridge as Elayne started to slow down many runners were passing her.

She knew that Jenny was running slower than she could just to be with Elayne.

By the time they got to River Street Elayne was laboring and had to stop to take on water and some refreshment.

"Come on Elayne, you are doing great. More than half-way there already" Jenny tried to encourage her.

"But everyone is passing us." Stated Elayne.

"No matter girl! Remember it's not where you finish, but that you finish!"Exclaimed Jenny.

"Yah, but I already witnessed at least four runners collapsing and one hit her head. I don't want that to happen to me" Elayne said.

"Don't worry. You are in great shape. That won't happen to you" stated Jenny.

Elayne could now see the North Harvard Street bridge and she knew they would be turning right just before John F Kennedy Park.

"Jam up, Jam up" proclaimed Jenny, as they ran

into a crowd of runners just before the park turn.

More running in place so the muscles would not relax. More drinking water, and some more water.

The stopped runners began to move, and Elayne and Jenny moved with them past the Harvard Square Parking Garage. Past Mt. Auburn Street and approaching Harvard Square and a short turn onto Mass Avenue and onto the finish at Cambridge Common Park.

Elayne was dead beat but pleased to finish. Almost four hours was not great but it was good enough as she had finished.

The short walk to the dormitory on DeWolfe Street was not easy but Elayne was happy and sore. Jenny was right about the rubbing. Her nipples were raw.

Thirteen

Elayne had chosen to live at the DeWolfe dorm because it was a short walk across the North Harvard Street bridge to the campus of Harvard Business School.

In her second year of the MBA program she was persuaded by Jenny to start running and she was happy to be with Jenny as Jenny had become like a sister to her. Jenny was also enrolled in the MBA program, although Jenny was writing for the Harvard Revue and had ideas of being a journalist or news reporter.

Jenny Munroe of Atlanta, Georgia, with seven brothers and two sisters, daughter of the Mayor of a small city just west of Atlanta, had high hopes perhaps pushed by her mother, a pioneer and activist of her own having participated in marches to promote equality not only for black African-Americans but for women of color. Jenny had worked her behind off to get through college and then be accepted at Harvard, being a black woman.

Elayne sensed Jenny was going to be someone important or at least accomplish some good things in her career and life.

Every morning on the days when Elayne and Jenny attended classes they would jog from the residence over the bridge and onto the campus, sometimes separating due to Jenny taking a different course than Elayne that day.

They would meet in the Baker Library , spend a few hours studying , and jog back home.

Jenny talked about the Hyannis Sprint Triathlon, and at first Elayne said "No. Definitely not. Running Marathons is enough. Running, swimming, biking. Definitely not. I'm not a good swimmer anyways. I don't own a bike. I get headaches and see ghosts and spirits when biking. I can't explain it. No absolutely, definitely no."

Definitely No turned to OK Yes!

Elayne loved Cape Cod.

She loved running up and down the sand dunes.

She loved Hyannis port. She loved taking the ferry over to Martha's Vineyard.

She relished eating lobster on Martha's Vineyard, and biking to Edgartown.

The scenery while biking along the ocean thru several towns until Edgartown and the view of the sunset or sunrise was phenomenal, breathtaking and she developed a love of biking.

One day a quick circumnavigating bike ride around the perimeter of Martha's Island with Jenny sold her on the idea of entering a triathlon.

It was seventy-five miles around, passing through several small towns, taking a small home made ferry across a river, and sprinting home to catch the last ferry across to the Cape that got her exhilarated.

Once she had said "Definitely No", now she said "Definitely Yes. Let's do it."

The water at Craigville Beach looked inviting however the wind was whipping up a few waves

The view was spectacular.

Elayne and Jenny splashed some of the cold water on their shoulders before wading into the blue water up to their waists, and stood beside the other two hundred or so participants.

The air temperature was around seventy degrees so it was not a big difference in air to water however it still felt cold in the water off Nantucket Sound.

One quarter of a mile race against some of the best Triathlon Competitors in the world.

Jenny was coaching. "Don't forget. Just take it easy. You know this is not the best part of you. Just keep swimming, and for God's sake don't go off course because that adds extra mileage to your race. Don't worry if you get out of the water last or near last, you will make it up on the biking and running segments."

"Sure. Ok." answered Elayne.

The starter had fired his pistol and we were off.

Jenny, who was a strong swimmer forged ahead and was swimming with the elite in front. Elayne fought to stay with the pack and got hit several times by flaying arms. Accidental, of course. However Elayne seemed to sense sometimes done on purpose. After all this was a competition.

The course was rectangular and at the first turn Elayne fought off three swimmers who were aggressive and flaying all over the place.

She could not see Jenny, and anyway was swimming with her head down or sideways most of the time.

Elayne spotted the red bobbing marker and turned right with 150 yards to go to the next turn.

Moderate choppy water was evident out there but did not bother Elayne.

Finally the second marker and another right turn while being kicked in the arms and head by some swimmer in front.

The beach was approaching and Elayne was happy this part was almost over.

As soon as she exited the water some swimmer stepped on the back of her heel and Elayne tumbled down onto the sand.

"You Idiot why don't you watch where you are going?" Elayne yelled out.

"Sorry" was the answer.

Elayne picked herself up and ran to her bike. A quick jump into her bike shoes, planting the helmet on her head, putting on the bike gloves and she was off.

A quick glance back and she could make out only about ten or so bodies behind her. Jenny was nowhere in sight.

The rolling hills bike course was just over ten miles long. The first village was Centerville and as she entered she could see the enthusiastic villagers and probably some tourists lining both sides of the street and cheering.

Elayne had very strong legs as a result of jogging, training, and running some Marathons.

She started to pass other competitors and as she passed them she would count them.

"One, two, three, four, five, six, seven, eight, nine" Tiring after nine she knew she was making up time lost in the swim portion as Jenny had said she would. Down South Main Street and past Four

Seas Ice cream. Past the Centerville Pie Company and the old Country Store.

The road then meandered out to the Village of Osterville and Elayne stopped at Dowses Beach to pee in the toilets near the beach. School children from the local Cape Cod Academy lined the street and were cheering on the participants.

"Hey!" Elayne thought she glimpsed Jenny up ahead as she passed the Oyster Harbors Club and the Wianno Yacht Club on West Bay.

She could just make out the Red Shirt with Harvard on the back but she wasn't sure. The road alongside the beach reminded Elayne of the road along the beach in Martha's Vineyard.

Elayne had passed maybe sixty or seventy riders in her estimate, and Craigsville Beach was approaching. The bikes stacked up at the finish made it a little difficult for Elayne to maneuver however she found where her bike was to be left. Two minutes to drop the helmet, change shoes, and drop the gloves and she was off towards Hyannisport.

A quarter mile on a flat road and then a climb up.

It was easy for Elayne and she again thought she spotted Jenny up ahead. Another quarter mile up and then some gentle rolling hills on the way through the four mile run to Hyannisport. Craigville Beach Road is great to ride on and the view of

Nantucket Sound is breathtaking,

Elayne could not spend too much time sightseeing as she had to make up time in order to finish near the top. The last mile into Hyannisport was a gentle downward slope and Elayne easily passed several more runners as Elayne passed Sixth Avenue, down to First Avenue and then the turn down to Scudder Avenue and down to the Hyannis Port Yacht Club and the finish line in the park.

Elayne was feeling a little light headed as she ran passed the finish line and into the park. She stumbled and crashed into a group of runners sitting on the grass.

"Sorry!" she exclaimed.

"That's OK. " answered Jenny, who was one of the runners sitting and resting.

"Jenny! Am I glad to see you. I thought I saw you several times ahead of me."

"Yeah. I got off to a good start in the swimming." Stated Jenny. "Anyway you survived and finished. How do you feel?" She asked.

"OK. I guess. I am a little dizzy. But I loved it. The scenery and all." answered Elayne.

"That's great! Let's plan our next Triathlon." Jenny said. "Please. I just survived this, my first one. We'll talk about it." Replied Elayne.

Fourteen

Elayne and Jenny talked about it and decided to enter the Nickerson State Park Triathlon.

Nickerson State Park is a state-owned public recreation area of more than 1900 acres located on Cape Cod in Brewster, Massachusetts. The state parks' sandy soil and scrub pines surround many kettle ponds which are dependent on groundwater and precipitation, The largest of these kettle ponds is Cliff Pond which is 0.7 miles across.

The land comprising the state park was once part of the estate of Samuel Mayo Nickerson who made a fortune as one of the founding fathers of the First National Bank of Chicago; and who in 1890 built a mansion a mile west of the present day park.

In 1934 his wife Addie donated that portion of the estate on the south side of Route 6a for use as a state forest park. The park offers more than 400 campsites including cabins and tents.

In addition to 8 miles of roads the state park has trails for hiking, cross-country skiing , horseback and mountain bike riding, and an 8-mile set of bicycle trails that connect the Cape Cod Rail Trail. The bike trails bring riders through white pine stands, spruce stands, a cedar Swamp. Pond views, and woodlands. Cliff Pond is stocked yearly with trout. Other facilities include a boat ramp, lakes for canoeing and swimming, showers, and an amphitheater.

Nowhere in sight are the sand dunes and salt marshes all over Cape Cod. Instead woods that slope down to the banks of eight crystal clear fresh water ponds.

Yet if you walk or cycle through the woods you will not find any rivers or streams feeding the ponds. These are "kettle ponds" among the more than 300 formed as glaciers retreated from the Cape over 10,000 years ago.

Completely dependent on groundwater and precipitation. The water level in the ponds fluctuates from season to season and year to year. Cape Cod Bay is within walking distance or bicycling distance.

Elayne and Jenny had driven down from Boston the night before the race and were at Cliff Pond at 7:00 a.m. stretching, and getting ready with maybe 500 other participants.

The starter gave the five minute warning, and everyone jostled for position on the edge of Cliff Pond, anxiously awaiting the start. The siren went off and so did the swimmers/runners/bikers running into the chilly waters.

A lot of thrashing and flaying of arms.

"Too crowded" said Elayne, pushing for space.

"Your right" answered Jenny.

Suddenly a big body crashed into Elayne pushing

her under the water. Elayne pushed back and maneuvered sideways to get up and breathe.

"Sorry" said this big boned red haired woman.

"Who was that?" asked Elayne.

"That's Susan Hargitty. She does that!" exclaimed Jenny.

"Well-Susan Hargitty,you'r not doing that to me." Elayne exclaimed as she jumped onto Susan Hargitty's back, and pushed her underwater. Susan reached up with one arm that looked like a mechanical crane and pulled Elayne down.

Elayne punched Susan in the side of the head, and managed to get away. Jenny begged" Stop fighting. Concentrate on the race." Elayne swam on ahead making the first turn at the marker.

Lifeguards were situated on rowboats just outside the race area but had not intervened. Elayne said to Jenny" They won't come over to help unless we are drowning. I guess just fighting is ok!"

"They know Susan. They know her tactics" Jenny replied. The second turn marker and Susan was nowhere in sight.

Elayne guessed she was left behind somewhere and suddenly like in the movie Jaws Susan appears and somehow in the deep water of Cliff Pond rises up and flops down on Elayne's back.

Jenny tries to pull her off but Susan's weight is too much. Elayne punches and kicks and breaks free to continue toward the beach. Elayne reaches the beach and runs to where her running shoes are, puts them on and starts the difficult 300 foot stair climb from the end of the swim up to the transition area. She looks around and sees Jenny climbing up but so far no Susan.

Change of shoes, helmet on, bike gloves on and she is off on a paved road narrow enough for only two or three bikers abreast, and very challenging.

The signs say *"Nook Road"* and the climbing starts. Elayne is thinking that this looked so easy driving in, but it is harder than Hyannisport.

About twenty riders including Elayne and Jenny are bunched up together and make the turn towards Area 7 when one rider loses control and spins off into the bushes.

"Well, one down" Jenny says.

"Yes. Gotta concentrate".

A spin into Area 7 and a loop around that goes back towards Nook Road.

Problem here is there is not enough room for two or three bikes side by side and specifically going towards each other because the stragglers are still heading up towards Area 7.

"Very dangerous. Very stupid." States Jenny.

"I agree." Mutters Elayne.

Making it back to the bike stop Elayne drops the bike, the helmet, the shoes, the gloves, puts on her running shoes and takes off with Jenny next to her.

Up the side of Cliff Pond on a narrow strip of land with Little Cliff Pond on the right side. Very narrow trails, no one can pass another. Rocks and roots underfoot require alertness and agility.

Surprise, surprise Big Susan appears and launches into Elayne and pushes Elayne into the bushes on the right side and down a short embankment.

"What the Heck!" cries out Elayne.

"Are you ok?" asks Jenny worried.

"Yes. Just bruised and bleeding a little."
Jenny reaches down and helps pull Elayne up. Elayne looks like she was in a car wreck. Limping she continues towards the water stop where she consumes a lot of water and washes the blood off her arms.

"I'm going to kill that Susan when I see her"
Jenny and Elayne continue up and around Higgins Pond towards Eel Pond and make their way to the next water stop. No sight of Susan.

Elayne's right leg is bruised and hurting now, and she is having trouble running. She can see the finish line but it is still too far. Putting her arm over Jenny's shoulder she limps in the rest of the way and crosses the finish line.

"Well we finished!" exclaims Elayne.

"Yeah Girl. We finished." admitted Jenny. "Now let's find that Susan."
They walked around the finish area and looked into

rooms and walked around the food areas and no sight of Susan.

"Let's go home" begged Jenny.

"Yeah and maybe to the hospital" Joked Elayne. Jenny was hoping Elayne was just joking, and wondered if this would be their last Triathlon. However Jenny had other plans.

Fifteen

Hawaii-Fire and Ice

'Owzit!" Jenny blurted out.

"Owzit? What?" Elayne inquired.

"Owzit?" Repeated Jenny.

"I don't understand what you are asking or talking about." Elayne put forward puzzled.

"Owzit in Hawaiian means How is it? And the answer is, it's good" Jenny explained.

"So what! What do I care about Owzit, whatzit, or any zit in Hawaiian?" Elayne questioned emphatically.

"Well" explained Jenny. "I am invited by National Geographic to go over to Hawaii for two months to help write an article about Hawaii".

"And?" queried Elayne, although knowing what was coming. "And, I want you to come with me!" Jenny answered.

"What! All the way over there? What will I do for two months?" Elayne asked.

"Come on! Elayne! Hawaii is supposed to be beautiful, and we will visit four islands; and run along the beach, and enter a triathlon or two, and maybe meet some interesting and handsome locals.

Listen to this description right out of Frommer's

Guide " Jenny deplored. "There's no place on earth quite like this handful of sun-drenched, mid-Pacific Islands.

The Hawaii of south seas literature and Hollywood films really does exist. Here you'll find palm-fringed blue lagoons, lush rainforests, hidden gardens, cascading waterfalls, wild rivers running through rugged canyons, and soaring volcanoes.

And oh, those beaches-gold, red, black, and even green sands caressed by an endless surf. Each of the six main islands is separate, distinct, and infinitely complex.

There's far too much to see and do on any short vacation, which is why so many people 'Return to the Aloha state year after year."

Elayne was excited."When do we leave? And where will we stay?"

"We leave in three weeks at the end of the semester, and we will stay with the National Geographic crew near Honolulu and on the big island of Hawaii."

Three weeks had passed ever so slowly for Elayne , and it was raining at Logan Airport in Boston however Elayne was excited and couldn't wait for the plane to take off for Hawaii. She fell asleep and woke up as the plane taxied in to the gate in Honolulu.

Elayne and Jenny hoped on the Wiki Wiki Shuttle

bus at Honolulu International Airport and were anxious to arrive at the Sheraton Waikiki on Kalakaua Avenue, after the long flight from Boston.

They arrived, checked in, absorbed the clear Hawaiian air and relished the bright sun beating down on their foreheads.

Elayne ran 3-5 miles every morning and today she decided to run along Waikiki Beach, with the 2-3 miles out being uneventful and Elayne maintained the pace she wanted too.

Coming back Elayne felt a little pain in her left thigh and was laboring on the return jog. As soon as she passed the convention centre she fell onto the sand. A kind gentleman assisted her in standing up.

"Hi! I'm Larry Christofaro. Are you hurt?"

"Not really Larry Christofaro! Just a pulled muscle." Elayne answered.

In front of her, and holding her arm was a very-well tanned, good looking, she observed, man about thirty years old, decent build, about five foot eight wearing one of those Hawaiian shirts with fish in many bright colors decorating the shirt, and a pair of Bahama shorts, and sandals. Blond Hair, Blue eyes, L.A. Dodgers baseball hat. The watch sort of gave him away. A Rolex President , she observed, probably worth $20,000 or so."Come to my abode. Come you can rest"as Larry directed Elayne to his tent at the rear of the beach under the pier.

Larry Christofaro was a true authentic beach bum. He lived on the beach, ate on the beach, and slept on the beach. The strange thing about him was that he was a millionaire.

One of those eccentric millionaires.

His father who had built a fortune in the food business in Los Angeles sent Larry over to Hawaii to start up and oversee a division of the L.A. food business called *Chocolate Gold* which Larry, even with his weird way of conducting business succeeded in establishing on the Hawaiian Islands and supplied most of the cruise ships that docked with chocolate for the chocolate fountains that the ships created during their midnight buffets.

Already having spent five years on the Islands Larry decided to set himself up on Waikiki Beach at the back under a pier. He set up a little tent with a couch, chair, television, gas bar-b-cue, and even hung up some of his favorite pictures of surfers and such.

He was untouchable as a few good old U.S. dollars and boxes of chocolates given to the local police left him to enjoy his makeshift home. He often left his Penthouse in the Hilton Hawaiian Village to spend the night on the beach.

"Hey! Let me massage that thigh for you as Larry sat Elayne down on a padded chair."

"I'm Ok! Just a little muscle pull." Explained Elayne.

"Chocolate?" Larry offered.

"All right" Elayne gave up. "This is good Chocolate! Buy this around here?" Questioned Elayne.

"Actually, My company makes it in L.A., and I distribute it on all four Islands, been doing it for five years. I also supply the cruise ships with liquid chocolate for their chocolate fountains that they set up at their midnight buffets."

"It doesn't look like you eat too much of your product-Your slim and trim!" Elayne noticed.

"Well, I consume too much, but I also jog every day. Keeps me slim." answered Larry.

"Hey, It's late. I gotta go! Larry, thanks for your help and the chocolate. Maybe I'll see you tomorrow or some day when I jog by" Elayne stated.

"Not maybe." Larry answered. "Pass by tomorrow around eight, and I will join you up to Diamond Head and back along Waikiki Beach"

"That's far. I'm not really a long distance jogger!" Complained Elayne.

"I'll teach you. I've been jogging for years." Larry responded. "OK. See you tomorrow!" responded Elayne.

"Where have you been?" Jenny inquired when Elayne returned to the Sheraton.

"Oh, just jogging on Waikiki Beach, and met a handsome local yocal!" "Native?" Jenny pushed.

"No. Actually from L.A., and has been here working the past five years, owns his own chocolate factory and we are going jogging tomorrow." explained Elayne.

"Already! First day here, and you managed to pick up a guy!" Jenny marveled. "Sorry, I can't go with you. Have to go over to Maui with the crew."

"That's all right. I can handle chocolate man." Elayne declared.

Elayne was up early and decided to walk the Ala Wai Canal. She could see the numerous row boats, canoes and rental kayaks.

The palm trees on both sides of the road framed the roadway and the view of the mountains in the distance were breath taking.

No wonder Hawaii is truly described as paradise. Elayne looked down and could see many fish swimming near the side walk. The short walk from Kalakuana Avenue past Ala Moana , down to the boat harbor was like walking in a fantasy land with flowers and fauna.

Elayne just passed the U.S. Army Museum and saw Larry ahead on the beach, stretching. His well tanned muscular back gleaming as the sun bounced off his torso.

"Hi Larry!"

"Well Hello Princess! Ready to rock?" Larry asked. "I don't know about rock. But I'm ready to run!" Elayne responded.

"All right. Let's go!" Stated Larry, and he was off along the beach towards Diamond Head. Elayne had difficulty in keeping up with Larry, and she had to stop continuously.

"Princess, how many marathons have you run? asked Larry.

"A few!" Elayne was able to push out the answer while trying to catch her breath.

"Well" Larry started. "Let's run this beach up to Diamond Head and back with a slow jog and tomorrow I will teach you how to train properly" Elayne was happy that the slow jog would be in her wheelhouse as she was used to running with Jenny, which was she guessed at a slow pace.

They jogged through Ft. DeRussy Beach and into Gray's Beach, and past Waikiki. Queen's surf beach was phenomenal as they jogged slowly while watching the surfers navigate the huge monster waves. Larry was nice enough to slow down every so often to let Elayne catch up.

Past the Waikiki Aquarium, through Sans Souci Beach with the tourists and locals most in bikinis and low rise swim shorts, with bronze well-tanned bodies starting to plant their umbrellas and lay their claim to their small square of sand.

Honeymooners, sun seekers, all in the heart of one of the most beautiful locations in the world. The Diamond Head Lighthouse welcomed Larry and

Elayne as if it's beacon would draw them in like a magnet.

"Let's rest here!" Larry stated, as he walked into the glamorous Hyatt Regency Waikiki on Kalakauna Avenue.

The Hyatt Regency Waikiki is one of Waikiki's biggest hotels, with two 40-storey towers and the hotel itself covers an entire city block, just across the street from the Diamond Head end of Waikiki Beach. The huge second floor lobby is decorated in koa and wraps around an atrium that rises 40 feet from the ground level. Parrots and waterfalls fill the atrium and you get the feeling you are in a tropical jungle paradise and in fact you are; man made of course.

"Come on, let's get a facial and body treatment while we are here!" Larry said.

"How can we? We are not paying guests here!" Elayne questioned."The hotel is one of my customers for *Chocolate Gold* and anyways you are with The Larry, didn't you know?" Larry trotted in like he owned the place

"Hello Mister Michael-How are you today?" Questioned the woman with the flowered white blouse and skirt at the door. "I'm ok! Can the two of us get one of your fantastic massages?" "Of course Mister Michael. Follow me."

Two hours of unexpected facial and massage and body treatment put Elayne in a relaxed wonderful emotional state.

"Larry, Why did she call you Mister Michael?" Wondered Elayne. "I don't know but the massage was great right?"

The jog back was uneventful and Elayne noticed that the beaches were starting to get crowded and soon a space of sand will not be available for any squatters, she decided. Back at Larry's beach tent under the pier Larry ended the day.

"OK Princess see you tomorrow same time and we will start proper training" "OK Larry". Replied Elayne. On the way back Elayne couldn't get that "Mister Michael" off her mind. What was that all about? Sort of strange.

Sixteen

Elayne was up as the saying is' at the crack of dawn.' Jenny was already up and packing for her trek over to Maui with the National Geographic Crew.

"Owzit? Asked Elayne.

"It's good." as Jenny voiced the usual answer.

Elayne moved over to the balcony, went outside, and from the thirty-fourth floor balcony she could just barely make out the figures down on the beach at Waikiki Bay. She could see someone dressed in a bright feather cape blowing on a conch shell and street vendors setting up to sell their

souvenirs and those necklace of flowers called'
Lei'.

Some of the vendors actually sit in their booths
and fashion leis by hand in various patterns, some
sewing tiny blooms or shells together. Some are
twisted, some braided, some strung. Every island
has it's own special flower lei-with the small orange
flower called a ilima popular in Honolulu. Leis say
Hawaii hello, or goodbye, or congratulations, or I
love you.

Leis as they say are the perfect symbol for the
islands. They are given in the moment. And their
fragrance and beauty are enjoyed in the moment,
but even after they fade, their spirit of aloha(or
greeting) lives on, long after, indeed long after.

Elayne could see the sun creeping over the
horizon over Waikiki Bay and thought, this is truly
paradise. The water of the South Pacific was
translucent turquoise and crystal-clear; calm and
inviting.

Elayne breathed in the magnificent air and watched
the first rays of sun streak across the beautiful baby-
blue sky. No spirits, no ghosts, no fears, no being
anxious or worried.

Elayne looked down onto Duke's Waikiki
Beach Restaurant on Kalakaua Avenue and could
just make out the employees setting up the colorful
beach umbrellas. It's always a party at Duke's.
Elayne thought she could hear Hawaiian music that

they play all the way up to the thirty-fourth floor.

A horse with a rider dressed up with numerous Leis. Leis probably for sale. The horse very slowly moved through the water next to the golden sand beach that contained sand as soft as powdered sugar.

Four individuals wearing bright orange Hawaii T-Shirts were pushing their outrigger canoe off the beach to experience the same feeling of riding the crystal-clear water as had been done here for centuries. The canoe was bright yellow and will most likely be seen for miles out to sea.

A Scene from Paradise and in an hour or two Paradise will be wall-to-wall beach towels.

Jenny said "Goodbye! See you in a few days" as she walked out the door.

Elayne decided it was time to go and meet Larry so she excited the balcony, grabbed her back pack and took the elevator down to the lobby.

The sun was hot and it was only 7:30 a.m. but after all this was Hawaii in the South Pacific, and the temperature would soon reach the standard 84 Degrees that was the average day after day, year round.

A quick jaunt down Waikiki beach and there he was lifting weights under the pier, next to his beach tent.

"Hi Larry!"

"Princess. How are you? It's a wonderful day"

stated Larry as he planted a quick kiss on Elayne's cheek. And Elayne didn't mind as she liked Larry and wouldn't mind getting closer to him both physically and mentally. Larry at the same time as the kiss put a Lei necklace of flowers over Elayne's head.

"What's this for?" Questioned Elayne.

"What's this for? What's this for?" Repeated Larry. "It's Hawaii Hello! and Hawaii "I love You!

"How can you love me? You've only known me for one day!" Questioned Elayne.

"It was love at first sight, as they say!" answered Larry.

"Who is they?" Elayne inquired. "They! What's the difference?" Larry stated. "Anyway how are you today, Princess?"

"I'm fine. Yes it's a great day!" Answered Elayne.

"Have some fruit. Some real Hawaiian fruit". Larry pointed to a bowl on his picnic table in his makeshift house-on-the-beach.

"What's this?" Elayne asked, as she held up a round fruit colored purple , green and white.

"Mangosteen" Answered Larry. "Mangoes are found all over the Hawaiian Islands and are sweet and delicious. And Papayas and Pineapples like those" Larry pointed to the fruit bowl.
Maybe next week I'll take you out to visit a Plantation. "Anyway, grab a mango and let's go!"

"Have you stretched?" Larry asked.

"Yes! And you?" Elayne questioned. "Me? I've been up and about since six thirty!" "Let's go!" And Larry was off jogging down the beach close to the sea, sometimes jumping over an incoming wave of wonderful blue-green translucent water.

"Larry...You're going too fast!" Yelled out Elayne "Elayne...You're going too slow!"Answered Larry. Larry stopped and waited for Elayne to catch up, then took her hand and ran a pace between her 'slow pace' and his 'faster pace'. Elayne enjoyed her small delicate hand being cradled in Larry's bigger hand and she tried her best to keep up the pace without falling. Past Kuhio Beach Park and then Hapuna Beach.

Down Kalakaua Avenue , past the Aquarium and Natatorium and through Sans Souci Beach.

"Larry, I need to stop. I need to take a short break." Implored Elayne. "Want some chocolate?" Larry asked, while digging into his backback.

"No thanks. Just need a short break." Answered Elayne.

At Kaluahole Beach Larry let go of Elaynes hand and began to run full speed up to the Diamond Head Lighthouse.

"I'll wait for you at the Lighthouse." Larry yelled back over his shoulder as he sped on.

Elayne was relieved that she could have a chance to take a rest as even Larry running a slower pace than he usually does was hard for her to keep up.

Elayne was huffing and puffing and hadn't realized that she was not in the best of shape, although running with Jenny in all those Marathons and Triathlons was at a very easy pace.

The Lighthouse rebuilt in 1917 after an inspection found cracks in the original 1899 structure, and the newer structure strongly resembles the original, and it is a spectacular sight, white 55-feet tall overlooking the clear blue Pacific Ocean. It's red color lantern dome looking like a candle flame lit and able to spread light nearly 18 miles out into the Ocean, with a 60,000 candle power Fresnel lens. The tower itself is square with a circular balcony.

Perched on the side of an extinct volcano , the lighthouse shines a powerful light to warn boats, ships and canoes to stay away from the reefs at Waikiki, and it had become a necessity due to ships running aground in the same area.

The lighthouse is not open to the public but can be seen from Diamond Head Road, sitting in a sea of green lush trees , palm trees and vegetation while spreading it's light like a parent protecting their children.

In 1825, British sailors ascended the defunct

Volcanic crater and found hard clear calcite crystals among the black rocks. Mistaking them for diamonds, the sailors named the crater Diamond Head. One of the Hawaiian names for Diamond Head is "Leahi" meaning "wreath of fire".

This name reflects the ancient Hawaiian practice of lighting a fire on the crest of the volcano to guide canoe fleets back to the island.

When Captain James Cook sailed the Hawaiian Archipelago in 1778 he saw no man made aids to navigation. In today's Hawaii however hundreds of modern aids such as lighthouses, buoys and radio beacons are in operation to assist the sea traveler. The Diamond Head Lighthouse is now automated, it stands as a sentinel to Honolulu, flashing a welcome to mariners from the east and west.

Though the days of the traditional lighthouse keepers are gone, the duty of the lighthouse continues, and like the hundreds of sentinels of the shore Diamond Head Light stands its watch guiding the weary mariner safely passed its rocky shore.

Elayne could just make out the neighboring island of Molokai as she made it up to the street near the lighthouse, and there was Larry reclined on a park bench.

"What took you so long?" He asked.

"Hey! I had to take a break. I'm not as in shape as you are!" Answered Elayne. "Well, Whatever shape your in, I like that shape." Exclaimed Larry.

Elayne was surprised at the comment. *Was Larry starting to come on to her? She thought.* "OK. Come on we are going to hike up to the top of Diamond Head Crater" Larry stated.

"Did you know that Ancient Hawaiians first named the extinct volcano Le'Ahi for its strong Ahi-Tuna-fish brow like appearance?"

"No! I didn't know that! And how should I. This is my first trip to Hawaii." Elayne replied."OK Princess! Don't get testy!" Larry shot back.

"Testy! I'm not testy! Are you implying I'm irritated or cranky because I answered you back?" Elayne asked.

"No. Princess-Just having conversation". Larry said."Come on we need to enter the Diamond Head Park from the eastern side through a short tunnel that will bring us into the center of the crater where we will start our 560 foot climb.

Larry and Elayne made their way through the tunnel and began climbing up the switchback dirt pathway that ascended up the Westside of the crater. Lots of loose gravel and dirt potholes on the trail make it dangerous to keep footing and many have slipped and fallen. Larry and Elayne passed four hikers wearing uncovered flip-flops meant more for the beach, and Larry commented to Elayne that these four were fooling around with disaster as those flip-flops provided no support or grip on the slippery loose gravel slope.

They quickly made their way up to the first lookout, and stopped to catch their breath and enjoy the beautiful ocean view.

Then stairs, lots of stairs. 99 steps leads up to a dimly lit 200 foot long tunnel that leads through the volcanic crater wall to the Pacific Ocean side.

Next Larry and Elayne climbed out of the tunnel and continued up more stairs until they finally reached the top viewing platform with its 360 degree views that are breathtaking.

The panoramic views of Waikiki to Waianae, the hugh Pacific Ocean, the Ko'olau Mountains and eastern views reaching out to the Koko Head Crater. The sign that Larry and Elayne read stated "Diamond Head Crater holds the record for the longest recorded land views in the world. On a clear day, that is definitely true.

"Oh Larry, this is the most beautiful place in the world! Thanks for bringing me up here!" Elayne said with emotion.

"Your welcome, and now we go down to Diamond Head Beach Park and you will witness some more beauty."Larry stated. "You promise?" Questioned Elayne.

"Yes! And surprises too!"And Larry was off before Elayne had a chance to inquire about what surprises.

The jog down was of course a lot easier than going up, and in fact in some places the pathway is paved as it winds down to the beach.

As Larry and Elayne got closer to the beach Elayne could pick out surfers out on the waves, and she noticed that the surf breaks outside the reef in multiple spots, which is located a good quarter mile out to sea. Even if the waves were flat around the island you could still count on some surf breaks in this area. The reef is shallow and extends right up to the beach for the most part.

The beach is semi private as huge amazing beach front homes that Elayne imagined are worth millions lined the beach.

The view of the beach and ocean was incredible and Elayne could see several beach combers with their metal seeking equipment combing the sand.

Even though the water was shallow in some spots there were some deeper sections of water where swimmers were splashing and playing like children in a sun-drenched paradise.

Larry and Elayne came upon the sign that read 'Cromwell's Cove' and Larry explained that this spot is a local weekend favorite spot that is less travelled, and has, as Elayne could see lots of sand and shady palm trees.

"Ok Princess, this is our spot" Larry exclaimed as he dropped his backpack onto the sand under a huge palm tree that was bent out in a u shape pointing towards the ocean.

Larry took a blanket out of his backpack and spread it out over the sand while flattening down the edges to make a perfect four foot square of blanket over sand.

"Sit!" Larry ordered as if telling his dog to sit.

Elayne was tired from the walk, jog, stairs, up and down so she just sat without comment. Larry next took out a thermos and two glasses and poured a cherry-red liquid into the glasses.

"Mimosa?"

"Amazing, Larry you have everything. What else do you have in that backpack? A candelabra and a piano!"asked Elayne as she reached for the Mimosa. Several Mimosas later and Elayne was a little dizzy.

"Is this the surprise you talked about?" Elayne asked.

"No. This is!" Larry responded as he removed his Hawaiian shirt, his cargo shorts, and except for his designer underwear, he was standing before Elayne as naked as a jaybird. Larry's deep dark tan could be easily distinguished from the white skin that framed his lower torso. White skin from below his belly button to the top of his thighs. He shone like a Greek statue in a museum on a pedestal.

Elayne was shocked and surprised and all she could say as she perused the scene was" You forgot to take off your socks, shoes and designer watch!".

Elayne could not help but notice again how

muscular and well built Larry was, and because she was wearing her sunglasses she suspected that Larry could not really tell her reaction to his swift and surprising undressing.

"My watch is waterproof!" Larry calmly said as he removed his socks and running shoes. "Come, take off your clothes and join me in the most refreshing swim you'll ever have, my Princess!"

"But Larry, can't people see us?" She questioned.

"Maybe, but they don't care, and they will mind their own business. Come on Princess, this is what life is all about! Take off your clothes and join me. I want you to come into the beautiful Pacific Ocean with me."

Elayne hesitated for a moment and then thought, 'Why not?'

She was thousands of miles from home, and on a beach in Paradise with a handsome good looking almost nude dude who probably if she did not undress would undress her himself, and actually she relished the thought of being almost nude and in the water with Larry.

First came the T-shirt and then the running bra which she gingerly hung over a branch of the palm tree. Then she removed her socks and running shoes and her watch, which was not waterproof. She decided to keep on her underwear as she removed her running shorts. There she was almost naked like a baby first brought into the world.

"Your hat" Larry stated as he viewed his exquisite Princess. What a body. Beautiful, flat stomach, white thighs, and a similar tanned body to match his with white skin from below the bellybutton to the top of the thighs.

He took her hand in his and started towards the blue translucent water, and dunked himself and pulled Elayne with him into the ocean resting in a small pool of water that he knew was deep enough to cover their almost nakedness.

Pulling Elayne towards him he wrapped his legs around her and put his chest against hers. Lightly caressing her hair he kissed her with passion, and Elayne did not resist or pull away.

"Larry, we've just met yesterday!" Elayne managed to say in between the kisses.

"Everything moves quickly in Paradise, my sweet!" Larry stated. "Come lets swim out to a reef"

Larry was a strong swimmer and Elayne as in running with Larry struggled to keep up. Elayne noticed the outrigger canoe with the six men paddling towards her and dove down into the water hoping that the men did not see her swimming almost nude. She held her breath and from deep down she could see the canoe slid by. Phew she thought its ok to go up to the surface.

Larry was resting against a reef and although it took Elayne a few minutes to reach the reef she was happy to reach Larry and slid next to him, putting her body next to his, feeling the warmth of his body.

"Princess, I have another surprise for you tonight!" Larry said.

"Larry, most of my clothes are already off. I can't take anything else off". "No we will swim back, get dressed, and a friend of mine has arranged for us to eat up in the lighthouse and spend the night there"

"I thought the public is not allowed in the lighthouse, right?" questioned Elayne. "Yes the general public. But I am Larry, the chocolate man, and I have friends"

"Ok Larry, It should be exciting." Elayne said.

Swimming back to the beach was uneventful, and actually Elayne relished the freedom of swimming without any bathing suit top, and could imagine how the nudists liked to be nude. In the water no one could see, but close to the beach a family of four including two teenagers had settled in near where Larry and Elayne had left their clothes. And in addition six men where sharing a picnic table just off the beach under a palm tree that was close to where Elayne's Bra and T-shirt were hanging.

"Larry, I can't get out of the water and walk nude on the beach showing everything I got to that family and those men at the picnic table. I need three hands to cover up whereas you only need one so I will stay in the water and you go onto the beach and bring back my clothes. I don't care if they get wet." Elayne stated.

"OK!" Larry answered.

To Elayne's surprise Larry got up out of the ocean and without covering up at all just strolled right past the family, including the two teenagers, and proceeded right to where Elayne's clothes were hanging. He quickly put on his shorts and pulled Elayne's Bra and T-Shirt off the palm tree and gathered up the rest of her clothes and walked back to the water.

He gave her the clothes one by one as she got dressed and then he returned to where his clothes were to complete dressing.

Elayne walked out of the water to put on her socks and shoes.

"Thanks Larry. That swim was wonderful!" Elayne stated while the picture of his well sculptured bronzed body remained stuck in her head.

Seventeen

The walk back along Kulamanu Street from Kulamanu Pl Beach and Diamond Head Rd was fairly easy and the Lighthouse could be seen in the distance with its fire red domed top glowing.

As they got closer to the gate it was locked to prevent the public from going onto the Lighthouse property. Elayne was surprised to see two locals unlocking the gate and opening the door for Larry and Elayne to pass through the wrought iron fence. One of the locals told Larry that the food and drink he ordered were up in the Lantern room and they would lock the gate behind Larry and Elayne and see them at 7:30 the next morning.

Larry and Elayne made their way through the manicured grounds, past the well trimmed palm trees and bushes and entered the lighthouse through the main door that was already unlocked for Larry. Up the circular stairs going round and round until they reached the Keeper's Quarters where a long natural wood table was placed in the middle with six chairs, surrounding the table. A nice chandelier hung from the ceiling.

A double bed rested against one wall and Elayne could see a small bathroom on the opposite wall.

Larry and Elayne deposited their belongings including Larry's backpack on the table and went outside onto the circular balcony and climbed up the ladder which was the only access to the lantern room.

The huge Fresnel Lens dominated most of the room and Elayne knew that the light that shone from this lense was extremely powerful. She had heard that Fresnel Lenses were developed in France around 1823 and that they are used by most lighthouses around the world. More than 400 lighthouses in the United States used Fresnel Lenses. Way back in 1300 B.C. the Trojans built an early fire tower or lighthouse at Sigeum. The Egyptians and the Romans built lighthouse towers way back in 280 BC and 50 BC.

The Romans built a lighthouse in England at Dover in 3 BC. Even with the bright light from the lens what a beautiful view of the ocean and of Honolulu itself from the walk around balcony. A wind vane on top of the dome pointed the way north.

Larry and Elayne carried the containers of food and drink downstairs to the Keepers' Quarters and unpacked the food onto the table.

Elayne was excited at the prospect of having a nice dinner up in the lighthouse with Larry, and spending the night.

To Elayne's amazement Larry unpacked a white linen tablecloth which he lay over the table like he was covering a table at the Ritz. Next came the candles and linen napkins and cutlery, silver of course. Roses put into a venetian glass vase that was lying on the floor were put onto the table in the middle with the candles strategically placed around them. A giant bottle of Mimosa and two long stem wine glasses, with strawberries placed in clear glass bowls set the scene.

The sun was just setting over the horizon and Larry and Elayne went out to view the magnificent scene laid out over the South Pacific like a painting created by one of the masters.

They could hear the sound of a conch just as the sun disappeared from the sky going below the ocean horizon. The beat of a sacred Hawaiian drum called a pahu could be heard all across the beach down below and the beautiful melodic sound crept up to their perch on the side of the lighthouse. The incantation of a Hawaiian chant followed. Elayne wondered what this all meant, the sounds of the conch, the beating of a drum, and the wondrous melodic sound that followed.

"Larry, what does all those sounds mean? anything significant?" Elayne inquired.

"Elayne, the sounding of the conch shell is as the Hawaiians say is to gather up all of the mana or energy from the four corners, and from our day, from our ancestors, and from ourselves. It signals to us that it is the time to reflect upon the day-what we have accomplished and all of our good deeds, but also what we're yet to accomplish. The things we shouldn't have said or thought or done, the promises we made but can't keep."

Larry continued and Elayne was mesmerized by Larry-his way of talking, his delicate speech, his actions, his handsomeness. "As the sun touches the ocean" Larry explained." You let all of these things go, so you can await the dawn and a new day. And the Mother tells you, you are forgiven" he said, "but to remember."

"The Chant calls on the gods and on our ancestors to give us wisdom, and to help us bid farewell to the day, whose light is represented through the heartbeat-like rhythms of the drum."

Larry pulled Elayne closer and wrapped his arms around her and planted a kiss square on her lips. Elayne kissed back and could feel the warmth of Larry's body as they stood perched on the edge of the lighthouse, with a little wind picking up.

"Princess!" Larry continued."The thought of releasing the day with the sinking of the sun is soothing-and the notion that whole families perform this ritual together feels powerful"

"With or without the kissing?" Elayne joked and inquired. Larry did not answer but continued his narrative.

"What if we all punctuated every day with a moment of reflection and intention?" "What if we could release ourselves from our mistakes, our failures, and our misgivings each evening and begin again, anew, tomorrow? And what if we did this with the people whose lives-whose feelings and thoughts and possibilities-are all tangled up in our own? What if we could collectively move forward refreshed and renewed, to try again-maybe to try harder-tomorrow?" Larry asked.

"That's beautiful! Larry. Just beautiful!" exclaimed Elayne.

"So bid farewell to this day, Elayne. Bid farewell."

Elayne's heart was beating fast as she bid farewell to her day. What was next? What plan did Larry have to follow this stupendous day and what was to come? Elayne was in a trance and this was just a fairy tale come true. Larry broke the silence. "My Princess Elayne. Come in for dinner!"

The escargot was exquisite. The Mimosa kept flowing. The pasta with shrimp and lobster was scrumptious. The bread was just baked and coated with cheese and bowls of Hawaiian fruit decorated the table. Larry cut up a fresh pineapple and fed Elayne small pieces of the delicious fruit.

"One pineapple for you, and one kiss for me" As Larry kissed Elayne. "Another pineapple for you, another kiss for me, and now some brandy" Larry stated, as he poured some into a glass and gulped it down.

Larry picked up Elayne and carried her to the bed against the wall, and slowly let her down onto the bed. Elayne rested her head on the pillow as Larry lay on the bed, and cuddled close to Elayne.

The Red Glow of the Lighthouse Beam swept over them in a continuous motion as the beam went round and round and shone out into the Pacific competing with the candlelight that was coming from the candles Larry had lit on the table top.

The sky was clear and moonlight flooded where they lay as 360 degree of windows allowed the light in without restriction.

After some hugging and kissing both fell sound asleep as the day had been long and physically demanding. Elayne had no thoughts of Spirits or Demons. No thoughts of Ghosts or goblins. Only wonderful memories of the day just past, and the thought of wonderful days to come, perhaps with Larry, The Chocolate Man of Hawaii.

Elayne was stirred out of her dreams and deep sleep as the strong morning Hawaiian sun pushed through the all-encompassing windows framing the Keeper's Quarters. At first she could not see Larry but after walking around the small area she spotted him crouching against the huge Fresnel Lens, inspecting it as if he was a lighthouse engineer doing a quality control check.

"Come down, Larry! Let's have breakfast!"

"What breakfast?" Larry responded. "You will see. I prepared it for us." Answered Elayne.

Larry was surprised to see what Elayne had put together, and they proceeded to finish off the rest of the Mimosa and Strawberries.

A quick descent down the circular stairs and before Elayne knew it they were back at Larry's tent on the beach.

"Princess, I've got to check on some of my merchandise downtown so how about if we jog tomorrow morning around eight?" "Sure, Larry, looking forward to it. See you tomorrow".
A little peck on Elayne's cheek and Larry was off walking briskly down towards Ala Moana Blvd.

A knock on the door interrupted Elayne's wonderful deep sleep as she dreamed of beaches, oceans, lighthouses and such.

"What time is it?" she asked to no one in particular, as she glanced at the digital wall clock. Her eyes still not focusing made out what looked like seven thirty.

Who would be knocking on her door at seven-thirty in the morning? Maybe Jenny was back.
Elayne put on her housecoat , buttoned up, and moved slowly over to the door wondering who was knocking at this early hour.
Opening the door she was shocked by the apparition

before her.

"Hello Ma'am." He said." I'm Sam Yakimoto, Michael's- sorry I mean Larry's Business Manager."

Elayne couldn't actually see anything past this creature as his huge body filled the complete doorway. A six foot plus something man of about thirty-five , with stubble on his chin that appeared to be two or three days old, jet black hair sporting a pony tail, draped in a grey suit that barely contained his massive shoulders. Something out of the World Wrestling Circuit.

A brown face that reminded Elayne of the local Hawaiians with two gigantic hands that obviously were battle weary and two tree stump legs that strained to tear apart the trousers wrapped around them. Oddly enough white Adidas sneakers that seemed completely out of place finished the picture blocking the light in her doorway.

"Why are you here? And where is Larry?" Elayne's thoughts were scrambled as she attempted to discover what was going on at seven-thirty in the morning.

"Larry had to go to L.A. suddenly last night on business. He will be back in three or four days so he asked me to tell you".

"Oh." Elayne was surprised. "Ok thank you" as she tried to close the door, but a size fourteen Adidas shoe blocked the attempt. Elayne suddenly got very nervous.

"Sorry Ma'am. I'll get out of the way" as the look like an ex pro wrestler stepped back into the hallway.

Elayne shut the door, slid the two latches and turned the knob to lock it, as she breathed a little easier, having been a little anxious with that huge creature almost inside her apartment.

She stood still and listened as she could hear him moving down the hall; and now wondering what Larry was up to in L.A. He didn't mention anything about going and in fact the plans were to jog again together this morning.

Elayne felt sleepy and exhausted after the lighthouse ordeal so she slipped into bed and fell into another deep sleep.

Eighteen

Jimmy" Mad Dog" Morales pushed open the thick stainless steel freezer door to check on 'the meat' on the hook.

Jimmy had made his mark in Acapulco while working his way up through the Mexican Mafia. At just seventeen he had shot and killed Arturo Guzman a high ranking cartel leader that had controlled the illicit drug market in Mexico and exported almost 70% of the *ice* being smuggled into Hawaii.

Mad Dog was short, about five foot five, with big broad shoulders and massive arms. Balding during his thirties he had decided to have the Yul Brenner look and shaved his head completely. His big black bushy eyebrows and his shiny bald head made him look like a cartoon character, however when once a local Hawaiian had mistakenly called him 'Bushy' he used his massive hands to turn that Hawaiian's face into pulp. No one had the nerve to challenge him after that. He had a reputation for being a little crazy at times and really crazy and violent at other times. He had personally strangled almost a dozen Mexicans during his rise up the Mafia ranks.

Mad dog had come over to the Islands almost twenty years ago to help supervise the distribution and control of the *ice* that his cartel was shipping over to Hawaii. In order to appear legitimate to the local authorities he had opened and was running a golf course on the Waianae Coast and had a 50% share in an illicit gambling house that the police left alone, some suspecting a little payoff happening to persuade the police to leave the gambling house alone, and the police were happy to comply as they perceived no major crime occurring at the house, and in fact it's operations, including some prostitution was good for Hawaii tourism.

What the police were not aware of, or ignored, was that Mad Dog's gambling house was a major source for distribution of drugs and specifically crystal meth (*Ice*) which fed Mad Dog an estimated $20 million per year.

Jimmy "Mad Dog" Morales pushed aside some sides of beef that were hanging and approached his meat that was hanging at the back of the freezer in a corner.

The human figure , arms tied behind the back, legs shackled, was strung up under the armpits with a massive chain that then hung on a hook protruding from the ceiling. A blindfold covered the eyes and the mouth was gagged with a towel.

Mad Dog used a meat hook to push and prod the human in the back making him spin around slowly.

"Michael, you still alive?" Asked Mad Dog.
A moan was all that came from the human meat, but a pool of blood was visible on the floor suggesting some wounds had been inflicted.

"Ok. Michael. Are you cold? It's only 38 degrees in here. I wouldn't want you to get sick!" Mad Dog stated with irony.

Mad Dog gave Michael, the human meat on a hook, a final stab in the side, and excited the freezer.

"Hey Boss. How's the meat?" Questioned Carl Lagusta, Mad Dogs' muscle on the Big Island, even though he didn't need any, he could take care of things himself, but he couldn't be everywhere so Carl managed the Big Island for Mad Dog.

"He's still alive, but barely. Should be dead meat by tomorrow morning". Mad Dog calmly replied.

"Great. I'll get the transport ready"

"Hey, let's keep this between the two of us. We don't want the Feds or local cops knowing we knocked off another *ice* competitor." Ya got me, Carl?".

"Sure Boss. Sure. Just you and me".

Hawaii's crystal methamphetamine problem was upsetting businesses, the economy and the community even though a lot of people were racking in millions as suppliers, wholesalers, retailers and resellers.

Some businesses that appeared to be legitimate were actually dummy business fronts for smuggling in the drugs and to manage the cash; and the Feds nicknamed the Las Vegas supply *"Ice"*.

It was easy to pack *ice* inside product that was shipped from the U.S. and Chocolate was the ideal product as it's Chocolate smell masked the smell of the drugs. *Ice* was packed inside crates of Chocolate and then put into containers to make the trip over by boat to Hawaii.

Various pick-up agents in Honolulu working as Chocolate dealers and distributors picked up packages at the warehouse in Honolulu where the containers were unloaded. The contraband would be passed down the chain until it got to a user; with the cash making it's way back up the chain to the importer.

A type of pyramid marketing scheme that was bringing in sometimes $25,000 to $30,000 or more per week and Larry Christofaro aka Michael Simons was having a tough time managing the cash flow. Some weeks he had to handle a suitcase full of cash and how many boats, cars or houses could he buy without law enforcement finding out that he was not importing Chocolate but *Ice*.

Also the Mexicans were major competition and deadly. Mad Dog had caused a lot of problems for any competitor since he arrived in Hawaii and several competitors had disappeared mysteriously in the past few years.

Mad Dog was not pleased with Michael Simons who as Larry Christofaro was cutting into Mad Dog's business with the Chocolate ruse. Anyway by tomorrow morning another competitor will have been eliminated.

Mad Dog excited the main building and could just make out two figures down at the first tee hitting golf balls out over the cliffs into the ocean.

Probably some teenagers! Thought Mad Dog as he made his way up the stairs to his bungalow.

Two beers later and Mad Dog fell onto his king-sized bed like a whale flopping down on the Pacific Ocean after rising up to blow air out of the blowhole.

5:00 am

Henry's Hawaiian Meat truck pulls up to the rear unloading door at the golf club; and Jerry Lupatoga adjusts his San Francisco 49ers cap to sit down tighter on his massive Samoan head.

Everything about Jerry is massive-His shoulders, neck, torso, legs, all over average from picking up slabs of meat and crates of vegetables; and also from his daily gym workouts.

Jerry, all six foot six inches of him was scary to look at, and he intimidated the opposing players when he played in the NFL for ten years. Now retired back on the islands he was happy with his 50% ownership of Henry's Meat and his daily routine which begins at four in the morning and ends around two in the afternoon.

Jerry rang the service bell as he usually did

three times a week at the golf course main building and was surprised when no one answered. This was unusual as in two years of delivering here this had never happened. Normally someone opens the door within a few minutes. Jerry rang again and pounded on the window covered so no one could see inside.

Almost ten minutes had passed and Jerry turned around trying to decide what to do next. The Hawaiian sun had not crept up over the horizon yet and only one dim light lit up the area around the door, when suddenly one door out of the two creaked open a few inches and Jerry turned back and asked" What's happening? I got a load of meat and other stuff for you!"

Jerry could not make out who was behind the door as it was only open ever so slightly so with his oversized left hand he grasped the edge of the door and pulled it open another foot or so.

"We don't need any delivery today. Come back tomorrow." A male voice ordered.

"Half of my truck is for you. I can't come back tomorrow!" Jerry pleaded as he tried to force his face further between the open and closed doors. " I have to be on the other side of the island tomorrow".

"Too bad. You go now!" The voice stated with authority. Jerry could make out something hanging from a hook and it looked to Jerry like something human. He tried to stall so he could get a better look. "OK. Can I use the washroom?".

"No sorry. Everything closed. No one here. Go use the public washrooms near the beach."

Definitely human form Jerry decided. Arms handcuffed behind it's back with legs shackled and Jerry could just make out the head with a rag wrapped around probably he thought as a blindfold. "OK. I'm going. Maybe see you tomorrow or I'll send another driver". Jerry pushed the door shut and could hear the sliding bolt being maneuvered into place.

Jerry was not involved in any crime or organized crime on the Islands however he knew some Samoans who were deep into racketeering, drug trafficking, prostitution, loan sharking, money laundering and corruption and were competing with the local Asian gangs- The Chinese Triads, Japanese Yakuza, Korean Khangpae. All fighting for a piece of the vast illegal economy that operates all over the Hawaiian Islands.

Jerry climbed into the cab of his truck, sat down on the oversized 'Jerry Seat', started up the vehicle and drove down to the beach where the public washrooms were. Of course he knew they were locked up until 9:00 when the local authorities would come and unlock them.

Jerry had John "JohnJohn" Hui's number on his speed dial and he pushed the button to make the call and after only two rings someone answered.

"Ya. Who does you tink you are? And what the Hell- why are you callin' so early in the a.m.- You crazy or someting?" "Maybees I wons the lottery-You tink? Is dat why you are callin'? You better has a good reason you sons of a bitch!" JohnJohn shouted out, using his best English.

"Hey. Calm down. It's Jerry Lupatoga- remember me from the NFL?"

"Yes. Jerry. Has you finally decided to join us? Business is boomin'-You could make a killing- A KILLING!" Emphasized JohnJohn with a little irony.

"No. Listen I was making a delivery to the golf course past Ewa Beach up there on Okupe Street and I noticed something unusual. First, for the first time in two years the place was closed and I couldn't make my normal meat delivery. Whoever answered the back door wouldn't let me in." Explained Jerry.

"So, what's so crazy about dat?" Questioned JohnJohn.

"I managed to pull the door open a little and I swear I saw a human figure hanging in the freezer next to the door."

"So what! Mad Dog Morales usually gits rid of his competitions by 'freezin' them out' and it's OK wit us cause it eliminates another one of our competitors too, so it's less work for us. Hey t'anks for calling-maybees they got Michael Simons all trussed up over dere. I heard he's been missin the past few days.

Maybe you should call his muscle guy-Sammy Yakimoto! And Jerry, don't call this fukin early in the mornin' again-you disturbed my baby sleep." JohnJohn slammed down the phone to emphasize what he had just demanded.

Jerry knew Michael Simons' business location where he operated as Larry Christofaro and where containers of Chocolate were coming and going. He didn't know the phone number so he drove out past Ewa Beach and down into Waikiki.

The Hawaiian Sun was now over the horizon and it was the beginning of another day in Paradise. By noon it would be eighty-two degrees, sunny, no clouds , with a little humidity being pushed away by a slight breeze coming in from the Pacific.

Jerry adjusted his sunglasses and turned on the truck radio to catch the latest news as he travelled down the H1 at a speed of seventy miles per hour.

"The DEA has just busted another Meth Lab and seized a significant quantity of cocaine at the airport, which was hidden in dolls apparently made in Mexico and destined for delivery to Maui and into the hands of the Mexican Cartel there." News burst out of the truck radio speaker.

Reports of drug seizures and busts of Meth labs and other drug seizures were a daily occurrence and most Hawaiians were used to the reports.

" Larry Christofaro, The King of Chocolate has been missing for two days, and is still unaccountable." added the announcer,

The Chocolate Gold warehouse was in among a series of warehouses that bordered the waterfront and at first sight appeared to be run down and neglected, and they were. The buildings were mostly three story brick with dirty, never washed windows covered with metal bars to prevent entry. Newspaper and trash moved down the street and settled in doorways that probably had not been opened in years. A favorite place for the unemployed street inhabitants to occupy the steps in front of the steel warehouse doors. Built almost sixty years ago with a few windows actually broken and neglected in disrepair.

Jerry looked for 76 Libby Street, found it and drove up to the stairs protruding from a grayish color non-descript two story building. One single spot light was still shinning over the parking lot even though the sun was now completely out overhead.

As Jerry exited his truck he could see four or five containers across the pavement probably waiting to be loaded or unloaded.

The words Chocolate Gold could be seen imprinted on the sides and backs of each container. Loose electric wires were strung on poles with one transformer perched up on a wooden pole. In the distance the mountain range was visible as it lined the area as if it was an attempt to fence in what went on here and keep it here.

One knock on the door and it was opened quickly, with force and Jerry was shocked to see a figure that mirrored himself, except for the pony tail. Sam Yakimoto, all six foot plus stood face to face, nose to nose with Jerry and sneered " What can I do for you?"

"It's what I can do for you, is the question?" answered Jerry.

"What do you mean, Sir?"

"Well I understand that your boss Larry or Michael, as he's known is missing!" Jerry pushed out the words.

"Yes. Why? You know something?" As Sam reached out with his gargantuan hands and pulled Jerry closer by grasping Jerry's shirt collar.

"Yes. I think I know something. But first let go of my shirt or I will have to hurt you-football style!" Jerry explained.

A moment in time when two well-built former athletes starred at each other and processed the next move which would be a full fledge fight or a back-off nicely situation.

Sam sneered. Jerry meaned up his face. Both looked eye to eye. Jerry reached into his back pocket for his pen knife in case.

Sam made one tug of Jerry's shirt towards him and then let go. Possible war had been averted and now Sam inquired" What do you know? And make it fast."

"I sell and deliver meat. See my truck over there?" As Jerry pointed to his truck, motor running in order to keep the meat frozen in his temperature controlled truck.

" I was making my usual delivery to the golf course down past Ewa Beach on Fort Weaver Road and for the first time in two years the place was closed and someone at thc back door wouldn't let me in."

"So What?" Yelled Sam impatiently. "What does that have to do with Larry?".

"Well, I was able to sneak a peek through the door and I am sure I saw a human trussed up and hanging in the freezer; and I know meat and that was a human torso, also gagged with hands tied behind it's back."

"Were you able to determine male or female?"

"No."

"Well what does this have to do with Larry?"

"Do you know Mad Dog Morales?"

"Yes! Man he's running some meth and other stuff out of that club!" Shouted Sam."

"Bingo! That's right. Everyone including the cops know that; and a lot of Hawaiians know that

Larry aka Michael is a big competitor to Mad Dog. It just fits." Explained Jerry.

"OK. Thanks for the tip off. I will get my boys together and go right out there. If it is Michael and we can save him he will be grateful, I know it."

"Just a couple of crates of Chocolate and I'll be paid back!" Jerry replied as he walked towards his meat delivery vehicle.

Sam Yakimoto shut the door and got on the phone with Vinny"The Juice" Mammato and then Gregory"The Russian" Lukovitch and then Steve"Baseball" Winters and explained quickly what they needed to do, and how important it was that they drop anything they were doing and meet him right away in Ewa Beach , of course bringing their guns, weapons, bats, and chains. It appeared that Michael's life depended on them, if he was still alive.

Only forty-five minutes later all four were perched on Fort Weaver Road looking down on the main building of the golf course.

"Vinny, you and me are gonna just drive right up to the front door and unload my golf clubs as if we are playing eighteen today. However instead of golf clubs I got a little friend in the bag.
Rus, you and Baseball make your way through the side property and try to get in the back door. If it's locked drop some of that dynamite which when

exploding might cause a diversion so we can get in the front. Anyway break some of those big picture windows and come in the side of the building if you can't get in through the back door. Cah-peesh?" Questioned Sam.

"Yah Sammy, we cah-peesh, we understand". Vinny replied.

Sam and Vinny drove down the circular driveway and stopped in front of the main building door, where Sam , who had golfed here several times, knew the pro shop was down to the right with the restaurant on the left towards the back of the building overlooking the 18th green and the ocean.

Some lights were on inside but when Sam tried the front door it was locked. He looked at his $20,000 Patek Phillippe Calatrava watch and in checking the time, which was almost 9:00, he remembered that Michael had given it to him on his birthday last year. 9:00 sharp and an explosion could be heard coming from the back of the building which was Rus and Baseball setting off the dynamite on schedule.

Vinny smashed the glass on the front door with a five iron and reached around and was able to turn the knob to unlock the door. He then kicked it open and as he went in two goons appeared from the pro shop area.

Sammy reached into his golf bag and pulled out the Mini Uzi submachine gun and began to spray bullets along the wall from the glass windows about two feet high. The goons retreated and hid behind the corner in the hallway leading to the pro shop.

Sam and Vinny had both served in Viet Nam and as Sam sprayed bullets into the lobby Vinny made his way around back of Sam and headed towards the restaurant. He could hear some gunfire coming from the back of the building and suspected that Rus and Baseball were in a firefight with Mad Dog or his men.

Vinny tried the restaurant door and it was locked so he shot at it with his pistol and after three shots he kicked it open. Vinny was surprised there was no opposition in the restaurant, no goons, no gunmen, no one.

Sam followed him in and they made their way past the circular tables decorated with white linen tablecloths, neatly folded white linen napkins, and silver cutlery all set out as if royalty was coming in for a feast fit for a King. Each chair was upholstered in an animal print that resembled Zebra skin. Each of the forty or so tables had a gold candelabra sitting in the middle.

Sam could see the kitchen door at the back and warned Vinny about going in. "Vinny, be careful. Crawl in".

As Vinny pushed open the door while crawling toward it a barrage of bullets came from within and out the door opening.

Sam immediately reached in and sprayed bullets all around the kitchen while Vinny crawled in and crouched behind a large stainless counter.

Vinny was firing using his pistol to create cover for Sam, who then burst through the door opening firing continuously with the semi-automatic Uzi.

There was no return fire and through the smoke Sam could see the freezer doors at the back of the kitchen.

"Over there!" He exclaimed and pointed to the back left.

Vinny made his way over to the freezer doors and stepped over the goon who had been firing at them. A shot in the forehead apparently did him in. Vinny slid over the bolt, opened the door and peered inside. The air was chilly, and as he glanced at the temperature gauge it showed thirty-eight degrees.

Exhaling air was being expelled from his mouth. Sam also came in and they made their way past several slabs of meat hanging from the ceiling. As they approached the back of the freezer Sam was shocked to see the human figure which he recognized as Michael's form. He hoped they were in time. He saw no movement.

"My God, it's cold in here!" Vinny pointed out the obvious.

"Help me take him down!" Sam asked.

Vinny put his shoulder under the legs as Sam pulled

the chain up and unhooked the body from the hook. Sam then pulled off the blindfold and pulled the towel out of the body's mouth. Michael's bluish face could be seen with no signs of life.

" Let's get him outside" Stated Sam, shaking with the cold and in despair.

Vinny unlocked the bolt and pushed the back door open and immediately the strong Hawaiian sun beamed down providing warmth. Sam and Vinny brought the body out and laid it down on the grass. They unshackled the legs broke the handcuffs and then Vinny put his head down on the body's chest and listened for a heartbeat. He had seen similar situations in Nam where men were shot or unconscious and appeared dead but were still alive, just barely.

"Where the hell is Rus and Baseball?" Sam inquired. "I don't know, but Sam I think I hear a heartbeat!" Exclaimed Vinny.

"What? Let's call an ambulance". As Sam said that he could see Rus and Baseball coming up from a stream that fed down and over the cliff into the ocean. They appeared to be all right, except for Rus having a a bandage on his right hand made from a torn part of his shirt with blood sprayed all over his shirt.

"We are ok boss. The dynamite didn't work too well." "That's fine. Michael's alive, but we don't know in what condition, he's unconscious.

We've called an ambulance. Thanks for everything Guys!". Sam shook their hands and waited for the ambulance, hoping that Michael would be all right. He was also wondering where Mad Dog was during all of this going on.

The ambulance didn't have to travel far as the nearest hospital was The Queen's Medical Center-West O'ahu on Fort Weaver Road. The Physicians put heat lamps all around the body, and special bandages on the toes and hands; however they determined after tests that cardiac arrest had not occurred . The body was immersed several times in hot water and Michael blinked, opened his eyes and smiled. The Doctors stated that because Michael was in great physical condition he was able to survive the extreme cold of the freezer and did not lose any fingers or toes, arms or legs.

Three days to recover and as he was released he said to Sam "Let's keep this business from Elayne. You haven't told her anything, Have you?". He inquired.

" No Sir Boss. No. What are you going to tell her? You were missing for five days."

"As far as she is aware I was in L.A. on business as Larry Christofaro. She knows nothing about Michael Simons. So let's keep it that way". Larry emphasized. "OK Boss. You're the Boss!". "I owe you, and the boys, big time!" Larry said.

Nineteen

"I'm home!"Larry yelled into the phone, Elayne was delighted.

"How was L.A.?" Inquired Elayne.

"A little chilly, business was good. How about we go to dinner tonight? I'll pick you up around seven-thirty". Larry asked.

"Sure, see you then" Replied Elayne.

Larry's limousine arrived at exactly seven-thirty and as Elayne walked out of the Sheraton she was met at the door to the limo by Larry dressed in a tuxedo with a dozen roses in his hand which he presented to her while saying "Princess, a dozen roses for a rose. I love you!"

"Thank You Larry. That's wonderful".
Larry opened the bottle of champagne, poured two full glasses and handed Elayne one. Elayne could notice he was shaking and his right hand seemed out of color and a little swollen.

"Larry, what's with your right hand? Why discolored and swollen?" She inquired.

"Oh hurt it in L.A. Just accidently got caught in between an automatic door that was closing. I'll be all right. Anyway drink up there's lots more to consume tonight, my Princess!"

"Why tonight?" She asked.

"Tonight's going to be special, I promise!"

"Oh, Oh. More nudity, fun and frolic?"

"You'll see. You'll see." He promised.

The limousine pulled up in front of La Mar down on Kalia Rd by the beach, and as an attendant opened the door for Elayne he couldn't help but notice her beauty and the sleeveless, white gown that was draped over her gorgeous figure like she was Venus going to a feast with the President.

Larry and Elayne were welcomed by Chef Yves Garnier himself, and he in his French accented English exclaimed" Monsieur Michael, how wonderful to see you, and with this beautiful creature, I am sorry Mademoiselle I am not aware of your name!"

"My name is Elayne." She replied.

"Ah wonderful-The Fire! I can see it in your eyes and in your hair. Welcome to La Mer. I will make something special for you tonight. Do you like fish prepared a la France?"

"Well, I don't know a la France. But I'm sure it will be delicious. I can't wait!" Responded Elayne.

The Maitre D' brought them upstairs to the second floor to a table in the open sided room where they could see Diamond Head and hear the sound of trade winds rustling the nearby coconut trees with leaves moving as if in a ballet.

La Mer is the only AAA Five Diamond restaurant in Hawaii and here is where haute cuisine shines, with fine dining that is romantic, elegant, and of course expensive.

"Larry, another person calling you Michael. Why?"

"Oh that's just my middle name and sometimes I prefer it" shrugged Larry.

"Well, Larry is the guy I met. Larry is the guy I know. So if you don't mind, you will always be Larry with me!"

"No problem Princess. And you'll always be Princess with me." He responded. "Have some wine- Brunello di Montalcino".

"Larry, isn't that expensive?"

"Only $249.00 a bottle. My Princess nothing is too expensive for you, my darling. Drink up" as he put his glass next to hers, and declared "Salute".

"Larry this wine is delicious, so warm and fruity!"

"Elayne, this Brunello is a great wine and as you consume more you begin to taste the cherries and red berries followed by a hint of flowers, minerals and mint. On your palate you sense it's beauty which is fine-grained , silky and just stupendous. It goes great with the wonderful dinner Chef Garnier will prepare for us." He replied with authority.

Elayne was mesmerized. Here she was in Paradise being wooed by a handsome, smart, worldly successful business man who, it seemed knew everything, from Chocolate to wine to jogging properly to living life at its' fullest. She wondered if anything could spoil this dream, or what was next.

This was so far from being Missy Shaw back home, it was like she was in another world, on another planet. Maybe this was not Earth, maybe it was Venus or Jupiter or in another solar system.

The exquisite looking food being put on the table interrupted her thoughts.

"Crispy-skin filet of onaga with truffle jam, tomato confit with fresh basil and local fish baked in a rosemary-salt crust for you to review, Mon Ami." Chef Garnier announced. "And for you Mademoiselle Seared Foie Gras, Garnish with Pineapple Coulis as an Appetizer".

"This is wonderfully delicious!" Exclaimed Elayne as she took in some Foie Gras while sipping the Brunello.

The delicacies kept coming as *Agneau Poche au Lait et Aromates, Caviar d'Aubergines, Presse de Raisin* were brought to the table , translated as Lamb Marinated and Poached in Milk Garlic Cream, Eggplant Caviar, Raisin Juice, Thyme, Lamb Juice.

Dessert was as scrumptious as the main meal with Illanka Chocolate Mousse, Morello Cherry Marshmallow, Pistachio Anglaise and Beetroot Sponge just melting in Elayne's mouth.

La Mer Specialty Pressed Coffee followed with Elayne choosing the Island of Hawaii, Koa Estate, 100% Kona Decaffeinated.

"Bring us a bottle of Remy Martin XO ,

Garcon!" Demanded Larry."We might have something to celebrate tonight!"

"What are we going to celebrate, Larry?" Elayne was inquisitive.

"Possibly a marriage!" replied Larry.

"Who's marriage?" Elayne asked.

"Well perhaps ours, if you accept this ring." as Larry reached into his jacket pocket and brought out a velvet ring box, opened it up and pulled out the sparkling 2 carat diamond crowns surrounding a stunning center 3 carat stone which radiated a light that was almost as bright as the light emanating from the lighthouse.

Taking one deep breath Larry asked" Will you give me the pleasure of marrying me, my Princess?" Elayne did not hesitate "Of Course, My Prince, Yes. A thousand times Yes!"

Larry slipped the ring on Elayne's finger and both got up and embraced with a longer than usual full- on centre kiss on the lips like two large lip *humphead* fish embracing. *The humphead wrasse is found on coral reefs in the Pacific ocean and can be easily identified by its large size, thick lips, two black lines behind its eyes, and the hump that appears on the forehead.*

"We are getting married Monsieur Garnier! Hitched! Attached! Tied! Coupled!" Larry announced happily.

"What was it? The Foie Grasse? The Remy

Martin?"

"Everything!"answered Elayne. "Everything!"

The limousine drove up to the Sheraton and Elayne kissed Larry goodnight and said" Larry, tonight was wonderful! Of course topping off everything was this ring and our engagement. I'm just chaffing to tell Jennie, if she's returned from Maui."

"Princess, I'm on cloud nine too. Tomorrow we will make plans for a fantastic perfect wedding, right here in Hawaii. I'll call you around ten and come by, ok?"

"Sure, Larry. Great. See you tomorrow morning." Elayne exited the vehicle as Johnny Glover, the driver that Larry always used held open the door for her, and Johnny couldn't help but notice the flash of thigh and leg that showed under the side slit of her dress as she got out of the car. What a beauty Larry has snagged, he thought. Good for Larry, he's a nice guy, even though he's running a smuggling ring bringing in enormous quantities of drugs including Meth, Cocaine, heroin, and smuggling out local grown Marijuana. All through his chocolate company.

Johnny was careful to keep his Glock G43 Pistol hidden behind him in its' holster attached to his belt, covered by his jacket. "You got the ammo with you, in case?" Asked Larry.

"Sure, Boss , you wanna see?" as Johnny walked

over to the trunk of the limousine, he was going to raise the trunk cover.

"No, Stupid, not here out in the open. Just tell me what you got."

Johnny was not too bright. He had made it into the Hawaiian Mob but stayed low level because he couldn't handle too much stress, and calculating gave him a headache. Larry used him as a driver and muscle occasionally when needed. Johnny had proven his usefulness several years ago when some Chinese traffickers tried to ambush Larry when he was over on Maui visiting one of his dealers, and the Chinese in two big Mercedes trucks tried to force Larry's car off the road, and over the cliff.

Johnny was driving and hi skill at making the curves in the road at speeds over one hundred miles-per-hour was right out of a James Bond movie. Larry was bouncing around in the back of the black limousine while Sammy Yakimoto was firing off shots through the smashed back window, aiming for the tires of the Mercedes trucks.

Sammy hit one front tire and the Mercedes flipped over and rolled against a cliff face.

One down, one to go.

The second truck was right up against the back bumper of the limo and pushing towards the cliff edge. Sammy put one bullet right smack center of the driver's forehead and suddenly the truck veered right and smashed into a slow moving auto coming up the mountainside. Both vehicles immediately caught on fire, rolled towards the cliff edge, jumped the guardrail and plummeted down the hundred foot drop.

Larry thanked Johnny for a job well done and promised him he would be taken care of. Taken care of by Larry meant a life time job and a condo to live in.

"So what do you have in the trunk?" Asked Larry.

"The regular couple of Berettas."

"M9's or PX4'S?" Larry inquired.

"PX4's of course." Responded Johnny, a weapons expert trained in 'Nam." And a crate of dynamite".

"What else?"

"Sammy's Uzi and a Kalashnikov Assault rifle given to you as a gift from the Russians".

"Oh Yea I forgot about that, and did you get the limo retrofitted?" Larry asked.

"Of course Boss. Curved Bullet Resistant Vehicle Glass level 3 that will resist a .44 magnum , and flexible Kevlar Vehicle Armor panels for all side doors, rear quarter panels and the rear of the limo. In addition I got Run Flat Tire inserts so if needed we can drive a minimum of 30 miles at 30 mph with all 4 of the limo tires flat; includes protection from road debris, potholes, air leaks all the way up to ballistics. This baby is safer than a Sherman Tank" Johnny stated proudly.

"What about bullet resistant vests? Got any?" questioned Larry. "Absolutely! What do you think, I'm stupid?" answered Johnny. "Look at this" as he opened the trunk.

Larry could see the vests taped to the trunk hood, and he recognized the Tactical Assault Vests which were tailored to fit most body styles.

"Lookin' good. Looks like we are ready for anything. One thing Johnny I don't want Elayne to catch on to anything concerning this business, got it?" Larry was looking for a confirmation from Johnny.

"No problem boss. My lips are sealed".

"Good. Now let's go down to the warehouse to see how shipments are going". Larry maneuvered into the front seat and Johnny sped off towards the *Chocolate Gold* warehouse.

Twenty

Elayne rode the all-glass elevator in the Sheraton up to the 34th floor and she was elated thinking about dinner, the engagement ring, Larry, and the future.

Arriving at the 34th and stepping out into the hallway she noticed a rather tall, looking like a native Hawaiian, well-tanned, muscular man in a Hawaiian shirt and shorts, standing near a window looking down onto the courtyard below.

Elayne had no thoughts about this individual and proceeded to her room, and while opening the door she called out" Jenny, Are you here?"

A familiar voice from one of the bedrooms responded. "Yes Elayne I'm in here."

Elayne proceeded to the bedroom where the voice came from and observed Jenny wrapped up in a Sheraton Hawaii enormous Bathrobe lying on the huge King sized bed with what appeared to be remnants of fruits and vegetables everywhere-on the floor, at the bottom of the bed, on a chair, on a night table.

"Welcome back! How was Maui, and why the hell is all this fruit and veggies thrown around?" Elayne continued. "You have an orgy here, or something?"

"How did you guess, Elayne! Bruce just left".

"Well, Bruce must be a vegetarian, right Jenny?"

"Sort of". Responded Jenny.: Any way enough about me and vegetables. How was your fling with Chocolate Man?" Inquired Jenny.

"Look!" Elayne answered while flashing the diamond ring at Jenny. "5 carrots".

"Now that's what I call a vegetable with class. A five diamond vegetable. What's going on Elayne? You've only know Larry for a few weeks."

" A few weeks or a few years, what's the difference. Time on Hawaii has no relevance. Larry is a true gentleman , romantic, and not only treats me like a Princess, but calls me his Princess. Anyway we have to plan a Hawaiian wedding"

"What's a Hawaiian wedding?"

"I don't know. But we are about to find out." Replied Elayne. In four days we visit Matilda, The Wedding Planner.

"Matilda?"

"Yes, Matilda. Now I'm hitting the sack. Elayne began to yawn as she said "Jenny I will see you tomorrow. I am beat".

"Sure Elayne, have a nice wonderful sleep".

The phone sounded louder than ever with the distinct ring-ring, ring-ring Hawaiian telephone ring sound that woke up Elayne as she was soundly asleep. She peaked up from under her light proof eye coverings and could just barely make out 8:15

on the clock radio sitting on the table across from the end of the bed, and wondered who the hell is calling this early.

"Hello! Hello! Who is it?" She was still half asleep.

"Surf's Up Princess!" Larry's cheerful voice stated with glee. "Come on down, we're going surfing".

"What? First of all, where are you? And second I don't know how to surf!" Elayne pointed out.

"I'm down at the pool. Come on down".

"There's no surfing at the pool, Larry! And it's only eight fifteen in the morning, what's the rush?"

"We're not surfing at the pool. I've got the limo, and Johnny's driving us out to the best surfing area in Hawaii at 'Pipeline' which is on the North shore. Yes, it's early but you know what they say- the early surfer catches the wave!"

No Larry, it's the early bird catches the worm!"

"Who cares! Larry exclaimed."Same thing different location. We work with water, the bird works with the worm. Anyway come on down. I'm waiting"

"All right Larry give me a minute to freshen up"

"Your fresh all the time, my Princess".

"Ok Larry fifteen minutes." Elayne closed off the conversation, crawled out of bed and made it to the bathroom to clean up, freshen up, and get dressed. Some make-up, lipstick and hairspray.

Jenny didn't feel like surfing so Elayne exited the apartment, was surprised to see the same Tall Hawaiian looking native still standing near the elevator, however she didn't think twice and pressed the elevator button, and went in when it arrived. A swift ride down from the 34th floor and Elayne met Larry who was standing beside the indoor pool.

"Larry, I have no idea how to surf, and I am afraid of the water out there-too many sharks!" Elayne explained. " and we are getting married next week, I wouldn't be able to live through any accidents."

"Princess. Princess. Don't worry, I will teach you how to surf, and there are no sharks where we are going, and there won't be any accidents." Larry assured her.

Elayne took in the surreal scene as she exited the Sheraton with Larry. Ahead was Larry's gleaming white Lincoln Stretch limousine, all 28 feet of it, with a pale blue surfboard lying upside down on the roof, with it's rudder pointing upwards, and the American flag decorations placed strategically on the surfboard reflecting a little moisture that had accumulated during the morning dew. The board was tied down to the limo in two places and the whole scene reminded Elayne of the California Surfers who brought their boards to Malibu and other California beaches in their wooden-sided station wagons.

Larry and Elayne climbed in the limo and Johnny said" Welcome aboard the Banzai Pipeline Express. Boss you sure you want to go out to Pipeline? We can go to Holualoa Bay where *Banyans* break except it could be dangerous as the hazardous waves and currents could be dangerous to us all specifically to Elayne, a beginner; or to Sandy Beach where the *shore break* breaks very close to the shore, and consistent *barrels* all along the beach. More injuries occur each year at Sandy Beach than any other beach in Hawaii, earning it the infamous nickname "Break-neck beach."

"So why are we even thinking of Sandy Beach as an option, Boys?" Questioned Elayne. "I like my little neck just as it is, unbroken. "And what are *Banyans* , *shore break*, and *barrels*?"

Larry decrypted the slang for Elayne. "*Banyans* are when surfers ride inside the curve or barrel of a finely-shaped breaking wave, and under the right conditions waves in some areas form a moving tube or cylinder as they break, as in the Banzai Pipeline where we are going; and *shore breaks* are obstructions such as a coral reef, a rock, or a shoal that causes a wave to break forming a barreling wave of water that can be surfed before it eventually collapses. The topography of the seabed determines the shape of the wave and type of break. A good surfer rides the break and must be ever vigilant as some surf breaks are quite dangerous, since the surfer can collide with a reef or rocks below the water.

One of the largest surf breaks in the world is *Jaws surf break* in Maui with waves that reach a maximum height of 40-60 feet."

"I'm getting more nervous as you explain more about barrels, cylinders and such. Larry why do we have to go? It's dangerous!" Elayne stated nervously.

"Danger, smanger. It's life. It's fun. It's a challenge. Let's go Johnny, move it." Larry ordered.

The limo, shinning all white and glistening in the Hawaiian sun looked spotless as Johnny had painstakingly shined it up the night before. He moved out and thirty minutes later onto the two-lane Kamehameha Highway, beginning at Kalae'o'io Beach at the base of the 2000 foot tall headland called Pu'u Kanehoalani, winding past Ka'a'awa's magnificent valley and narrow ribbon of beach, and around the perfectly placid bay at Kahana; then along the coconut-shaded beach colony at Punalu'u and the fisherman dotted reefs of Hau'ula.

Johnny then pulled the limo over to the side of the road to take in all this panoramic splendor." Boss and Elayne, isn't this view unbelievable?" He asked.

" Stupendous." Larry responded.

"Gorgeous" Elayne replied as Larry grabbed a quick kiss on the lips.

"Look" Johnny pointed out. "shacks on the beach so you can just lie around, and slow streams of water running down from the mountains emptying into turquoise reef water, with greenery all around and a valley laced with a waterfall- This is paradise, you can't deny it. The slight trade winds blowing in off the ocean , moist and salt-laden provide a cooling effect that reduces the Hawaiian sun to just the exact temperature to enjoy nature."

Elayne was surprised to hear such delicate words and flowing emotion coming from such a huge monster of a man, but it's true she was convinced this Paradise hypnotizes and mesmerizes everyone. She could see down the road an old lava-rock wall and a gate that opens to a lush overgrown estate, spread out under a towering coconut grove. Small rock-lined ponds and pathways sit next to breadfruit trees.

Johnny put the limo into gear and it slinked away just like a giant snake slithering around in the sand trying to make its' way towards wherever it's goal was.

Ehukai Beach loomed up ahead as Johnny announced "Well here we are home of the Banzai Pipeline. Johnny pulled the limo up to the largest and only commercial hotel on the North shore, the

Turtle Bay Resort, and as Elayne steps out she takes in the spectacular fresh ocean fringed air. She hears a gentle roar and guesses it's the surf rolling in on the wide Hawaiian beach. No automobiles screaming and roaring on a freeway here, just the sound of the surf.

Larry began. " I have arranged for you to take surfing lessons with Aloha Surf School. They will meet you in the lobby. Johnny will drive me down to Ehukai Beach, and I will see you later this afternoon."

"OK Larry, but please be careful. I've heard that some great surfers have died on that beach over the years" Elayne cautioned.

"I'll be all right; but if something happens to me you'll be transformed from a Princess into a Queen, a Chocolate Queen, because I would want you to take over running my company!" Larry explained.

"Come on Larry, don't joke like that". Elayne stated nervously "I wouldn't want to live if something happened to you, or even think of running your company. I have no experience."

"The boys will help you! Right Johnny?" Larry asked with implied authority.

"Sure boss, anything you say, is all right with me!" Replied Johnny.

"Come on, please Larry. Now I'm afraid to see you go. I'm worried now".

"Don't worry Princess .I've surfed that beach

dozens of times. I'll be OK". Larry tried to assure her.

Elayne reluctantly walked up the steps and past the porter, who opened the door for her. She had terrible thoughts in her head about Larry having an accident while surfing. The big bodied women in the Mau Mau full color dress broke her thoughts while blocking her way forward.

"You are Princess, right?" Asked the Mau Mau Woman. "Well, yes, actually my name is Elayne".

"Welcome to Aloha Surf School, Princess Elayne!" "Just call me Elayne, Please."

"OK Dokey. No problem. Anyway you will have a good time with us learning to surf. You seem tense. Any problem?" She asked.

"No. I'm just worried about my fiancée going to the Pipeline".

"He'll be all right. He's an experienced surfer dude, I know him". Mau Mau responded. "Let's go out back to meet your instructor", as Mau Mau took Elayne's arm and steered her out towards the back of the lobby, through the glass sliding door, and out into the Hawaiian sun. Johnny eased the Limo into drive, stepped on the gas and drove out towards Ehukai Beach on Ke Nui Road.

"Park over there at the Sunset Beach Elementary School. Larry ordered. " You won't get any closer!"

Johnny parked the limo, opened his door and helped Larry untie the board, and then with the board on their shoulders, Larry in front, and Johnny in back they walked across the road and onto the smooth white beach sand, and down to the water.

Larry peeled off his shirt, removed his sandals, threw his straw hat on the sand, put his watch and sunglasses in his hat, picked up the board and told Johnny "Watch I'm gonna kill this pipeline!"

"Sure boss, enjoy yourself, but remember what Elayne said, be careful!"

Johnny watched as Larry put the surfboard down, crawled aboard and started paddling out to meet the monster-waves that occasionally reach heights of over 30 feet. It's no wonder the beach is one of the most famous surf spots in the world-and as you might expect, also one of the most dangerous.

Johnny could just barely make out the Red flag on the pole down the beach which he knew was the warning sign for dangerous shore break. He could see two lifeguards standing half in the water and half on the beach sand with binoculars scanning the waves for possible signs of anyone in distress.

"Larry! Larry! The Red flag is up!" Johnny yelled but Larry was already in the water paddling out and didn't even look back to see Johnny trying to warn him. Johnny knew that the lifeguards were well trained in treating broken bones and pulling bodies out of the surf but he didn't want any such thing happening to his boss, so he was nervous, and started pacing back and forth along the shore.

The deep blue and translucent turquoise ocean appears to offer a wealth of beauty and fun. The beauty is deceiving. The fun is easily and instantly turned to sorrow. Everyone enjoys looking at the ocean and a lot of people take risks because they ignore signs as if they were hypnotized.

Larry was paddling out and all he could see was the giant waves rolling in, and he was determined to get out past the crest and turn around and ride one monster wave in, as he had done on this beach dozens of times before. Larry picked out the peak of the break he wanted to ride and paddled out while making sure he went through the wave in the green portion.

Larry turned his board around, lay flat and started paddling to catch the peak of the wave. Larry concentrated on his take-off and since he was a long boarder he easily gained the speed/momentum to drop in on the wave that he had his eye on-the one he wanted to ride. Larry worked to get into the green part of the wave and stood up on the board at the same time the wave appeared to hit a reef as it started to throw a lip, and Larry could feel the power and force of the water rushing towards the surface as the wave rose rapidly about five feet, and because Larry was experienced he used this boost to drop in on the wave. Still even though Larry had been here many times before he still had that "your heart drops moment" as he was about to drop and could see it was a long way down. It seemed like he was gazing down into the Grand Canyon without a parachute except this was a chasm of water-tons of water which could turn fun into sudden death in an instant.

Larry could just barely see out of the corner of his eyes the peak next to him. He could see how vertical the face of the wave was. It didn't look that bad, didn't look that high, didn't look that destructive as he sped down his chosen wave to ride; and suddenly he was airborne. He had lost contact with his board. He was flying down the face of his wave without a board. He knew this was called an 'air drop' and he knew this could be disaster in the making. Larry had more than average skill and he managed to catch his board , connect with it, and continue on this magic watery ride, down the slippery ocean water slope. Larry knew he wasn't in charge here, the ocean was and it was sometimes scary.

Johnny could see Larry riding the giant wave, and he saw Larry first losing contact with his board, and then miraculously making contact. Larry cruised in onto the beach, jumped off the board, and exclaimed "Johnny, that was amazing". I'm going back out.

"So soon? Can't you take a break?" Johnny asked. "Nope. I'm here to surf. The waves are monstrous, and you know what?"

"What?" answered Johnny.

"I bet from the beach it looks like I'm going a hundred miles an hour, but you know on the board, surfing a big wave, it almost feels like time has stopped. It's almost like slow motion. And it feels great. Everything slows down so a five-second wave feels like an hour. It's like I'm in a hypnotic state."

Larry hoisted up the board and put it into the water, climbed aboard, lay flat and started paddling out. He reached the crest of another big wave, managed to paddle over, turned the board around and started to paddle hard to catch the crest. As soon as he did he crouched on the board, throw out both arms for balance, and stood up riding the board like it was a galloping horse in a stampede.

Larry did not immediately see the two surfers making their way towards him; one on his left, and one on his right. Then he had a glimpse of the one on his right who was moving fast at a 45 degree angle towards him. Like a runaway locomotive barreling down the tracks without a driver. As he kept focused on the well build barrel chested rider on his right, the surfer on his left crept up within two feet , and with one swing of his elephant like arm hit Larry so violently that Larry flew off sideways off his board, which then flipped up appearing to be completely vertical, as no human weight to hold down the board caused the board to go airborne.

Larry was doing somersaults and trying to keep above the surface, which he was not, and suddenly his head hit an obstacle, probably a reef, and he was knocked unconscious.

Johnny yelled for the lifeguards, while he himself was fighting the fierce water as he struggled to move through the ocean current to find Larry.

"Larry! Larry! Come on up! Larry where are you"

Johnny was frantic as the two lifeguards arrived. One dove in under the surf and at first could not spot a body; however then all of a sudden a trail of fresh blood made its way up to the surface and pinpointed to the body below, a body that appeared with a gash on the forehead which was expelling blood like a tap was broken.

The two guards and Johnny were able to bring Larry onto the beach, and lay him flat. Guard number one checked Larry's chest and stated "Well he's breathing. Let's get the ambulance" as he applied a towel to the forehead gash.

At the Queens' Medical Centre in the Emergency Ward Dr. Joseph Harmony briefed Johnny and the boys, Sam, Vinny, Greg and Steve as they had rushed to Queen's as soon as Johnny had contacted them.

"I have to tell you that your boss is still unconscious , however we have been able to get him in a stable condition , but he must be monitored for the next 24 hours, at least, so he must stay here".

Dr. Harmony explained." He should come out of being unconscious within the next few hours, and then we will send him for an MRI to determine if there was any brain damage or any other potential damage that we may have to operate to release the pressure."

"What pressure?" Johnny inquired. "You didn't mention anything about any pressure."

"Well , I am now. Preliminary tests showed an imbalance in the right side of his brain near the speech center". Dr. Harmony stated. "We cannot determine if there is any damage right now so we are calming him down with sedatives, and when he wakes up we can test his verbal and visual skills to see if there are any impairments, as well as sending him up for an MRI."

"All right. Thank you Doctor, I guess I will call his fiancée to break the news to her." Said Johnny with reluctance.

"Good luck, I'll keep you updated every few hours." Dr. Harmony confirmed.
Johnny went over to the payphone to make a call that he knew would cause a lot of stress for Elayne.

"Miss Elayne, there is a phone call for you in the front lobby." Mau Mau informed Elayne, who was standing on a fixed surfboard bolted to the floor , as she practiced turning her body left and right while keeping her feet on the board; while a ferocious fan spit wind at her to duplicate the conditions out on the ocean water while surfing. Her arms were raised to be horizontal as she practiced her balance. The giant poster behind her on the wall appeared as if she was on the beach, on the ocean, surfing like a pro.

"Who would be calling me here? Only Larry and Johnny know I'm here. Something must have happened, I can sense it. I warned Larry not to go. Oh my god, what if he is dead? What am I going to do? Stuck here in Hawaii on this make believe surfboard." Tears were starting to flow from Elayne's eyes, and Mau Mau could see Elayne was having some kind of episode like she was having a breakdown.

While Mau Mau slapped Elayne hard on the right cheek she yelled out " Miss Elayne, calm down! I'm sure nothing happened to Larry. I told you he is an experienced surfer. Probably just calling to tell you he will be late for dinner. Go to the lobby and take the call. Now go!" She ordered.

Elayne stepped of the board, walked past the enormous fan, which blew her hair all over the place, opened the glass door , and walked out to the lobby with an anxious look on her face that could foretell the bad news she was about to get.

Johnny was on the phone. "Elayne" he began.

"Johnny, Please don't tell me Larry is dead. Please tell me he is in the washroom ,and asked you to just tell me he will be a few minutes late for dinner. Come on Johnny, the suspense is killing me. What's going on? Larry's dead , right?" Elayne was frantic. She couldn't wait for the bad news. She didn't want to hear any bad news. She was in Paradise. She was engaged to a wonderful kind soul. God wouldn't let anything happen to spoil this dream that was a reality.

"Elayne, shut up, and let me speak. Larry is not dead, but he had a terrible surfing accident, that actually was not his fault. He was not reckless or careless. He had surfed a wave first, and did a magnificent job-you should have seen him, like a pro."

"Johnny, get to the point. What's with Larry?"

"Elayne, he was knocked off his board by two local surfers and he flipped head over heels and hit his head on some rocks or a reef, which caused a gash on his forehead and knocked him unconscious, but he's alive." Johnny explained.

"Oh! Thank God he's alive. Where is he now?"

"He's at the hospital in Honolulu, Queens Medical Centre". Johnny replied.

"And?"

"And he has to stay there at least 24 hours so they can conduct some further tests including an MRI. The Doctor said he should come out of being unconscious within a few hours."

"And what if he doesn't?" Elayne asked.

"I don't know. The Doctor was confident he would be conscious in a few hours. He is stable, with a gash on the forehead, and a giant bandage around his head."

"What else? Come on Johnny, tell me the truth." Elayne implored. She suspected Johnny was not telling her everything.

"Well, the Doctors noticed some abnormal pressure on the right side of his head just near his speech center so they will be doing tests over the next few hours to diagnose him further." Johnny added.

"So , he may not be able to speak. Right?"

"The Doctor never said that. Elayne you are guessing and speculating with no knowledge".

"I guess you are right. Anyway Johnny I need to go to the hospital right away. Can you pick me up soon?" Elayne asked.

"Of course. I will leave right away. Depending on traffic I should be there in an hour or so."

"Johnny, hurray as fast as you can." She deplored.

Traffic was dense going out to the beach and it took Johnny over two and a half hours to reach the resort. Elayne jumped out of the lobby door and opened the limo back door simultaneously as the limo slowed down and parked at the curb.

"Johnny, any change in Larry's condition?"

"Nothing new when I left the hospital. Maybe he is conscious now. I left Sammy and the crew at the hospital in the Emergency Ward waiting lounge. Don't worry, Elayne, he will be all right". Johnny stated trying to calm her down.

"That's what you and Larry told me when you drove off to the beach for Larry to surf the big waves, and look what happened." Elayne replied.

The drive back was as hectic as the drive down with traffic very dense, and stop and go. Johnny saw through his rear view mirror that Elayne had conked out and was fast asleep lying across the back seat.

"We are here. Elayne wake up. We are at the hospital. Elayne!" Johnny raised his voice and shook Elayne by the shoulders until she sat up, smoothed her hair and proceeded to exit the limo.

"Follow me up to the lounge."
Elayne followed Johnny up to the Emergency ward waiting room and immediately viewed four large muscular men playing poker with potato chips lying all over a make-shift table they had put together by using two coffee table type tables put together. Elayne recognized Sam Yakimoto but she didn't know the others. It looked like the waiting room at a World Wrestling Federation event where all the over exaggerated muscle men were waiting for their

time in the ring.

Johnny introduced the crew. "Elayne, you've met Sammy. Over there with all those potato chips is Vinny, And next to him is Greg, we call him the Russian. Steve on the right, with no potato chips. Hey guys, what's with the potato chips?"

Sammy answered." Well we needed some chips to bet in the poker game so Steve went down to the store and brought back real chips, actually real potato chips; and Vinny has had some phenomenal luck. He keeps getting aces and kings, so he has been winning all the chips, as you can see."

"Ok never mind about chips, potato or not. Any news about Larry from the Doctor?" Asked Johnny.

"Yes, Some good news. Larry is conscious and they are putting him through tests right now." Explained Steve. "Thank God. What about his speech? Can he talk?" Elayne asked.

"Too early to tell. The Doctor should be coming back in maybe in an hour or so with an update." Steve replied

"Mister Larry. What you doin' here again?" asked Martha, the head nurse when she saw Larry being wheeled into the MRI area. " You like us so much you decided to have a repeat visit?"

Larry could not speak but he had a paper and a pencil and he just barely eek out an answer " Yes Martha, the treatment here last time was just like the Ritz, and I enjoyed it so much I came back for more, but my head is killing me." He wrote. As Larry mentioned his head he reached up and could feel the bandage wrapped around his head and forehead.

" Your lucky your alive , Mister Larry. You know how many men have died trying to surf the Pipeline?

Apparently Martha had been told by someone what had happened to Larry, and she had enough experience to know that usually when someone was brought to their Emergency Section wearing beach clothes or a swimming suit that something had happened on one of the numerous beaches. It was almost a daily occurrence.

Larry couldn't answer as the attendants pushed his bed on wheels into the MRI room.

Dr. Harmony came out and briefed everyone.

"The MRI didn't show anything but the wound required ten stitches , and it will hurt for a few days."

"What about speech, Doctor? Is he able to speak?" Elayne asked anxiously.

"Well not yet. The swelling and pressure on the right side of his head has subsided so he could be speaking soon, maybe tomorrow. I cannot tell you if there was any damage to the area of the brain that controls his speech. We will have to wait and see, but I don't foresee any major problem" The Doctor responded. " Time heals all wounds".

Elayne wanted to stay at the hospital overnight so she curled up on a sofa , and a nurse brought her a blanket. Johnny and the crew decided to leave and Johnny told Elayne he would come back in the morning. It was a tough night for Elayne as Paradise seemed to have some cracks in the foundation. What if Larry's ability to speech does not come back as before, she pondered.

It was early in the morning, perhaps 6:30 am, Elayne guessed, as she heard a familiar voice, coming from behind a curtain that separates those being treated from those being attacked by images of their loved ones dying , maimed, sick and/or ill. Elayne slid open the curtain. It was Larry talking nonchalantly with a nurse. He appeared to be all right, except for a giant bandage wrapped around his head as if he had just excited from a Roman Bath. And to Elayne's surprise Johnny was there sitting on a chair, looking very uncomfortable and half asleep.

"Martha. I was ok alone on the board, but two thugs attacked me, and apparently tried to kill me." Larry told Martha.

"Mister Larry, those thugs were probably the surf gang that patrols that beach. They don't want nobody surfing their beach. It's their territory and they will protect their turf, so to speak, although it's water. They don't like outsiders enjoying themselves on their beach. Did they have black surf shorts on?" Martha asked.

"I don't know. I was concentrating on keeping on my board and I was sideswiped by one of them".

"Boss". Johnny spoke up." I saw them from the beach, and yes they had on black surf shorts".

"Oh my god!" Martha screamed. " Da Hui. You've been knocked off your board by the local surf gang named Da Hui or Black shorts, as they are known. They were set up to keep foreign surfers out of their water at that beach."

"What the hell! They don't own the water, and they don't own the beach". Larry stated with anger.

"They don't allow drop-ins" Explained Martha.

"Well, this is one drop-in that they shouldn't be messing with, Martha!". Larry stated. "Johnny bring the limo around, we're going black short hunting".

"But, Mister Larry, it's too soon for you to be leaving the hospital."

"Martha-It's not soon enough. I have a hankering for a pair of black surf shorts, or two, or three".

"Larry, you seem all right. How's your head?" Elayne asked, feeling relieved at seeing Larry and hearing him talking in a normal voice.

"Princess , am I glad to see you. Come here for a hug". Elayne hoped on the bed and lay next to Larry, with her arm around his chest. He kissed her gently on the forehead.

"Larry, I hope what I heard is not true. That you want to get discharged so you can go after those hooligans, the Black Shorts. Tell me it's not true!" Elayne begged.

"Princess, I'm ok and yes my head hurts a little, but I'll be all right" Larry assured her." I have to go after those thugs. They can't be allowed to do this to someone else. They will kill someone. They have to be stopped or taught a lesson. Johnny call the Doctor, tell him I want to be discharged and get the boys back up here. We need to teach some Surf boys how to surf."

"Sure, OK Boss. Right away." Johnny answered.

"Elayne, Johnny will take you back to the Sheraton, where you can rest until I come back".

"But Larry I don't want to be alone, without you."

"Elayne, probably Jenny will be there, so you won't be alone." Larry pointed out, "and we won't be long , maybe one hour max." Larry said, trying to reassure her.

Johnny drove the limo up to Ehukai beach without incident, and as in the day before he parked in the Sunset Beach Elementary School parking lot.

Steve, Vinny and the boys arrived a minute later in the Hummer, parking half on the side of the sidewalk, and half in the parking lot.

"Johnny, you and Vinny take the Uzi and see those five boards leaning up against the cement wall?" Larry inquired.

"Yes Boss. We see them." Responded Vinny.

"Well, make toothpicks out of them! I don't want any piece bigger than my little figure, Ya got me?"

"Got you boss!" Vinny replied as he walked over the hot sand with Johnny keeping up the pace. As they approached the boards Vinny opened fire with a rat-a-tat-tat sound while the Uzi disgorged hundreds of bullets a minute, hitting the top of the boards, the middle , the bottom, shattering all five into splinters.

Johnny scooped up several surf shoes and threw them in the air while Steve shot at them like he was at a shooting hall taking practice.

Greg "The Russian" , in his best English" picked up a piece of chalk and scrawled on the concrete wall housing the washrooms, " Don't F with us, you Surf Monkeys" as he drew a pirate symbol.

"Nice art, Rus". Complimented Steve.

"Ya, Real nice!" Larry stated as he walked back to the limo. "Thanks for comin' out boys".
Larry fell into the limo back seat exhausted and grabbed some Mimosa that was in the ice chest. After finishing off half a bottle he collapsed sound asleep with a little snore here and there. Johnny made it back in good time , with the boys in their Hummer providing some escort until they reached Honolulu , and the boys waved off, as the limo cruised to Larry's Penthouse.

Two days passed and Elayne called Larry to hear how he was. "Larry how are you" She asked when he answered the phone.

" I'm perfect. No towel wrap, just a little bandage." He replied.

"Larry. Jenny and I have an appointment to see the wedding planner. Can you send Johnny with the limo". "Sure, Princess. He'll be there in an hour". The drive to Waimanalo, Matilda's village by the sea was uneventful and Elayne and Jennie could not keep their eyes off of the ocean views. Through Kalakaua Avenue past the multitiered Dillingham Fountain and around the bend in the road, which now becomes Poni Moi Road. Past Diamond Head Road and the steep climb up the side of the old crater. Continuing down Diamond Head Road and through the rich community of Kahala. Johnny had driven this route many times and he knew to veer right at the V in the road just before Fort Ruger Park and continue on the palm tree lined Kahala Avenue; and then he made a left on Hunakai Street and proceeded down past the H-1 highway to the Kalanianaole Highway, which was a four lane highway with beach parks on the right side and shopping malls on the left. The landscape here was more moonscape, with prickly cacti decorating the shore.

"Look, over there!" Elayne was excited. "Do you see the whale sprouting out there in the ocean."

"Yes. Elayne how beautiful." Jenny responded.

Past Hanauma Bay and to Sandy Beach where Jenny spotted the ambulance.

"Johnny, why is there an ambulance up ahead? Was there an accident?" Jenny asked.

" No Ma'am. Sandy Beach is the most popular and at the same time the most dangerous beach for wave catchers and body boarders in all of Oahu, and an ambulance is on stand- by all the time."

The coast looks raw and empty as the road weaves past old Hawaiian fish ponds and the famous formation known as Pele's Chair, just off the highway and from a distance , the lava-rock outcropping looks like a mighty throne; and local legend has it that it's believed to be the fire goddess's last resting place on Oahu before she flew off to continue her work on the other Hawaiian islands.

Johnny pointed out "Ahead lies 647 foot high Makapuu Point, with a lighthouse that once signaled safe passage for steamship passengers arriving from San Francisco. The automated light now brightens Oahu's south coast for passing tankers, fishing boats and sailors."

The windows were open in the back of the limousine and Elayne and Jenny could feel the cool trade winds coming in off the ocean. Up ahead the coastal vista included many fluted green mountains and strange looking peaks, edged by golden beaches and the blue, deep blue Pacific Ocean.

Johnny provided more commentary. "The 3000 foot high sheer green Koolau mountains plunge almost straight down into the ocean. The mountains actually separate this side, the windward side of the island from Honolulu and the rest of Oahu. Look see the waterfalls?" As he pointed forward and to the left. Johnny continued to steer the limousine towards Waimanalo Beach.

Waimanalo Beach is a country beach town of nurseries and stables, fresh-fruit stands and some of the island's best conch and triton-shell specimens at roadside stands,
 Less than 5,000 people actually live here with half Native Pacific Islanders. The rest is a mix of white, African American, Native American, Asian, with some 7% Hispanic or Latino.

The beach itself stretches for more than 5 miles and is Oahu's longest beach. The waters are turquoise and great for swimming when the waves are not too big, however the ocean gets deeper quickly and strong currents sometimes create an undertow that is hard to fight off. There are no lifeguards so every swimmer is on his or her own guard. The offshore reef makes this beach good for swimming.

Johnny turned the limo onto Laumilo Street and stopped at 1100 , a non descript two storey white house with skylights and what appeared to be roof mounted solar panels and an antenna to receive satellite communications. In the two car driveway, amongst the lush green vegetation surrounding the property was what appeared to be a twenty year old grey Buick station wagon automobile with the words Great Hawaiian Wedding Planner painted on the side door panels.

A short walk past the wooden fence and at the side door someone appeared who identified herself as Matilda.

"Aloha Kakahlaka! Good morning"
Matilda Onakuau stood in the doorway and Elayne and Jenny were shocked by her beauty. Long black hair down to her waist. Beautiful Hazel Green eyes. A stunning figure and a gorgeous smile, tanned, with a flower perched on the left side of her head. Draped in a white floor length linen dress with a flower design down the length on one side, with a slit up on to her mid thigh. Slim, trim and a wonderful descendant of the original Polynesians who populated the islands centuries ago.

"Welcome. Come in." Matilda welcomed them to her abode. "Sit down here" , as she pointed to several sofa seats decorated with flowers-It seemed everything is decorated with flowers in Hawaii-Elayne thought.

"It's a wonderful day to be talking about a wedding and a Hawaii wedding is wonderful in itself. Matilda spread out a brochure and pointed out to Elayne and Jenny.

"Look! Look what this brochure says. A beach ceremony is usually the first thing that comes to mind when considering a Hawaiian wedding and there are many gorgeous beaches for you to choose from on every island, but of course I am partial to our beach right here, Waimanalo Beach, where I myself got married."

Matilda went on. "The stunning sunset ceremony is why you should get married right here, but keep in mind that beaches in Hawaii are public, so there is no way to keep strangers from walking past or stopping to watch your ceremonies. You may or may not mind this. And a right-of-entry permit will be required."

"That's OK. Larry has some people that are big and strong, so they would keep intruders away". Elayne pointed out.

"Good. Now whose the lucky one?" Asked Matilda.

"Huh? What do you mean?" Inquired Elayne.

"Which one of you is getting Hitched?"

"Me!" Answered Elayne. "I'm hitching myself to a Prince".

"Great. A royal wedding. I haven't planned one in a while. Now do you want the barefoot ceremony?" Matilda inquired. "On the beach or on the grass next to the beach?"

"Barefoot, of course. Whatever that means!"

Answered Elayne" As long as we are barefoot but wearing clothes. Although knowing Larry he would probably prefer the unclothed wedding".

"Well we can arrange that too. We have conducted wedding ceremonies for Nudists."

"No, No. No Nudism. Barefoot is fine".

"OK. We normally do ceremonies on the grass under the shade of the coconut trees as this makes for the best lighting for photography. We recommend ceremony times between 4-6 pm as sunset will enter into the time of the ceremony.

It's nice to just finish as the sun is going down over the horizon. We can provide you with our Rolls Royce Silver Cloud III limousine to pick you up in Honolulu." Matilda explained.

"No. I think Larry and I would just prefer to come out in our own limousine." Answered Elayne.

"OK. No problem." Matilda now stated. "Our ceremonies are straight forward, simple, and follow a basic traditional western and American wedding format appropriate for beach weddings." She continued. " Hawaiians did not actually get married. There is no "traditional" Hawaiian wedding ceremony. Many of these "traditions" are simply made-up by wedding websites, officials, or so-called "Kahu". With that said, there are some modern "Traditions" like the giving of lei and local Hawaiian elements that are a nice addition to any beach wedding in Hawaii.

Our ceremony styles are the following: Romantic-Which is non-religious with no mention of God in the religious sense. You must be aware that our officials conduct a lot of weddings of all styles and sometimes a reference to God will slip out. If you absolutely hate the mention of God, I suggest you find another Wedding Planner."

"No. I got no problem with God!" Stated Elayne. "You got a problem with God, Jenny?"

"Me? No. In fact I love God. I got no problem either". Answered Jenny.

Matilda went on with her explanations of ceremony styles. "Romantic Christian non-denominational is a traditional non-denominational Christian based ceremony"

"It is what it is!" Jenny butted in.

"Yes". Matilda emphasized. " While we don't do "preaching" we do acknowledge that God is part of the ceremony and ask for his blessing!"

"Yeah. Ask for his blessing! I'm all for that". Jenny pointed out." Ask for him to bless all of us. Every man, women and child. Every Hawaiian and American, and Filipino too. Every Australian and Mexican and Great Britoner-Is that how you say it? Great Britoner? "

"Jenny. What have you been drinking? Great Britoner?" Elayne asked.

"Ok. All right drop the Britoners!" Elayne responded.

"Then we have Romantic Hawaiian or Christian Hawaiian accented ceremony". Matilda began.

"Oh. I like that. Christian Hawaiian. You mean like when Captain James Cook came over here in 1778 and the Hawaiians attached religious significance to the Europeans' visit." Stated Jenny.

"How do you know this?" Elayne asked.

"Well, I've been doing some reading about Hawaii" Jenny continued. " At the time of Cook's arrival the locals were engaged in a festival dedicated to Lono, the fertility god of the Hawaiians. Cook and his men were welcomed as gods and for almost a month they exploited the Hawaiians' good will. After Missionaries from various Protestant sects swarmed the islands and began transforming Hawaiians into Christians. Ancient Hawaiian religious practices disappeared completely and today many Hawaiians practice Buddhism, Shinto and Christianity."

"Well whatever ceremony you choose there will be flowers, lots of flowers. Both you and your Prince will wear elaborate leis-necklaces of flowers, nuts, seeds, and other plant material woven together. " Matilda explained." Our Christian Hawaiian accented ceremony will incorporate Hawaiian elements which will give your ceremony a uniquely Hawaiian feel. It includes in addition to our standard ceremony structure, Hawaiian verse, and a conch shell blowing, called a "Pu" by the official conducting the ceremony. Some of your guests will wear a Hawaiian theme attire wrap called a "Kihei", others will wear Hawaiian lei. By the way we don't do hula dancers, fire dancers, sacrifices, or any other stupid stuff, which is not traditional Hawaiian elements."

"No sacrifices?" Asked Jenny with sarcasm.

"No. We add Hawaiian elements that work and are an appropriate addition within the framework of a wedding ceremony which will give your ceremony a uniquely Hawaiian feel." Matilda explained.

"You said that already. What else?" Elayne was getting impatient with all the explaining.

Matilda continued. " Each official that conducts a ceremony has his or her own proprietary "words" and these may vary from ceremony to ceremony depending on the specifics. We may assign an official and that person may change by wedding day, because of their schedules and having to travel amongst the islands. Also don't wear any pearls. No earrings, no necklaces as they resemble tears and Hawaiians who are very superstitious believe pears will cause the marriage to be filled with sorrow."

Elayne began. "Can we exchange our own vows in our ceremony?"

"Yes. Of Course. Let the official know that you have special words to share. We usually have couples do this during the lei exchange. You must know that as a matter of official duty and the law in Hawaii , the official is required to ask you, Do you take, Larry, in this case, to be your husband?"

Elayne continued "Can we approve the ceremony words and what's said?"

"No. When you get married in a church or by a judge they don't tell you the words." Matilda went on." Nor do you get a copy for your inspection and approval. Our officials operate under the same principles. Also each licensed official has their own ceremony and most have it memorized. Ceremonies are proprietary to the official. Actual words spoken vary with the specifics of your ceremony. And in addition if you prepare and or authorize a certain wording that official may be replaced at the last minute by another who uses different terminology.

So there is no written ceremony that we have to share and there's no way we'd want to be tied to an exact script. That's it, that's all. That's the way it works."

Elayne was beginning to think this was dictatorial but she liked the beach area, and in spite of Matilda's very blunt explanations she was sold by Matilda's appearance, beauty and dress.

"Don't worry" Matilda continued. "Your wedding ceremony will be upscale, elegant yet simple and reflect exactly what a Hawaiian Beach wedding is, and of course if you don't want to use us then there are dozens of other beaches and other

Wedding Planners that you could use."

"No Matilda. I like you, and I like your frank explanations of the various options-so I will talk to Larry but I'm pretty sure he will go along with me in choosing your services. Thank You for your explanations and hospitality." Elayne said with passion.

Johnny drove back to Honolulu with Elayne and Jenny mostly quiet in the back seat area as they were a little tired with the long discussion with Matilda.

Elayne and Jenny waived goodbye to Johnny, and he waited until they entered the Sheraton lobby before he drove off, as were instructions from Larry, who was now a little paranoid about possible attacks by his drug smuggling competitors.

Twenty-One

The day of the wedding had come quickly and Larry had been picked up first by Johnny with Sam, Vinny, The Russian and Steve following in a van; with Johnny easing the limousine up to the Sheraton main entrance.

Elayne and Jennie had been waiting impatiently in the lobby as Larry was late thirty minutes, which was not usual with Larry, however Elayne did not know that an unexpected stop had been made to pick up more bullets required for Sammy's Uzi, now stored in the limousine's trunk.

"Hello Princess. Ready for the big day?" Larry asked.

"Yes, of course Larry. This is the biggest day, ever!" Exclaimed Elayne as she entered the limousine. Jenny went around the other side of the limousine and entered. Larry climbed in and pulled the door shut. Johnny eased the limo onto the street and proceeded past Diamond Head.

"We'll take the scenic route. Ok Boss?"

"Sure Johnny, Sure" Larry replied.

Johnny checked for traffic and drove along Diamond Head Road past Kaluahole Beach towards the Diamond Head Lighthouse glancing very quickly out the right side to see the spectacular blue Pacific Ocean and seeing a few sail boats out in the distance with full sails blowing in the wind. Their mainsails catching the South Pacific breezes and tipping over to 45 degrees to speed up and take full advantage of the wind.

Johnny could see one catamaran poised on one wing like a circus performer on a tight rope balancing and causing ohs and ahs from the audience as the tightrope balancer seemed almost always ready to fall over, but doesn't.

Several speedboats pulling water skiers filled out the picture, and surfboarders riding the waves completed the scene.

"Larry, can we go surfing sometime together?" Elayne asked. " I learned a lot from Mau Mau.

"Of course, Princess! Now? Or after the wedding?" Larry joked.

"Larry-you know what I meant. Sometime after the wedding, of course."

The limo eased past Kaalawai Beach as it moved along Kahala Avenue and onto Magic Island adjacent to Ala Moana Beach Park. Past the sailing clubs, the rows of long canoes, and past the clear, calm turquoise water Johnny maneuvered the limo to the park end, where the sunset views were the greatest. Two very tall palm trees sheltered the man made Hawaiian Wedding Arch that was decorated with silk floral arrangements and a white draping to form the top of the arch.

Twenty chairs for guests draped in white stood like soldiers arranged row by row and standing ready for duty. A ukulele player slowly strung his instrument.

Reverend Sally Parker stood, back to the green/blue ocean holding the traditional Hawaiian Leis, and awaited the happy couple who will soon be united by marriage.

Larry wearing a pure white linen suit, and Elayne dressed in a traditional Hawaiian Wedding Gown walked hand in hand barefoot across the grass from the limo to the front of the Wedding Arch.

"It's wonderful to see you here today." Started Rev. Parker. " Did you bring the State of Hawaii issued marriage license?" she inquired.

"Johnny, the license." Bellowed Larry.

"Right here, Boss". As Johnny produced the document, the guest chairs were being occupied first by Vinny, Steve, Greg and their wives, girlfriends, concubines, lovers, all not exactly in that order. Several invited guests took possession of chairs, and one or two uninvited guests managed to sit down, as they were warned that the beach and the ceremony is open to the public, and any of the public can attend.

Jenny took her place next to Elayne, like a bridesmaid. The sound of a Conch shell bellowed into the wind as Rev. Parker motioned to Larry and Elayne to each take a Lei Necklace and drape it over the head of the other; and then the Reverend began the blessing for the marriage.

"May your marriage bring you all the exquisite excitements a marriage should bring, and may life grant you also patience, tolerance, and understanding.

May you always need one another-not so much to fill your emptiness as to help you to know your fullness. A mountain needs a valley to be complete, the valley does not make the mountain less, but more; and the valley is more a valley because it has a mountain towering over it. So let it be with you and you." As Rev. Parker nodded first to Larry and then to Elayne. The sun was beginning its decent into the Pacific as Rev. Parker continued.

"May you need one another, but not out of weakness. May you want one another, but not out of lack. May you entice one another, but not compel one another. May you embrace one another, but not out encircle one another.

May you succeed in all important ways with one another, and not fail in the little graces; and may you look for things to praise, often say, 'I love you!' and take no notice of small faults; and if you have quarrels that push you apart, may both of you hope to have good sense enough to take the first step back.

May you enter into the mystery, which is the awareness of one another's presence-no more physical than spiritual, warm and near when you are side-by-side, and warm and near when you are in separate rooms or even distant cities. May you have happiness, and may you find it making one another happy. May you have love, and may you find it loving one another.

Larry , Do you have the Wedding Rings?"

"Yes, Of course. Johnny the rings!" Larry yelled. Johnny dug into his pocket and picked out the two identical gold bands and handed them to Larry.

"Larry, place the ring on Elayne's ring finger, and Elayne, Please do the same. Place the ring on Larry's ring finger. Now by the power vested in me by the State of Hawaii, I pronounce you Husband and Wife. Mr. Christofaro you may kiss your bride." Rev. Parker stated as the Sun was just disappearing over the horizon, and golden streaks travelling horizontally lit up the sky.

"Let us give thanks for this day and let us look forward to tomorrow. Larry and Elayne please sign this marriage license". Rev. Parker insisted.

As Larry and Elayne signed the paperwork flowers were being thrown in the air over them and two white doves were released from a bamboo basket to make their way together towards the Sunset, just as Larry and Elayne would from this day on make their way forward together.

Twenty-Two

The beautiful surreal scene with only the sound of the wind whistling through the Palm trees was suddenly disturbed by the chopping and whirring sound of a helicopter that suddenly appeared over the top of some distance palm trees.

At the same time two Hummer H2 SUV's swiftly travelled onto the grass and towards the wedding party.

Johnny and the boys could sense trouble. Johnny ran to the limo, opened the trunk , and took out the UZI while Steve, Greg and Vinny armed themselves with Berettas and Sammy picked up the Kalashnikov assault rifle. There was firepower coming from the windows of the Hummers and the boys fired back, while taking cover behind the palm trees, although because they were out in the open along the beach there was little cover available.

Johnny used the limo itself for cover and crouched down next to the hood where he could reach over and fire some rounds with the UZI. Greg was able to shoot out the two front tires of one Hummer which stopped it dead in its' tracks. Vinny lit some dynamite and hauled the two sticks right into the blown out front windows of the Hummer, which after the explosions, no sounds were heard coming from within. The other Hummer was being driven at full speed towards the wedding party.

The helicopter was now close and bullets were being sprayed all over the ground coming from the helicopter. Johnny pointed the UZI up and fired several hundred rounds of ammunition towards the helicopter.

Larry pushed Elayne aside , and yelled "Jump" as Rev. Parker leaped towards her left.

The Hummer pummeled through the space just vacated by the trio and dramatically leaped up and over the grass covered edge and plunged down towards the rocky reefs below with shots still being fired, although intermittently and not actually hitting anything.

Johnny and the boys all reached into the trunk to obtain new weapons.

Now that the two Hummer were gone, the helicopter became their main target and it was now flying directly overhead firing down on the wedding party. Johnny could see blood being sprayed all over the white guest chairs and Rev. Parker was hit and down. Larry, Elayne and Jenny could not be seen.

Johnny looked up and he recognized the shooter in the copter-It was Mad Dog Morales, their old drug smuggling competition.

The helicopter was directly overhead and Mad Dog was spraying the ground with what appeared to be some semi-automatic machine gun.

Johnny ran towards what was left of the Wedding Arch, half destroyed, half hanging sideways, and aimed his UZI up and directly towards the copter. He heard tinging sounds as his bullets hit the rotor blade. He could now see Larry on the ground lying over Elayne protecting her from gunshots but his white linen suit was perforated with blood oozing out from several holes. Jenny was lying back a little and to their right , not moving.

Suddenly Johnny took a bullet in his right leg which pulled him down; and another to the shoulder.

"Sammy, use the Kalashnikov" he yelled.

Sam pointed the AK-47 towards the rear of the helicopter where the gas tank was, and fired a round of bullets into the tank. The copper-plated steel jacket , large steel core, with some lead between the core and jacket were excellent in penetrating through heavy walls or a vehicles metal body and Sammy's bullets found their mark. The copter exploded with pieces of metal raining down everywhere but luckily the main body was over the right side of the cliff over the ocean and it plunged down and hit the rocks with a further explosion.

Mad Dog was gone but he had done a lot of damage.

Johnny motioned to Vinny. "Vinny go check on Larry. I think he was hit several times. I can't move. I have a bullet and metal shrapnel in my leg and a bullet in my shoulder."

Vinny and Greg could see that Larry was not moving. They pulled him from covering Elayne and there was no visible signs of life. Greg could see at least 12 bullet holes with blood spurting out without stopping. His Viet Nam experience told him the truth-Larry was gone.

"Larry, get up. You've gone through tough situations before. Come on get up!" Elayne was screaming, and shaking Larry.

Sammy and Greg had to use all their force to pull her away from Larry and Sammy said" Elayne, he's gone. That's it. He's gone".

"No! It can't be!" Elayne cried out."Jenny, tell me it's not true!" Elayne begged. Her beautiful Hawaiian Wedding Gown splattered with Larry's blood. Jennie , also had taken a bullet in her arm, but was now up, holding a napkin to stop the bleeding.

"Elayne. He's not breathing and he's lost a tremendous amount of blood." Jenny confirmed.

"Well. Call an ambulance. Maybe they can bring him back. I can't believe this. This was supposed to be Paradise-Now it's hell!" cried out Elayne.

The ambulance came and took Larry to the hospital however the Paramedics did not see any signs of life and he was declared dead on arrival. Johnny was treated for his wounds. Rev. Parker was gone. Two wives of some guests were killed. Johnny did some checking and was able to find out that the perpetrators in the Hummers were the Surf Gang Black Shorts looking for revenge for their surf boards being destroyed.

A funeral had to be planned and Elayne was dreading the days ahead. She had to make preparations, plan the funeral and grieve at the same time. She was sick. She could not handle this.
Johnny came in and provided the relief she needed.

"Miss Elayne!" He began. "Larry was a mainlander, but he spent his past five years on these Islands ,and yes he was our boss, but he was also our friend, and we considered him Hawaiian. He respected our culture, our native ways, and the boys and I would like him to have a traditional Hawaiian funeral in the form of an ash-scattering ceremony."

"Well, Its true he was Christian but he was not religious" Elayne remarked while wiping tears from her eyes.

"Hawaii is truly a magical place, and a wonderful site for recalling memories and making new memories. I feel your hurt right now, but you have to remember the good times you spent with Larry, short as it was, and a traditional Hawaiian ash scattering ceremony will truly be remembered by us all; and our memory of the way he was will be forever embedded in our minds.

"Miss Elayne, a Hawaiian funeral reaches out to natural beauty to console the sadness in our hearts, and for that reason a lei or flower petals will traditionally be floated on the water where the ashes are scattered. You or I can say a few words, as we will be a part of the ceremony, and not just merely witnesses. We will hire a singer who will sing or chant a poem that includes images of nature." Johnny continued. "A Hawaiian singer who sings songs that can be considered a prayer, although the poem structure , Hawaiian style, will not explicitly address God as Christian prayers do, but I think the type of poem I know the singer will chant will work for your purpose."

"Sounds wonderful, Johnny". Elayne declared between sobs.

"I'll make the preparations." Johnny said. " I'll get it done so we can say a Hawaiian *'Aloha Oe'* or farewell to thee , in your language to our beloved Larry." Johnny completed his words as he excited the suite, and then took the elevator down to the Sheraton Waikiki lobby , and out the front door to his limo. He drove away with sad, morose thoughts but swore to himself that he would give Larry the best most memorable Hawaiian funeral, and that Elayne would be proud and ultimately happy after the sincere services.

The Oahu Mortuary on Nuuanu Avenue handled the cremation and delivered the ashes to Johnny in the Classic Bronze Cremation Keepsake Urn, with elegant black banding, and 'Larry' in a Lucida Calligraphy font engraved in bronze on one side. Enclosed in a velvet bag, it was handed very carefully by the Ohau Mortuary employee over to Johnny, who placed it carefully in the back seat of the limo over near the left door.

The sun had risen in Honolulu as it does every day and the beginning of a great day in Paradise was commencing. Johnny started up the limo and began the twenty minute drive over to the Sheraton to pick up Elayne and Jenny on this funeral day, when they would say goodbye to Larry. The boys, Vinny, Greg, Steve, and Sam Yakimoto were following in Sammy's Hummer.

Meanwhile Jenny was penning a letter on behalf of the just deceased Larry, as if Larry had written it himself. She intended to give it to Elayne, but she also wanted it put into the Urn as if it was a final goodbye from Larry to Elayne, which he himself was not able to say, as his death was so sudden.

Miss Me But Let Me Go

When I come to the end of the road,
And the sun has set for me

I want no rites in a gloom-filled room,
Why cry for a soul set free?
Miss me a little but not long
And not with your head bowed low.
Remember the love that we once shared
Miss me but let me go.
For this is a journey that we all must take
And each must go alone
It's all a part of the Master's plan
A step on the road to home.
When you are lonely and sick at heart,
Go to the friends we know,
And bury your sorrow in doing good deeds,
Miss me, but let me go.

Jenny put down the writing instrument, read what she had penned, and was satisfied with the writing. She rolled up the paper and tied a pink ribbon around it, a ribbon that she normally used to tie her hair. Johnny had just called from the lobby so Jenny went into the bedroom, where Elayne lay on the bed, and said" Elayne, it's time to go. Johnny's downstairs."

Elayne got up slowly, and reluctantly moved towards the front door, without making a sound. Jenny opened the door and locked it after they both excited the suite. The ride down the elevator was in silence, and nothing was said as Johnny, first met them in the lobby, and guided them out to the limo.

He held open the rear door for them, and as Elayne eased into the limo she caught a glance of the velvet bag leaning against the left side door, and she started to sob.

Jenny got in and tried to comfort her, but Elayne was crying all the way out to Kailua where Johnny had booked the service.

They arrived at the beach and Jonny parked partially on the sand. He ran around and opened the door for Elayne and Jenny who got out and began the short , but what seemed like a long walk down to the water. The boys parked their Hummer behind and followed the two women, dressed in the traditional Hawaiian white wrap. While they made their way down to the water's edge Johnny had almost forgotten the urn. He had made it halfway to the water, then ran back to the limo, opened the left rear door and removed the velvet bag which contained the Bronze Urn, cradling it carefully in his left arm, while shutting the door with his right.

The outrigger canoes were awaiting their precious passengers. Flower leis were put over the heads of Elayne, Jenny and Johnny who gingerly stepped into the lead outrigger canoe, and two native Hawaiians commenced paddling out onto the Pacific.

Two more canoes followed with the boys. Johnny had removed the Bronze Urn from the Velvet Bag before getting into the canoe and slowly gave the

Urn to Elayne to hold.

The paddlers knew they were carrying a "Haole" as they called foreigners, nevertheless, there was an honorable history of foreigners adopting ethnic customs that are not part of their genetic heritage. Consider celebrations of St. Patrick's Day and Columbus Day by people who are not noticeably Irish or Italian any other days of the year. For that matter , Christmas is a holiday whose non-religious aspects have been adopted by many non-Christians.

The paddlers stopped paddling at the spot where it had been decided to scatter the ashes. Johnny had recruited Liana, a Hawaiian singer, with a wonderful, tender voice who commenced to sing *'Aloha Oe'* translated as Farewell to Thee, written in 1878.

> " *Ha'aheo e ka ua I na pali*
> *Ke nihi a'ela I ka nahele*
> *E hahai (unhai) ana paha I ka liko*
> *Pua 'ahihi lehua o uka"*

And then in English.
> *"Proudly sept the rain by the cliffs*
> *As it glided through the tress*
> *Still following ever the bud*
> *The 'ahihi lehua of the vale.*

Aloha 'oe, aloha 'oe
E ke onaona I ka lipo
One fond embrace,
A ho'I a 'e au
Until we meet again
'O ka hali'a aloha I hiki mai
Ke hone a'e nei i
Ku'u Manawa
'O 'oe no ku'u ipo aloha
A loko e hana nei"

As Liana continued in English Elayne removed the cover off of the Bronze Urn, gave to to Jenny to hold, and began to scatter Larry's ashes into the beautiful green/blue translucent sea.

" *Farewell to thee, farewell to thee*
The charming one who dwells in the
shaded bowers
One fond embrace,
'Ere I depart
Until we meet again
Sweet memories come back to me
Bringing fresh remembrances
Of the past
Dearest one, yes, you are mine own
From you, true love shall never depart"

Elayne had emptied 60 percent of the urn and

she started to cry again, so she handed the Bronze Urn to Jenny to finish scattering Larry's ashes, as Elayne grabbed a towel from Johnny to wipe her tears.

> *Maopopo ku'u 'ike I ka nani*
> *Na pua rose o Maunawili*
> *I laila hia'ia na manu*
> *Miki'ala I ka nani o ka liko*

> *I have seen and watched your loveliness*
> *The sweet rose of Maunawili*
> *And 'tis there the birds of love dwell*
> *And sip the honey from your lips*

As Liana completed the song Jenny had completed scattering Larry's ashes into the sea and screwed on the top to the Bronze Urn. Jenny couldn't help it, tears started to develop in her eyes as well as emotion, and her intense feelings for her friend. She had only met Larry once, but she grieved for her friend Elayne, who had loved and lost in such a short time. Jenny felt a little guilt , as she was the one who convinced Elayne to come to Hawaii with her in the first place.

"Johnny, I feel terrible. I'm the one responsible for this. I brought Elayne to Hawaii, and look what has happened to her." She cried out.

"Jenny, come on. Don't talk that way. You did

not introduce Larry to Elayne. You were not a matchmaker. You had no responsibility for what happened, and besides Elayne had two or so of the most wonderful weeks of her life. Elayne will have wonderful memories of Larry for the rest of her life. You know what they say, it is better to have loved and lost, then to have never known love at all". Johnny answered, although almost ready to break out in tears himself.

The mourners in the canoes threw flowers and flower leis for Larry. Soon the ocean was a blanket of flowers and Rev. Asonga spoke amongst the tears" Larry was a man of Aloha. God gave him to us as a gift from the sea, and now we give him back from whence he came."

A rainbow formed over the island as the canoes made their way back to the beach.

"Johnny, I want you to keep the Bronze Urn. I wouldn't be able to see it every day, it would only cause heartache." Elayne said, as she handed the urn to Johnny." You keep it , and shine it up when it needs shinning."

"OK. Miss Elayne, If you insist."
The mood that permeated the air in the limo on the journey back was similar to that when they were headed towards the beach and the ceremony. Subdued , each one starring out their own window, no discussion.

Johnny turned onto the Sheraton driveway and

stopped the limo at the front door. Elayne and Jenny got out on their own, and waved goodbye to Johnny with Elayne saying" Johnny, thank you for arranging the funeral ceremony, it was wonderful. I will contact you in a few days. I need some shut-eye time." "Good idea, Miss Elayne, I think we all need some." Johnny drove off, and Elayne and Jenny made their way through the lobby, up in the elevator, and into their suite.

"Goodnight Jenny, Thanks for everything."

"Goodnight Elayne, Enjoy your rest."

Five days of sleep, lying around the suite, some swim time, and a lot of balcony gazing and Elayne decided it was time to call Johnny and the boys.

Elayne called a meeting at the Sheraton and asked the boys to come. Johnny, Sam Yakimoto, Vince, Greg and Steve. Johnny had told Elayne about *Chocolate Gold* and how it was a front for smuggling in drugs, cocaine, heroin and shipping out Hawaiian grown Marihuana. Johnny explained how many attempts there had been on Larry's life and that Mad Dog was truly a mad dog, however if Mad Dog hadn't got Larry, then the Chinese or the Koreans or the local Hawaiian gang or the Mexicans would have got to him. It was like playing Russian Roulette- aiming a loaded gun with one bullet at your head and pulling the trigger; eventually you get hit in the head.

Johnny informed Elayne about the limo and it's armor and how Chocolate smell disguised the drugs in the crates so even drug-sniffing dogs were thrown off by the chocolate scent.

"Boys, It's been five days since we scattered Larry's ashes, and I've been doing a lot of thinking." Elayne started. "I am going to take Larry's place and run *Chocolate Gold*, The Company." "But Elayne. It's a tough, down and dirty business!" Johnny explained. "Not only are the competitors murders and thieves but the Feds and local Hawaiian Police are breathing down our necks everyday. Larry had a large payroll to handle every week to take care of the police and politician's."

"Yes, I know it's tough, but look I loved Larry and I was only with him a few weeks but I need to do this. I remember when he was going surfing and I thought it was dangerous, and I said what happens if you get killed. Well he said, Princess you will become the Chocolate Queen, and take over the company, and run it, and that's what I am going to do." Elayne emphases. "Now is everybody with me? Or does anyone want out?" she questioned.

Each man in the room pledged his allegiance to Elayne and agreed to run the business like Larry had, and like Larry wanted.

The Chocolate Queen was where she wanted to be. It wasn't Paradise but she had to move on with her life, and what a life that was going to be.

Twenty-Three

"Johnny, you're going to run the warehouse and the business here in Honolulu for a week or so while I go over to Maui and straighten out some of our distributors over there." Elayne stated.

"No problem Miss Elayne, just be careful and holler if you need any assistance". Answered Johnny.

Elayne brought Jenny with her over to Maui explaining that they were running in the Maui Marathon and that at the same time Elayne was meeting some *Chocolate Gold* customers and distributors.

"Although its only 75 miles from bustling Oahu, Maui is a very different island-a collection of mostly small towns, plus natural wonders like Haleakala National Park that is a slower way of life than Honolulu." Jenny stated, having just spent almost two weeks there with the National Geographic Magazine team. "Tumbling waterfalls, and a climate that varies from region to region. A very lush island equal to an equatorial rainforest in Hana, and hot and dry as Mexico in Lahaina, and as cool and misty as Oregon in Kula.

A 10,000 foot volcano, Haleakala, is the highest peak on Maui, and can be accessed by car going up a 37 mile long road to the summit."

Elayne and Jenny checked into the Sheraton Maui Resort on Kaanapali Parkway in Lahaina to rest up before the next days' marathon.

They had to be up at 4:00 a.m. as the marathon starts at 5:00 a.m.

5:00 a.m.   The fire dancer performed during the opening festivities and provided a good clue how warm the race was going to be. It was already 72 degrees at the start, high humidity with light wind from the northeast. They started at the Queen Kaahumanu Center, and proceeded through a pair of Kahului neighborhood streets before turning onto the Kuihelani Highway, where the runners were given one lane of the four-lane divided highway that took them by the sugar cane fields.

Before mile 7, they headed south on the Honoapilliani Highway as the sun began to rise. Elayne and Jenny felt the wind at their backs as they had their first glimpse of the Pacific Ocean and the neighboring island of Kahoolawe, as they approached Maalaea, located at the southern end of the isthmus that connected the two main lands of Maui, formed millions of years ago by two separate volcanoes, with the land created by them fusing together.

They stayed on the side of the two-lane road to Lahaina for another 15 miles, sharing it with traffic going in both directions, which was not really any problem, as by then most of the marathoners were spread out along the course. Up to this point they were on level ground, but that changed beginning at mile 8 when they encountered the *Pali* ('cliff') and they started their ascent. They would climb approximately 100 feet over the next three or so miles, and at around mile 12 they encountered the tunnel that would signal their descent back to sea level. It also meant they would no longer feel the benefit of the wind to cool them down, which is exactly what happened, and with the sun beating down in full force it started to get hot. Now running westward they were able to view surfers and paddle-boarders with neighboring island Lanai in the background.

Elayne and Jenny were enjoying the run but they had to be constantly aware of the traffic cruising by. They were happy to see mile markers positioned along the course at every mile which kept them up to date as to how much road they had travelled.

They were on the leeward part of the island where it was fairly dry, with few trees around to give them cover. They stopped at almost every course aid station to pick up the water from Menehune Water Company, and occasionally took some Gatorade for refreshment and to avoid dehydration. Elayne stopped twice at the Porta Potties while Jenny only needed to stop once.

At mile 16 they briefly departed from the coast as they entered the village of Olowalu, with the course now heading northwest. The heat started to take its toll as the mile splits were getting longer and longer.

"This is definitely a lot hotter than the Cape" Jenny stated". "Oh Yea, for sure", gasped Elayne as she was trying to keep pace." I'd say it feels twice as hot-probably close to 100 degrees when on the Cape it was only 50 or 55".

At mile 22 they entered the aptly named *Lahaina* (Hawaiian for 'cruel sun') detouring from

Honoapiliani Highway on Front Street. The protection provided by the homes, retail and dining establishments from the wind made this the hottest part of the course , and Elayne was starting to feel like she was hitting the wall. She was slowing down and said to Jenny "I'm afraid I might not finish. The heat is just too much."

"Drink some more water, breathe easy, eat that banana that you are hauling, don't worry we are almost at the finish line". Jenny answered.

They left Lahaina and returned back to Honoapiliani Highway at mile 24. Only 2-12 miles to go , thought Jenny. Heading north they could see neighboring island Moolokai on their left side as they headed to Kaanapali Parkway and Whalers Village, their final destination. Elayne passed a sign that she could swear was flashing 94 degrees and she didn't need the sign to tell her it was unbearably hot and humid. They cruised through the finish line and easily picked up their souvenir bright orange/peachy tee shirts and refreshments, wolfing down fresh fruit and large quantities of water.

"Well, we can check off Maui Marathon off of our bucket list!" exclaimed Elayne.

"Absolutely. Wasn't it great? Jennie asked. "A little hot but what scenery, unbelievable. A fantastic experience. Did you see all the Japanese runners?". Elayne wasn't paying any attention as she was headed straight for Kaanapali Beach walk and the ocean." Come on, Jenny! The big beautiful blue ocean is waiting." Jenny followed as fast as she could and both dove right into the sea feeling absolutely refreshed by the relatively cool water compared to the 90 degree Hawaiian Heat.

Elayne rented a car and drove over to Wailea, the playground of the stretch-limo set. Just 4 decades ago this was wall-to-wall scrub kiawe trees, but now Wailea is a manicured oasis of multimillion dollar resort hotels along 2 miles of palm-fringed coast. The warm, clear water off the five outstanding beaches are full of tropical fish, and with year round golden sunshine and clear blue skies, Wailea is more than paradise.

Larry and *Chocolate Gold's* most successful dealer owned and ran a multimillion-dollar resort hotel, with beachfront property on one of the six beaches, which was spectacular, and attracted the richest, most well to do clientele, who could drop from thousands to millions in a day devouring Larry's product. One Saudi Sheik alone dropped $500,000 last month.

Elayne drove up the circular driveway and stopped at the main entrance. She excited the Mercedes Convertible and flipped the keys to the valet.

"Park this somewhere." She said with authority.

"Yes, Ma'am." The valet responded.

Elayne strode past the automatic doors and as soon as she stepped onto the marble floors in the lobby she took in the aroma of the flower-filled lobby; and she could see the big blue Pacific Ocean outside framed by a hugh dome of glass and was overwhelmed again by Hawaii's beauty. You know there is no doubt you're in Hawaii when you are in that type of scene. She walked over to the concierge.

"How do I find Madame Picard's Villa" she asked.

"Just walk past that pool on the left, out the door and it's number seven on the right."

Elayne followed the concierge's instructions and knocked on door number seven.

A football-type player opened the door. Elayne looked up at his massive well-tanned face, as she only reached his mid chest, even in her staccato heels. Sporting an Hawaiian short sleeve shirt she spotted huge forearms and shoulders.

"I'm here to see Madam Picard".

"She's not available". The football player stated.

"Well, make her available. I'm from *Chocolate Gold.*" Elayne responded .

Madame Picard appeared in a two piece very skimpy swimsuit and a Hawaiian towel wrapped around her waist and flowing down to the top of her beach sandals like a wedding gown. Decorated with bright flowers, pure white, it was exactly opposite to her dark features, brown skin, unusually red hair, and she had at least four flower bracelets on her right wrist, and two leis around her neck. Gold earrings, and a headband twisted round with flower decoration adorned her forehead.

"Oui, Bonjour. Who are you? And what do you want? Mademoiselle!" Madame Picard blurted out.

"I was married to Larry Christofaro , you probably knew him as Michael Simons, President of *Chocolate Gold.*" Elayne began. "May I come in?"

"Of course, Madame. Excuse me for calling you Mademoiselle. I did not know! But what do you mean , was married? Is the marriage over? And call me Michelle."

"Well, Michelle, the marriage was over in five minutes when Mad Dog Morales broke into our wedding party, let's say with a bang. Larry took several bullets and died almost immediately." Elayne explained.

"Ah Yes, I heard something went down on Oahu, and Mad Dog had gone down in a helicopter".

"Well Larry went down also, and I decided to take over running *Chocolate Gold* like he would have wanted me too." Elayne continued. "Now you , Michelle, have been *Chocolate Gold's* best distributor for almost four years but last year your purchases were down almost 50%. What's happening?" questioned Elayne.

"First of all Mad Dog and the Mexicans were hassling us all the time and threatening us that if we don't switch to buying their merchandize , and replacing Larry's they were ready to 'let's say, remove some of my limbs, one at a time." Michelle Picard explained.

"You don't have to worry about Mad Dog anymore, he's gone." Stated Elayne.

"And the DEA have been sniffling around. I think they are targeting my operation here on Maui, because we are seeing a lot of new law enforcement Officers, both in the open, and undercover, although they are very sloppy undercover officers, who we can spot very quickly. We had one of our dealers in Hana busted three months ago and we lost a big shipment of crystal meth. We suspect the Mexicans had something to do with it." Michelle reported.

"Michelle, first of all, like I said, Mad Dog is gone, so the Mexicans are hurt, and probably won't be able to apply any muscle real soon; and we can take care of the DEA and any local officers. I need you to switch back to us right away. You understand?" Elayne explained, but at the same time demanded, and Michelle could see that Elayne was all business and tough. Maybe toughened by a five minute marriage that was torn apart by bullets.

"I wouldn't want anything to happen to those beautiful arms or legs of yours, understand." Elayne repeated.

"Sure, no problem, Madam. You just handle the Feds for us and business will be back to usual."

"Ok. I was sure we could come to an understanding". Elayne responded. "I'll expect to see those orders coming in starting tomorrow. Have a nice day" as she stood up and excited the Villa.

"Whew, she's tough." Michelle stated to her football player.

The drive back to Ka'anapali was enticing as the road hugged the coast and the blue Pacific Ocean contrasted with the Hawaiian lava fed earth. The sky matched the deep blue ocean, and it was hard to see where the sky and ocean met as they appeared to be one. Elayne's blonde hair was moving and flying around as the wind flowed through her hair. She drove the Mercedes Convertible with the top down, and decided not to wear a hat, as she felt free and easy with the cool ocean breeze flowing through her hair. The wind breezed past her ears and the sun was filtered through her Armani sunglasses. She for a fleeting moment remembered a movie when Marilyn Monroe had driven a convertible with her blond hair flowing in the wind, and Elayne imagined herself as Marilyn, driving down a curvy Hawaiian coastal road.

Past Kihel and Maalaea, and left onto Route 36 towards Lahaina. The Pacific Ocean view continued.

Into Ka'anapali and directly to the Sheraton, where to her surprise, Jenny was sitting outside the main building, sunbathing.

"How was your little business trip?" Asked Jenny.

"Oh great. I was very persuasive and to the point. I think I made a good impression and I may have saved one of our most important distributors of *Chocolate Gold,* anyway I'm beat. I'm going straight to bed." Elayne answered.

"OK Elayne. See you tomorrow".

Elayne didn't know Michelle Picard. Neither had Larry. No one except Michelle's football player/body guard actually knew the truth about Michelle.

It appeared to everyone that Michelle was big time. That she ran an exclusive Hawaiian Resort on Maui, and secretly was a *Chocolate Gold* distributor.

Probably everyone would be shocked to learn that not only was she a meth addict, but she also was an undercover vice cop working with the Maui Police Department.

She joined the Maui Police Department when she was 25 years old and rapidly worked her way up to being a cop in the narcotics division. Every day she would investigate the big time meth dealers including the Mexicans, the Koreans, the Chinese Mob, and even Larry himself. She would go on search and destroy missions with various Police agencies, including the DEA, and hit the worst slums in Hawaii looking for illegal drug activity.

She had been recruited right out of university where she was working on a PHD and had experimented with soft drugs, marijuana and such. Then tried Heroin and Cocaine eventually becoming hooked on Hawaii's most popular drug, Methamphetamine. She also used and abused Ecstasy as a teenager which was being used in increased amounts by young adults ,20-30 years old, because it was readily available at raves, nightclubs, and some hotels. In fact when Michelle was just 19 she was hooked up with an Asian boyfriend, who through his contacts brought in to Maui large quantities of YABA tablets from Thailand. Her boyfriend worked at the Honolulu airport and was deeply involved in smuggling in Ecstasy and other drugs.

Michelle's boyfriend was taken into custody by the Feds when they discovered a shipment of YABA tablets hidden in some lockers at the airport that were under her boyfriend's control. He in turn in a plea bargain, identified her as his associate, and deeply involved in sales and distribution of the drugs. Michelle was given a choice-spend ten years behind bars or go undercover and work with the DEA; she picked the latter.

She was a native Hawaiian, father French, mother Hawaiian. Exotic, dark skinned beauty with unusual Hazel Green eyes. Dark black hair down to the small of her back. She didn't look like a cop, didn't look like an addict, she fooled everyone.

Michelle dyed her hair red, had it cut back to shoulder length, and excelled in shooting class, became a sharpshooter with her Glock 27 police issue pistol. She would go out on searches with other officers, and occasionally cuff some lowly drug user, being satisfied that she was contributing to cut down the drug use on Maui, but knowing that she really had no choice-it was either drug busting or sitting in the slammer.

At night she would return to her small one room apartment overlooking the beach in Hana, take out her pipe , fill it with meth and light up.

Michelle was leading a double life , Vice Cop by day and Meth Addict by night. It couldn't last. She worked her way up the ladder in both occupations.

Michelle was extremely attractive and she knew it so she used her beauty to get promotions and favors form her fellow officers, and her fellow drug users and dealers. After only a year being part of the Maui Police Department she had an affair with a Hawaiian cop who just happened to be on the vice squad and was responsible most days in tagging the drugs seized, filing in storage, filing reports and testifying at court hearings.

Michelle was able to, after a night of sexual activity with the officer, in the police station , and after all other officers had left for the night; was able to remove a small percentage of the meth, with her lover's knowledge and approval, to use and abuse at home in her small one bedroom hideaway near the beach. This continued for several months, until their relationship broke off when she discovered he was married with two young children. The problem was Michelle was addicted to meth. She couldn't brazenly go out looking to buy it on any streets in any village on Maui because she was known as a cop busting Meth Labs and dealers.

Michelle made deals with the big boys, the big dealers, on the Island. She promised them that she would not raid their locations, and only bust small insignificant users to make her look good, but leave their big Meth Labs alone, in exchange for a regular supply of Meth.

She needed Meth every day. Problem was she had no appetite because of Meth abuse. She started losing weight and looked gaunt, with black circles under her eyes. Working 12 hour shifts with the Vice Squad and wolfing down Meth every night didn't help her appearance. Only so much make-up could hide her ghastly appearance. She took a leave of absence from the Police Department and hid out at a Wailea Resort that catered to drug users.

Sheik Hassan Yamani , one of the Princes' from Saudi Arabia, let her use his Villa, in return for sexual favors. She didn't care. He supplied her with the Meth she needed, and she in turn helped distribute Meth, Cocaine and Heroin to the tourists staying at the resort. After a few weeks her Captain at the Maui Police discovered where she was and inquired when she would be returning to her duties.

She replied "never". "I'm through working the Vice Squad." Her Captain had another idea. He told her emphatically "Either you work for us, as your deal with the DEA dictates, or you are against us, and I will have to take you in, and send you back to be incarcerated. Prison life you know is not fun; it's not Paradise. You will be living in a hell in Paradise-a cell on a Hawaiian Island. So what's your choice?" He asked.

"I'll think about it and get back to you." She answered.

Michelle couldn't take it anymore. She couldn't live the double life, and actually the Meth use was slowly killing her. She searched for a solution, and then Elayne dropped into her life.

Twenty-Four

Michelle fiddled with the Captain's card, turning it over and over, flipping it back and forth. She looked at the phone numbers of the Maui Police Department and even though she knew the numbers she still looked at them printed in black on the white card. She studied his extension and finally decided it's time to act. It was four days since he had contacted her with his ultimatum, and she now knew what she wanted to do. She had to escape this life, both of them, and survive.

She dialed the phone number, and when prompted punched in his extension.

"Hello, Captain Stenson speaking!"

"Captain, it's Michelle."

"It's about time. I expected you to call two days ago." He stated.

"Well, I've been mulling around in my head what I wanted to do and I have decided." Michelle said.

"Good. Can you come into the precinct tomorrow? I want to pair you up with a rookie, that I think will be good. He needs training." The Captain said.

"No. I have something else in mind. Can you come up to Wailea? I have an idea."

"Ok. What kind of idea?"Captain Stenson inquired.

"I will tell you when you get here. I need to discuss with you privately, where there is no possibility of anyone eavesdropping. You understand?" Michelle asked.

"Yes. I can be there in a couple of hours. Where can I find you?"

" Villa Number Seven." Michelle responded.
She heard the click of the phone hanging up, and Michelle pondered- was she doing the right thing? Only time would tell.

It was drastically humid by the time Captain Stenson walked past the pool and down towards Villa Number Seven. His blue police uniform shirt was stained with sweat, with huge embarrassing circles of wetness under his armpits and a circle of sweat on his back that resembled a target. Sweat was pouring down the sides of his face like water escaping a broken faucet. He loosened his tie and unbuttoned the top button so he could pull his shirt open at the collar. He wiped his forehead with his sleeve, and dabbed his eyes to remove the salty sweat water away from his eyes. He removed his police issue Glock 27 and banged on the door with the gun butt, ignoring the bell button that was clearly visible next to the door.

An oversized male opened the door and said" You must be the Cop Miss Picard is waiting for!"
The rush of cold air-conditioned air hit the Police Captain right in the face. " That's right. Can I come in? It's boiling hot and humid out here." For a moment while Captain Stenson waited for the obvious answer he looked at the oversize male, up and down, and figured he had to be an ex-football player, or one of those wrestlers in the WWF, or EWF, whatever, as Captain Stenson didn't follow what some refer to as Professional Wrestling.

"Sure, come in, and close the door quick-like, the cool air is escaping." Stated the oversized male who in the same moment looked at Captain Stenson, up and down. Tall, maybe 6 foot, thin, but with muscles bulging under that sweat soaked police shirt, turning it ,in spots from Blue to dark Blue, almost black. Bald except for a circle of shaved hair running above his ears and probably around the back of his head. The color of a Hawaiian as skin color with big bushy eyebrows, and a firm wide mouth.

The Captain did as he was told and stepped into Villa Number Seven , shut the door; and then felt the full blast of cold air as it settled over his body and actually made him shiver slightly as the cold air met with the warm sweat. He could hear a female voice beckoning.

"Captain, welcome, come through the living room and out to the back." Michelle yelled out.

Captain Stenson was a fourth generation Hawaiian and his ancestors were mostly farm and plantation workers. He himself had worked several part time jobs to raise the money to put himself through Police School. He had worked hard, stayed on focus, and after twenty years , with seven years as a Vice Cop had been made Captain, and he relished the job, and did his utmost to bring honor and success to the Maui Police force. Captain Stenson had stayed in some Holiday Inn's and Sheratons in his travels, whether on business or vacation; but he had never experienced or had even seen the opulence that permeated a suite like this Villa Number Seven.

Wall to wall, ceiling to floor mirrors covered one side of the Villa, and reflected the gold chandeliers hanging from the ceiling. The ceilings were probably ten feet high, and the Captain immediately viewed the marble staircase, with glass sides and polished bronze hand rails, that rolled up in a circular fashion to the second floor that appeared loft like. The carpet covering the floor wall to wall was white Berber that seemed like pure sheep wool. Picasso- like paintings adorned the walls, and the mahogany bar on the right side of the room was stocked with Bourbon, champagne and vintage wine. Three tall bar stools with polished bronze gold-like legs, and thick cushion seats guarded the bar like soldiers guarding royalty.

"Here, sit down!" Michelle ordered."Like a drink? Some wine? A beer?"

"No thanks, maybe just some cold iced tea, if you have." He responded.

"Sure, Raphael, get the Captain some iced tea, and some for me too." Well the oversized man had a name- Raphael. Thought Captain Stenson.

"So, what is this idea you have?" questioned the Captain. Michelle waited for a minute, thinking about what she would say, and how to present it to the Captain; and then she began.

"You want me to return to work with the force. You want me to work with the DEA. You want me to continue taking down Meth dealers and work undercover, which is extremely risky. My problem with all that is that I enjoy the risk, the bust, the taking down of some high-end dealers, but what you don't know is that I am a meth addict, and I have been for a few years. I can't buy the drugs here on Maui because I am known as a narcotics vice cop so I have to go to Honolulu once a month to buy my one month supply.

Look at my face carefully. My pupils are dilated. I've lost fifteen pounds. My face is thin and emancipated. Black rings under my eyes are only hidden by makeup. I'm only thirty-two years old and I am walking a tightrope, balancing between succumbing to the Meth, Heroin, Cocaine that I am feeding myself, and in danger everyday of being knocked off, either in one of those drug busts, or anywhere, here, in the Villa, or out on the street by any of the gangs running the drug scene on Maui.

I can't take this scene anymore." Michelle , as tough as she was, began to cry, accepting a hanker chief from the Captain to wipe her eyes.

"So, what do you propose?" asked the Captain.

"First, I need to go into rehab." Michelle explained. "Probably around four weeks."

"And then?" The Captain inquired.

"Then I will work with the Maui Police and the DEA, but only on one major bust, and after that bust I retire, and you leave me alone. I retire from the police force. I retire from the drug scene. I leave this Island forever." Michelle replied.

"What major drug bust?"

"You are aware that Michael Simons aka Larry Christofaro , former President of *Chocolate Gold* got wiped out on his wedding day by Mad Dog, who also died in a helicopter crash." Michelle started.

"Come on, that's old news". The Captain stated.

"Well, what you may not be aware of is that his widow has taken over running the company, and she just dropped in on me to explain 'how things were gonna go down from now on, in the business'." Michelle continued. " So, what I am bargaining with, is this. I will go undercover, wear a wire and help the DEA destroy *Chocolate Gold* completely. I will get enough evidence to convict all the top people and close down the company forever. I will even be a witness at any trial that is necessary; but for all this I want to be free, and leave this Vice Busting business for good."

"Sounds good Michelle. Let me clear this with the top guys at Maui, and with the DEA."

"No Captain! No talking to anyone at the Department. I'm afraid there are moles there and some are on *Chocolate Gold's* payroll, because it's strange that in four or five years of operations in Hawaii *Chocolate Gold* and Larry Christofaro has not even been given a speeding ticket. Someone's getting paid off. You can negotiate with the DEA and the Justice Department, but say nothing to anyone on the Maui Police Force, or I'm not agreeing to anything." Insisted Michelle.

"OK Michelle. I will handle this your way. I hope everything works out for you. I will speak to the DEA, clear everything, and get back to you in a few days." The Captain promised.

The heat hit Captain Stenson like a punch in the face by a prizefighter as soon as he opened the door to Villa Number Seven , and walked outside into the burning Hawaiian sun. He had thoughts of everything working out with Michelle, and he would be credited with a major bust which could reward him with a promotion.

Captain Stenson rushed to his automobile, quickly dropped into the driver's seat, started up the vehicle, and turned up the air conditioning to high, while turning the air ducts toward his face and body.

He couldn't stop thinking about a promotion as he entered the highway and drove back to headquarters.

Twenty-Five

"Michelle, It's Stenson. I have good news. I cleared everything with the DEA and the Justice Department. Everyone is in place and we also have Judge Smallman who will handle the warrants and the arraignments." Captain Stenson explained to Michelle. "I have also arranged for you to be flown to a rehab near L.A. to spend the four weeks there."

"That's great , Captain. I will make my way to Honolulu next week , Monday. Have someone meet me at the Airport with my flight tickets and rehab info." Michelle responded.

Four weeks went by quickly and Michelle, completely sober was back on Maui, sleeping comfortably in Villa Number Seven.

A DEA Mobile Enforcement Team consisting of three tough looking men and one petite female officer arrived at the Villa to prepare Michelle for her meeting with Elayne. Michelle had called Elayne to tell her she was coming to Honolulu and wanted to visit Elayne at the *Chocolate Gold* warehouse to place a big order as Elayne had demanded. Michelle insisted that she wanted to meet personally with Elayne and didn't want any of Elayne's people handling the order. Elayne agreed, and stated she was looking forward to the resumption of a great business relationship between *Chocolate Gold* and its' biggest dealer on Maui-Michelle.

The female DEA officer sat with Michelle in a large bedroom in Villa Number Seven, and taped the wire under Michelle's Bra strap, ran it around her waist to the transmitter taped to her lower back. The microphone was hidden in her left Bra cup. She explained that Michelle could not wear a see-through blouse or light colored blouse because, obviously the wires could not be seen, so Michelle picked out a bright red blouse with some Hawaiian Leis on the front breast pocket.

Raphael, Michelle's bodyguard, chauffeur, and all around chief assistant parked the Mercedes Limo as close to the door at 76 Libby Street, Honolulu, which was the *Chocolate Gold* warehouse and headquarters. He checked his pistol that was holstered under his left armpit, and ran around the car to open the door for Michelle.
Michelle exited the Mercedes and explained" Raphael, I want to meet with Elayne alone, so you stay here with the limo"

"You sure, Miss Michelle? You sure you will be all right?" questioned Raphael.

"Raffee, Elayne is tough, but I'm tougher. I will have no problem. Get yourself a coffee. I'll be meeting for about an hour. If I don't come out in an hour then you can come in and get me" She stated as she walked up the stairs and opened the warehouse door. It seemed like ex football players or wrestlers were all that Elayne and others in her business employed, as what looked like an ex running back blocked Michelle from proceeding as soon as she entered the warehouse. Short, maybe five –six, squat, compact, thick legs, broad shoulders, wearing a suit that probably was size fifty-two short. The equipment he had in addition was an UZI submachine gun.

"Who are you and what do you want?" he asked. "A rather big gun to just guard Chocolates, don't you think?" Michelle asked.

"That's my business, not yours!" He replied. "Now who are you and what do you want?" He repeated. "I'm your biggest dealer on Maui, Michelle Picard".

"What are you French, or something?" He asked.

"Yes, half French. That is not important. I have an appointment with Elayne. Could you bring me to her?" Michelle asked.

"Mais oui , Mademoiselle. Suivez moi." He said as he walked past crates marked *Chocolate Gold* and down past dozens of opened crates towards a light that shown through a dirty window, from what appeared to be an office. Michelle followed.

He opened the foggy glass door, and motioned to a metal staircase near the corner. "Up there!" Michelle climbed the stairs and before opening the next door, paused to take a deep breath, knowing that the next forty-five minutes would be stressful.

As Michelle entered the office she noticed Elayne lounging on a red leather three seat chesterfield. She had a glass of wine in her right hand, and the bottle of Batasiolo Bosc Dia Rei Moscato D'asti in her left. Half the bottle remained full, which meant Elayne had consumed half. Two more bottles rested on the glass table in front of her.

"Michelle. Hello. How are you? Come sit down and enjoy some great wine!" Elayne promised.

Michelle dropped into a black leather chair opposite Elayne, picked up a wine glass, and poured herself some Moscato D'asti. She put her glass forward and said "Cheers" as Michelle and Elaynes' glasses clanged together.

"Elayne, I am going to be up front with you and honest as to my intentions, and why I am really here". Michelle began.

"Michelle, you don't have to explain to me, I have the paperwork all prepared right here." Elayne picked up ten papers that looked like purchase orders."Elayne, explain to me what those papers are, and can you go more into detail what you want me to do, going forward, because on Maui at the Villa you didn't provide details" Michelle asked.

"Michelle, *Chocolate Gold* appreciates your purchases in the past but now we want you to double your commitment, and triple after one year."

Michelle knew she had to get Elayne to talk specifically about certain drugs, otherwise continuing to talk about chocolate will not allow the DEA or Justice Department to lay charges ,and succeed. No one will be indicted for selling chocolate.

"Elayne, what are you identifying specifically? Meth, Cocaine, Heroin, Oxycontin, What?" asked Michelle.

"Michelle, you know we are the biggest Meth importer and distributor on the Hawaiian Islands. We are seeing a lot of competition from the Mexicans and the Asian cartels. Your buys were way down last year so this year we want it increased and specifically in 'ice'. Our 'ice' is 96-99 percent pure and we are bringing in pound quantities every week. We also need you to set up and supervise a meth lab on Maui so we can convert cheaper right on Maui. We also are bringing in Ecstasy, which is easy to stuff into our crates of chocolate.

We found that supplying Ecstasy to young people creates a base for the Meth user, and teenagers and young adults between twenty to thirty years old are increasingly using Ecstasy, which we are easily dealing at raves, nightclubs, and some hotels, including yours on Maui." Elayne detailed.

"Elayne, are you yourself involved in the business, or just your underlings?" Michelle asked.

"First of all don't refer to my business associates as underlings, and yes I am personally involved. I have taken over all of Larry's former duties; and this is for you to know, I have been taking shooting lessons at the local gun club. You never know when a girl needs to defend herself." Elayne answered.

"Now sign these documents which lists exactly how many and what quantities of the Meth and MDMA you will commit for and I will sign and give you your copy. We have to run this business like a business. Here sign here."The ten pages were put in front of Michelle and she signed and initialed each page, which Elayne then signed, initialed and kept five pages, then handing over the five duplicate pages to Michelle.

"Well it's been a pleasure doing business with you Michelle. I knew you would come around to my way of thinking. Let's look forward to a long and profitable relationship!" Elayne finally stated.

"Sure, Elayne, sure!" remarked Michelle.

Michelle stood up, stumbled a little, but did not fall, as she was feeling the three glasses of Moscato she had consumed in a short thirty minutes.

"Are you all right?" Elayne inquired.

"Yes. No problem. A little dizzy, but I'm fine", as Michelle reached the office door, pulled it toward her, walked out, and pulled it shut. Down the metal staircase, through the warehouse past the open and also yet to be opened crates, past the short man with the UZI, and out into the sunlight.

She exhaled in relief as she entered the limo.

"How did it go?" Raphael asked.

"Very good. Raffee. Very good."

Michelle knew that if everything that was said was transmitted Elayne was finished and soon would be out of the *Chocolate Gold* business completely.

Twenty-Six

The DEA cops working with the Honolulu Police Department had confiscated a warehouse across the road, and had set up the communications devices they needed to monitor Michelle as she talked with Elayne. Raphael drove off the *Chocolate Gold* parking lot, across Libby street, down past a row of warehouses and turned right into the row of offices and warehouses up to #5. A guard stood outside with his hand on his hip as if he was ready at any time to pull out a pistol.

Michelle stepped out of the limo, glanced across the street, noticed the high wire fence topped with barbed wire and the sailboat, she estimated at 36 foot, sitting on a stand probably waiting to be repaired or serviced. Ethel's Grill was over on the next street, an establishment that Michelle had busted many times. Not the Grill itself, but some of the dealers and users that hung out there. The food was delicious. The steak special with chimichurri was scrumptious with its' lurid green sauce. Served pupu-style on a bed of rice, the plate comes with a garnish of highlighter pink pickled onions, a nice complement to the tangy chimichurri. Michelle usually ordered the daily sweet potato, topped off with a sweet Carolina-style barbecue pork.

The baked goods are insane with Minaka, the owner taking a slice of Bread shop city bread, slathered with Nutella, and toasted marsh mellows with rainbow sprinkles. Its' a must have finish to a great Hawaiian meal. Although technically its' Japanese food with Hawaiian flavor.

The DEA female officer tapped Michelle on the shoulder, and as Michelle turned around she said" Hi, day dreaming a little? We need to go inside to remove the equipment, the wires and stuff."

"Yes, I was just remembering the great food around the corner at Ethels' " Michelle answered.

"Ya, I've been there. Good food. Anyway my name's Jo-Ann. Let's go inside."

Michelle followed Jo-Ann up two concrete stairs, past the warehouse door that Raphael held open for them, and into the semi-lit warehouse that smelled as if it contained olives, pickles, and such. Down past some wooden containers and into the office where the DEA had set up their listening equipment.

"Hello. I'm George Espinola head of the DEA deployment team that is assigned to this case." George was obviously Hawaiian. Tall, good looking, brownish skin color, and he directed Michelle to computer equipment and screens that were flashing and spitting out data.

"We picked up your transmissions 100% and we are good to go. Elayne Christofaro and *Chocolate Gold* will soon be a thing of the past; and you will have helped to eliminate one of the biggest drug smugglers on the Islands." George stated as he signed some official looking documents that Michelle knew were warrants, pre-signed by Judge Smallman. George then handed the warrants to Jo-Ann and instructed her to go scoop up the fish.

Michelle also knew that was code for, go across the street and serve the arrest warrants, arrest anyone who was there, and specifically Elayne Christofaro, and lock up the warehouse. Jo-Ann excused herself, left the room, excited the warehouse with three DEA officers and dialed up the Honolulu Police.

"Ok. We're ready to go. Send about four squad cars with two or three officers each; and don't forget the vests and UZI's." Jo-Ann ordered like she was ordering an all dressed pizza with cheese covered garlic bread. Jo-Ann and her DEA officers just made it across the road and down to 76 Libby Street when the four Honolulu White and Blue Police cars pulled up to the warehouse. Eight officers, wearing bulletproof vests, helmets, and carrying assault rifles jumped out with four running around back of the warehouse building on the left. Two officers went out right side of the building, and two went to the front door with Jo-Ann, and the three DEA officers.

No guard confronted them at the door as Jo-Ann rang the bell. A thin wide slot opened and as the brown eyes looked through the slot the human behind the eyes asked "Who are you? What do you want?"

"I'm Jo-Ann working with Michelle, and Michelle sent me to meet with Elayne. Can you open the door?"

Three bolts slid, and the door swung open. Two Hawaiian Police jumped in first, and with an UZI pointing at the human behind the door, allowed the others to move in to the warehouse.

Jo-Ann and the officers moved towards the office, opened the door, and immediately viewed Elayne sitting on the red couch, sipping wine. She was shocked when Jo-Ann threw the warrants at her and said" You're under arrest, don't move."

"What am I under arrest for?" questioned Elayne.

Jo-Ann didn't answer but motioned to one of the DEA officers to bring a medium sized wooden crate over. The officer then smashed the crate with an axe and pried open the rest of the crate with a crowbar. Turning the crate upside down he extracted thirty or forty chocolate bars.

"Your arresting me for importing chocolate bars?"
Elayne laughed out loud, but then the bags of drugs fell out. Ten bags of white powder-"Probably Cocaine, we'll get them tested at the lab." Jo-Ann declared. Ten bags of another substance-"Looks an awful lot like Meth, Crystal Meth." Jo-Ann pointed out." Finally we see the Ecstasy pills" as a few hundred pills tumbled out onto the warehouse floor.
"Or could be Molly, another drug that hits young adults , aged 20-30 years old. You are not being arrested for importing chocolate bars, Elayne Christofaro, but for operating one of Hawaii's largest drug importers and distributors. Hands behind your back please!" as Jo-Ann took out her handcuffs and expertly handcuffed Elayne's hands behind her back.

Telling one of the DEA agents to bring Elayne out to the Police Cars, she grabbed the bottle of Moscato d'asti and took a swig. The other officers combed the warehouse, let in the other Police waiting in the back, and came across two *Chocolate Gold* employees trying to hide behind some crates. They were immediately searched for weapons, and handcuffed and led outside to be put into the Police Cars.

The locksmith was waiting at the front door for Jo-Ann who ordered "OK. Gerry, Change the lock, and give me the only key!"

By 5:00 p.m. Jo-Ann reported back to Captain Stenson. " Operation Chocolate went off without a hitch. We have Ms. Christofaro in custody, and a locked warehouse full of evidence."

"That's great-Jo-Ann. Bring Ms. Christofaro into court tomorrow to be arraigned." The Captain replied.

Courtroom #14 at the Honolulu Court House was packed at 8:30 in the morning. After a few of the unfortunates were paraded across in front of Judge Smallman, who directed them any which way, so as to just disperse them as fast as possible; a constable brought up Elayne who appeared with messy hair, no makeup, and prison attire-orange jumpsuit.

She identified herself and the duty counsel acted for her, putting the matter over for three days so Elayne could dig up a person to bail her out.

The Assistant Warden at the Women's Prison in Waikiki spoke first " Ms. Jenny Monroe , we have an inmate that has requested she speak with you, and I am putting her on the phone now".

"Jenny, its' Elayne!" her voice seemed dispirited and tired.

"What? What are you doing in prison?"Jenny asked.

"I was arrested and charged with smuggling or importing hard drugs into Hawaii. Jenny I'm scared. I'm afraid of the other inmates in here. You've got to get me out. The court appearance is in two days"

It seemed Elayne was begging and pinning her hopes on Jenny.

"Don't worry Elayne, I'll get you out. I'll get the best Lawyer in Honolulu and see you in the court on Thursday. Just relax. We'll get you out." Jenny tried to assure Elayne that she would get her out.

"That's easy for you to say. I'm in here with criminals, and you're out there free." Elayne remarked. The phone clicked off.

Jenny called her friends at the National Geographic and asked if they knew anyone who knew the best criminal lawyer in Honolulu. They referred her to James P. Hogsworth, a name to be remembered. A name that was easy to remember. Jenny called the number and asked for Lawyer Hogsworth.

"James here!" He answered.

"Mr. Hogsworth I have a friend who just got arrested and is in the Women's' Prison. She will be in court Thursday for a Bail hearing. Can I hire you to handle the hearing? I heard that you are the best." Elayne commented.

"Well I am the best and you must be aware I charge the highest fees. I charge $5000.00 for a Bail hearing with no guarantees, and I require cash up front." Hogsworth pointed out.

"Mr. Hogsworth can you do better?"

"No. You want better. Get someone else!" Hogsworth answered with roughness.

The hearing lasted fifteen minutes as James Hogsworth worked his magic and got Elayne released on a $100,000 bond with her passport surrendered, and an order to stay in Hawaii until her case is resolved. Two hours later she was led up out of the cells and collapsed in Jenny's arms.

"Elayne did you eat anything while in that hellhole?" Jenny inquired.

"Almost nothing. Just drank some water that looked suspiciously not clear for three days." Elayne managed to cry out. Jenny take me to the hotel. I need a shower, some good food, and a plan how to handle this disaster that has come over me! I escaped being raped twice, and fought off a lunatic giant ape who wanted my shoes. Jenny if I ever have to go back to a jail like that I will kill myself first."

The bronze plaque read James P. Hogsworth, Criminal Lawyer. The ride up in the all glass outside the building elevator was a thrill ride as it hugged the thirty-floor First Hawaiian Center at 999 Bishop Street in downtown Honolulu. Elayne could see all the way to Diamond Head, and the greenery contrasted with the always deep blue Pacific Ocean.

The Makai side of the building facing the ocean featured horizontally louvered windows that framed views of the sea, while the Mauka side facing the mountains had vertically proportioned windows facing the mountains. The glass elevator stopped at thirty-four and the polished mirrored doors opened to reveal a wondrous sight. A short hallway framed on each side by white leather couches, sitting on bronze colored marble floors, polished to a mirror finish. At the end of the short hallway was a door surrounded by water falling from the ceiling, with rainbow colored fish jumping up the waterfall but not succeeding, and falling back into the pools that remained close to the wall.

"Is this real? Or digital?" Elayne asked Jenny.

Jenny put her hand under the waterfall and said" Its' wet and real!" They stepped towards the door and it slid open, it seemed sensing what they wanted, and they moved through into another world.

James P. himself was sitting on the left side of a room that was decorated as Elayne could not imagine. He was sitting at the end of a long boardroom table with a green felt top like you see on billiard tables. Beautiful mahogany sides were obviously stained and polished every day. Eight lawyers' office mahogany chairs with armrests and plush red pillow seats guarded the table. The room itself was enormous, with wrap around ceiling to floor windows surrounding the exotic room. Five trees in large pots were placed strategically in several corners of the room. An enormous flat coffee table made from a Hawaiian tree sat two steps down in a oblong hole with coffee cups and a coffee maker sitting on it. A king sized round bed was fitted against a wall on the right side, with gorgeous white polar bear rugs decorating the top.

The sunlight beaming in through the skylights framed the stainless steel appliances along one wall.

"Put on those Hawaiian slippers" James P. motioned to a row of plush slippers sitting just beside the entry door. Elayne and Jennie complied. They shuffled over to the boardroom table and each pulled out a huge chair to sit on. The plush red pillows sighed as they sat down on them.

"Mr. Hogsworth, I don't want to go to jail" Elayne started. "I spent almost three days locked up courtesy of the Hawaiian Police Department , and I almost died in there. I am told that I may be facing twenty years in prison, because I am charged with numerous drug charges, including as I am sure you are aware, intent to distribute, cultivation and manufacturing of drugs, conspiracy to possess with intent to distribute, running a criminal organization with intent to distribute, and assault charges, threatening death, conspiracy, and I don't know what else. I don't know how I could have committed all those crimes in less than six weeks, while I was running *Chocolate Gold.*
Mr. Hogsworth , can you help me?" Elayne pleaded.

"Mr. H will help you!" Jenny threw in. "He's the best on the Islands. Right, Mr. H?"

"I will do my best!" James P. Hogsworth, the top criminal lawyer in Hawaii confirmed. "But as I told you before we got Elayne out on Bail, I'm expensive."

"What do you mean, expensive? How expensive?" Jenny asked.

"$20,000 to do a deal, and an extra $25K if we have to conduct a trial! Cash up front, of course!" James P. reminded the girls.

"Of course. Cash up front! I'll get you the money in two days." Elayne stated. " Can you guarantee me no jail time?"

"I'll try, but I know the prosecutor here, and the DEA will be pushing for a long sentence. The mitigating circumstances in your favor is your short time running the company. I have to tell you though, part of any deal will involve you telling the DEA everything you know about your deceased husband's business, and the involvement of the goons that were arrested with you." James P. pointed out.

"They are not goons. They are nice guys." Elayne stated.

"Well those NICE GUYS smuggled a crap full of drugs onto the Hawaiian Islands, destroyed many families and lives of young men and women; caused millions or billions of dollars earned by hard working Americans to be flushed down the toilet. They caused suicides and shootings, and probably committed some killings themselves. Nice Guys like that we don't need. I will be paid to get you off of the charges, and no jail time, as you request. Whoever we use or whatever we need to do to complete our task, we will do. Ms. Elayne keep focused in your mind how Paradise in jail was , and that you will need to follow my instructions and my lead, because that will be my requirement, if you can come up with the cash." James P. Hogsworth stated.

"I'll get you the money, see you back here in two days." Elayne stated emphatically, as she motioned to Jenny to move towards the door. They dropped the slippers, put on their street shoes, and excited the room. Quickly between the white sofas, and onto the glass elevator. The ride down was in silence. Jenny wondered where Elayne would raise the money. Elayne knew exactly who to ask.

"Dad, its' me Elayne. I'm in Honolulu".

Raeburn Shaw had not heard from his daughter for at least six months, as he could remember. He thought she was in school in Boston. He knew she was running triathlons and marathons, but every phone call back home was to Elayne's mother.

"Elayne, what are you doing in Hawaii? I thought you were in Boston at school." Questioned Raeburn.

"Well I came over two months ago with Jenny. You remember Jenny, my roommate? Well she brought me to Hawaii because she was asked to write a special piece on Maui for National Geographic." Explained Elayne. "The problem is ,I am in big trouble. I could go to prison for twenty years."

"What! Why?" asked Raeburn inquisitively.

"It's a long story but I got involved with someone who deceived me, and he was smuggling heavy drugs into Hawaii, and the DEA scooped me up. I've hired the top criminal lawyer in Honolulu, and he's expensive." Elayne explained.

"How expensive?" Raeburn asked.

"Twenty thousand to do some plea bargaining and try to keep me out of prison."

"Will he take fifteen?" Raeburn always negotiating.

"I'll ask him, if he does I give you the $5000 difference back right away; but I might need the full twenty thousand." Elayne stated.

"OK. Where are you staying? I'll wire transfer the money, but you have to promise me one thing!:" Raeburn pointed out.

"What?"

"I have faith that you will get out of that horrible problem you got yourself into." Raeburn said." and when you do I want you to promise now, that you will come home to Port Perry, and to mom and me. If you don't promise I'm not sending any money."

"Thanks Dad. I really appreciate you helping me. Yes I promise, as soon as this nightmare is over I will fly out of Hawaii as fast as I can."

"and come home" added Raeburn.

"and come home" repeated Elayne.

The $20,000 showed up the next day at the Fedex counter in the hotel. Jenny helped Elayne to cash the draft at a local bank that National Geographic was doing business with. Elayne called James P. Hogsworth to confirm that she has the money and would come up to retain him the next day. She had trouble sleeping that night, and had to resort to a bottle of Vodka mixed with Orange Juice to help her sleep.

Two o'clock the next day Elayne and Jenny were back on the ride up the side of the tower in the all glass wrapped around elevator. The ride stopped, the door opened, and the familiar white sofas lining the hall walls appeared in view. The only difference today were the two Honolulu Police in uniform standing one on each side of the elevator door, as if they were standing guard outside Buckingham Palace. The only thing they were missing were those bearskin hats, and the uniforms of red tunics.

Elayne began to panic. Were these two here to re-arrest her? Were they here to take her off to prison? What kind of super-lawyer was James P? Two days ago he spoke of charging $20,000 and maybe no jail time; and today he brings in the cops to take her away.

A character that resembled Charlie Chan had moved down the hall between the white sofas, and approached Elayne. He took her by the elbow of her left arm and said " Ms. Elayne don't be alarmed by these two Egyptian looking statues. They are just here to make sure our discussions are private."

"What discussions?" Elayne asked, as she was being led down the hall, with Jenny a step behind.

"The discussions that James and I have started , and you will participate in, for your future depends on the outcome of those discussions." Mr. Chan declared.

The door to the magical room slid open and Mr. Chan, Elayne and Jenny walked through the opening and sat in chairs next to the boardroom table. James P. was at the end, in his usual spot, nursing Iced Tea.

"Welcome back, Ms. Elayne. You have an envelope for me, I presume. "James P. stated.

"Yes, here it is" Elayne replied, as she slid the envelope stuffed with $20,000 in hundreds across the table towards James P.

"Very good. Looks all there" remarked James P. "Now let's introduce Mr. Chan." He started.

Elayne thought how coincidental, Charlie Chan, one of the greatest made up characters in fiction, fighting crime and injustice; and here in real life, another Chan. James P. broke through Elayne's thoughts.

"You might think how coincidental, another Chan, but in real life to replicate the fictional Charlie Chan.

Well let me introduce you to Harry Chan, Head of the DEA in Hawaii. Harry oversees twenty-two mobile enforcement teams, and he has been responsible for 10,342 arrests. I have personally known Harry for twelve years and he is a tough yet at the same time generous, willing to co-operate human who I have done some deals with in the past." Explained James P.

"Harry is very interested in shutting down *Chocolate Gold* completely and to put in place certain safeguards so that *Chocolate Gold* doesn't rise up like the proverbial Phoenix in another form. He actually has been working the past year trying to discover enough evidence to shut the company down; and he knows to do that he must be able to gather enough evidence to put away the main men that were running the company.

Harry is of the opinion that he has discovered a gold mine in you. That he can use you and your knowledge of the operations of *Chocolate Gold* to put away the masterminds for a long, long time."

"What does Mr. Chan mean to me. And my personal welfare?" asked Elayne.

"Elayne, I thought you were smarter than that!" answered James P. "Its' obvious, that in order to put away the four or five masterminds that ran *Chocolate Gold* Mr. Chan will need you to tell him and his associates everything that you know, and that you have learned in the past six weeks."

"And then what?" Elayne inquired.

"Then, after you co-operate, Harry will do everything in his power to make sure you get a plea bargain deal that will allow you to avoid jail. Let me tell you that Harry has a lot of power, so the chances of him succeeding are high." James P. explained.

"All right, what do we do next?" Elayne asked.

"We will arrange a meeting at Honolulu Police headquarters and you will be interviewed by some of my DEA officers in conjunction with the Honolulu Police. You will be asked about each and every person involved in *Chocolate Gold*, and what you are aware of their involvement in all kinds of crimes and misdemeanors. I have to warn you that the interrogation could get rough as those questioning you won't be privy to any deal we made." Explained Harry Chan, DEA Head, Hawaii.

Twenty-Seven

The fog had just been burned off and the sun was beginning to heat up the Hawaiian landscape. Elayne, Jenny and James P. Hogsworth relaxed in James P.'s limo as it slowly approached the gates to the Honolulu Police Department compound. James P. explained to security at the gate the reason they were there , and was directed to the second building on the right, where Harry Chan would be waiting for them.

The interrogation room appeared to be too small as it was approximately 10 feet wide x 30 feet long with a long metal table taking up most of the room and as Elayne entered the room she could see the group awaiting her. The DEA agents including Jo-Ann; three men in suits that she didn't know; two women at computers; Harry Chan; and one person in a Honolulu Police uniform. Elayne was directed to sit exactly on a chair in the middle of the table, with James P. sitting down beside her. He arranged his documents and yellow legal sized note pad in front of him.

Harry Chan began the discussion. "Elayne Christofaro, you have been charged with some of the most serious Federal Criminal charges that are available to the DEA and local authorities concerning drug smuggling and drug distribution. In my estimate you will definitely be sentenced to a minimum of twenty years in Federal Penitentiary."

Elayne started to shiver and put her hand out so Jenny could hold her hand and comfort her. What was this big old Hawaiian trying to do, scare the hell out of her? She thought.

"I, I" she stammered. "I was only involved in the business for a month and a half!"

"Yes, we are aware of that, but your associates have been operating the business for at least five years, and it's them that we want to put away for a long time, and its' the business that we want to shut down" explained Harry Chan. " Now I have had the opportunity to get through to the Attorney General and he has agreed to the deal that I will reveal to you in a minute." Harry Chan walked over to the water cooler and filled up a glass of water."Want some water, Ms. Elayne?"

"No thanks." She replied.

James P. Hogsworth was taking notes quickly on his legal size yellow notepaper.

Elayne, if you co-operate 100% with our investigation, and we are able to accomplish what we started out to do, that is bust *Chocolate Gold* down to size, and that size is dust; then I have arranged for all charges to be dropped against you. Of course you will be on probation for perhaps two years."

Elayne gasped, as she heard all charges to be dropped."That's great, I will co-operate for sure."

"Good. Now I have to take care of some department business elsewhere so I will turn you over to Jo-Ann, who you've met; and Christopher Walker, who will be asking you some questions." Harry Chan pointed out.

Christopher Walker , dressed in a designer suit with high lapels and wearing Clark's Brown Leather Oxfords held his pink shirt and red tie in place. He placed his 3 inch thick binder on the table and opened the contents into approximately 200 sheets of note paper bound together by the circular holes perforated in each one.

"Elayne Christofaro, what school did you attend when you were a teenager?" He began, with a simple question.

"Port Perry High School, until the age of sixteen." Elayne responded. "Then I attended a private boarding school until age 17, and I was accepted at Harvard Business School in an MBA program." Elayne blurted out the answer.

Chris Walker continued his easy going interrogation style." What brought you out to Hawaii, the beaches, the night life?"

"Actually, it was Jenny here" as she pointed to Jenny sitting next to her. "Jenny was hired by National Geographic to write a special article on Hawaii and since she was my roommate at Harvard she invited me to go along, and well I'm here!"

"So how long had you known Larry Christofaro before you came to Hawaii?"

"I never knew him before I came here about six weeks ago." Elayne responded.

"Never knew him? Come on Ms. Christofaro, you expect us to believe that? You come here six weeks ago, shack up with him, get married, and take over his company in such a short time. No one works that fast." Exclaimed Chris Walker.

"Well, apparently I do!" Elayne responded. "I met him the first day I was jogging on the beach, and I guess it was love at first sight. He was a perfect Gentleman, suave and sophisticated, and like they say, he swept me off my feet. He had money, and was well known all over Honolulu , and he had connections. I never knew what *Chocolate Gold* was really all about. He never talked to me about his business, never."

"We will get to *Chocolate Gold* later. Let's stick with when you arrived, why you came here, which you explained, and when you met Larry, and what you and Larry did for those two or so weeks when you were together." Chris Walker stressed his point.

"How is it possible that you spend over two weeks with a man, and you don't know what business he is involved in. You spent a lot of hours with him, both day and night, and overnight. You must have seen or suspected something or overheard something. Come on Ms. Elayne, you said you would co-operate fully." Chris Walker emphasized.

"Well, several times people would call him Michael, and when I asked him about that he said it was his middle name, so I just forgot about it." Elayne revealed. "Never did I suspect he was involved in drug smuggling. He described his chocolate business to me, and the fact he supplied the cruise ships with liquid chocolate for their chocolate fountains. He called himself the chocolate king."

"So. Let's get this straight. In the weeks you were hanging around with him, you never knew he was involved in one of the largest drug smuggling operations on the Hawaiian Islands?" Chris Walker repeated.

"No never. How many times do I have to tell you?" Elayne asked.

"What about guns and ammunition? What about the arsenal we discovered in the trunk of his Limo? You didn't know about that either?"

"No not until after Larry had been killed and Johnny his associate showed me the UZI and other guns." She responded.

"Ok since you brought him up lets' talk about Johnny. What did he do?, what was he in the organization? How much control did he have? Did you ever see him do a hit?" asked Chris Walker.

"A hit? You mean a killing? No never. I knew him as Larry's Chauffeur and best friend. I don't even know his last name, but he was terrific when Larry got killed. He was the one who suggested a Hawaiian funeral , and after I agreed, he arranged it all. After Larry was gone and I took over managing the company Johnny was devoted to me and helped me with every facet of the operations. He arranged for me to take shooting lesions at the local club. He was wonderful, I can't imagine him being a killer or a gangster." Elayne stated.

"Elayne for your information your friend Johnny is a Native Hawaiian, has a long history of violence and has served close to eight years in prison for various drug smuggling and minor misdemeanors. He also was convicted as an associate in a murder case. Johnny "Big Hawaiian" Jones is certainly not one to be friendly with." Chris Walker explained.

"Well , he was ok with me, a pussycat." Elayne threw in.

"What about Vinny as we know him Vinny "The Juice" Mammato?" asked Chris. "Convicted of murder twice and served a total of fourteen years in the slammer."

"I really didn't know much about him. Only met him at my wedding and at the funeral. Got to know him a little bit after I took over. I think he ran the importing part of the business."

"Next Greg Lukovitch". Chris inquired.

"Same thing. Saw him at both places, but didn't know him very well." Elayne explained.

"You will be surprised to learn they called him Greg "The Russian" Lukovitch and he was brutal, vicious and savagely violent. Used to kill off competitors and then cut off their arms and legs and throw the remains out to sea. He also served five years at the Halawa Correctional Facility. I was personally responsible for bagging him one year" Chris Walker proudly exclaimed.

"Steve Winters is our next topic" What do you know about him?" asked Chris.

"Nothing. Only met him twice briefly" Elayne said.

"Steve got the nickname 'baseball' cause he would tie his victims up, and then throw baseballs at their heads until he killed them off. Used to pitch in the minor league for San Fran. Had a great fastball!" Chris explained."Last topic is Sam Yakimoto. Know him?" questioned Chris, walking over to grab a bottle of Hawaiian Springs natural clear water.

"A little' Elayne began.

"A ha! "Chris yelled out. "Finally someone you knew a little! I thought we were going through this exercise without you providing any information but I guess I was wrong, because now you knew him a little. Let's proceed. How little? Did you know he was native? And did you know he was ex pro football? And did you know he murdered two tourists with his bare hands, just strangling them?"

"No, I didn't. And to be frank with you in the short time I was running the company I don't think and I was not aware of any violence against anyone committed by my boys." Elayne emphasized.

"Your boys, you call them, continued to bring in thousands of kilos of drugs, including Meth, cocaine, oxycontin , and other illegal substances." Jo-Ann interrupted." and exported Hawaiian grown marijuana. *Chocolate Gold* was not just a chocolate company Elayne, and you know it."

James P. Hogsworth had heard enough. Four hours of interrogation, and it appeared that Elayne knew very little, and in some instances nothing about her co-accused. He was beginning to think that the Feds had very little to convict her on, so no wonder they were so anxious to make a deal.

"That's enough for today. Chris, let's break for the day, and you and I and your boss Harry Chan can have a talk tomorrow to see where we go from here!"

"All right James. We break now. Elayne Christofaro, stick around. We will have more questions tomorrow or the next day" Chris stated.

"I'm not going anywhere. Besides you have my passport as well as my promise to co-operate."

James P. Hogsworth's limo dropped off Elayne and Jenny at the Sheraton, and James explained to Elayne that tomorrow he is meeting with Chris Walker and Harry Chan to work out a deal for her. He is going to push for an all-out release but he can't promise anything. The Feds have been in a terrible mood lately and good plea bargains have been hard to get. He let her know that all 'the boys' were detained, and have their own lawyers representing them. He couldn't because it would be a conflict of interest by representing her, especially if she is a witness for the Feds against them. He told her that he wouldn't be seeing her tomorrow so she can get some rest, maybe some rays, eat well, and prepare for the day after when they will return to Police Headquarters for more questioning; and then he barked out to his driver to get going as he closed the window.

Elayne and Jenny walked through the lobby and rode the elevator up to their suite. When Elayne went in she immediately started to sob and cry and grabbed a towel to wipe her face.

"Jenny, I am having a breakdown. I can't take this pressure. I can't go to prison. I told you I will die. I would rather jump off the balcony out there, drop 31 floors and splatter myself all over Kalakaua Avenue street then go to a Hawaiian prison for even a day." Elayne cried out.

"Elayne you're not going to prison. I believe James P. He's the best Criminal Lawyer in Hawaii , and I bet you he will make a deal where you won't have to spend a minute in prison!" Jenny said with conviction, and also hoping at the same time that she's right.

"Well, I hope your right." Elayne replied."Really, you think he's the best?"

"Not only do I think he's the best-I know he's the best. I asked around and all I got was wonderful stuff being said about him. If there's anyone that will work a deal for you, it's him." Jenny tried to convince Elayne not to worry."Now let's hit the sack, you're beat, and so am I. Tomorrow we can relax on the beach. Goodnight."

"Night, Jenny. Thanks for everything."

Next day Elayne and Jenny first had some breakfast of fresh Hawaiian fruit and cottage cheese and then went out to the beach, laid down a blanket and lay on the blanket dozing and taking in the sun. It was 10:00 in the morning, and James P. was wolfing down four poached eggs, five strips of bacon, and half a plate of potatoes, with several glasses of Mimosa to wash down the enormous breakfast, that was his standard every day. A mango cut in four for dessert with a satisfying burp and he was ready for his guests that would be arriving soon. He was modestly attired in a terrycloth pair of shorts, with no shirt, and his hairy chest and pumpkin sized belly hanging out to dry. Even though he was inside and in his penthouse, he wore dark black sunglasses as yes the sun beamed down through the skylights and it was very sunny and bright in any area of the huge room. You could not escape the Hot Hawaiian Heat.

James P. was thankful that the air conditioning running full blast kept the suite cool.

Harry Chan and Chris Walker arrived on time at 10:30 as had been arranged. Jo-Ann entered the luxurious hallway a step behind. She had never been up on the Thirtieth floor and never saw a suite with so much opulence. White leather couches, a waterfall, and the almost suite long table covered in felt with beautiful leather chairs at the tables' side.

The three officers sat down as James P. said "get comfortable, my friends. Mimosa, anyone?" fruit, mango, anything you want just ask. Remove any clothing you want to make you feel comfortable!" He exclaimed looking at Jo-Ann , whose body under her Hawaiian Police uniform was slim and trim. wonderful tan, blonde hair with streaks of silver with a pony-tail under her regulation HPD hat. The Glock 27 in a holster on her right erased all thoughts that she was a gentle, passive female. Actually she was terror wrapped in a pink package. She had already been disciplined twice by the Police Review Board for using excessive violence while on a drug bust.

A wolf in sheep's clothing. She was not just there to negotiate , work out a deal, and let a drug lord escape any form of punishment. She personally wouldn't let it happen.

Three Police Officers along one side of the table, opposite James P. who started his pitch. "Gentlemen, and Jo-Ann. You've conducted the first four hours of questioning and I put forward that you can see you don't have too much on Chocolate Queen. She replaced Larry but during her short reign she didn't commit a real crime, and she doesn't know squat about her boys' criminal activities. The most you will get a Judge to sentence her is maybe two years for some minor guilty plea. I propose the following: Milk her for what you can get, any details about *Chocolate Gold* that she can give you , and any info about dealers or procedures or the whereabouts of their labs on the islands. Let her loose for a couple of weeks so she can be undercover and perhaps bring in some worthwhile hoods. But after you've used her, then set her free. I suggest a life-time ban from the Islands. What do you think? Is that a plan?" He threw out for the three senior officers to ponder.

Harry and Chris agreed that it was ok. Jo-Ann opposed it and talked about all the havoc that Larry had brought to Hawaii, all the kids on the streets that were addicts or had died of overdoses. All the families that had their dreams explode with money being taken from their savings and hard earned funds by some grazed drugged up member of the family. A leech hiding among a family full of love only to be destroyed and torn apart by Larry's drugs.

No Jo-Ann wouldn't agree. She emphasized someone has to pay for the crimes that Larry committed. He had escaped punishment by dying but his wife shouldn't escape and should pay for the sins of her dead husband.

Harry Chan argued that she should not be punished for what Larry had done in almost five years when she was only in charge for a few weeks. Put away her 'boys' for a long time. The company would be shut down, probably permanently, and most of the dealers would be shut down. Hell almost 50% of Meth coming into Hawaii would be shut down. That was a great accomplishment.

Chris Walker agreed with Harry but Jo-Ann could not be convinced so it was up to Harry to make an executive decision, and he decided what was the best way to proceed under the circumstances. He made up his mind and he delegated Jo-Ann to meet with Elayne the next day at Police Headquarters and relay his message to her.

James P. was excited" Some Mimosa folks?"
None of the three professionals took up his offer. They all kept their clothes on, despite James P. being half naked, and they walked together to the elevator, and rode it down to the ground. Harry saying" Jo-Ann good luck tomorrow with the Chocolate Queen."

"Don't worry Boss, I can handle her with one finger!" Jo-Ann stated with confidence.

James P. had high hopes the next day as he rode his limo over to the Sheraton to pick up Elayne and Jenny. They were waiting outside and jumped in as soon as his driver stopped the vehicle.

Elayne was anxious to hear what had happened the day before in his meeting with the DEA and Hawaiian Police. "James what happened yesterday. Will I be going to prison? And for how long?"

"I don't actually know the answer to that question. We had a good meeting and I presented your case. I don't think they have enough to put you away for a long time, but they may have enough for a short sentence." He replied.

"What's a short sentence?" she asked.

"Probably two years so you can be in a Federal Prison"

"No. No. No. I wouldn't be able to handle that." Elayne pleaded. "You promised me no prison. What happened?"

"Nothing is decided yet. Or maybe it's decided but they haven't told me. We will be told at Police Headquarters in about an hour. So relax in the meantime. It could be good news. I haven't lost a drug case yet. Well didn't lose technically, although two of my clients are in the slammer for five years each; but not on drug convictions, that was tax evasion" He explained.

"Oh great! So I don't get two years for drug smuggling. Maybe for chocolate smuggling!" Elayne cried out.

The limo pulled up to security at the front gate, and was let in, and eased up to the same building as two days before.

Elayne was afraid to go in. She was having terrible thoughts of never coming out. Of not breathing the beautiful Hawaiian air for at least two years. She would not feel the warm sun. Would not be able to run along the beach, and smell the Hawaiian leis being sold by street vendors. Probably the fruit in prison would be none existent or days old and rotten. She would be on a diet of stale bread and rancid water instead of fresh mangosteens, pineapples, and 12 grain bread. If she survived two years she would come out fat and ugly, and her youthful appearance would become that of an old hag. Her perfect teeth would rot and fall out one by one. She would have to eat insects to survive. She probably would become some monster's girlfriend.

Elayne banged into the door frame and Jenny caught her and said" Elayne stop daydreaming. Let's go in."

"Jenny, I'm night dreaming or to be more exact I'm hallucinating or having a nightmare about being in the slammer."

"Stop. We haven't got the news, and it could be good. Let's keep our hopes up." Jenny tried to perk up Elayne, but she could see Elayne was really stressed out, and on the verge of a breakdown." Elayne had told her it happened when she was a teenager. It could happen again. Jenny thought Elayne could escape this horror by having a breakdown and being put in an asylum.

They entered the interrogation room and sat in the same chairs as two days before. All the same players were there. The DEA agents, the two women on the computers, Jo-Ann and Harry and Chris Walker, and the unknown Hawaiian Police Officer.

Jo-Ann stood up and made sure she was opposite Elayne across the table before she began her speech.

"Elayne Christofaro we met with your Attorney , the famous James P. Hoggsworth yesterday and he did a good job in presenting your case.

My associates , Harry Chan, who is actually my boss, and Chris Walker, here." She motioned to Chris sitting several persons down the table. "We reviewed the evidence that would be used against you at trial, and the short time you have actually run the company, and we reviewed the Criminal Code and what we probably would be able to obtain a conviction against you, and frankly two out of three of us believe you have suffered enough, and with your assistance, as limited as it is, is enough for you to be set loose without prison."

Elayne could not believe what she was hearing. Does this mean she will be free? No prison time?

Jo-Ann interrupted Elayne's thoughts.

" I was the one who objected to setting you free. I was the one who pushed for you to be punished for the short time you ran the company but also for the five years that Larry ran the company. Somebody has to be punished for the monstrous drugs that you and Larry have rained down on us Hawaiians. Larry escaped punishment by dying but you won't escape, you bitch!"

As Jo-Ann spit out the words she simultaneously pulled the Glock 27 out of its holster on her right leg aimed at Elayne and fired two shots. Elayne moved as quick as she could. One bullet hit her chest just above the heart. The other struck her arm just above the elbow. The force of the blows pushed Elayne back and she fell down beside the table.

Chris Walker and the unknown Hawaiian Police Officer were first to react. At almost the same time as the shots rang out they lunged at Jo-Ann and knocked the gun out of her hand and Chris fell on top of her on her side of the table. Chris quickly pulled both of her arms back behind her, and with the unknown officer's help, and handcuffs, subdued her.

Jenny looked down at Elayne and panicked.

"Oh my God, She's shot dead. Now she has escaped punishment and will join Larry wherever he is." Then Jenny walked around the table to where Jo-Ann was being pulled upright and punched her right in the right side of her face, while yelling" you're the bitch, and your gonna serve Elayne's time in prison. I hope you are tortured and die in there. You have taken a wonderful women's life."

Harry Chan leaned over Elayne, put his head down over her chest, ignored the blood, and could hear a heartbeat. He exclaimed" Call an ambulance, she's still alive."

Elayne survived. As the Surgeon stated, probably because she was in such great physical shape. The bullet had missed her heart. She required a minor operation to stop the bleeding, an operation to pull out the bullets in her chest and arm, and with her arm in a sling, and her chest wrapped tight, so tight she could hardly breathe, she left the hospital five days after she was brought in.

James P. had sent his limo to pick her up , and with Jenny pushing the wheelchair Elayne took in the fresh Hawaiian air, and blinked as the hot sun struck her face. She was assisted by the driver in getting into the back seat of the limo, and Jenny slid in beside her.

It was mid day and the limo driver , even though the traffic was very heavy, knew the route to get to the courthouse, where Elayne was to appear at 1:30 PM. They drove up to the entrance and Jenny jumped out and removed the wheelchair from the trunk, and set it up next to the rear door. The driver again assisted Elayne in getting out and into the chair. Jenny maneuvered the chair up the handicap ramp and into the courthouse, stopping at Courtroom #2 and entered.

Elayne's case was the 3rd called and Jenny wheeled her up to the microphone where she identified herself with the help of the clerk.

Harry Chan himself appeared for the prosecution and announced that all charges were dropped, that Ms. Christofaro was free to go, and as part of the deal she had to leave Hawaii within 48 hours , and never return.

The Judge echoed what Harry Chan had said. " Ms Elayne Christofaro, you have heard the prosecutor, all charges against you are withdrawn, and you are free to leave Hawaii, and in fact you must leave Hawaii within 48 hours, and are not permitted to return. Do you understand?"

"Yes, I do. Thank You." stated Elayne.

"All right Ms. Christofaro. Best of luck, and I don't want to see you in this courtroom in the future." The Judge emphasized.

"Don't worry, Your Honor, you won't see this pretty little face again. Thank You." Elayne repeated.

Elayne called her father to give him the good news, and to tell him she was coming home.

He was elated.

Jenny went to the airport with Elayne and transferred her to a Hawaiian Airlines wheelchair, with 'Aloha' stenciled on the back rest.

At the gate Elayne and Jenny embraced.

"Jenny, thank you for all you have done. I couldn't have survived this ordeal without you. I plan to go back home, as I had promised my father, and apply for a job in the library or at city hall, and relax for a few years. I hope to see you soon. Promise me you will come up to visit." Elayne asked.

"Of course I will visit, and Elayne I feel a little responsible for your ordeal as I was the one who dragged you out to Hawaii. I'm truly sorry." Jenny apologized.

"No. come on Jenny. You invited me, but I made my own decision to come. I could have refused, and Hawaii is beautiful, it is paradise. I actually fell in love with the state and a handsome charming gracious Prince. Of course the fairy tale didn't turn out like Disney would have told the story, but never-the-less I'm grateful to you for giving me the opportunity to come out here, and you have to admit it was some whopper of a ride these past six weeks or so!" Elayne exclaimed.

"What a whopper!" Jenny repeated. They hugged again and both had tears coming down their cheeks as the boarding call was announced.

"Well gotta go. Attendant wheel me aboard".

Jenny waived goodbye with the same tissue that she was using to wipe her eyes. She wondered when she would ever see her best friend again.

The plane climbed up and Elayne could see Diamond Head and the crater. She could make out tiny figures on the beach and the deep blue/green Pacific Sea. As the plane made it's turn left she lost sight of Honolulu and Hawaii all the while knowing she would never be back here in paradise again.

She fell asleep quickly and dreamed of home where she would be in a short fifteen hours.

Twenty-Eight

Cornell Law School Moot Court Trial

Ithaca is a small town perched on the edge of one of the finger lakes in Northern New York State.

Cornell University, with over 20,000 students and Cornell Law School, one of the Ivy League Schools is ranked 13th in the United States and was started in 1887 and Cory was one of 600 students accepted to study law; and going into his second year he participated in the Moot Court Trial Program/Contest.

Professor Anderson picked nine students to participate/communicate/articulate/fight/a legal issue that had been argued in a Court in Michigan in 1952.

Cory was picked to be the Defense Attorney for an Army Lt. Mitchell Grange, who had been charged with murder; and Johnny Red Bear was Cory's assistant and investigator.

He was to prepare a Defense and conduct a trial copying the way the trial went in 1952 although in this Mock Trial the jury, which were 3rd year law students, could rule any way depending on the arguments and evidence presented.

This was to provide practice for when the students graduate and are actual licensed Litigators. The first item on Cory's agenda was to meet again with his client (Law Student Richard Bliss) and review the case; as he had, as the Professor instructed) had met with him once before in pretend Jail and he had retained Cory.

Fortunately he was able to put a $15,000 (Mock Trial Money) down with the retainer.

"Mr. Grange, you are charged with the murder of Barney Milton, the owner of the bar called New Lake Michigan Cocktail Lounge and Bar, and as we have discussed previously we are going to defend you by stating you were criminally insane at the time you shot Mr. Milton, because frankly, I don't see any other way for you to get off the murder charge, with all the witnesses against you, the gun, and other evidence. You understand?"

"Yes" answered Richard Bliss as Mitchell Grange. After meeting with Richard Bliss aka Mr. Grange Cory sat down with Johnny Red Bear to prepare their defense based on the defense in the real trial back in 1952 in Michigan.

"Were you able to get a copy of the Transcript of the 1952 Trial? Cory asked"

"Yes. Here it is-thousands of pages" answered Johnny.

Cory started to glance through the Transcript and realized that because there were so many pages and they were to begin a trial in two days so he would have to pull an all-nighter in order to be ready in time.

"Johnny, I will only have enough time to read Lieutenant Grange's testimony and prepare so can you review Archibald's testimony and make notes for me?"

"Sure Cory, no problem" Johnny reassured him.

"And I am sure the trial will last several days, not as long as the true trial, however after we rest after the first day I can read the other materials". Cory pointed out.

The sun was just starting to disappear over the horizon when he settled down to read Lieutenant Grange's testimony which was very important to the case as it was central to his defense and was an opportunity for the lieutenant to tell his version of the events.

A crucial point is what the lieutenant does and does not recall about the evening he shot Barney Milton. Very important also is how the lieutenant obtained the Luger.

Cory glanced at the small table top clock radio and was surprised it was already 3:05 a.m. More coffee was required.

Cory would have to rush through the rest of the materials in order to finish by morning.

He couldn't believe it but 8:00 a.m. came so fast and he had just finished reviewing the lieutenant's testimony. A quick call to Johnny was necessary.

"Johnny I need you to get a hold of the student, I think his name is Winston some-thing-or other, maybe Winston Sikaris. He is acting as the Army Psychiatrist who is key to our defense. I need to spend time preparing him for the trial"

"OK boss. I will get him" replied Johnny.

The rest of Cory's day was spent reading his law books and reading cases where temporary insanity was a defense presented, and in some cases was successful, and in some not.

Johnny got back to him around 4:30 with good news. He had been able to find and speak with the Law Student Winston, who agreed to meet that night to review and prepare for the trial.

In fact Johnny had also arranged to remove from the transcripts the actual transcript of the Army Psychiatrist witness statements and answers from the trial , and had delivered these to Winston to read before he met Cory.

8:15 that evening and Winston and Cory were deep into preparation for the Mock Trial.

He wanted to impress the Professor and be awarded a top mark as he was not doing that well in his mid-term exams and needed to boost his marks in order to continue in the program so he was lucky that he was going to have a chance to do a great job and in turn that would shine a light on him.

They reviewed the hypothetical questions and then the responses and his opinions based on the hypothetical questions; all based on the transcripts of the real 1952 trial.

Cory couldn't expect Winston to make up anything based on psychiatric knowledge as he was a law student not a student of psychiatry, however he urged him to go to the Cornell library and read up on psychiatry, which he said he would do.

"Johnny, I need to interview the student who will be acting as the witness Julien Barbote who was a bartender at the Cocktail Lounge, and is the prosecutor's main witness."

"No problem boss. I will find him. Do we need the approval of the prosecutor?"

"Well, not exactly approval. But we must inform the prosecutor-he may want to attend or have someone attend" Cory replied.

"Boss, you don't remember but the student acting as the prosecutor is Susan Yang, your classmate"

"Great, we should have no problem"

Twenty-Nine

The Great Hall at Cornell Law School had been converted into a courtroom complete with tables for the Prosecution and Defense, Judge's Chair, twelve chairs for the jury, rows of chairs for the audience and of course the witness box with chair where all the action would take place.

10:00 am. and we were ready to begin.

The Judge , which was Professor Anderson, entered the courtroom and all stood until he was seated.

The court clerk (3rd Year Law Student Amy Greenstead) called everyone to order and announced that Justice Anderson would preside and please turn off all communication devices, remove hats, and don't talk.

"We are here today in the presiding of the People versus Mitchell Grange , who is charged with the murder of Barney Milton on July 31, 1952 in Orchard Bay , Michigan and Mr. Grange in a previous appearance had the charge read out to him and his plea of Not Guilty was recorded." Explained the court clerk.

"Justice Anderson presiding and all of the Jury have been sworn in, we are ready to proceed."

"Your first witness, Miss Yang"stated Judge Anderson.

Julien Barbote, witness for the people , being duly sworn, was, as they say, under direct examination by Susan Yang , 2nd year law student acting as Prosecuting Attorney.

"State your name, please" Susan Yang started.

"Julien Barbote" the witness answered.

"Where do you live?"

"Orchard Bay, Michigan."

"Where are you employed?"

"At the New Lake Michigan Cocktail Lounge and Bar."

"Wow , That's a mouthful!" exclaimed Ms. Yang. *That didn't follow the actual court transcript but Professor Anderson had told us we can ad-lib or throw in anything we wish to add so Susan , who was a top law student did just that.*

"In what capacity? " she continued.

"Manager"

"Were you on duty during the early morning hours of July 31st, 1952?

"I was"

"Did you know Barney Milton in his lifetime?"

"I did"

"How long did you know him?"

"For seventeen years."

"Did you know the defendant, Mitchell Grange, prior to July 31st, 1952?"

"I did."

"How long did you know him?"

"Approximately three weeks."

"Had he been a patron of the Bar? The New Lake

Michigan Cocktail Lounge and bar?"

"Occasionally"

"Where did you meet him?"

"In the Bar"

"Can you identify in this court room the man known to you as Lieutenant Mitchell Grange?"

"Yes"

"Will you point him out please?"

"That gentleman sitting in the Army uniform next to defense counsel" and the witness pointed to Lieutenant Mitchell Grange.

"Mr. Barbote, how long was Mitchell Grange in the Bar prior to the shooting?"

"I don't know. The first I saw him was about 11:35 the night of the 30th."

"Did you ever serve as a police officer?"

"I did"

"How long did you serve as a police officer?"

"Thirteen years"

"In what organization?"

"Michigan State Police."

"Where were you in the Bar when the shooting occurred?"

"I was sitting at the front table on the north side, the bar,-facing the front of the bar."

"Who was seated at that table?"

"Mr. and Mrs. Brownberg"

"The elderly couple?"

"Yes"

"Are they in their nineties?"

"Yes. I believe so."

"I ask you,-Did you see the shooting?"

"No, not the actual shooting."

"Did you hear it?"

"I heard cartridges being fired, Ys, sir." Responded the witness.

"Where were you when you heard the cartridges being fired?" asked Susan Yang.

"At the table and rising up from the table; while I was sitting at the table and pushing my chair back to get up."

"Please will you describe what you saw at the time of the shooting?|

"During the first and second sound I had my head down explaining some pictures in my State Police scrap-book to Mr. and Mrs. Brownberg and the first impression I had was fire-crackers were fired and as I pushed the chair back and raised my head the first thing I saw was some man in what appeared to be an Army uniform bending down over the bar. And I could hear three sounds that sounded like fire crackers going off but I could see no gun at that time." Detailed the witness.

" You saw this man in Army uniform leaning over the bar?"

"What did this man in the Army uniform do then?" Susan Yang continued.

"Raised up, turned, and strolled out the front door."

"Did you see him walk out the front door?"

"I did"

"By the front door which door do you mean?"

"The main entrance to the Cocktail Bar."

"When this man in Army uniform walked out did you identify him then?"

"Not positively." He responded.

"What did you do then?"

"I rushed to the front door and followed whoever left outside."

"And did you see this man outside?"

"I saw a man outside."

"Were you able to identify him?"

"He turned and faced me and his face was exposed to the light coming from the Bar windows."

"Who was that man who faced you?"

"Lieutenant Grange"

"The man sitting at that table to the left of his attorney, dressed in an Army Uniform?" Susan Yang probed.

"Yes, ma'am."

"That's all the questions I have for this witness, Your Honor." Stated Susan Yang.

"All right, we will take a thirty minute break, and Mr. Defense Attorney, you can cross examine,

if you wish". Judge Anderson pointed out.

I could see the snow starting to fall outside the windows of the Great Hall as had been predicted by the weather channel, and actually a snowstorm was coming, which was standard in the Ithaca area.

"Johnny, I hope we can finish my cross before we shut down for the snow storm"

"Don't worry you have plenty of time." He tried to reassure me.

After thirty minutes the Judge returned and we were ready to continue.

"Mr. Barbote, did you say anything to Lieutenant Grange before he turned around?" I asked.

"Yes" confirmed the witness.

"What did you say?"

"Just the word 'Lieutenant'"

"And with that word he turned around?" questioned Cory.

"Yes, sir."

"Please can you tell the court what it was he said?"

"What he said,-He asked me if I wanted one through the head."

"And was he then holding a pistol?"

"I believe he was."

"You have , of course told us what he had said, and what you had said, to the prosecutor before today, have you not?" questioned Cory , the Defense Attorney.

"Yes" responded the witness.

"The prosecutor knew that the Lieutenant had turned and reputedly made this remark to you concerning whether you wanted one through the head, you told that to Susan Yang, the Prosecuting

Attorney?"

"Yes, the Prosecuting Attorney and her assistants."

Susan Yang states " The Defense Attorney is trying
to infer that the prosecution is trying to conceal
something. The reason that was not brought out by
the Prosecution is that there might have been-it
might result in error because of bringing a second
offense committed by this defendant-which would
put him in a position of two offenses when we
started with one."

Judge Anderson "I think it has been covered but I
will take the answer to this question and then that is
far enough."

"I told the Prosecuting Attorney; yes, sir." The
witness repeated.

"I ask you whether or not the Prosecuting Attorney
warned you not to mention that because it might be
erroneous." Inquired Cory.

"No, I don't think she said that to me."

Or anyone connected with the Prosecution here?
Such as an assistant?"

"No."

"OK let's move on"

"You say you knew Barney Milton about seventeen
years."

"Yes Sir."

"Was that largely that you first got to know him
when you and he were in the State Police?"

"Yes, sir."

"You were stationed in Marquette County one time when you were in the State Police, is that correct?"

"Yes, I was"

"Was Barney Milton there also?"

"No , not at the same time when I was at Marquette. We were stationed together outside Detroit for five years."

Were you a member of the State Police when I was Prosecuting Attorney in the County?"

"Yes"

"So we know each other." Stated Cory.

"Yes, sir" affirmed the witness.

"Would you say you knew the deceased intimately?"

I glanced out the windows and the snow was intensifying.

"Yes, I think so"

"Would it be fair to say that you knew him as intimately as any man not of his immediate family?"

"I believe so; yes."

"Now I ask you, Mr. Barbote, if from your intimate knowledge and acquaintance with the deceased that you were able to tell when he had been drinking or not?"

"How much?" questioned the witness Barbote.

"Well, heavily" answered Cory.

"Yes, if he had been drinking extra heavy I could tell." Stated Barbote.

"And I ask you whether or not you observed that the deceased had been drinking extra heavy on the night in question?"

It was time for Susan Yang aka Prosecutor to step in to the ring.

"I object. I don't see where it would be material or relevant. There is nothing involving drinking and certainly whether he had been drinking or not would not enter into this case." Susan emphasized.

Judge Anderson replied" I think it is right but there has been other questions and answers concerning the state of the deceased with reference to his imbibing in intoxicating liquors. I don't like to let a part in now-cut it off-at that time I saw no reason for it and I see no reason for it now, but in view of the situation I will take the answer." The Judge ruled.

The Judge himself could see the snow intensifying and stated

"It seems that the snow storm that was predicted is here so we will see how everything goes however we may have to stop earlier than we intended. Let's continue. Mr. Witness please answer the question."

"I do not believe he was drinking exceptionally heavy that night."

"I ask you whether or not the deceased had been drinking heavily that night?"

"No."

"I ask you whether or not the deceased had been

drinking heavily that day?"

"No, I don't recall of paying any special attention to his drinking exceptionally much that day."

"Had he been drinking that day?"

"I presume so. Because he did the days before"
Susan Yang jumps in " I ask that that be stricken. That is a presumption."

Judge Anderson in reply" If that is a mere presumption it would be properly objected to. If he did not say exactly what he meant to say I have no objection to asking him further. If he is guessing I will strike the answer" the Judge explained" Witness please respond"

"I don't remember any definite time when he took any special drinks throughout the day. I meant he was in the habit of drinking each day"

"And for several days prior to this night how much would you say he drank on an average? Each day?"
Susan decides to jump in" I object. I don't see where this line of questioning is leading. The deceased is not the one on trial here. I don't see what difference it makes what he was drinking, how much he was drinking, when and where he was drinking. It is all irrelevant to the case at hand, and the charge at hand. "
Judge Anderson " I can see a reason for an objection, however I am going to allow a few more questions on the subject. Mr. Defense Attorney, can you get to the point?"

"Yes, your honor" I replied.

"So for several days prior to this night how much would you say he drank on an average ? Each day?"

"I don't believe I could give an honest estimate. I don't know."

"Could you give us an estimate?"

"Oh, possibly eight to ten double shots a day."

"And a double shot is how much?" queered Cory.

"Two ounces."

"So on a day when he was drinking heavily he would take from sixteen to twenty ounces of whiskey?"

Susan "I object to that line of questioning. It has been shown by this witness no evidence he was drinking heavily on this day, and this is the day we are concerned with, July 30th and 31st. Any other days would be too remote and we should not concern ourselves with it. I don't even think we should be concerned with July 30th or 31st.

Obviously even though Susan Yang is a top law student, and probably will be a top Criminal Lawyer, either Defense or Prosecution, she read the transcript , studied her lines, and knows what to say.

However Judge Anderson (Professor Anderson) had been a top Criminal Lawyer for twenty years before coming to Cornell and has been a Professor here for ten years so he knows the case, has read the transcript and replied" I don't think it is too material, and this last question has to do with what two double shots, or what ten double shots a day amount to. I thought that was the question. You may answer, Mr. Witness."

So far we are winning-let's see if we can continue on our winning streak. Cory thought.

"Eight shots a day was not heavy drinking for Barney Milton"

"What would be heavy drinking for Mr. Milton?" Cory asked.

"About the only way you could tell was when he would retire and go to bed. I never watched how many he took to get noticeably drunk."

"He could stand quite a charge of drinks. Is that correct?"

"Yes, sir"

"And the average person, that was not acquainted with Mr. Milton, might not realize what a cargo of whiskey he was carrying, correct?"

"Yes"

The snow was coming down very very heavy and Cory could hear the snow cleaning equipment being used outside the hall.

"Would it be fair to say that the deceased could carry quite a lot of whiskey without showing it?" Cory continued with the same line of questioning echoing the court transcripts.

"Yes"

"To the average person?"

"Yes"

"But from your long acquaintance with the deceased you could generally tell?"

"I could generally tell when he had an extra heavy load."

"In view of your long acquaintance with the deceased I wonder if you would be willing to tell us more about his habits and characteristics so that the jury could get a better idea"

This time Susan Yang's assistant, Dave Buchold steps in." I object to answers to such a broad question"

Judge Anderson " Objection sustained. Mr. Defense Attorney. Narrow down your question." He ordered.

"I ask you then, more narrowly, whether the deceased was an expert pistol shot?"

Susan Yang " No showing any self defense whatsoever. From the evidence up to this time the defendant was questionably the aggressor. It would be immaterial and irrelevant"

"I would like to argue this whole proposition out to the court" Cory responded.

Judge Anderson " If there are other questions, well we might continue on- If the balance of your examination is premised on this I may as well excuse the Jury."

Cory" I am quite agreeable" We will try to make progress"

"I ask you whether or not the deceased owned a number of pistols."

"He did" responded the witness.

Susan: "I object, on the same ground; incompetent, irrelevant and immaterial, whether he owns pistols or anything regarding them. It is just as immaterial as to whether he was an expert shot" she emphasized.

Judge Anderson " Objection sustained"

Oh no we are starting to have decisions against us. Cory thought.

Cory: "I would prefer to argue or present our views on the admissibility of this type of question now, if the court is willing."

Judge Anderson" We will excuse the Jury as the storm is raging outside anyway and we would probably have stopped any minute. The Jury is now excused. Come back tomorrow afternoon at 1:30 as we will take the morning to handle this argument."

"Gentlemen and Susan see you here tomorrow at 9:30 am."

Johnny had difficulty in pushing the main door open as a lot of snow was against it on the other side, however after several attempts he was able to get the door open and we pushed through the snow to retire in our dorms.

Thirty

9:30 The Great Hall- Day Two of the Mock Trial

"The defense is prepared to show that the deceased threatened, assaulted and raped the wife of the defendant a short time before the deceased met his death." Cory opened.

"We are prepared to show under what circumstances and with what frame of mind the defendant went to the Bar. We are prepared to show among other things that he went there to take the deceased into custody; to hold him for the Police."

Susan Yang pushed in" Come on, Is this just some tirade supposed to be put in the Press?"

"I will ask the court to ask the Counsel for the Region Prosecutor's Office to wait until I finish"

Judge Anderson" I would like to hear one at a time, if you don't mind. It will be more satisfactory"

Cory continued" If the defendant went to the Cocktail Lounge and Bar among other things to take the deceased into custody for a felony that night I believe and submit that under Michigan Law he had a right to do so. Provided that certain things were true-that, first, that a felony had indeed taken place and that the defendant or the deceased was guilty of it, and, second , that a felony had indeed taken place and there was reasonable cause to believe that the deceased had been guilty of it. I believe that it is a law of this State, substantially of the right of a private person to make an arrest without a warrant-"

"And do you call that an arrest?" Susan asked.

"I will ask the court to warn counsel not to interrupt me. It throws me off. It makes me angry, and I cannot think so well."

Judge Anderson " Go ahead with your argument."

Cory" Please don't. Please don't"

Cory continued" Now it seems to me, it also appears and will appear that the defendant in this case went there armed. He had a gun. It seems to me that it is important to the defense to be able to show that he knew or had reasonable cause to believe that the deceased was an expert pistol shot, if he was, that he had guns about the premises, if he had them. That he had been drinking excessively for several days before this occurrence. In other words to show the reason why the defendant went to the bar armed as he perhaps may have had a right to do under these circumstances. Now we have on the stand a man that has known the deceased for seventeen years and perhaps as intimately as any other person outside of his family. I believe it is fair to assume that he can shed some light on some of these things that we consider so vital. To project our defense. That is the reason that I would like to get that testimony in. I feel honestly that we have a right to show the kind of man, with respect to guns and pistols and drinking-the kind of man that he was going to do whatever he was going to do-and this is why we feel that we should have the right to pursue this line of questioning. I am finished."

Judge Anderson obviously quoting from the transcripts says" I can only say, until those issues are raised I will not permit those questions. That is the first I have heard that he was on his way to arrest the deceased-I have heard previous testimony and read a lot of information and theories about this case but this is the first time I hear about your theory about the defendant on his way to arrest the deceased-It was not presented previously in the Defense position.

If these theories come out we will go into those things and I will allow both parties to sled length as far as any rule of evidence will permit but until they are brought out by competent evidence they will not be received." And Judge Anderson seemed to be final on this matter.

"Does your honor take the same view as to this type of evidence as to any evidence of any alleged rape or assault? Asked Cory.

"I do, and I repeat, that if these matters do come out and if these witnesses are necessary to either prove or disprove any of those matters the court will be at perfect liberty to call them back and permit counsel to examine them further. Judge Anderson explained.

I will not excuse them. They are under subpoena

and I will not have them leave the jurisdiction of the court. They can be called out but I don't like to treat these issues until they are properly before the court. That is the court's ruling and it will be that way until someone tells me something to the contrary. If there are any decided cases or rules I shall have to see them and if I am in error I will change my mind. Until then I know nothing to the contrary. That is the court's ruling."

Susan Yang "Nothing further"

The court was recessed until 1:30 in the afternoon.

Cory continued" Mr. Barbote, you remember you are still under oath?"

"Yes"

"I wonder if you could tell us something of the behavior of the deceased on the day he was killed?"

"The day he was killed or the day before?" Barbote asked.

"And shortly before? A few days before?"

Dave Buchold, Susan Yang's assistant " I object to anything that does not concern the time of this alleged killing. I fail to see any basis to establish materiality or make it competent"

Cory began" I think the time has arrived for the defense to object to the objections of the People.

The way they are made. This witness was being examined by the Prosecuting Attorney, Susan Yang. I may be mistaken but it is my understanding that when there are two counsel representing a side it is procedure for that counsel to carry through including any objections that should be made to testimony of that witness. I am willing to take on two attorneys, but one at a time, I don't want both of them putting spit-balls at me"

Judge Anderson rules" I will lay down the rule on that, so there will be no misunderstanding. The court will rule that in the case of the examination or cross examination of any witness that examination and all of the objections incident to the question and answer, examination and cross examination and re-examination must be conducted by the attorney conducting the examination. If the associate counsel desires to suggest further questions and objections the court will have no objection to that.

On motions I have no objection to hearing all of the attorneys on all of the questions that come before the court, on motions and things like that, but anything that has to do with the evidence being offered by a witness it is better to confine it to one attorney and the court will so rule and if we can follow that we will get away from that objection.

I will rule on the objection made by the Assistant Attorney General. I think that the time element is important, as he pointed out. However the court is of the opinion that we should take into account and into consideration all of the facts and circumstances which may be brought out by either side at the time of the shooting and immediately prior thereto and in certain cases immediately after-ward. Whether or not it is material I suppose resolves itself into a question of fact for the Jury to determine.

So the court will have to be a little liberal on the time element. Under the circumstances at the moment and not knowing what the line of questioning is going to be I feel that I must overrule the objection and take the answer.

And, Mr. Prosecutor and Attorney General, if you feel we are going too far afield don't hesitate to object. Take the answer"

I don't know how many times Professor Anderson has acted in this same trial but he sure knows the case and the testimony, thought Cory.

"Mr. Barbote. Please answer the question"

"Remind me. What was the question?"

"Tell us the behavior of the deceased on the day of and in the days shortly before he was killed"

"There isn't anything unusual that happened that I can recall other than he drank more than I think he should have. Being a businessman. But that was usual for quite a few days there."

"And you made that statement on the basis of your long friendship with the knowledge of the habits of the deceased?

"Yes, sir"

"And would it be fair to say that on the day of the shooting that as a result of excessive drinking shortly before the shooting that the judgment of the deceased was somewhat impaired?"

"I would say yes" responded Barbote.

"May the court inquire of whether or not the defense has the right to further cross-examine this witness in the light of other facts that may be brought out."

Judge Anderson responded" There may be elements of defense of which the court is not aware at this time and if so it would appear that this witness would be a material witness to those facts as well as what has been brought out and the court will require that this witness keep himself within the jurisdiction of the court. He is not released from subpoena and is under oath in this case and if it should develop that he is a material witness the court will call him back for further re-direct or re-cross examination as the case may be."

Cory put forward" With that understanding we have no further questions now"

Susan Yang, Prosecuting Attorney " No further questions."

"Madame Prosecutor, do you have any other witnesses? Inquired Judge Anderson.

"Not today, however your honor , I would like to reserve the right to call any rebuttal witnesses that are required should the defense bring forward witnesses that testify to or bring out statements that have not been disclosed; and of course I will object

to any evidence being brought out that has not been properly disclosed to the Prosecution"
Susan stated.

"And in addition, we anticipate that the defense will be putting Dr. Matthew Smith on the stand and we will be requiring our witness Dr. Joseph L. Archibald to bring rebuttal testimony"

"Of course, your request is granted Ms. Yang. Now we retire until tomorrow at 9:30 a.m."

Day Three of the trial and the weather had cleared up. Twenty-two fresh inches of snow had fallen and the area around the Great Hall looked like the Antarctic and not Northern New York State.

Cory didn't actually have cabin fever and he wasn't keen on being inside for another day but he was determined to conduct a trial almost exactly as in 1952 when the original trial was done.

They were all ready when Judge Anderson announced" Ladies and Gentlemen, let's continue. Mr. Defense Attorney, your witness, please!"

Cory decided tt was time to put his client on the stand and begin putting forward a defense.
Lieutenant Mitchell Grange was sworn in and settled into the witness box and into the uncomfortable wooden chair. The chair was uncomfortable, a little creaky, thought Cory perhaps to make the witness uncomfortable so it may shorten his or her testimony.

" Lt. Grange can you remember back to July 30th , a Wednesday I believe?" as Cory opened the questions.

"Yes, of course , it was early evening, about eight o'clock, and I was at home taking a nap, as I had a tough strenuous day and I was feeling tired" started Lt. Mitchell Grange.

"Go on, tell us what happened" prompted Cory.

"Suddenly I woke up when I thought I heard the sound of screaming."

"Yes, and then?"

"Well, I got off the bed and went to the door and then Jessica fell into my arms."

"Jessica, your wife. Please describe what you saw."

"She was hysterical; her face was swollen, her skirt was torn, her hair was in her eyes; and she was crying and couldn't speak."

"What did you do?" Cory inquired.

"I got her in on the day bed and got some cold cloths and tried to quiet her down and find out what happened."

"Did you finally find out?"

Quietly Lt. Grange said "I did"

"Now" asked Cory" without going into details now, will you tell us what your wife told you had happened to her?"

"Yes" replied Grange. "She told me she had been

beaten and raped by" Lt. Grange paused as though he hated to say the words, and indeed he fairly spat them when he spoke-" by Barney Milton"

"What happened after that?"

"I stayed and tried to comfort her and quiet her down. Then I tried to get her out of her clothes-she was helpless, and still half-hysterical-and then I, I saw the evidence on her legs. Well-"

"What evidence?" Cory pressed. Again the words were spat out "Seminal fluid" he said." That's how the Doctor termed it; Dr. Josephson."

"What did you do when you saw that?"

"To trust my recollection-I got my wife on her feet. She walked into what we call the kitchen in our trailer, a little semi room between the bedroom and living room. I wiped the fluid off with a cloth and burned it in our incinerator." Responded Grange.

"Then what?"

" I went to a little stand and took my pistol out of the drawer and put it in my pocket and left the house"

"Now as your wife was telling you what happened, to you that night, did she say anything about telling the deceased , Barney Milton that if he did this to her you would kill him? Do you remember?"

"She didn't tell me completely that night. That happened after we got back. It was either when I came in the County jail early that same morning or the next morning or the next time I saw her, I don't recall."

"Did you tell your wife you were leaving or to your knowledge did she see you take the pistol?"

"No, I said nothing and I don't think she knew I was leaving. She was in the kitchen. I don't know whether she saw me or not."

"Then what did you do?"

"I stepped outside the trailer we were living in and stood in the dark for a few minutes to adjust my eyes. I also wanted to make sure that-that Barney Milton wasn't lurking around out there, Then I went to the bar."

"Walk or ride?" asked Cory

"I rode in my automobile."

Cory paused as he was coming, he though, to the crucial parts of the defense case as he had read interpreted from the transcripts, and he wanted to get it right and make sure the jury heard it.

"What was your purpose in going to the Cocktail Lounge and bar?"

The Lieutenant flushed darkly as he spoke. "I was going to grab that individual, so help me."

"What were you going to do with him?" Cory pushed on.

The Lieutenant now spoke rapidly.

"I'm not quite sure. Grab him and hold him. A man like that could not be at large."

"I ask you whether or not you had any intention of

killing or harming him?"

"I had no intention of killing or harming him but if that man had made one false move I would have killed him." Stated Grange emphatically.

Cory now pondered-well it was in now; for better or worse our man had now declared that he had gone to the bar to 'grab' Barney Milton, an assertion which Cory hoped gave the defense sufficient evidence to warrant an instruction from the court on the right of arrest. If so, it would answer many perplexing defense questions; so Cory continued.

"When you got to the bar with your car what did you do?"

"I remember I got out of the car and walked into the bar. I wasn't even in the bar when I saw him watching me through his rear bar window. I watched him, and he kept watching me. Then as I approached he whirled around on me."

"OK then what happened?"

"I can't-from there on it is a jumble. My next recollection is back in the trailer. My next coherent recollection is back in the trailer." Lt. Grange blurted out.

"Can you illustrate for us, Lieutenant, what position Barney Milton assumed when he turned around?"

"As I say, he turned, to the best of my recollection, to his right. His left hand on the bar, And I cannot recall seeing his right arm."

"You say his left hand on the bar or arm and hand?"

"His left fore-arm. He kind of leaned."

"State whether or not you remember driving back to the trailer."

"No, sir; I don't"

"Did you know that when you got back to the trailer, you were seen standing outside your trailer holding the gun in your hand?"

"Yes, sir"

"And that the gun was empty, no shells?"

"Yes, sir"

"Is that substantially as Detective Sergeant Quigley's written Affidavit explained it?"

"It was near it. I think he knows more about guns than I do."

At this point Cory purposely did not get into how the Lieutenant had got the Luger as Cory, just like in the real trial, had a little trap set out for that question; and if the cleaver Susan Yang evaded it Cory could still bring it out on re-direct.

"OK Lt. Grange, let's go back to the bar that night, the 30th." Cory began.

"How many people did you see in the bar that night?"

"Only one-Barney"

"There has been witness statements filed that there were a number of people in the bar and at the bar, and that some of them greeted you. Did you observe any of them or were you aware of their greetings?" Cory inquired.

"I saw and heard nothing." Responded Grange.

"Now you of course saw the affidavits of the eye-witnesses that was filed in court, didn't you?" Judge Anderson " Mr. Defense Attorney. You realize that we had agreed in order to conduct this trial in the short amount of days we have that affidavits were filed instead of actual witness testimony. Right?"

"Yes Professor Anderson! I mean Judge Anderson!" answered Cory meekly,

"So go on, don't spend any more time on the witness statements"

"Yes, Your Honor" Cory replied however he needed to make a small point.

"So, Lieutenant Grange, did you know prior to that night some of those who claimed to have greeted you?"

"Yes, mostly by sight, but I had spoken to them on previous occasions. The people up there were very friendly."

"Did you speak to anyone that night?"

"No, sir"

"To your best recollection did anyone speak to you?"

"No, sir"

"Including the deceased Barney Milton."

"That is correct."

"Do you remember leaving the bar?"

"I do not"

"or talking to the bartender or anyone outside?"

"No, sir"

"Do you remember returning to the trailer?"

"No, sir"

"What was the first thing you recollect?" Cory continued.

"Well, after standing outside for a few minutes, I entered the trailer.

"I first recall sitting in the trailer with my wife and telling her I guess I had probably shot Barney Milton or someone and then I got up and went over and told Mr. Abbot what I had done."

"That is the deputized caretaker of the trailer park, correct?"

"Yes, sir"

"Why did you go to him?"

"Well, he was the only one who seemed to be in charge, either there or in the village for that matter."

"Did you go to him because he was a deputy sheriff?"

"I may have. At that rate I went to him"

Susan Yang was scribbling furiously and Cory knew she would pounce on all this deputy business.

"Did you think of Mr. Abbot being a deputy before you went to the bar that night?"

"I did not. I did not think of Mr. Abbot or his

being a deputy or about anything but grabbing that man."

Cory paused and then pitched the fast ball, as much for Susan Yang as anyone. Of course he was following the original trial as closely as possible, throwing in a few things here and there to show he had actually learned something in almost two years at Cornell Law School.

"If you had thought of Mr. Abbot and remembered he was a deputy would you have gone to him?"

"No sir, I would not have, any more than I'd have got my old father out of bed to gather in this-this man, this son of a bitch"

"Do you recollect what you told Mr. Abbot?"

"Not exactly. I assume I told him what he put in his Affidavit filed here."

After that Cory quickly took the Lieutenant over his knowledge of Barney Milton's prowess with pistols; his medals; the fact that it was common knowledge that he possessed pistols and sometimes carried them; his experience at judo; and finally that the Lieutenant possessed the knowledge that night when he went to the bar to 'grab Barney Milton, Cory purposely avoided his war record, feeling Susan Yang would bring it out by digging it out. Cory then brought out, over Susan Yang's objection, that Lieutenant Grange had been obliged to retain an Army Psychologist for financial reasons.

"Lieutenant Grange" Cory started. " On the night of this shooting did you love your wife?"

"I did sir." Answered Grange. "Do you still love her?"

"Very much, sir"

Cory then turned to Susan Yang "Your witness, Madame Prosecutor" Cory then retired to his defense table, exhausted, but happy.

Judge Anderson" Before we start cross-examination, a fifteen minute break."

The clerk announced "All rise" and everyone stood up as Judge Anderson left the room.

"Johnny, were you able to review Archibald's testimony in the transcripts and prepare notes for me?" Cory questioned Johnny who had been relatively quiet during the proceedings.

"Yes boss!" replied Johnny. "And why do you call me boss, Johnny?" asked Cory. "Well , in this make-believe Mock trial you are the boss, so we make believe, ok?"

"OK!" responded Cory.

Fifteen minutes exactly and the Judge returned which as anyone who has been in courts when trials or other proceedings take place, is unusual. Usually fifteen minutes turns out to be thirty minutes or more. But this was a make-believe Mock trial so fifteen minutes was fifteen minutes.

Thirty-One

Susan Yang, top law student acting as Chief Prosecutor and secret bloodhound began with an ominous tone to her voice. She was a great actor and top Law Student. Maybe you need to be both to succeed in the Law Profession.

"Lieutenant Grange let's go back to the trailer when you woke up and found your wife so hysterical, sobbing and you weren't sure she knew what she was talking about, and you couldn't believe what she was telling you about Barney Milton having beat her and raped her, correct?"

"Yes , Ma'am"

"I object to the answer of the witness" Cory stated" He can tell what he saw. If he wants to tell what he saw I will not object" Judge Anderson" We'll strike that out"

Cory" the characterizing"

"What happened then?"

"I thought she was so hysterical that I wasn't sure she knew who had done this to her. I made her swear that it was the deceased Barney Milton." "Did she?"

"She did, Ma'am." Confirmed Grange.

"When you saw this fluid you describe as Seminal fluid"

"Not me Ma'am. the Doctor who examined my wife." Jumped in Grange. "Ok , tell us again what you did when you saw the fluid?"

"I had got my wife on her feet and I wiped it off as best I could." "Do you recall what you did? What you used, and what you did? That you wiped this fluid off with?"

"No Ma'am I don't" responded Grange, under pressure.

"And exactly when did your wife tell you she had warned Barney Milton that if he did this to her you would kill him? Do you remember? Susan was on a fishing expedition.

"I didn't say she said that" replied Grange.

"Well what did you say Lieutenant Mitchell Grange? Susan raised her voice uncharacteristically.

"I believe I said she did not tell me she had warned Barney"

"You don't remember much about that night in the trailer or after you left the trailer, do you Lieutenant?" she continued.

"Now there has been some information that there was a locked gate on the main road into the trailer park.

"Do you remember opening the gate?"

"I don't recall opening the gate."

"Do you remember the route you took to the bar?"

"There is only one route to take."

"Do you remember taking that route? Do you remember unlocking the gate?" "I do not" "Or anything about the gate?"

"No, Ma'am."

Cory had to jump in" Your Honor I object . I submit this line of questioning is leading. I believe she should ask him what he did and it would be much better."

Judge Anderson" It's cross- You know leading questions are OK. Anyway proceed Ms. Yang"

Susan Yang just shrugged and proceeded. Maybe her opponent was just trying to mess up her rhythm or thought process. Whatever she stayed on track.

"Now Lieutenant, I ask you whether or not you were angry when you heard of what had happened to your wife and what you observed yourself-when you went toward the bar?"

"I would say I was long past that stage." Explained Grange.

"I object" Cory stated. "I ask that that be stricken from the record. It states the conclusion of the witness."

Judge Anderson" It may stand".

Oh no thought Cory. Lost another one.

"What was your purpose in going to the bar?" continued Susan "I said it before. I was going to grab that bastard, so help me." "You were going to grab him?" questioned Susan.

"Yes , ma'am" "What were you going to do with him?"

"Your Honor, I answered that before!" Grange pleaded for assistance. "Answer the question, Mr.

Grange"

"At that stage-I couldn't say exactly what I was going to do. I suppose I planned to have some help with an individual like that. Obviously a criminal"

"I ask that that be stricken and the Jury be instructed to disregard it" shouted Cory.

"Objection sustained" Judge Anderson confirmed.

"I ask you whether or not you had any intention of killing or harming him."

"I had no intention of killing or harming him but if that man made one bad move I would have killed him" responded Grange.

"Come on, Lieutenant Grange, you bring your pistol with you, loaded, and state that you had no intention of killing or harming him. You expect the jury to believe that you had no intention of killing or harming him; why bring the pistol?"

"To protect myself. I knew he owned lots of guns and had them hidden at the bar" answered Grange.

"Well when you got to the bar with your car what did you do?" "I got out of the car. Walked into the bar. I wasn't even in the bar when I saw him watching me through his rear bar window. I watched him. And he watched me. And close to the bar he whirled around on me."

"What happened after that?"

"I can't –from there on it is jumbled. My next memory is back in the trailer." "You don't remember too much about that night, do you

Lieutenant Grange?"

"Well, Ma'am, just as I have testified before here" The Lieutenant paused, and Cory noted that the Peoples' psychiatrist had at last come to life and was making some notes.

"Can you illustrate for us, Lieutenant, what position the deceased assumed when he turned around."

"Come on, I already told the court. When I saw him-If you could picture a mirror and standing here-apparently he was watching me through this mirror-and he turned to the bar this way" "And with the left arm up and across his body-and the bar-and his right hand-" Susan started.

Cory" I object to the leading question"

Judge Anderson" Ask him what the position was."

Susan Yang" Can't I suggest for the record that the witness-"

"Just ask him-" Judge Anderson repeated.

"Will you describe the position you just indicated so that it will appear in the record?" "As I say he turned, to the best of my recollection, to his right. His left hand on the bar. And I cannot recall seeing his right arm."

"You say his left hand on the bar or arm and hand?"

"His left fore-arm." Grange explained.

"State whether or not you remember driving back to the trailer." "No. ma'am, I don't"

"What happened when you got back to the trailer?"

"I guess I came to." Answered Grange.

Cory in his great acting as the Defense attorney jumps in. "I object to that and ask that it be stricken; not responsive to the question" he stated. "Cory is the only one who will object for that reason" Judge Anderson says.

"It is improper" Cory states. "Came-to?" Susan questions.

Cory "It is for the jury to determine. I believe the answer invades the province of the jury-conclusion of the witness. I ask a ruling, your honor."

Judge Anderson " We will let this question and answer stand"

"What were you doing when you came to" Susan pushed on.

"I was standing with an empty pistol in my hand" Grange answered. "How do you know it was empty?" Susan asked.

" And before you answer I would like to show you People's Exhibit No 3 (other documents were #1 and #2) and I ask you if this is your pistol."

"Yes , it is mine, Ma'am." "Now how did you know it was empty?" "This is a semi-automatic pistol-it is recoil operated. This gadget sticks up on the top of the magazine when the last round goes off-and there is not another shell-the pressure holds it back-you can't aim it and you can't release this."

Lt. Grange stated with confidence.

"In other words by looking at it you could tell it was empty?" "Yes, Ma'am."

"Where did you get this German Luger?" "In the last war."

"And by' last war' what do you mean?" she asked. "In the Vosges Mountains of France. World War II"

"It is a souvenir of World War II?" "Yes"

"Under what circumstances did you get it?" She probed.

"At the time I was an infantry rifle platoon leader." Cory " I will submit that that would be immaterial and irrelevant how he got it. There is no question he had it and that is all we are concerned with at this time."

Judge Anderson confirmed" I think it is admissible if Ms. Yang wants to go into it. There are other reasons why it would be admissible also." Answer please.

"The pistol was property of a First Lieutenant in the German war. I removed it from his body." "Under what circumstances?"

"He had been sniping at the platoon-and that pistol takes a rifle stock-well he was shot in the foot-and with a carbine-" Grange started to explain.

Susan was losing patience with this witness. "Anyway that's how you got this German Luger?"

"Yes, ma'am." "How did you happen to take it in your trailer?"

"It was there for my wife's protection and had been for months." "State whether it was loaded or empty."

"It was always loaded." "Why?" She questioned.

"She can shoot the pistol but it is impossible for her to load it. The spring is too strong." "On this night do you recall or know how many bullets were in the Luger?"

"I do not. There could be no more than nine completed loaded." "If you completely load it you put quite a strain on the spring?"

"Not necessarily but to completely load it you must put one in the chamber" he explained.

"Did you have it that way?" "There was one in the chamber but to the best of my knowledge I am not sure."

"State whether or not that was the usual way you left it in the trailer for your wife's protection." "Yes, it was always there." He confirmed.

"With one in the chamber?" She asked.

"With one in the chamber. Yes , Ma'am."

"How many people were in the bar that night when you went up there?"

"I don't know. I have heard many stories as to how many."

"I mean from your observation that night,-How many did you see?" "None, To the best of my knowledge, one."

"That was who?" Susan asked.

"The deceased , Barney" He responded.

"There have been reports that there were people at the bar. Do you remember seeing them?" "No-one."

"Would you deny that they were there?" "Yes, Ma'am."

"Or do you remember?"

"I don't remember seeing anyone there."

"Then you would not be in a position to say whether there were or no, would you?" "No, Ma'am."

"Do you remember seeing a lady called Mrs. Brownberg standing at the end of the bar?" "No, Ma'am."

"Do you remember anyone saying or greeting you "Hi Lieutenant", "Hello", or anything on that order?" "No, Ma'am."

"Did you speak to anyone?" "To my knowledge, no, Ma'am." "Did anyone speak to you?"

"No, Ma'am." "Including the deceased?" "Yes, ma'am."

"When you got back to the trailer and observed that the gadget on your pistol was in position indicating it was empty what did you do?"

"I believe I asked how my wife was. She was sitting at the end of the sofa. I told her I shot someone."

"What were the words you used? If you remember?

"I don't remember the fact but some of it has come

back to me while I sit here in this court room, but I did tell her that."

"So you are saying that you have a memory lapse from the time you saw Barney Milton at the bar until you came to at the trailer park"

"Have you ever had similar lapses?" Susan continued.

"None other than the ordinary lapses a man might bump into from combat!: stated Grange.

"What do you mean?" Susan probed.

"Well, quite often after an action had been completed and we got back to talk it over, if there were ten survivors there would be ten different stories of what happened" stated Grange.

"Can you give a specific instance rather than generalities?"

Cory thought that Susan Yang would surely have had objected had he tried to bring this out, and yet she was diligently wrapping the flag around our man on her own.

This had been done in the original trial and Susan had the option of leaving it out of the mock trial but she either foolishly or unknowingly decided to continue on the line of questioning.

"Yes, I recall one incident in Korea" Grange began."One of my half-tracks was supporting the infantry. I had eight in this action and a Chinese mortar round dropped in and wounded all eight. I happened to be far enough away to see what happened without getting wounded. Two or three more rounds came in. When we'd silenced the mortar fire and the meds could work on our men, all of them told a different story. From one to a hundred rounds had come in, There were actually four." Grange concluded.

Cory glanced at the Jury/law Students and he noticed one of them was hanging on the Lieutenant's words, evidently reliving some private remembrance of his own. That Law Student Cory was aware had served two years in the army overseas before starting at Cornell. That may help the defense when the jury deliberates.

"How long did you serve in Korea?" Susan continued.

"Nearly sixteen months." Grange answered.

Susan Yang then asked the Judge if her Assistant Deputy Prosecutor could continue as she was feeling a little ill. The Judge agreed and Cory had no objection. Dave Buchold , Susan Yang's assistant jumped out of his chair like he had been catapulted over a wall, as he was anxious to make points with Professor Anderson aka Judge Anderson.

He took the obliging Lieutenant through World War II, from Sicily up through France and Germany and wound him up on VJ day on an island in the far Pacific. As Dave Buchold pressed on Cory began to see what he was getting at, although the price he was paying seemed a little high.

"Now did you see action in all those places?" Buchold continued. "I did , sir"

"Now were you in constant combat?"

"No, sir, no soldier is ever in constant combat. None that survive, anyway. We were under constant to intermittent barrage, constantly in a sweat,, you might say"

"And you had skirmishes from time to time?"

"Oh yes." Confirmed Grange.

Cory thought that Buchold was also, and not so subtly, demonstrating his own familiarity with combat conditions, and Cory had to concede that if he were a soldier he wouldn't want Buchold gunning for him. Did Professor Anderson know that Buchold had military experience in combat situations, and had picked him to assist the prosecution for that reason? Probably, Cory determined.

"Did you participate in the skirmishes?" "Yes, sir as the platoon leader I had to" "About how long?"

"Sometimes a day, three days, even from sometimes it was three or four days in the hole." Dave Buchold paused to hurl another bolt.

"And during this time did you experience any unusual mental state of any kind?" "No, sir. I once had a concussion from shell fire but I was back in action the next day"

"Were you ever treated for mental disease?" Dave

Buchold threw out that question like a Major League baseball pitcher throws a fastball.

"No, sir" responded Grange, as if he was fouling off the fast ball pitch. Dave Buchold continued " Were you ever hospitalized for mental neurosis or psychosis?" "No sir"

"OK! Lieutenant Grange. Let's review what happened when you went back to the trailer park and after you told your wife what you think you had done" "Sure" replied Grange.

"Tell us again what you did after you told your wife what you did." "I didn't do anything at the time. I sat there, I guess, is all. I told her I would have to get the Police. And I don't remember to be the truth whether it was myself remembered that Mr. Abbot was a deputy or whether my wife informed me. At least I went over and got him."

"That was the Caretaker at the trailer park?"

"That is right" confirmed Grange.

"Who provided evidence by way of Affidavit because he is unavailable for trial?" "Yes, sir."

"And what did you do?"

"I left the trailer and walked over to Mr. Abbot's house. It was completely dark. I don't recall the exact time. I knocked on the door and finally aroused him. I gave him an idea of what had happened and he said' just a minute, I will be right over'. I think I walked back to the trailer door and waited outside my trailer for him until he could get some clothes on, and he came to the trailer."

"Where was your wife then? When Mr. Abbot came to the trailer. If you remember?"

Cory thought- not too professional cross-examination. In fact this assistant prosecutor was laying the foundation for the defense by asking ' If you remember?".

"She was in the doorway" Grange responded.

"Do you remember whether your wife and Mr. Abbot exchanged words as he approached?"

"Something was said but all I know is what Mr. Abbot put in his Affidavit filed here."

"You have no recollection? None? Nada? Nothing?" the words rattled off of Dave Buchold like bullets from a machine gun. "I do recall him saying something."

"Now some of the people who say they were present in the bar that night and they provided evidence here-I ask you if you knew them at least by sight before the night in question."

"Yes, sir." Affirmed Grange.

"I ask you whether you remember seeing any of those people or recognizing them while you in the bar? On this night that you went down with the pistol?"

"No, sir. I had already said that, several times." Grange responded. "Although you previously knew them at least by sight, correct?" "Yes, I did."

"Did you know Barney Milton before that night?"

"Yes, I did. And I have also stated that several times in this court. Why are you asking the same question, over and over?" Grange asked.

"Mr. Grange." Judge Anderson interrupts. "It is Mr. Buchold's job to cross-examine and he just wants to make sure you are telling the truth, and for sure the Jury are going to review your testimony to see if it differs from one examination to another. Remember you are on trial here for murder , which I don't have to remind you is the most serious charge, and the potential consequences to you, should you be found guilty are in the laws of this State , perhaps terrible to imagine. So let's continue, Mr. Prosecutor"

"Thank You, Your Honor. Under what circumstances did you know Barney Milton before the night of July 30th?"

"I knew him as proprietor of the New Lake Michigan Cocktail Lounge and Bar. And I knew his wife" stated Lieutenant Grange."What was her name?" inquired Buchold.

"Her first name, I don't know,-we always called her Mrs. M." "Did you occasionally go in there and have a drink or two or more?""I did, sir."

"I ask you, how, up to the night in question, you and the deceased got along?" "Very well."

"Had he ever called at your trailer?"

"One day when I was at work Mr. and Mrs. Milton stopped at the trailer and talked to my wife. I wasn't there at the time. Friday night-toward the 30th of July,-my patrol commander and the deceased stopped in for a few minutes."

"Who was your patrol commander?" "Lieutenant John Simpson."

"Would you say that you were on friendly but not intimate terms with the deceased?" "Yes, sir"

"Now there has been some evidence here that the deceased was an expert pistol shot. I ask you whether or not you knew anything about that when you went to the bar with your Luger that night."

"It was common knowledge in the Village. That it was his medals that were displayed on the back wall of the bar. At least I assumed they belonged to him." Grange replied.

"And I ask you whether or not you had any knowledge as to whether he carried or possessed pistols." Buchold inquired.

"As to whether he owned them, I don't know. But I do know that that was common knowledge in the Village also that the deceased carried, or had carried them."

Cory jumps in." I object to that. He said of his own knowledge he didn't know".

"Objection sustained" Judge Anderson replies.

"That is all the questions I have for this witness" Dave Buchold, Assistant Prosecutor states.

"No re-direct at this time. However I request the courts indulgence in allowing me to bring this witness back if rebuttal evidence is required" Cory points out.

"Of course. Witness you can step down" Judge Anderson confirms. Before we proceed a twenty minute break is required. We need to give the court clerk and others a chance to take a break. See you in twenty". Judge Anderson proclaims.

A twenty minute break and Judge Anderson states:

"Ok Mr. Defense Attorney. You have been given , I am sure, the Will- Say of Dr. Joseph Archibald, Psychiatrist who is scheduled to testify for the Prosecutor and is delayed due to a snow storm outside our area." Judge Anderson begins.

"Since you already are aware of what Dr. Archibald will say at trial I ask you if you have any objection to presenting your expert witness Dr. Smith now, in order to expedite the trial?"

"I have no objection as long as when Dr. Archibald does present evidence he sticks strictly to his Will-Say statement and or provide rebuttal only to what Dr. Smith states, and not introduce new evidence which we are not party too." Cory explains.

"I agree" Susan Yang replies.

"Fine. Then Mr. Defense Attorney bring forward your witness." Judge Anderson ordered.

Thirty-Two

Dr. Matthew Andrew Smith, at the real trial, did not look like a member of the medical profession.

Of course one of the reasons was that he was a professional football player for the Green Bay Packers for ten years before he retired and completed his studies and took up the profession of a Psychiatrist.

Huge shoulders and arms and a barrel chest that overtook the witness box as he sat down. Muscles bulging everywhere and a face tanned from a lot of muscle beach appearances. His suit, tie and shirt were just containing his muscular physique and it looked like buttons were about to snap at any time. The only part of Smiths' physique that was small was his height-he was less than five feet seven inches tall so it seemed that he was hanging onto the edges of the witness box to prevent from falling into the box itself. An almost cartoon like appearance, and in this Mock Trial Professor Anderson had recruited a Cornell Student from the Cornell Football Team.

No Law School experience , and Cory was aware of that, so Cory hoped he would do a good job and stick to the script as presented in the transcripts.

"Dr. Smith, I ask you whether or not you were assigned by your superiors in the army to conduct a psychiatric examination of Lieutenant Mitchell

Grange." Cory began.

"I was" replied Dr. Smith.

"Did you conduct the examination?" "I did"

"Where?" "At Harry Weaver Army Hospital, Detroit."

"When?" "From September 3rd thru the 5th , 1952."

"And will you tell us, Doctor, some of the things that were done in connection with this examination."

"This man received complete physical examination, which means that he went through each of the specialty clinics in the hospital and examined by a specialist in the particular department. And complete social history performed by a man specially trained and qualified in that field. He received an electro encephalogram study." Dr. Smith explained.

"What is that?" Cory inquired.

"Because there was in the history the fact that the Lieutenant had been unconscious as a result of a concussion efforts were made to determine whether or not there might be some residual effects. These would have shown or probably would have shown up on an electro encephalogram. It was a perfect, normal encephalogram." stated Dr. Smith.

"Go ahead" "He also received-" "By a technician?" questioned Cory.

"The imperceptions test-and was interviewed on the three days he was there with me. This was my primary assignment during the Lieutenant's hospitalization."

"I ask if some of the tests were conducted by men working under you-a person working under you?"

"Taken by technicians trained for the purpose. The responses were examined by me."

"Did you say technicians?" asked Cory

"Yes. The test itself , the responses to the test were examined by myself and interpreted to the extent that they were interpreted." "And state whether or not you, yourself, spent time examining Lieutenant Grange."

"I spent the major part of five days during his hospitalization examining him. There would be three rather extensive interviews."

"Now I ask you Doctor, whether there is psychiatric facilities and equipment at the Harvey weaver Hospital."

"Yes there is, yes sir." "And how do they compare with other equipment of that nature in other hospitals?"

"It compares favorably with that in any other hospital I am acquainted with." "Are you aware of any equipment or facilities that are better?" "I am not" replied Dr. Smith.

"Doctor, you and I have gone over the hypothetical question together. I should like to read the question." Asked Cory.

Judge Anderson" You may read it."

Cory began slowly reading the question.

"Doctor, assume that a man of thirty-eight is a First Lieutenant in the United States Army. That he was a combat veteran of World War II and the Korean War. That he returned to this country from Korea in March, 1952 and was assigned to military duty in various places. That in June 1952, he was assigned to duty in a remote logging resort village in the Upper Peninsula of Michigan. That he was married to an attractive and vivacious women four years his senior. That these two were and are much in love with each other. That they lived in a trailer in a public park in said village. That the social and recreational facilities of said village were limited. That one of the few public recreational places they could go to was a neighboring bar. That the proprietor of this bar was friendly to said Lieutenant and his wife and that in company with his own wife he had called upon them at their trailer.

That because of his long overseas service the Lieutenant had few acquaintances among local Army personnel. That he occasionally went to said bar when off duty and that his social relations with the proprietor were friendly and cordial though not intimate. Assume further, Doctor, that at approximately 6:00 P.M. on Wednesday, July 30th, 1952, the wife of this Lieutenant went to the bar to get some Beer and play shuffleboard and that the Lieutenant went to bed and slept because he had a long day and was taking a nap and he slept and that soon after that evening he was suddenly awakened. That he hurriedly got up and thereupon heard a scream. That he ten met his wife at the door of his trailer. That she was sobbing and breathless and hysterical. That she finally told him that the proprietor of the tavern had threatened her life and assaulted and raped her. That he had again just assaulted her and beaten and kicked her. That she was badly bruised and beaten. That her skirt was ripped and her underpants were missing.

That the Lieutenant spent upwards of an hour attempting to calm and comfort and minister to his wife. That during this time she told him the details of the threats and assaults and beatings. That during this time he wiped a fluid from his wife's leg, which he believed to be semen.

Assume further, Doctor, that this Lieutenant believed that the man whom he believed had just assaulted , threatened and raped his wife was an expert pistol shot and that he kept pistols about his premises and possibly on his person. That he himself kept a loaded Luger automatic pistol in his trailer for protection.

That his mind was in a turmoil over what he believed had just happened to his wife and over her present condition. That he finally determined to seek out said bar proprietor and take him into custody and hold him for the police. That while he felt considerable anger and loathing and contempt for the bar proprietor he had at no time any intention of killing or harming him.

That he went and got his pistol without his wife's knowledge and left his wife in the trailer and proceeded toward this bar. That he does not remember what time it was or precisely how he got to the bar. That he finally got to the bar and entered it. That he saw the proprietor standing alone behind the bar closely watching him. That he then advanced to the bar and produced his pistol and pointed it at the proprietor and emptied its contents into his body, leaning over the bar to do so. That he had and has no conscious recollection of this act. That he then turned and left the bar and proceeded toward his trailer. That he does not remember anything after he entered the bar other than that as indicated until he got home to the trailer. That he then first observed that his pistol was emptied. That he then told his wife that he had shot the bar proprietor. That he then notified a deputized caretaker of the trailer camp and said caretaker called the police. That he was subsequently arrested and charged with first degree murder.

Assume further, Doctor, that aside from his boyhood escapades that this man had never before in his lifetime ever been arrested for or convicted of any criminal offense, including any act of violence toward another human being.

Doctor, assume all of the facts hereinbefore stated to be true, have you an opinion based upon a reasonable psychiatric certainty as to whether or not it is probable that the hypothetical man was in a condition of emotional disorganization so as to be temporarily insane?

Or was he suffering from a temporary mental disorder at the time that the deceased met his death so as to be unable to distinguish right from wrong?"

Susan Yang breaks in" I object in view of the fact that I have not had opportunity to look at the question and that we certainly would like to study it to determine whether or not the necessary factors and facts and evidence are in it. I believe that we should be permitted time to look it over and discuss it with our psychiatrist."

Judge Anderson" I would like to hear the finish of the reading of the question. I want all of the question on the record before I consider the objection"

"Very well." Sighed Susan.

"Did he at that time know, understand or comprehend the nature and consequences of his acts? Cory continued. "Was he in such a state of mind that he did not have the benefit of his conscious reasoning mind, and rather was dominated by instinct and the unconscious mind?

Is such a condition know to psychiatry and if so describe and define it, and further tell us what effect did it have upon his mind. What effect did it have on his mind?"

"OK Ms. Prosecutor. Now renew your objection. Susan Yang" Yes. In view of the hour-if we could-" Judge Anderson" I was anxious to complete the examination and cross examination of Dr. Smith tonight if possible. He made no request on me and I did not discuss it with him but I assume as a general proposition that he would be glad to get away if he could and get back to his work. I don't want to work any hardship on counsel for the People. I want to give them a reasonable opportunity."

Cory" Defense is ready to proceed."

Judge Anderson" I wanted to make one suggestion. And this is entirely for the assistance of the court and I don't want to be considered as suggesting how you should try your case. But I wish that for my benefit each of those separate questions, of which it appears there are several, could be taken up one at a time. I don't care to have the facts repeated. We have gone over those. But it would appear there are several questions. I wish each question might be propounded to him and then take his answer, yes or no, and then the conclusion and if he wishes to explain. I should be glad to have him do it rather than try to have him answer all at once and then go into explanation. I think I would be better satisfied if it could be handled that way. I suggest it for what it is worth."

"There is no objection before the court. I am willing to do that" confirmed Susan Yang.

"I would like to have the Doctor answer each question and then without further discussion recess until 9:30 tomorrow, Then if there are any objections before that time I will be glad to hear them the first thing." Stated Judge Anderson.

"Then as I understand we will have an opportunity to undertake specific objections to the various questions and it will be considered as though made before the question is answered.

Judge Anderson: "And also to the fact. I thought you might as well study the question and facts and study the answer and if you want to raise objection I will be glad to hear it. And if we omit or emit something I will strike it and instruct the jury not to consider it.

I felt if stopped there it couldn't be anything too prejudicial if I had to strike it. I am familiar with the fact that damage might be done but I have followed it carefully and saw nothing too much of material harm tonight. Then you can get together and be prepared to come in the morning, otherwise we will have to take a recess in the morning so that you can study over those things. If you could do it that way it would give you opportunity to do it over the recess and finish with this doctor and he could be on his way. Unless it is necessary for him to be held for re-direct. I only suggest it. It occurs to me as what I would like but I don't want to tell you how to try your case."

"It is agreeable to us" stated Susan.

"Anything that will get this case over, help get it over I am agreeable to." Confirmed Cory.

"That is the way it strikes me, unless there is some serious objection on the part of either party." Judge Anderson confirmed.

"May I go ahead then?" asked Cory.

Thirty-Three

Judge Anderson" With each question , and get the answer, but not go into any explanation tonight. He may in the morning but not tonight."

Cory began again" Assume all of the facts hereinbefore stated to be true, taking into consideration all that occurred, and based upon reasonable psychiatric certainty, is it probable that the hypothetical man was in a condition of emotional disorganization so as to be temporarily insane, or was he suffering from a temporary mental disorder at the time that the deceased met his death so as to be unable to distinguish right from wrong?"

"I believe he was" responded the Doctor.

"Did he at that time understand or comprehend the nature and consequences of his acts? Cory asked.

"I do believe that he did."

"Was he in such a state of mind that he did not have the benefit of his conscious reasoning mind and rather was dominated by instinct and the unconscious man, the unconscious mind?"

"I believe he was?" confirmed Dr. Smith.

"Is such a condition known to psychiatry and if so describe and define it and tell us what effect it has upon his mind."

"The condition is known to psychiatry. It is not uncommon. At the present time the nomenclature is known as disassociated reaction. The condition that you described certainly constitutes a psychic shock. This shock disturbed the mental and emotional equilibrium of the Lieutenant and was responsible for creating an almost overwhelming tension. In this state the one object the Lieutenant could have would be anything, something that would reduce the tension or alleviate the tension. His past history indicates he is a man of action and it was natural at this time that he should turn to action.

It would mean that at this time he could not consider an alternative course. It would mean he would not be fully capable of understanding the significance of any course of action he followed.

Though he might well have been told what it would be he was not at this time in a state where he could fully appreciate it."Doctor Smith continued" At such a time the only right that an individual may understand is the right that will reduce the unbearable tension. In this instance it was responsible for certain phenomena, in other instances responsible under circumstances having similar remarkable phenomena."

"Can you give us example?"

"This is a condition that I have seen in men who have come back from combat-this is a condition I discussed with men who experienced it during combat. After they were out of it some time. Considerable time. Some of the most remarkable heroics take place in this state , as well as some of the most remarkable cowardice." The Doctor explained.

"In this state you described-this state you described-is it sometimes known as irresistible impulse? Cory inserted.

"I object to that. That is invading the province of the court to define." Susan pointed out.

"I withdraw; it is probably leading." Cory stated and continued.

"Does this mental state that you talk about have any other label or tag?"

"It may be considered and know as an irresistible impulse" confirmed the Doctor.

"I object to that and ask that it be stricken because that is in the same category as the former one?
Cory replied. " The Doctor began by saying the current nomenclature-known as disassociated reaction and I asked him if this condition is known

by other names."

"Maybe it will clarify it if you were not referring to the legal term of irresistible impulse." Susan stated.

"I will not so confine it." Replied Cory.

"Then it would be objectionable as invading the province of the court." She answered.

Judge Anderson steps in with "Do I understand the question was-what is another common name for this situation-and you stated what the common name for it was. Is that where we are at?"

Cory "That is the substance of the question"

"Yes , sir" confirmed Susan.

Judge Anderson" The answer will stand"

Cory was relieved because this was a key point in this trial and even though the question put to the Doctor testifying for the Defense could have been ruled' leading the witness', it was not ruled that way, and if it was then Cory would have a difficult time going forward as he would not be able to mention those two words again. Cory knew, after reading the transcripts of the original trial that this was a key point, and he had handled it well, had presented it well, and the Judge did his part in confirming that 'the answer will stand".

"Doctor, during the time you examined Lieutenant Grange and after you concluded did you form an opinion as to whether he was then sane?" Cory asked.

"I did. I felt at the time of the examination he was sane and competent" replied the Doctor.

"And what is your opinion as to his sanity or insanity now?

"I have seen enough in the last four days to indicate that I should change my mind."

Susan then inquired" Does the court desire that the objections to the hypothetical question be made in the presence of the Jury?

"There are some matters which counsel presumably can agree on in changing the hypothetical question and some were mutually agreed on and others we feel that the court can decide, and if the court so desires we would suggest that the jury be excused until we form a hypothetical question and-"

Judge Anderson" I suppose the question of the admissibility of any evidence is for the court. The weight to be given it after it is admitted is for the jury. The jury may be excused."

The twelve jurists left the room and Susan commenced as soon as the last one exited.

"There are some things we are agreed on. The only thing as far as the first part is concerned-"

Cory" Could we retire to chambers?"

And in chambers Susan repeated" The first page is alright.:

Judge Anderson" I have copy of the Defense questions."

"Here is a corrected copy as the Defense Attorney handed it to me" Susan remarked.

"We are now all set on page 1. Now on page 2."

The discussions that followed ironed out any areas of disagreement and it was agreed to continue before the Jury, who were then summoned.

Cory" Your Honor, regarding the hypothetical question, counsel for the prosecution and I have ironed out certain areas of disagreement and the objection to the original hypothetical question and being thus in agreement I should like to read the question."

Cory then handed a copy to the court reporter.

Judge Anderson" read the question."

"Doctor" Cory began. Assume that a man of thirty-eight is a First Lieutenant in the United states Army; that he was a combat veteran of World War II and the Korean war; that he returned to this country from Korea in march 1952, and was assigned to military duty in various places. That in June 1952 he was assigned to duty in a remote logging and resort village in the Upper Peninsula of Michigan.

That he was married to an attractive and vivacious women four years his senior. That these two were and are much in love with each other. That they lived in a trailer in a public park in said village. That the social and recreational facilities of said village were limited. That one of the few public recreational places they could go to was a neighboring Cocktail Lounge and Bar.

That the proprietor of this bar was friendly to said Lieutenant and his wife and that, in company with his own wife, he had called upon them at their trailer. That because of his long overseas service the Lieutenant had few acquaintances among local Army personnel. That he occasionally went to said bar when off duty and that his social relations with the proprietor were friendly and cordial though not intimate.

Assume further Doctor, that at approximately 9:00 P.M. on Wednesday, July 30, 1952, the wife of this Lieutenant went to the bar to get some beer and play shuffleboard and that the Lieutenant was in bed sleeping when shortly after he was suddenly awakened. He hurriedly got up and thereupon heard a scream. That he then met his wife at the door of the trailer. That she was sobbing and breathless and hysterical. That she finally told him that the proprietor of the bar had threatened her life and assaulted and raped her. That she was badly bruised and beaten. That her skirt was ripped and her under pants were missing. That the Lieutenant spent upwards of an hour attempting to calm and comfort and minister to his wife. That during this time she told him the details of the threats and assaults and beatings. That during this time he wiped a fluid from his wife's leg which he believed to be semen.

Assume further Doctor, that this Lieutenant believed that the man whom he believed had just assaulted, threatened and raped his wife was an expert pistol shot and that he kept pistols about his premises and possibly on his person. That he himself kept a loaded Luger automatic pistol in his trailer for protection. That his mind was in turmoil over what he believed had just happened to his wife and over her present condition. That he finally determined to seek out said bar proprietor and grab him and hold him for the police. That while he felt considerable anger and loathing and contempt for the bar proprietor he had at no time any intention of killing or harming him but if the man made one bad move he would have killed him.

That he went and got his pistol without his wife's knowledge and left his wife in the trailer and proceeded toward the bar. That he does not remember what time it was or precisely how he got to the bar. That he finally got to the bar and entered it. That he saw the proprietor standing alone behind the bar watching him. That he then advanced to the bar and produced his pistol and pointed it at the proprietor and emptied its contents into his body, leaning over the bar to do so. That he had and has no conscious recollection of his act. That he then turned and left the bar and proceeded toward his trailer. That he does not remember anything after he entered the bar other than as indicated until he got home to the trailer. That he then first observed that his pistol was emptied; that he then told his wife that he had shot the bar owner.

That he then notified a deputized caretaker of the trailer camp and said caretaker called the police. That he was subsequently arrested and charged with murder. Assume further, Doctor, that this man had never before in his lifetime ever been arrested for or convicted of any criminal offense, including any act of violence toward another human being.

Doctor, assume all the facts herein stated to be true, have you an opinion based upon a reasonable psychiatric certainty as to whether or not it is probable that the hypothetical man was in a condition of emotional disorganization so as to be temporarily insane?"

"I have." The Doctor replied.

"What is that opinion?" Cory asked.

"That he was temporarily insane."

"Doctor, have you an opinion as to whether or not he was suffering from a temporary mental disorder at the time the deceased met his death so as to be unable to distinguish right from wrong?" "I have."

"What is your opinion? Cory again asked.

"That he was unable to distinguish right from wrong."

"Have you an opinion as to whether or not at that time he knew, understood and comprehended the nature and consequences of his acts?"

"I have" "What is your opinion?" "That he was not."

"Was, or did not?" questioned Cory.

"That he did not" replied the Doctor.

Cory continued "Do you have an opinion, Doctor, as to whether or not he was in such a state of mind that he did not have the benefit of his conscious reasoning mind, and rather was dominated by instinct and the unconscious mind?"

"I have an opinion" stated the Doctor.

This was like pulling teeth, thought Cory. Why didn't the Doctor come out and state exactly what the Defense Attorney wanted him to state, instead of all the going around and around.

"State your opinion"

"That he was dominated by the unconscious mind"

"Now , Doctor , would you state on what you base these opinions?" "Upon my personal knowledge of this hypothetical man" replied the Doctor.

Susan interrupted" May it please the court, if I understand the Doctor-he is not basing it on the hypothetical question, he is basing it on something else. In which case I would have to object and ask that his answers be stricken."

" I am not quite sure that the Doctor- " Judge Anderson began.

"We will reserve our decision on the answers to the question propounded after the statement of facts and the last answer may be stricken. I am not quite

sure that the Doctor understood what you are getting at, Mr. Defense Attorney. He has answered these preliminary questions and as I understand what you want to know is how he arrived at that or what he uses as a basis for his answers. They are not particularly based on any examination that he made of the respondent in this case. He may have some psychiatric explanation for certain behavior which might or not apply to this man but would give the basis for his answers to the question.
I think that is what you are getting at-"

Cory states" I'll try again"
Judge Anderson sticking to the script states" I don't think he understood. Ask it over again."

"Doctor, state whether or not you have a psychiatric basis for these opinions." "I have" replied the Doctor

"Tell us about that. These psychiatric basis?"

"The situation that you described in this question is one that would constitute a psychic shock for almost any man. It is one that would so disturb the equilibrium , the mental and emotional equilibrium of a man that would result in an almost unbearable tension. As a result of such a tension a man would have to seek some immediate means of alleviating it" explained Dr. Smith.

"Now, Doctor, going back to this hypothetical man-you may state whether or not the thing that this hypothetical man appears to have done would be consistent with the opinions you have given" Cory stated.

Susan jumps in" Are you still referring to the question and not his personal examination?"

"I said the 'hypothetical man'" replied Cory.

Susan sighed "Very well"

"It would. Now in psychiatry is there a name to what you believe to be the mental state of this hypothetical man at this time and of which we are speaking?" Cory inquired.

"There is. It would be a dissociative reaction."

"Doctor" Cory continued" Is this mental state or condition-has it ever been alluded to or described in other words?"

"It may be known in lay language as a trance-like state or spell"

"State whether or not, Doctor, that this mental state which you are describing is sometimes known as irresistible impulse?" Cory was pushing to have this label.

The Doctor replied" in this mental state that I refer to the individual is very likely to be driven by an irresistible impulse or an overwhelming urge. It is specifically this urge that |I referred to when I said that the man would have to seek some means of alleviating this tension. The necessity to alleviate this tension is irresistible."

"I ask you whether or not, Doctor, in your opinion this hypothetical man in the mental state you have described could have or would likely have gone to a fifty-eight year old unarmed caretaker and asked him to grab the bar owner and hold him for the police?" Cory asked.

"Such behavior would have been incompatible with everything else you enumerated in this hypothetical question. The things you have enumerated in the hypothetical question indicate that this is certainly a hypothetical man of honor, a man who would sense that personal security depends upon self respect, self esteem, ideals and honor. To have such a man at this particular point turn to a fifty-eight year old caretaker would have been simply incompatible with the hypothetical man up to this point. The Doctor continued" I would not attempt to explain any circumstances under which such a hypothetical man could do such a thing".

Cory continued this line of questioning" Doctor, I ask you whether or not in your opinion this hypothetical man would have gone to seek to grab and hold the hypothetical proprietor of this hypothetical bar-whether or not he, the Lieutenant,- "Susan interrupted" This is supposed to be hypothetical. We should keep it that way".

Cory responded" it is hypothetical Lieutenant all through."

"No" stated Judge Anderson.

Susan states" He is the hypothetical man"

Doctor Smith inserts " In the state in which this

hypothetical Lieutenant was at the time he would have gone to the hypothetical bar with or without a gun, whether or not the hypothetical proprietor had any hypothetical guns available, and whether or not he knew that they were there.

I think it is important to understand that the very essence of this hypothetical man's manhood was at stake here. And in that the presence or absence of an alternative course-consideration of its significance or any course of action could not have prevailed against this over-powering need of alleviating the tension under which he was. The need to alleviate this tension took precedence over everything else."

"Doctor, can you explain why this need involved the hypothetical bar owner?" Cory asked.

"It was the most natural thing under the circumstances that the efforts to alleviate this tension would be directed against the hypothetical cause of the tension.

The hypothetical precipitator of this tension. In your question you indicate only such conditions that would make it clear that this is a man of action. This man could not suddenly have started to behave in a condition so completely foreign to him as to philosophically have thought about this matter. Action was the thing that was essential." The Doctor outlined.

"You may state whether or not this hypothetical

Lieutenant might have done this while feeling angry toward the hypothetical bar owner."

"This man might have felt anger among all the other emotions he would be capable of feeling at that time." The Doctor stated. "I would think it would be impossible to limit that emotion-there would be an appeal to anger"

"Doctor, I ask you whether or not this mental state or condition of which you speak would necessarily interfere with the manual or physical abilities or manual dexterity of the hypothetical lieutenant, as for example his ability to produce a gun and aim it accurately"

"It would not" explained Dr. Smith." Indeed it might even facilitate whatever activity this man was following."

"Have you seen such phenomena in your experience as a psychiatrist?

"I have seen and I have heard-I have heard of it from those in whom the phenomena took place."
"Give us an illustration; an illustration-" Cory began.
Susan Yang" may it please the court, I don't believe we should go into illustrations or we may be here six months"

"Objection sustained as to the illustrations" Judge Anderson ruled. Cory changed tactics.

"With the courts' permission I would like to move away from the hypothetical man and get back briefly into the other. As to what the Doctor did with the real Lieutenant..

Doctor, you may state whether or not intensive and extensive psychiatric observation and examination of the individual is important in reaching psychiatric conclusions about his mental state"

"I would say it was essential" The Doctor stated.

"Can you explain that? More?" asked Cory.

"To understand that a particular experience would be a shock to one man or to another man does not necessarily require personal observation" The Doctor explained.

"To understand why the particular shock would result in a particular intensity observation would be absolutely necessary"

"You may state, Doctor, whether or not you would venture or attempt to pass a psychiatric opinion on the mental state of either the hypothetical Lieutenant or the real Lieutenant Grange on the basis of sitting here during the days of this trial." Cory probed.

"I would consider it impossible to pass my professional opinion on the state of this man's mind on or about July 30th and immediately thereafter on the basis of what I have observed here in the past few days" The Doctor pointed out.

"You may state whether or not in your opinion you would consider valid a psychiatric opinion-"

As Cory was speaking Susan interrupted" I object. I

see what it is headed for"

"Objection sustained" Judge Anderson ordered,
Cory thought Oh no! Now there is a stop sign for the defense. All this hypothetical stuff. This hypothetical Lieutenant and hypothetical bar owner and hypothetical case and hypothetical man stuff was going to lead to a hypothetical loss for the defense.

"You may state whether or not you have attended some of the sessions of this trial"

"I have attended some portion of each session since the beginning" responded Dr. Smith.

"You may state whether or not if you had just come in this door from Detroit and had not attended any of the sessions whether it would have affected your psychiatric opinion in this case." Cory imputed.

"I believe that would be unintelligible" Susan stated, and she continued" There are several opinions. Some based on one thing and some on another."

Judge Anderson rules" We have two angles of attack with this witness, one on the hypothetical question and the other based on actual examination over a period of some three days. I have no objection to the form of the question if you will restrict it a little bit. I did not want a broad question which might apply to all. It might make a difference but ask the Doctor."

"I ask you whether or not you consider your presence at this trial is necessary to pass the psychiatric opinion you have on this hypothetical man." asked Cory.

"Up until I stepped on the stand yesterday afternoon my presence was not necessary for me to pass my opinion." The Doctor explained.

"And that-State whether or not that was on the basis of your intensive and extensive psychiatric examination of the real Lieutenant Grange." "It was" replied Dr. Smith

Cory continued" You may state, Doctor, whether or not your answers to this hypothetical question are based upon your examination of the real Lieutenant Grange." "They are"

Susan "I object, and ask that they all be stricken from the record and the Jury instructed to disregard them"

Judge Anderson" I am not sure"

Susan " That would take them out of the realm of hypothetical question and would not be admissible"

"Your honor , all of the testimony of Dr. Smith, and all of the time we spent on a hypothetical case, and all of the negotiations between us and the Prosecutor should be honored and this is the basis for our defense. It should be allowed and not stricken from the record. We had an agreement that our expert Dr. Smith would testify and that the Prosecutor's expert psychiatrist could also testify;

and if the Prosecutor's Psychiatrist as a witness testifies to the contrary to what Dr. Smith testified then the Jury will have to take both Doctor's testimony into account when deliberations begin" Cory explained.

" I will let the questions and answer remain" Judge Anderson states. "In that case I have no more questions for Dr. Smith" Cory states.

"And I have no questions as I would rather present my expert psychiatrist, Dr. Archibald with what I feel will be rebuttal evidence" stated Susan.

"Fine. Dr. Smith, Thank You and you may step down" Confirms Judge Anderson."And we will take a one hour break for lunch

Thirty-Four

After the 'one hour break for lunch' which of course was one and a half hours we commenced.

"Dr. Joseph Archibald can you tell the court what your credentials are? You are the head of Psychiatry at Philadelphia General, is that correct?" asks Sara.

"Yes, that is correct. I have worked as a Psychiatrist for over twenty-five years and I head up the department at Philadelphia General"

"Now Dr. Archibald, your Statement under Oath

was given to the Defense and filed with the court and will be in the court record so we don't have to spend a lot of time on the contents so I would like to ask you some questions concerning the presentation and testimony of Dr. Smith, which I ask you, are you familiar with?"

"Yes, I read a transcript of his testimony, and I was actually present today when he completed his statements" replied Dr. Archibald.

"Good. Let's proceed". Stated Susan Yang acting as Prosecutor.

"First what is your opinion of this hypothetical presentation of a case that was entirely hypothetical and linked somehow to the real case, the Trial of Lieutenant Grange for a real murder"

"I object to the phrasing of that introduction and it is a leading question!" Cory insisted.

"Well , Counsel, I will allow it. Let's get on with this trial, otherwise we will never finish" Stated Judge Anderson.

"OK. Dr. Archibald Can you tell this court your opinion as a psychiatrist of the case that has been presented as a hypothetical case; and also your opinion concerning the theory of the Lieutenant being temporarily insane while committing the murder of the bar owner Barney Milton?"

"Well first of all, I will review and discuss the hypothetical case theory. It is fine to put forward a hypothetical case and ask a number of questions concerning that hypothetical case however it is as it is named hypothetical and not based on true fact. In a hypothetical case you can insert any facts you want, and you can bend the truth to lean towards your intended message. This is not a finding of fact but a finding of facts anyway it is presented"

"Yes but Doctor, wasn't the hypothetical question based on true facts in this real case?" Susan queried"

"Sort of. A lot of the information was put into the hypothetical case based on the real case however a lot of the information was never presented to the Jury through witnesses but only presented as hypothetical so really the Jury should disregard most of the story"

"I object. I object to this witnesses' summary of the case" stated Cory. "Doctor Archibald is supposed to be giving alternate psychological theory based on Dr. Smith's testimony solely and not bring in new information, as we had agreed, or give his own personal comments about the case. His testimony should be struck."

"Mr. Defense Attorney is correct, Dr. Archibald. Please stick to your testimony as a psychologist, not a court reporter." Judge Anderson ruled.

The defense which the Defense has been able to pull out of their Doctor and have him call it irresistible impulse has not been used in this state since 1886, and there is a good reason. That defense suggests that the accused was sane and only temporarily insane during a short period of time during which he committed the act of murder , and by some miracle the accused shortly after committing the murder recovers from the 'spell' and returns to his normal self.

I have reviewed the statements of both the accused and Dr. Smith and I state that the Lieutenant's state of mind before, during and after he pumped a whole lot of bullets into the bar proprietor's body was that of a sane person who , after picking up his pistol at his trailer had planned all along to kill the bar owner in retaliation for the bar owner in assaulting, beating and raping his wife whom he loved unconditionally.

"Well, Doctor Archibald, Can you explain why the Defense theory is flawed? What do you have to tell this court about the defense theory of irresistible impulse?" Susan prompted.

" Well , in my professional opinion we must apply the right and wrong test. The Defendant here , it is stated was a soldier participating in World War II and the Korean War. He had participated in many killing sprees and had seen numerous and terrible killings of human beings. He was law abiding. He was never charged with a criminal act. He never before exhibited any symptoms of mental illness, and he was not being treated for any signs of stress or post war symptoms.

He observed the law in all his everyday living, and he definitely knew what was right and what was wrong. Most of the courts in this country adhere to this right and wrong test, and they continue to disregard all criteria of mental depravity.

The Lieutenant had many options open to him besides grabbing his Luger and going direct to the bar and shooting the owner. The Lieutenant was not under the influence of alcohol or narcotics and more than the ordinary person knew what was right and what was wrong. The Lieutenant had not been diagnosed, ever, or even by Doctor Smith, who testified here today, as having psychoses or neuroses. It appears that the Defense Attorney picked neurotic behavior as his preferred defense.

The Lieutenant's defense lawyer, respectfully did his own analysis of his client to discover a diagnosis of a neurotic behavior in order to put forward the defense of temporary insanity."

"Please go on" Susan urged.

"Well , what I oppose is that the Lieutenant was never diagnosed with any form of neurosis or any other even symptoms of possible dementia or any psychoses so why does he suddenly have it for perhaps sixty minutes of his life.

The Lieutenant because he had been in the Army most of his life, and because of his strict adherence to right and wrong would not have grabbed a pistol, and would not have gone to the bar alone, and would not have pumped all the bullets in his Luger into the body of the bar owner or into any human body; it was not in his demeanor. He had options. He could have searched out the deputy caretaker of the trailer camp and , after telling him the story, they both could have gone to the bar to confront the owner. Or the Lieutenant could have called the Police immediately and have them accompany him . The village is small, and the distances close. The police could have arrived quickly.

The symptoms of dementia were not present in Lieutenant Grange. He was not frustrated, nor was he failing in life. In fact he had lived the life he loved in the Army, and he now had a wife who was not only beautiful but who he loved and she loved him. Insanity whether permanent or temporary was not in this persons' DNA. Any passion or temporary eccentricity that was present due to the fact he learned that his beloved had been assaulted, beaten and raped did not warrant exemption from responsibility for his act of shooting the bar owner. He cannot be classified as having Intellectual insanity as he was fully aware of right and wrong. He was not classified as having perceptional insanity as he was not and did not suffer from any illusions or hallucinations; for if he did and they were determined to be real that would be a valid defense.

He may have been diagnosed with emotional

insanity however his long career in the Army probably would have offset any possible diagnosis as Lieutenant Grange definitely showed that he had sufficient capacity to recognize that the act of murder was wrong, then mere passion or emotional insanity caused by anger or jealousy could not be brought forward as a defense to relieve him from criminal liability for his act of murder."

Doctor Archibald rested and asked for water, which was brought to him, and then he continued.

"In this trail the Defense has picked volitional insanity or as he has been able to get into the record irresistible impulse. The problem is this defense must be accompanied by a measure of intellectual insanity where the defense fails, as Lieutenant Grange definitely knew what was right and what was wrong.

Now let's look at some of the tests we use to determine criminal responsibility if there is a defense of temporary insanity; First there is the wild beast rule and this was laid down in 1724. The accused , in order to take advantage of it, had to exhibit traits of a wild beast. The accused

Was either a raving maniac or he was completely sane. This rule was in use before the advent of any psychiatric research and was never recognized by the courts of this country.

Second the Lord Hales rule is that a man to be responsible for crime must have the capacity and understanding of a normal child of fourteen years of age, but this rule is not in use as the courts have never recognized mental depravity as a defense in criminal prosecutions.

Last the right and wrong test is used in all the courts of this country except in Rhode Island and New Hampshire, where no legal test of irresponsibility by reason of insanity exists.

Irresistible impulse as defined by the courts is an impulse "induced by, and growing out of, some mental disease affecting the volitive, as distinguished from the perceptive powers, so that the person afflicted while able to understand the nature and consequences of the act charged against him and to perceive that it is wrong, is unable, because of such mental disease, to resist the impulse to do it."

Irresistible impulse is not to be confused with mere passion or an overwhelming emotion not connected with a diseased mind. The State of Wisconsin , notably reject it by court decision. Those repudiating it state it is harmful because it gives too great immunity to the accused."

Doctor Archibald then summarized.

"Here we have an act of passion, committed by someone who definitely knew right from wrong and was not diagnosed with any form of mental illness; and who as we stated previously had the time and ability to select any other form of punishment without shooting many bullets into the body of Barney Milton. He was not under any pressure to shoot or kill in a specific time nor was he under stress to kill in a limited time. He was not in my professional opinion and by the profession of psychiatry temporary insane or under an irresistible impulse in his act of killing Barney Milton."

"Thank You. Dr. Archibald" Susan put forward.

"I have no questions" Cory stated.

Cory was of the impression that his Dr. Smith's testimony and three day intensive testing of his client would stand up against Dr. Archibald's review and there was no reason to cross examine Dr. Archibald as that might bring up new evidence that might help the Prosecution.

"You sure you don't want to ask any questions?" Johnny inquired.

"No , Johnny. We are fine." Replied Cory.

"All right! Your next witness please Mr. Defense Attorney" called out Judge Anderson.

Now the proper procedure at trial would be for the Prosecutor to bring out Jessica Grange (Lieutenant Grange's Wife) as a witness for the Prosecution , however Susan Yang knew that if she did that she wouldn't be able to ask leading questions or act as cross-examiner because Susan actually suspected there was more than meets the eye in the statements by Lieutenant Granges' wife about being assaulted, beaten and raped by Barney Milton.

Jessica Grange was a vivacious , knock-'em-dead, woman who had a reputation of foolin' around with various men in the area.

If you talk about some men who couldn't keep their thing in their pants, well Mrs. Grange couldn't keep her pants on. Any breakdown of Jessica Grange's evidence could severely harm the defense's position. So an agreement was made that Jessica Grange would be brought forward as a defense witness; and Cory had to agree because he needed the Lieutenant's wife to state on the record that she was assaulted, beaten and raped by Barney Milton in order to collaborate her husband's story.

Lieutenant Granges' wife Jessica takes the stand and is sworn in by the court clerk.

She is dressed in a white pantsuit with no makeup and white shoes with a red rose pinned to her jacket. Her hair is done up in a beehive, and she is wearing black horn rimmed glasses, looking like a library assistant who possesses at least one or two master's degrees.

Cory begins with easy questions.

" Mrs. Grange. How long after you told your husband what had happened did he leave the trailer?"

"I don't know exactly. Everything was a blur. I was very tired and lying down on the bed in the trailer and he was sitting beside me. I thought he had gone out to get a doctor and then suddenly he came back in. I must have fallen asleep. The next thing I saw him sitting beside me on the bed with a gun in his hand and I said "What are you going to do?"

He said " I think I've already done it. I think I killed Barney Milton!"

"Are you sure he didn't say I've killed Barney Milton" Cory inquired.

"No. I remember exactly. He said I think I've killed Barney Milton"

"What happened then?" Cory asked.

"I put my arms around him and started to cry and I said you better go to see the deputy caretaker here at the trailer camp." And he said " I forgot about him"

"What did he mean- forgot about him?"

"He meant he forgot that the deputy caretaker was a Deputy Sheriff and he could talk to him"
He said " OK I will turn myself in to him"

"That's all the questions I have for this witness" Cory states.

"All right Madame Prosecutor, your witness" the judge proclaims.

Thirty-Five

Susan Yang, who's head was buried in transcripts and notes, looks up and gets up and starts her cross-examination like she was smashing potatoes in a pan on the stove; and was nearly starving, so she had to smash those potatoes quickly.

No fooling around just go right for the jugular.

"Mrs. Grange, May I complement you on your pantsuit today! Is this what you were wearing on the night of July 30th ?"

"No"

"What were you wearing, Mrs. Grange." Susan inquired.

"Well it was really hot, so I had on my shorts and a blouse" answered Jessica Grange.

"What was your job before you were married to Lieutenant Grange?"

"Housewife" replied Jessica Grange.

"You mean you were a housewife before? So you were married before?" inquired Susan.

"Yes, once"

"What happened to your first Husband? Did he pass away?"

"No"

"Did you divorce your first husband to marry Lieutenant Grange?" Susan knew the answer.

"Your honor, if counsel wants to know the grounds for Mrs. Grange's divorce-let her ask that question" Cory interrupted.

"What were the grounds for the divorce of your first husband. Mrs. Grange?"

"Mental cruelty" Jessica Grange replied.

"Naturally. How long was it after your divorce that you married Lieutenant Grange?"

"I'm not sure. I don't know!" stated Jessica Grange.

"May I refresh the witness's memory for the Prosecutor?" Cory asked.

"By all means." Susan replied.

"I believe she told me they were married three days after the divorce" Cory says.

"Judge, is my attorney allowed to say things that I told him. I thought what we tell our attorney is private and secret and cannot be divulged" Asked Jessica Grange.

"Well first of all, you are not on trial here Mrs. Grange. Your husband is. And the Defense Attorney is your husband's attorney so what you told him is not in confidence. But anyway do you dispute what he said?" Replied and asked Judge Anderson.

"No, he is correct" sighed Jessica Grange.

"So unless yours was a whirlwind courtship you must have know Lieutenant Grange before your divorce from your first husband. Is that correct?" asked Susan.

"Yes"

"What is your religious affiliation, Mrs. Grange?"

"I am a Catholic" replied Jessica Grange.

"A Catholic in good standing?" Susan inquired.

"Well, no-the divorce-you know."

"You mean that you have been ex-communicated because of the divorce?"

"Yes". Jessica confirmed.

"Mrs. Grange, If I say to you that a Catholic who completely ignores a cardinal rule of her church can also easily ignore an oath taken on an affidavit or an oath such as you took today to tell the truth, that you would agree?" Susan fishing.

"No, I don't agree" answered Jessica Grange.

"But wouldn't you agree that there might be some doubt about the integrity of such a person?"

"No. I don't think so. I don't know. All I know is the Catholic faith means a lot to me and I stick to its' rules" Jessica tries to explain.

"I see. Well. Let's go on to something else" Susan finalizes.

Susan had stood between Jessica Grange in the witness box and Cory at the witness table so Cory moved a little to his right, but Susan moved again and blocked Cory's view.

"Mrs. Grange, on the night of the 30th you left the trailer when your husband was sleeping, correct?"

"Yes, he was asleep" answered Jessica.

"Was part of the reason for going to the bar without telling him was that you were upset with him?" Inquired Susan.

"A little. I was ironing and cleaning all day-and he come s home and goes to sleep-yes, I was upset."

"Mrs. Grange have you ever gone before to the Bar or anywhere else in the village or close to the village before-alone at night?" Susan fished.

"Yes. Sometimes" Jessica replied.

"Did your husband know when you went out alone? Or where you were going?"

"Not always. He goes to sleep early and sometimes I'm restless."

"Where did you go on those occasions?" asked Susan.

"I used to walk by the lake or sometimes I went to the bingo place or maybe to the Cocktail lounge and bar"

"Did you ever go to meet another man?

"No. No I did not. Never. I never did that!" Jessica Grange raised her voice. "And I don't like what you are asking or suggesting"

"Well Mrs. Grange, It's my job to get at the truth" Susan replied.

"So, Are you saying I'm not telling the truth" Jessica asked.

"Mrs. Grange, do you mean to say that a lovely women like yourself, attractive to men, lonely, restless-that you never.."

"Objection, Your Honor" Cory jumps in and interrupts. "The witness answered the questions about other men. Counsel is now making a veiled suggestion for the jury"

Susan "I withdraw the question. Now Mrs. Grange , on these occasional travels into the night , did you always go and return alone?"

"Absolutely.   Definitely " responded Jessica Grange.

"Mrs. Grange, in your affidavit you stated that you got into Barney Milton's car that night because you were afraid to go home alone. Why on that night?"

"Because Barney had told me that bears were seen around the village."

"Was this the first time you had heard of bears being seen around the village?"

"No" replied Jessica

"Had you ever seen bears around before?"

"Yes"

"So then that night was the first time that you were actually afraid of them?

"No. I was always afraid of bears."

"Then this was the first time you were afraid enough to allow a man , who you know was drinking heavily, to not only take you home, but to drive drunk and take you home from one of your evening excursions as you prowled the night"

"Objection" Cory began."The use of the word 'prowl' is intended to mislead the jury."

Judge Anderson." Sustained. Ask the question again

without the use of the word prowl"

"I apologize Mrs. Grange. I didn't intend to imply that you were a huntress-so let's say , 'evening stroll'. Was this the first time you were scared enough of the bears to let someone take you home from an evening stroll?"

"But it wasn't just that-it was a sort of-" Jessica began.

"Come on, Mrs. Grange, you must be able to tell us right straight off. It's a simple question. Please tell this court with a simple answer. It's simple Mrs. Grange-Was this the first time you were scared enough of bears to let someone take you home or did it happen before? Mrs. Grange have you been taken home before by other men? Tell us the truth, Mrs. Grange." Susan pushed for an answer.

Cory inserted. "Your honor, my friend, the Prosecutor is badgering the witness. She is not allowing Mrs. Grange to answer. How can the witness answer if counsel interrupts? And in addition I object to the 'have you been taken home before by other men' question which is leading, misleading and implies something to the jury which has not been proven nor was it brought up in pre-trial hearings. I would like the whole question struck from the proceedings"

"The witness seemed rather slow in answering to me, Mr. Defense Attorney." Judge Anderson rules. "However I will let the witness complete a statement and answer if she can. Madame Prosecutor, please do not interrupt the witness, and let her answer one question at a time."

"Definitely, your honor. Anyway the Defense Attorney's objections have given Mrs. Grange lots of time to ponder an answer to my question. Mrs. Grange you have an answer, don't you?"

"What I was going to say" Jessica Grange commenced. " was that I didn't want to get Barney upset by making him think I was afraid of him, or that I didn't like him. He had been very nice to my husband and me whenever we visited his bar."

"So you purposely put yourself in danger by entering an automobile which was to be driven by a drunk through the woods in the dark to your trailer. Good Mrs. Grange. Very good" replied Susan.

"Your honor" Cory started.

"Attorney for the People will save her comments for the summary arguments" Judge Anderson stated.

Susan continued" I ask you this question, Mrs. Grange. Was this the first time you had been in Barney Milton's car at night?"

Jessica Grange hesitated and looked around the courtroom.

"Mrs. Grange, did you hear the question?" Judge Anderson asked.

"Yes, I heard. Yes it was the first time" Jessica said while looking down.

"Mrs. Grange. I believe the Jury did not hear you. Can you raise your voice a little and answer?"

"I said it was the first time" Jessica Grange repeated.

"OK. Mrs. Grange let's talk about the lost panties. Can you describe the panties to the court?"

"They were just underpants" replied Jessica Grange.

"What color? What material? Anything special about them. Where did you buy them? Susan blurted out like a machine gun.

"They were nylon and had lace up the sides. They were white I believe. I bought them in Los Angeles at a shop called *Under there*."

"What do you mean I believe. Don't you know what color underpants you were wearing?"

"No. I have white and pink. I don't remember which one I was wearing that night."

"You are not sure? Haven't you checked your lingerie drawer to see which pair of panties is missing?" Susan asked.

"No"

"When your husband came home from work and before he fell asleep and you went out were you already dressed to go out?" Susan I inquired.

"No"

"When did you dress?"

After he was asleep?"

"There have been reports and in affidavits from witnesses that you were bare-legged in the bar. Is that true?

"Yes."

"In your rush to get out of the trailer once your husband fell asleep and you being a little upset with him , maybe you didn't put on any panties, is that possible?" Susan asked.

"Objection. The witness has already testified as to what she was wearing." Cory inserted.

"Sustained." Judge Anderson
Susan continued." Do you always wear panties, Mrs. Grange?"

"Your honor, I object to this line of questioning. It's not material what Mrs. Grange does all the time. It's only important that on the 30th of July when she was attacked that she was wearing panties. That's all we're concerned with." Cory imputed.

"Your honor" Susan explained." Mrs. Grange seems uncertain about what kind of panties she was wearing and since these panties have not been found I submit that it's possible she wasn't wearing any and has forgotten. That's what I'm trying to get at."

"Take the answer, Mrs. Grange"

"No. I don't" replied Jessica Grange with tears building up in her eyes.

"On what occasions don't you wear them?— when you go out alone at night?" asked Susan.
Cory "Your honor, we've been deceived. The prosecutor says she is only after one thing and then she goes after another"

"The objection is sustained. Strike the last two questions and Mrs. Granges' answer. Now get off the subject of panties, Ms. Yang. You have done enough damage." The Judge states.

"Yes, your honor. Is your husband a jealous man, Mrs. Grange?"

"Well, he, he loves me."

"Yes he has told us that, but is he a jealous , excessively jealous lover?

"I object to the question, your honor" Cory breaks in" How can the witness answer that? How is jealously measured?"

"Can you put your question in another way, Ms. Yang" asked the judge.

"Has your husband ever struck you in a jealous rage, Mrs. Grange?" asked Susan.

"Your honor, I think Ms. Yang is fishing. What is the relevancy of this question?" asks Cory.

Susan replies. "Your honor, this is a murder trial not a high-school debate. It's a cross-examination in a murder trial."

"Well, get to the point quickly, if you have a point in this line of questioning, Ms. Yang!"
The Judge was explicit and for some reason had changed from referring to the Prosecutor as Madame Prosecutor or Prosecutor to Ms. Yang, but anyway that didn't matter.

"Mrs. Grange did you ever go out socially when your husband was stationed in Green Bay?"

"Yes, a few times."

"And when your husband's outfit moved into Green bay, didn't Barney Milton throw a cocktail party for the officers and their wives in a small bar he owned in Green Bay?"

"Yes, he did" answered Jessica Grange.

"Did your husband hit a young second Lieutenant at the party?"

"There was a little scuffle, it wasn't much" stated Jessica Grange.

"What was it about?"

"I'm not sure. I don't remember."

"Was it because you were too drunk to remember?" inquired Susan.

"No, I was not drunk. I think the Lieutenant was cutting in too many times when I was dancing with my husband."

"And isn't it true that shortly afterwards didn't your husband slap you hard enough that you fell against the wall?"

"He was drinking." Explained Jessica.

"And apparently so were you, excessively!" Susan stated" And wasn't this a jealous rage when he struck you?"

"I don't know"

"Do you remember why he struck you, Mrs. Grange?"

"Well, yes."

"Wasn't he enraged at you because he thought you

had encouraged this young Lieutenant?"

"He might have thought so." Replied Jessica.

"Mrs. Grange, there are witnesses to this whole affair. I'll ask you again—wasn't this jealous rage?"

"I supposed it could be called that" responded Jessica.

"Now I will ask you –on the night of the shooting, what did you swear, in your affidavit, what did you swear to?"

"It was about Barney Milton raping me."

"Why did you swear that he had raped you, Mrs. Grange?"

"For the reason that my husband said-I was hysterical" Jessica replied.

"That was the reason he gave you to ask you to swear an affidavit? What was your reason for swearing the affidavit?"

"So he would believe me." Answered Jessica

"Why shouldn't he believe you?" asked Susan.

"Objection, your honor" Cory interrupts. "The reason for the swearing of the affidavit have been answered. These questions are immaterial."

"No, I think the witness should answer. Ms. Yang proceed"

"I ask you again, Mrs. Grange, why shouldn't he believe you?"

"I guess – I guess because I wasn't making sense. I was hysterical and I was mumbling.

I couldn't repeat exactly what had happened .

Perhaps I was in shock" replied Jessica.

"Did he think you were lying about a thing like that?" Susan asked.

"Objection." Cory " Lieutenant Grange has already testified as to what he thought"

"Sustained" The Judge ruled.

Susan continued" Did your husband strike you that night?"

Jessica Grange did not respond. Her lips moved but no sound came out. Tears were starting to make their way down her cheeks.

"Did he hit you that night?" Susan repeated.

"He—maybe—he might have slapped me because I was so hysterical."

"And so didn't you swear to a lie to keep him from hitting you again, Mrs. Grange?"

"No—I didn't—I did not." Answered Jessica Grange. "Didn't he already beat you up at the gate to the trailer park when he caught you coming home from a trip down lovers' lane with Barney Milton?" probed Susan. Cory jumped up faster than Susan could finish her question" Objection. The witness has testified that she was beaten by Barney Milton."

"No more questions" Susan finishes. Jessica Grange is in full crying mode now. Tears flowing. Tissues out. Nose wiping. "I think the witness has had enough, your honor." Cory puts forward.

"The witness may step down. We will break for lunch and continue after." The Judge announces.

Thirty-Six

Lunch was quick, the sun was shining, and the recent snow storm was forgotten.

Several of Johnny's relatives , including his sister had decided to join the audience and were sitting in row three, although Johnny's sister was so big she took up three available seats , and two of the public had to sit outside.

Judge Anderson asked" Does the prosecutor have other rebuttal witnesses?"

"Yes we will call Robert Hunter to the stand" Susan replied. "Will the Sheriff please bring in the witness?"

Bill Bob Jones, a real Deputy Sheriff assigned to Cornell for the past twenty years always relished his part in these Mock trials, where he could act as a Sheriff , even for a few minutes, it was his fifteen minutes of fame , well actually three minutes, and he dutifully went out of the room and returns with the witness. In the meantime Lieutenant Grange appears to be pale, lips dry, eyes afraid. The Sheriff returns back into the room with the 3rd year student who will act as Robert Hunter; and he has a crooked smile on his face, and struts into the room , and is sworn in at the witness box.

"What can he tell?" Cory asks Lieutenant Grange.

"Nothing-he can't tell nothing" answers Grange.

"State your name for the record"

"Robert J. Hunter" answers the witness."Folks call me Bobby"

"Where do you presently reside, Mr. Hunter?" asks Buchold.

"Across the alley, in the jail".

"Do you know the defendant. Mitchell Grange?"

"Yes, Definitely, sure"

"How well do you know him?" asks Buchold.

"I got to know him the last few weeks. His cell's next to mine."

"Being neighbors , I suppose you frequently have conversations with each other. Is that true?"

"Yeah we talk" answered Hunter.

"What was the last conversation you had with him?"

"Well, except for a hello this morning, the last one was last night." Answered Hunter.

"Are you sure Mr. Hunter, that the Lieutenant said, "I've got it made—Buster?"

"I object to this line of questioning-It is leading" Objected Cory.

"Sustained. Mr. Prosecutor you cannot put words into this witnesses mouth- He has to come up with "I've got it made-Buster. Not you. Re-word the question so it is not leading." The Judge ruled.

"OK. Mr. hunter last night did the Lieutenant talk about this trial?"

"Yes , sir. And he said 'I've got it made-Buster!"

emphasized Hunter.

"And did he say anything else?"

"Yes sir. He said that when he got out the first thing he was going to do was beat and kick that bitch from here to Milwaukee." Replied Hunter.

"Do you know who he was talking about?"

"His wife" responded Hunter.

"Your witness, counselor" Buchold said with confidence.

Cory looked around the room and looked at the Jury and they were fidgeting and slouching and leaning. It looks like a couple of days of trial was too much for them, thought Cory. Time to wake them up with some theatrics.

"Mr. Hunter, what are you in jail for?" Cory began.

"Arson. I made a deal and copped out and I'm waiting for sentencing" Hunter replied.

"How many other offences have you committed?"

"You mean how many I committed or how many I got caught or how many I am in the

Clank for?" asked Hunter.

"Never mind. Did you discuss this trial last night?"

"Some. A little."

"Tell the court what Lieutenant Grange had to say about the trial, Please." Cory demanded.

"Well, I said how are things, are they looking up, Lieutenant?

And he said "I got it made, Buster.' He said I fooled my lawyer and I fooled that head shrink and I'm gonna' fool that bunch of hicks on the jury." answered Hunter.

Cory was ready to ask another question when Lieutenant Grange jumps up and yells"

You're a liar. You're a lousy stinkin' liar! You bum!"

The Judge raps for order and Cory pulls Grange back down into his chair.

"Your Honor, I don't know who is the worst offender-Grange or his lawyer.." Susan shouts.

The Judge rules" Look we are close to the finish. Can we have peace and courtesy for these last few hours. Cory you will continue your interrogation without comment. Ms. Yang will not object at every opportunity and the defendant will remain seated and keep quiet." The Judge raps his table with a bang of his gavel.

"How many times have you been charged with offences?" Cory asked.

"Huh-Oh – well, I was in reform school when I was a kid. That's all." replied Hunter.

"Your honor" Cory starts" I would like to see this man's criminal record"

Judge Anderson "Do you have the record, Mr. Clerk?"

"Yes, Your Honor, here it is."

Cory flips through the cards and states" Mr. Hunter, this record shows you've been in prison six times in three different states. You've been in three times for arson, twice for assault with a deadly weapon, once for larceny. It also shows you've done short stretches in four city jails for the charges of indecent exposure, window peeping, perjury, and committing a public nuisance. Is this your true record?"

"Well, them things are never right" Hunter says.

Cory walks back to the Prosecution table, angrily tosses the record on the table. Susan acts embarrassed, but Buchold says nothing.

Cory asks " Mr. Hunter, how did you get the ear of the prosecution in order to tell them about your conversation with Lieutenant Grange?"

Hunter replies " The District Attorney was taking us to his office.."

"Taking who to his office?" Cory asks.

"Us prisoners in the jail." Hunter responds.

"He took you all at once or one at a time?"

"One at a time. Him and that other lawyer took us to his office and asked us questions about Lieutenant Grange." Confirmed Hunter.

"Were you promised a lighter sentence if you would go on the witness stand?"

The People object, Your honor, to being…" Susan began.

"Overruled. Take the answer" The Judge demanded.

"I wasn't promised anything." Stated Hunter.

"Perhaps you just thought it might help your own troubles if you dreamed up a story that would please the D.A?, right?"

"I didn't dream up nothing" Insisted Hunter.

"And you're sure that's what Lieutenant Grange said?" asked Cory.

"Yep, I'm sure."

"Just as sure you were about your criminal record?"

"Well , I kind of forgot that."

"I don't feel I can abuse the court resources and all the participants here by asking this criminal any more questions." Cory states.

"No further questions, Your Honor" confirms Buchold.

"Your Honor I would like to bring my client back as evidence to the contrary concerning Mr. Hunter" Cory states.

"Of course, bring him up" The Judge responds.

"Lieutenant you heard the testimony of the last witness, Mr. Hunter?"

"Yes"

"Is any part true?"

"None"

Lieutenant have you ever talked with this man?" Cory asked.

"Yes"

"What did you talk about?"

"Nothing important. Certainly nothing about my personal life"

"That is all I wanted to ask." Cory finished.

Dave Buchold started" Lieutenant Grange , Have

you ever had any sort of trouble with Hunter?"

"Trouble? I don't know—you mean an argument—something like that?"

"Did you ever attack Hunter—physically attack Hunter?" asked Buchold.

Lieutenant Grange looked over at Cory for help.

"Your Attorney can't answer the question for you, Lieutenant Grange. Did you ever physically attack Hunter?"

"I wouldn't call it an attack. I pushed his head against the bars one day" answered Grange.

"Why?"

"He said something ugly about my wife."

"Do you clearly remember pushing or bumping his head against the bars? Because it is recorded by the jail staff, Lieutenant?"

"Sure. I just told you"

"Then that was not an irresistible impulse. Right?"

"The defendant is not qualified to answer that question" Cory states.

"Sustained" The Judge chips in.

"Lieutenant Grange, wasn't your action against Barney Milton, the bar owner the same as your action against Hunter or the 2nd Lieutenant you slapped at the cocktail party—all done in the heat of anger, with a willful, conscious desire to hurt or kill to get back at whoever angers you?" asked Buchold.

"I don't remember my actions against Barney Milton"

"How long did you know your wife was meeting up and hanging around with Barney Miller?"

"I never knew anything like that. I trust and love my wife."

"You just occasionally beat her up for the fun of it, I suppose." Buchold states.

Cory jumps up and yells" Objection. Objection. Objection. There has been nothing established to permit a question like that. The Assistant Prosecutor should be ashamed for taking such liberty. He keeps trying to insinuate without ever coming to the point or proving his point.

Let him ask the Lieutenant did he ever beat his wife."

"I will sustain the objection." Judge Anderson says."Mr. Buchold please refrain from those type of questions. Do you want to re-phrase your question?"

"No thank you your Honor. I'm finished."

"Did you ever beat your wife Lieutenant?" Cory asks.

"No sir"

"Is there any doubt in your mind that Barney Milton assaulted and raped your wife?"

"No sir." Replied Grange.

"That's all" Stated Cory.

"Nothing additional" stated Buchold. "And no other witnesses."

Lieutenant Grange , after stepping out of the

witness box and sits next to Cory asks" I'm sorry, I should have told you about Hunter. Are we hurt?"

"Bad" answers Cory.

"Does the defense have any rebuttal witnesses?"

"Your honor, before I answer that can we take a short recess?" Cory asks.

"Of course, see you in forty-five minutes."The Judge replied.

Forty-five minutes and more had passed and everyone was back except Cory.

As per the transcript of the real trial he stayed away a little longer.

Susan looked at her watch and asked the judge" Your honor respectfully, how long are we going to wait for Defense Counsel?

"Clerk of the Court , will you see if our Defense Attorney has gone fishing?"

The Judge inquired.

Just then Cory enters the room. "Your Honor, I apologize for being late. I know have a rebuttal witness. The defense calls Barbara Quinn to the stand."

Dave Buchold states" Your Honor, we must protest this witness being brought forward at this late time in the trial. We were not previously advised. We cannot be blindsided like this.

This is just another trick by the Defense to influence the jury. It's another back country lawyer shenanigan."

"Cory replied. "Your Honor, I don't blame the Prosecution. I'm just a humble country lawyer trying to do the best I can against this brilliant Prosecution team from the big city. If the Prosecutor wants to delay this trial we can have the witness prepare a statement by affidavit and a Will-Say statement, however that means a delay."

"No. we don't want to delay. In fact we want to finish soon."Stated Buchold.

"Present your witness"

"Where do you live, Miss Quinn?" Cory began.

"At the New Lake Michigan Inn."

"Is the Cocktail Lounge and Bar in the Inn"

"Yes. On the main floor facing the lake." She confirms.

"How long have you lived there?"

"For two years" Barbara Quinn answered.

"What is your occupation Miss Quinn?"

"I manage the inn"

"Was Barney Milton your employer"

"Yes."

"How is the laundry handled in the inn?"

"It's sent down a chute into the laundry room." She stated.

"Where is the chute located on the second floor?"

"Between room 42 and 43."

"Who lives in those rooms?" Cory asked.

"I live in 42 and Mr. Milton had lived in 43."

"Would Mr. Milton, coming up from the lobby have

to pass the top of the chute on the way to his room?"

"Yes."

"Could he easily drop something into this chute as he passed by?"

"Yes. Just open a door and drop whatever in." She confirmed.

"Now in the laundry room, what is done with the laundry?" Cory asked.

"The sheets and slips are sent out and the towels are put into a wash and dry machine there in the room." Barbara explained.

"When are the towels checked?"

"As they are taken from the wash and dry machine."

"Do you check them?"

"Yes. That's part of my job."

"Will you tell this court what you found among those towels on the day after Mr. Milton was killed?" Cory prompted.

"I found a pair of women's panties." She responded. There was a hush in the room and most of the jury were shocked by this revelation.

"What did you do with them?"

"I threw them in the rag bin"

"When did you learn of the importance of those panties?"

"Here, during testimony."

"Did you go to the Inn and get them from the rag bin?" Cory inquired.

"Yes. I was afraid that after so much time they wouldn't be there, but there they were."

Barbara Quinn opens her purse, removes a pair of women's panties and hands them to Cory.

"Please enter this as exhibit for the defense your Honor. They are white, have lace up the side and are badly torn—as if they have been ripped apart. The label reads: *Underthere/L.A.* " Cory proclaimed.

"If there are no objections the exhibit will be received in evidence as an exhibit for the defense." The Judge announced.

"Thank you Miss Quinn, That's all the questions I have." Cory says.

Dave Buchold gets up" Did you ever talk to any of the investigators concerning Barney Milton's killing?"

"Yes. Under questioning did you tell my assistant that you didn't believe Barney Milton assaulted and raped Mrs. Grange?"

"Yes" replied Barbara.

"Did you ever talk to the Defense Attorney or anyone working on the Defense?" Asked Buchold.

"Yes."

"Was this also in connection with the shooting of Barney Milton?"

"Yes"

"Did you also tell them you didn't believe Milton had assaulted and raped Mrs. Grange?"

"Yes"

"How many times did you talk to the Defense Attorney or his staff?"

"Twice" answered Barbra Quinn.

"When was the last time?"

"Last night" she responded.

"Now have you changed your mind about Barney Milton?" Buchold probed.

"I, I, don't know now. I think he may have."

"When did you change your mind-was it last night?" He asked.

"No—I, It was here, this morning."

"When were you given the panties? Was it last night, Miss Quinn?"

"Wait a minute, wait. I object to that question which insinuates that Miss Quinn was given the panties" Shouted Cory. "Actually, wait, I withdraw the objection. Miss Quinn answer. "

"No. I was not given the panties last night or any other time. I found them , exactly like I said."

"Did you know for a fact that Barney Milton dropped the panties into the laundry chute or did you just assume that he did, Miss Quinn?"

"I assumed it" responded Miss Quinn.

"Is it possible that perhaps someone else had put them in the chute? Someone who wanted them to be found in the Inn laundry, Miss Quinn?" Buchold raised his voice every time he ended his question with Miss Quinn, as if promoting the fact that what she had been saying was lies, all lies.

"I hadn't thought about that" said Barbara Quinn.

"And the fact that the Defense Attorney put forward several theories about the shooting/killing of Barney Milton and the panties were brought out through questioning the witness Mrs. Grange you decided to rush in here with the panties because you wanted to crucify the character of the dead Barney Milton-isn't that right, Miss Quinn? Demanded Buchold.

"No, I decided it was my duty to…."

"Your pride was hurt, wasn't it? "You found the panties and didn't realize anything was associated with that, however when you heard in court what the witness said about Barney Milton assaulting her and raping her and tearing off her panties that your thoughts then was that Barney Milton might have raped Mrs. Grange—or was it that he may have been hanging around with Mrs. Grange" Buchold pushed.

"I don't know what you mean. Your Honor what does he mean?" asked Barbara Quinn.

Judge Anderson says " Mr. Buchold Please ask the witness with a question that is straight and simple and not confusing."

"This is a straight question. Were you Barney Milton's mistress, Miss Quinn?" Buchold asked.

Barbara Quinn started to cry.

"No. No. I was not!" She insisted.

"Do you know that it's common knowledge in the

village that you were living with Mr. Milton?"

"That's not true. Barney Milton was---" Barbara Quinn was sobbing.

She looks at Cory hoping he can jump in-but he can't."Come on Miss Quinn, admit it, Barney Milton was your lover." Buchold pushed.

"He was my father" she cried out.

Dave Buchold is stunned and doesn't know how to proceed.

"No more questions, Your Honor"

"That's it for me" Confirms Cory.

"The witness may step down" The Judge states. " We will recess for fifteen minutes and then we will hear closing arguments.

I ask both counsel to be brief and to the point."

Both counsel were brief and to the point and the Judge gave instructions to the Jury.

Four hours later the Jury returns with their decision.

The foreman speaks for the jury.

"We find the defendant not guilty by reason of insanity"

Cory thought about what had happened after the real trial and after the jury had brought in their verdict.

Two days later the Lieutenant was examined by a psychiatrist who judged him sane, and he was released. The Lieutenant and his wife were divorced soon after.

Cory and Susan both received high praise from

Professor Anderson.

"Johnny let's go home. I'm exhausted" Cory proclaims.

"Yes, sir. And my sister says she is ready to give you a great massage , which obviously you need." Johnny says.

"No Johnny. No. Anything but that. Anything" Cory insists.

Thirty-Seven

There was fog on Island Road like the fluffy clouds that you fly through ,and there was morning mist with enough remaining to make the road a little slippery. The spray coming up from the back wheels of Cory's Honda sprayed dirt in the air, as the speedometer needle hit 60.

"Cory, please slow down" Elayne implored.

"I thought you liked going fast?"

"Ye, but I also like living!"

"Ok , Elayne. Anyways we're almost there".

Cory turned left onto Fralicks' Beach Road and into the parking lot adjacent to the Baagwating community center. He parked the Honda in front of The Great Totem.

"I'm home. I missed it".

"What?"questioned Elayne.

"That. The Great Totem. I grew up with it.

See the markings and drawings portray my people, The Ojibway".

"What do they mean?"

"Well, at the very top is the symbol for Ke-che-mun-e-do, The Great Spirit. Under that is the symbol for An-ish-in-aub-ag, who lived when the Earth was new, and they congregated on the shores of a great salt water. From the bosom of the great deep beings appeared in human form, and from them originated the five great clans. Today eight-tenths of my people are comprised of ,from the top, Uj-e-jauk, the Crane; Man-um-aig,the Catfish; Muk-wah, the Bear; Waub-ish-ash-e, the marten; Mah-een-gun, the Wolf; and Mong, the Loon".

"Cory, What clan are you from?""Bus-in-as-see, The Crane ,of course!"

"But, I thought you said Uleejak,or something like that meant Crane".

"Uj-e-jauk. Yes ,but Bus-in-as-see literally means 'Echo-maker', pertaining to the loud, clear, and far reaching cry of the Crane. Our clan possesses a loud, ringing voice and we are the chieftains over all the other clans. That is why my grandfather is the chief , and his father before him, and his father before him, and so on".

"Oh, Ok". Elayne sighed. She knew the significance and had an idea of the history around Cory's disclosure but right now didn't want to pursue Cory with any more questions about the Totem as she was lost after the first "Kecheemando" or "Muncimundo" or "Couchee-Couchee" , or whatever.

Cory and Elayne approached the dilapidated wooden structure that served as an-all-in-one community center, hospital, dining hall, and meeting place for the once mighty Mississauga of the Ojibway Nation.

"Don't be shocked or surprised by what you see". warned Cory.

The never-oiled hinges squealed as Cory pushed open the wooden door leading into the community center. Lit only by some daylight filtering through the never cleaned windows along the wall on the right side Elayne stumbled and almost fell, catching herself at the last moment, and avoiding crashing onto the dirty, rotting floor.

Elayne could hear the loud chatter from what she recognized as a television coming from a room at the far left end of the big room that served as a meeting hall.

Cory and Elayne entered that room with trepidation of what they may find. Something was wrapped up in that white Hudson's Bay Blanket , and as Elayne and Cory approached Elayne could just make out the features on the very wrinkled, weathered face.

Elayne had met Chief John Littlehorn several times before, but not in the past ten years, and his current appearance startled her. He was eighty-seven but he looked one-hundred-and seven. More wrinkles than face, she thought. He had the distinct hooked nose of the Ojibway; the always-tan, and the straight black hair-mixed with grey and balding on top.

Hair down to his shoulders, and a one inch wide beaded head band across his forehead. One beaded and feathered earing in his left ear with nothing in his right ear except the remnants of a hole that had an earring, previously. Unshaven, perhaps for three to four days or more. Elayne was really surprised by his thinness, for it seemed he was only skin and bones; perhaps not more than ninety pounds by her estimate, and she recalled him as a big man. His head was down with his chin resting on his chest. His eyes were closed and Elayne feared the worst.

"Is he ok? Is he alive? Is he breathing? Check his breath. Is he moving? Elayne's staccato-like questioning was irritating Cory "Wait a second, will-ya?"

"Elayne, turn down the volume on that television so I can check him out-it's too loud".
Elayne gingerly tried to remove the remote control from the Chief's right hand and was more than startled when the Chief slapped her hand with his left. She jumped back as if seeing a corpse come to life. The dry, course hand had scrapped across her hand like sandpaper going across a peach.

"Who are you? And what are you doing here? And what do you want?"
Elayne was shocked with the strength of that voice that had just come out of that emancipated being wrapped in that blanket. Good English too!

"Grandpa, It's me, Cory!" yelled out Cory ,trying to compete with the television.

"Elayne, turn down the sound. Forget the remote-use the buttons on the TV" He shouted.

Elayne pushed the down volume button just as Dustin Hoffman was going into one of his long speeches in his role in Little Big Man. Chief John Littlehorn rattled off the speech and mimicked every word perfectly as if he were playing the role himself.

"I could play that role better than that Hoffman guy, and be more authentic" explained Chief John."What is more authentic than an authentic Indian? What the hell is a Jewish guy, probably from Brooklyn, New York, doing playing an Indian from Wyoming, or Utah, or New Mexico or whatever. I don't understand it, Hollywood uses more non-native Indians to play Indians than real Indians. That's why all the native Indians are unemployed-because they can't play themselves in the movies or on television; and nobody uses them to play white folk so what the hell. Who's going to believe some Jewish guy or white guy with makeup is a real native Indian".

"You're right Pa" Cory placated.

Chief John continued, as if he was wound up" Did you hear about that guy 'Tonto' who played The Lone Ranger's sidekick? They never let him speak in the movies, and he was educated. The only thing he could do was grunt. Twenty years of grunting-no wonder we all got a bad rap. The white man thinks that all we can do is grunt. It's ridiculous".

"Your right Pa" Cory repeated.

Chief John Littlehorn never addressed his grandson by his adopted white man's name. As far as he was concerned his grandson, the future chief was to be known by his Ojibway name, and that was that.

"Boozhoo Kineu. Aaniin ezhi'ayaayan? "asked the Chief of his grandson.

"Nimino'ayaa"Cory-answered"Grandfather please speak the white man's tongue for this girl , Elayne does not understand the talk of the Ojibwa."

"Waenaesh k'dodaem?" inquired the Chief.

"She has no totem. I asked you to speak English. Elayne is not of any clan. She's Italian"

"What the hell kind of clan is that?" shouted the Chief.

"It's a special clan from across the great salt sea". answered Elayne.

"Uh, huh. "exclaimed the chief, "anyway grandson, I'm pleased that you have come to sit with me before I am called away by Gitche Manitou. Now listen I have much to tell you".

"Who is Gitche Manitou?" questionned Elayne.

"Gitche Manitou is the Maker of Makers, the Master of Life, he gives life and permits all things. I think my Grandfather is preparing for his last journey, and that is the reason I am here-to sit with him, and to listen to what he has to say. It might take some time. Do you want to go or stay?"

"I'll stay! Hell I might learn something".

"Go ahead Grandfather we're listening".

Chief John Littlehorn began." More than a century and a half ago, the country about Scugog Lake was clothed in virgin forest, and the great silences were disturbed only by such sounds as the whoop of our people. We were truly the First Nation. The other sound to be heard was the cry of the wild fowl. We called this place Wuh-you-wus-ki-wuh-gog to denote shallow muddy lake. At that time we were absolute Monarchs of all we surveyed. Your great great grandfather and The Mississauga, all sixty-four of them came from Balsam Lake near The Great Lakes, one called Lake Huron to make a permanent home on Scugog Island and this was the beginning.

Our history here is inscribed in the rocks, hills and valleys. We had for centuries before hunted, fished and trapped here in this fertile valley. And we traded furs with the white man who visited our camping ground just seven miles to the south of Nonquon Island.

But we knew not what the thin white man that we called Whites could or would do to harm our existence and one day in the white man's year of 1821 they came with their tools, their skill, and their purpose, and they came to have domain".

Cory had heard some of this before, but Elayne was mesmerized.

The Chief continued, "Gradually, where the forests were, there appeared the great open spaces, and the sounds that were only the whoop of our people and the cry of the wild fowl gave way to the white's scream of industry.

Wuh-you-wus-ki-wuh-gog, spoken slowly by our nation became Scugog, as though it was regurgitated at such a fast pace so as not to waste any time in saying it, for the white man did not at some point want to waste any time. And our sacred burial ground on the island was overrun by the whites, and the stones marking the spot broken and scattered.

The tide of white invasion flowed on both sides of the Scugog, north and south for many dawns. Before the whites came our home was clothed with forest and there were no roads or clearings, nor any other marks of man for we roamed and hunted the island amongst the animals that walked on four legs. We survived and prospered until your cousin Whistling Duck's brother O-go-ton-og-cut got a taste of the white's justice and The Battle of Purdy's Dam was the beginning of the end of our mastering of our island home. Purdy's Dam backed up water for miles flooding our homeland, and forcing us to retreat to this small island the whites called Scugog Island. Many fowl and fauna were drowned, and our life was changed forever.

We were forced to grow and cultivate our food from the land, and live off of the whites' charity and hand outs. We were once several hundred and now are reduced to sixty poor souls, and are destined to be eliminated one by one as we are called up by Gitche Manitou.

Grandson, as you know I wanted to restore our nation to again be Monarch of all we survey. I have tried and did not succeed; and now the body I am in is too feeble to achieve the task.

Son, you are named Kineu – War Eagle and in our tradition you have not spoken this name yourself; but I must tell you it is I who bestowed this name upon you as a gift and it is uniquely yours. Now I am asking you to take up the task that I could not finish. I do not want you to make war on the whites, but I want you to act as a Kineu, and 'see your vision.' Do you understand my son?'.

"Well, grandfather, what do you mean 'see my vision?'

"Kineu, No man begins to be until he has seen his vision. You will understand when the time comes, and I know you will act correctly, for you are the grandson of a Chief, who is the grandson of a Chief, who is the grandson of a Chief, and so on.

Kineu, take my hand in yours" implored Chief John Littlehorn. Cory moved closer and took his grandfather's hand in his.

"Kineu, you are now Chief . You are courageous and with foresight, and I want your promise here that you will restore our nation to again be sovereign over our lands and property, and be prosperous and grow with dignity and respect, as we once were."Cory hesitated. "Coreee!" exclaimed Elayne.

"Ok. I promise. I promise. Grandfather I promise!"

"All right Elayne get into your bathing suit and let's go meet the chiefs!"

"Why my bathing suit?" asked Elayne.

"Because where we have to meet them is in the sweat lodge" Cory answered. "Here, put this paint on my forehead, cheeks and chin."

The steam coming from the grass bunches on the hot rocks was so thick in the sweat lodge that Elayne could not tell how many Chiefs were in there; but she could barely see the outlines of at least four or five human-like figures in the mist. One was sprinkling water over rocks in the room's center.

"Boozhoo "Cory exclaimed.

"Aaniin ezhi'ayaayan?" One of the chiefs inquired. "Naimino'ayaa" answered Cory to tell the Chief he's fine. "My Grandfather has named me *Kineu War Eagle* , and he has entrusted me with the task of restoring our nation to again be sovereign over our lands and property , and I know he has talked to all of you to prepare for this day; and this day has come. In the tradition of our people now is the time to share the burden in order to have our people again become *"Anishinabeg"* or *"first people"* as is our calling.

Now is the time to bring your white man's money to help build the Great Blue Heron. Now is the time to instruct the Ottawa, the Pottawatomi, the Ojibway; and the Sauk, Menominee and Algonquin –now is the time to build. I ask for your help now !" Cory waited for the response he knew had to come. Sharing is a highly valued virtue among his people. Ensuring the well-being of the entire community and support of the Totem was paramount.

One by one each Chief moved out of the steam to approach Cory. Without talking each dropped his drumstick in front of Cory, which is the ultimate form of respect. After all six had passed Cory exclaimed, "Miigwech , Mino'ayaag!". And Cory knew he had their support.

"What did you say to them? Asked Elayne as they exited the sweat lodge. "I thanked them and wished them all be well". "What now?" She asked.

"Now we have their support in money and workers but I need your help as well". "I can't do too much" Elayne stated. "Whatever you can do, you can do. OK?" "Sure Cory, I'll help." "Thanks, now let's go visit the Mayor".

Thirty-Eight

The town council of Port Perry consisted of five elderly, conservative church going men and one woman ; and Mayor Kay Aldred who as Mayor for the past twenty-one years ran her town with an iron fist. In the past two elections she has had opposition by both Baxter Smith, the local Minister, and recently from Raeburn Shaw , the real estate multi-millionaire , who moved to Port Perry ten years ago and acquired a lot of property to develop. Mayor Kay has been able to hold off any challenges by these two men because of her popularity, but in council disagreements and posturing happen.

Cory and Elayne were ushered into the basement of the old church just as the meeting had started.

"Cory, nice to see you again. How's Ithaca?" inquired Mayor Kay.

"Great!" answered Cory.

"All right. Now before we give you two minutes to explain yourself I just want to inform you that the Town will remain neutral, just as we did ten years ago, on construction of the Blue Heron. But any bad publicity for Port Perry will not be tolerated!"

Mayor Kay Aldred was firm on that matter. She was forever protecting her town. She knew that she has no jurisdiction over what goes on in "Indian

Territory" however she could make it difficult for the "Indians". She had heard about the meeting Cory had with the Chiefs. She knew Cory was placed with the burden of building the Great Blue Heron Casino by his Grandfather; and she knew it was an almost impossible task.

Mayor Kay was also against gambling . She was aware that if the casino was built probably it would bring the dregs of society to, or through Port Perry; and in addition her people would succumb to the evils themselves.

"Ok Cory! What do you want to say?" as Cory surveyed the room. He did not necessarily need council support; he just did not want them to oppose building of the Casino.

Five conservative Church attending men and one women. Pasteur Baxter Smith definitely opposed the casino.

Cory was not so sure about Multi-Millionaire Real Estate Magnate Raeburn Shaw. Mildred Pierce worked at the bank and might vote his way.

The other council members were George Fitley, a garage mechanic; Sidney Waterson who ran a restaurant on Main Street ; and John J. Smitherson , Jr., whose family had lived and worked in and around the area for at least one hundred years. John, Jr. owned and controlled probably five or six local businesses. A Casino opening would benefit John, Jr., Waterson, and George Fitley. Port Perry was a quiet town, only recent construction of new homes and townhouses were bringing new residents. Probably seventy-five percent of the population were elderly. A Casino would bring much needed dollars into local business.

"You have heard that I have been entrusted with completing the building of the Great Blue Heron Casino by my Grandfather; and I have the support of all the Chiefs and my people."

Cory explained. "We will start construction in the next few weeks and finish hopefully within four months. I am asking for your support as I know that the Casino will be good for Port Perry. Can we count on Police, Fire and Emergency Services doing their job? Can we have your support?"

Baxter Smith jumps in quickly." We will not support any Casino in our area because this causes an increase in crime; brings in prostitution and undermines my work at the church. I am losing parishioners as it is. I don't want to compete on Sunday Morning with the Blue Heron. I will vehemently oppose construction just as I did before".

Raeburn Shaw is next." Cory, even though a Casino would help my real estate business, I must oppose it due to my principles and support of our church and the good work done all these years by Baxter. I'm warning you now. If construction starts we will do everything in our power to stop it."

"All right! Let's vote on the issue." Mayor Kay stated." All in favor?"

Three council members meekly raised their hands. John, Jr., Sidney Waterson, and George Fitley. All businessmen and Mildred Pierce was about to join them when Raeburn Shaw whispered to her that he held the mortgage on her house.

"All against?". Asked Mayor Kay and three council members raised their hands. Mildred Pierce, Baxter Smith and Raeburn Shaw. A tie so it was up to Mayor Kay.

"I won't vote on this issue. It does not change any by-law, alter any street, move any monument, or change Port Perry today in any way, shape or form. I believe the casino will not be built. There is too much against it. However I must warn you Cory, again. We don't want any bad publicity for the town. Everything is running smoothly. The residents are happy here. I will keep the council neutral , but don't upset the apple cart or I will get involved. Do you understand?"

"Yes, Ma'am". answered Cory. Outside the Church basement Cory and Elayne were reviewing the council decision when Raeburn Shaw stepped up to Cory.

"Cory! Can you come over around seven?"

"You mean to your house on fifth?" Cory inquired. "Yes. And come alone".

Thirty-Nine

Raeburn Shaw had bought an old mansion on fifth street and had added at least ten rooms, an outdoor pool, a tennis court, and a garage for seven of his vehicles. It was outrageous as it overpowered the street and the townspeople always wondered how he got this all approved by council.

Cory parked on the circular driveway and went up the circular staircase to ring the bell at the front door.

Audrey, Raeburn's trophy wife , opened the door. Raeburn was in the midst of an awful divorce case with his wife of twenty-five years. A case that was dragging on and costing Raeburn hundreds of thousands. Audrey was Raeburn's wife , and half his age.

"Hi Cory. Come in. Raeburn is in the library."
Raeburn Shaw had made millions developing real estate in the big cities and had moved to Port Perry ten years ago to semi-retire. His idea of semi-retirement was to dump his wife, marry his secretary half his age, acquire one third of all available land in and around Port Perry, and live in his mansion while developing the land he acquired.

A tall man, gray almost white- haired , handsome for his age of sixty-three, with modern glasses looking like a banker in a three piece suit.

An MBA at Harvard had prepared him well for his vocation; and wealthy parents didn't deter from his evolution.

Cory turned left into the cavernous library where Raeburn perched eating a sandwich and sipping green tea.

"Tea, or a sandwich?" offered Raeburn Shaw , the Real Estate Magnate.

"No thanks. Why did you want to see me?" queried Cory.

"I have an offer that you shouldn't refuse. I will build the Blue Heron for your people however I want control of the shares." Exclaimed Raeburn while picking his teeth for sandwich remnants.

"No thanks. I cannot give up control. We will build it ourselves. Thanks for your offer-but no thanks. So long.".

"Cory. The only way that you will build that casino is with my help. I promise you that without me you will not succeed. In fact not only will you not succeed but I will make sure you fail and bankrupt your nation. I will break you and your people down and stomp them into the ground and you will suffer humiliation like never before. Your holy burial ground will be overflowing Do you know what I am capable of? Do you? You little son of a bitch." Raeburn demanded an answer.

"Goodbye Mr. Shaw". Cory stormed out of the library and headed for the front door.

"Cory, Answer me. Do you know what I can do to you? Your finished without me!". Cory ignored the demand for an answer, went out the front door, down the circular stairs jumped into his car, drove out of the circular driveway, and headed for home.

Raeburn Shaw picked up the telephone in his library and dialed a number he had not called in ten years since he moved to Port Perry.

"Yeah." Exclaimed Homer Webb.

"Who's calling?"

"It's Raeburn! Get over here right away."

"Okey-dokey". Responded Homer.

Homer Webb had resided on the island near the Indian land since he was born forty-two years ago to illiterate parents who had never married. A farmer and alcoholic, Homer consumed at least ten beer each day. This was his life. Never married. Lived alone. worked the field in the morning while consuming as much beer as he could; and consumed as much beer as he could in the afternoon while sleeping it off in the field or on a hammock behind his farmhouse. Homer never shaved or groomed. His black beard rested on his chest and his shoulder length pitch black hair was tied in pony tail style behind his head. His black horn rimmed glasses were broken on the top left and held together with a band aid.

Homer was referred to by the town residents as "a

little touched". He had currently no friends and drank alone.

Homer parked his pickup truck in the circular driveway of Raeburn Shaw's mansion and hobbled up the circular stairs. He belched once up the stairs and once before ringing the bell. He dusted off the cow dung and field dust from his overalls and was surprised when Audrey opened the door.

"Holy Shit. Who are you?" he asked.

"I'm currently Raeburn's wife. Come in. He's waiting in the library, over there."

Audrey pointed to the first room on the left.

Homer entered the library and noticed Raeburn in the far corner. He hadn't seen him for several years but he still remembered how much he detested the rich son of a bitch.

"Homer. I have a job for you. I am sure I don't have to remind you that I own your farm and house and that you are living there rent free for the past ten years because of me. I promised way back then that I would not divulge your little secret to anyone and I won't if you do this work for me." Stated Raeburn.

"Yeh but you said ten years ago that everything was finished and that I could live there forever in peace and quiet."

"Well I've changed my mind." responded Raeburn" Now if you don't do what I want I will tell everyone what happened back then. And you know I can do that and will without hesitation!"

"Yes Sir. I understand. What do you want me to do?". Raeburn moved closer so he could whisper to Homer, and the exchange would remain with them.

Antonio Briganti had supervised the building and had built a lot of casinos in his twenty years of construction experience since he developed and sold the eighty store Little Italy Pizza Chain. Antonio looked at the skeleton of the Blue Heron from a distance; walked around it twice, climbed up a temporary ladder to view the beams and said to Cory "No problem we'll get it built!"

Cory had signed a contract promising Antonio Briganti that the Chiefs would finance the construction and Briganti would wind up with five percent ownership upon the casino opening. Antonio Briganti in turn promised construction would be completed in four months. "Where can my men stay in the meantime?". Asked Antonio.

"We will find them space with our families." answered Cory.

Meanwhile Baxter Smith looked out over his congregation. He personally knew about seventy-five of the one hundred in this community. They listened to him intently during his Sunday sermons. Homer Webb gave up farming and drinking on Sundays in respect of the church and Baxter Smith who he liked and honored.

Homer always attended Sunday Mass and sat in his regular seat two rows from the back waiting for Baxter to start.

"Welcome to church today!". Baxter Smith began." We have a problem that is starting to surface in our community-and you all know what I'm talking about. I'm talking about a casino that is being built. A casino that will bring horrors into our midst. A casino that will bring prostitution, gamblers, gangsters and the like onto our streets. An institution that is diabolical and opposite to our beliefs. We cannot allow this casino to be built. Unfortunately, your town has no jurisdiction over the Indian territory so we must act in other ways to stop this evil. You will descend into fiery hell if you allow this casino to be built. Mark my words you are allowing your homes and families to destruct".

Baxter Smith's face was a deep red color and sweat was pouring down the sides of his head and staining his white shirt as he worked himself up while giving this sermon. He continuously wiped his head with his old cotton handkerchief.

Baxter Smith continued his diatribe and filled his words with streams of abuse, bitter harangue and a verbal onslaught many of this assembly had never heard before coming from a Minister such as Baxter Smith. He was clearly agitated.

His face became more red with anger as his denunciation continued.

Homer Webb had heard enough. He was

mesmerized. He was hypnotized. He knew what he had to do, and remembered the instructions from Raeburn Shaw as he slid out of his pew, walked quietly to the exit, exited into the early morning air mixed with a little mist hanging around from dawn and opened the door of his truck , entered and drove towards Island Road, with determination to complete his nasty task.

Forty

Mayor Kay Aldreds' phone rang four times before she could get to it. She wasn't happy being disturbed on a Sunday afternoon by the Chief of Police. Sunday was her day with the grandchildren and her day away from politics and the running of the town.

"Kay. I've got some bad news". The Chief began.

"John Keane of the 10th Concession found the skeletal remains of a body lying in a field along Ghost Road".

"O no!". exclaimed Mayor Kay." Who is it?" she asked. "We don't know yet. John was headed out early in the morning to collect bottles along the road which he does every weekend. About half a mile south of the 10th he noticed what he thought was a bottle in the field on the west side of the road. He approached it and noticed it was a pair of running shoes not a bottle. Moving closer he noticed blue jeans and what appeared to be the upper part of a skeleton of a person. He thought at first someone was playing a prank which is not uncommon along Ghost Road. He looked again carefully and was convinced it was a decomposed body so he called us. We questioned him and he hadn't seen the body ever in the past weekends when he was walking that route.

As you know Ghost Road is a real dumping ground for garbage. You just never know what you'll find there along those ditches. Of course John is really shaken about this finding."

"This is terrible!" exclaimed Mayor Kay. "Who is handling the case?".

"Well the case is being treated as a homicide so the investigation is being handled by Regional Police Detectives Timothy Clister and Roger Mitchell."

"Thanks Bill. Let me know if anything develops". Mayor Kay was more than upset with this news. She checked the phone book for Cory's home number , found it and dialed it immediately. The phone rang twice. Cory wondered who was calling him at this number. No one knows he's here in from

Ithaca. He picked up the phone with anticipation.

"Hello this is Cory".

"Cory , this is Mayor Kay Aldred. Things have started to happen and I want you to stop construction of the Blue Heron".

"Why? What happened?". "A decomposed body has been found on Ghost Road. I warned you about this.". "We will not stop construction. That body probably has nothing to do with our casino. No one is missing as far as I know. Don't blame us for something that has nothing to do with us or the Blue Heron!"

"Cory, I smell something. I told you I didn't want anything bad effecting our town and it's good people; and I don't like that construction guy Briganti , either." Mayor Kay hung up before Cory could say anything more.

The next morning the story appeared in The Port Perry Star. 'Police suspect a Homicide- Find skeleton of man on Ghost Road' 'Police say "left-handed person struck and killed person with repeated blows to right side of head.'

A story also appeared in The Tribune. 'Motorcycle myth?- Spooky legend haunts Ghost Road'' Police yesterday interviewed a local resident who had discovered a headless decomposed body along Port Perry's famed Ghost Road. The head was discovered a short distance away but was too decomposed for forensic officers to identify.

Long time Island Road resident Brenda Stroud believes that the body is that of the famed Ghost Road rider. Apparently around Halloween every year hundreds gather in Port Perry to look across the lake and see a dancing light that flickers down Ghost Road for several minutes. "It's a Ghost, says Mrs. Stroud matter-of-factly. There's definitely something out there, a spirit of some kind."

The Island's claim to supernatural fame is known as Ghost Road, an isolated dirt side road where some say a young motorcyclist was decapitated in an accident decades ago. As the legend goes , the rider so enjoyed the sensation of speed that his spirit continues to frequent the road. Some area residents believe the story while others say its hogwash.

The legend of the Ghost Rider began to spread in the late 1970s, but some say it has been around much longer. Mrs. Stroud has lived here for thirty years and she believes it's a Ghost. So do visitors as far away as the southern United States who flock here to do a little ghost watching by the picturesque shores of Lake Scugog. Police and hospital officials have no record of a motorcycle accident in the area however now with the finding of a body perhaps the Ghost story will be solved.

Julia Dixon , Star Reporter looked at the teletype in her office at The Evening Star and looked away with disinterest as she had for the past ten years . Another story coming across the wire ; another story that was already news. She glanced at the headline- 'Motorcycle myth-Spooky legend haunts Ghost Road'. She noticed it was out of Port Perry , that sleepy little town where nothing happens. Then she noticed the information about a body being found. This got her attention.

Julia came from a small town . She had an affair with a local , mothered a child and moved to the big city. Her daughter Amanda was now nine years old and on summer holidays. Maybe Julia will combine some investigative reporting with a little outing for her daughter.

"Jim". Julia tells her boss. "I'm heading up to Port Perry to check out that Ghost Story".

The Lazy Susan Restaurant was smack dab on Main Street corner of Lakeshore Road overlooking the park where the faithful gather on Halloween's eve to view the Ghost Rider. Julia started her interview of Brenda Stroud by asking her to tell her story. Julia is shocked and calls her boss and asks for funding to stay two weeks to further investigate. He refuses saying "No one is interested in another Ghost Story".

Julia believes this could be her big break. She calls her old school chum at Niagara College and tells her about the story. Three students are sent up to film on Ghost Road. Julia also calls fellow reporter

Jenny Munroe , now at CNN who says' keep me informed.' Julia also brings in Psychic Sondra Whyte who visits the scene on Ghost Road.

"Definitely a motorcycle accident occurred at the intersection of Ghost Road and Island Road. The light everyone sees is the spirit of the man in his early 20s with light brown , curly hair. He drives an old motorcycle. The rider, which Sondra sensed was a Dan or Dave Sweeney , supposedly lost control of his machine at high speed and was beheaded by an old rusty barbed-wire fence. Definitely his spirit remains riding the road."

The three Niagara College film students set up beside Ghost Road in a tent and make a short documentary which they called *Ghost Light on Scugog Island* .The third year students Marcy Ebert Stacy Mathers and Bill Witherspoon are not afraid. Bill takes a still photo of the light approaching him and brings the film to a lab in Port Perry and develops the film with Julia anxiously awaiting the result. Marcy and Stacy stay at the tent. The photo is developed and Bill and Julia are shocked.

"Look here , Julia. I've enlarged the photo and it is the outline of a human figure bathed in a bright aura."

"I've got to call Jenny at CNN". "This is big". exclaims Julia as she rushes to use the phone.

Jenny confirms to Julia that she will be' up

there' next week. Bill and Julia drive back to the tent at Ghost Road and find it empty.

"Where the hell is Stacy and Marcy?" asks Bill a little worried.

"I don't know". Julia Dixon , Star Reporter drives up to the compound and is shocked by the huge totem pole. After being directed to Cory's place she gingerly knocks on the door. She is surprised to see a handsome tall black haired well groomed man with slight Native Indian features.

"Cory Littlehorn?". She inquires.

"Yes, that's me".

"Julia Dixon from The Star".

"Oh Yeh , Right, Come in". Cory had put the phone away in a drawer but he could faintly hear the ring. After four rings he decided to answer.

"Hello it's Cory".

"Stop the construction of the casino or there will be trouble for you and your Indian friends".

"Who's this?". Cory asked.

"Never mind. Stop the construction immediately or else". The click of the phone being hung up lingered around longer than he wanted it to.

"Who was that? "asked Julia.

"I don't know" answered Cory.

Julia was a beautiful women. Thirty years old with blonde hair, blue eyes , and a wonderful light –up-your- life smile. Cory could not stop looking at her. "Want some homemade wine?". "Sure".

Julia was enticed by this good looking, black haired , native Indian with a well-built physique. She sat on the couch so close to him their thighs touched. He noticed the closeness of this stranger but didn't mind. Consumption of a second bottle of wine and some conversation and they were even closer. Julia tried out a quick kiss and after receiving no objection she continued her attempt to seduce him.

Cory was in no mood to object, and clothes came off quicker than soft pork coming off the rib bone . And then without knocking at the door in came Elayne.

"O my god! Cory , Who's this?".

Cory rushed to put his pants on and smooth his hair while Julia grabbed for a sheet to cover her white no tanned nakedness.

"Uh , Elayne this is Julia Dixon , Star Reporter. Julia , Elayne, local Psychic.".

"Pleased to meet you ". Julia uttered in apology.

Elayne Christofaro had never moved so fast. She bolted for the door like an Olympic runner in the half mile sprint, as tears started appearing on her cheeks before she exited and Cory noticed her distress.

He knew she cared but he never knew she cared so much. He blocked her way out. "Cory I need to find my Spirit!" exclaimed Elayne.

"What?   Why?" asked Cory, surprised. "Just

because you walked in on me with Julia, with our clothes off?""

"Partly, but mainly because I was living as someone else most of my life, and I need to find my Spirit and find out about who I really am. I am not Missy!"

"Who's Missy? Cory asked." and I thought I was hunting for my Spirit, my vision, as my Great Aunt Sara keeps screeching"

"Never mind. Missy is a long storey. Now that we are in the village bring me to the Mississauga at the Medical Centre"

"No! Let's go visit Great Aunt Sara" Cory replied.

Forty-One

Great Aunt Sara was one of the eldest, if not the oldest of the tribe. Her house was near the Medical Centre, consisting of two rooms in a wooden shack. The front door was unlocked , actually no lock, and Cory pushed open the door and peered inside.

"Great Aunt Sara. Are you here?"

A faint sound came from a bundle in the far corner.

" Yes. Who is it?" "It's Cory and my friend"

"You mean Kineu-War Eagle and a friend" Great Aunt Sara corrected Cory.

"Come closer" she requested.

"OK"

A small dim light bulb provided enough light to see Great Aunt Sara's face. Pockmarked, granite-like, eyelids half covering her eyes. All in all a well weathered, bronze collection of skin and bones mirroring a human in her nineties. Evidence of being a Native Indian with no make-up or any white man's trick cosmetics.

"Why you come here today, Kineu? I haven't seen your face for many moons?

"My friend is looking for her Spirit and since you are the oldest in our village you probably have the answer she seeks" explained Cory.

"Come closer girl! Come right close to me!" demanded Great Aunt Sara.

Elayne moved to within inches of Great Aunt Sara.

Great Aunt Sara then reached over to her left and picked up a tray with chalk, crayons, paint, markers, brushes, large and small.

"Sit still and do not be afraid as I apply some markings to your face, and then you will know your Spirit and who you are" explained Great Aunt Sara.

"I am afraid!" Elayne cried out. "Don't be afraid my young one. This will be your answer to your search, and from now on you will know who you are, and you will be pleased, and you will leave here in peace", answered Great Aunt Sara.

Great Aunt Sara's hands shook and were unsteady.

She first picked up a small brush and dipped it into the colors in the tray and she started to apply a blue color to Elaynes' right eyelid, with a swoosh a few inches long and one inch high towards the top of her ear, and black color under the right eye. Now using a brush dipped in green color Great Aunt Sara put six lines of symbols extending right from Elaynes' forehead top of her right eye down to her cheek and extending several inches below her right eye with one line of symbols extending drown her cheek almost level with her mouth.

The colors applied to Elaynes' face contrasted greatly with her pale white face and dyed blonde hair and the color around her right eye spoke of mystery and required explanation.

Great Aunt Sara put away the brushes, the tray, the other colorants, and Great Aunt Sara began to unravel the mystery.

"Twenty-six white man years ago our tribe searched for a new chief and a birthing took place in the Medical Centre.

"The first born was a girl and was removed quickly by scooter and delivered to that bastard Raeburn Shaw's house, in return for payment and secrecy; and that girl was you".

A twin was born next ,and was a boy and that was Kineu standing here next to you.

The Tribe needed a new Chief desperately to survive, and all the midwifes were sworn to secrecy, and to this day the truth has not been revealed".

"If you truly care for our community, that now you have learned is your community, I deplore you to also not reveal the truth".

"Your mother was Emily , a great woman who lived and worked in our community and taught us how to sew and produce crafts to sell".

 Unfortunately she drowned several years later."

" I have written and painted some symbols and words on your face just as our ancestors had many centuries ago, and I will now explain what these words and symbols mean".

Great Aunt Sara paused , drank some herbal tea she had in front of her, and continued.

" When you were born, and just before you were sent away by scooter ,we, the midwifes, scratched a symbol on a pendant and attached it to a silver necklace to protect you.

That symbol was not a wolf. It was a wolverine, and that is your Spirit Animal.

Of course you probably know that a spirit animal is meant to be a representative of the traits and skills that you are supposed to learn or have; and we believe that an animal who chooses you or you choose it to get guidance and learning to help you through life.

The wolverine is ferocious, strong, cunning and is a messenger between the real world and the spirit world.

Your totem spirit guide , the wolverine, can teach you to respond to challenges of life with great focus, and it looks like it has already taught you as you have had challenges of life, and you have responded with great focus. Part of the wolverines ferocious way is its tenacity and persistence.

Once the wolverine grabs onto something, it digs in with its sharp long claws and sinks its teeth in and seldom lets go. This tenacity will help guide you to a deeper understanding of your personal spirit." Great Aunt Sara was getting tired and started to close her eyes.

"Continue! Great Aunt Sara!" He demanded.

"The medicine of the wolverine is powerful, sometimes too powerful for the situation. It can teach you to regulate your relationships to maintain

an even hand, not too hard and not too soft"
explained Great Aunt Sara.

"Learning how to utilize your power in a
balanced way is one of the teachings of the
wolverine. Because of the wolverines cunning,
focus and tenacity it arranges its energies in a
straight, balanced line. This alignment allows them
to know the exact moment they should act and
when they should retreat. Knowing the situation is
what makes the wolverine such a worthy and
capable guide.

The endurance and strength of the wolverine
teaches us to have a stick-to-it attitude in life and go
the last mile to get what we want." Great Aunt Sara
irrigated her dry mouth with her herbal tea.

"Wolverines are slower than most of their prey,
but their cunning and willingness to be a scavenger
suits them and keeps their bellies full.
They are known to be nature's best survivor by all
who know them well because wolverines can make
do with whatever nature provides.

The wolverine is a master of its domain and its
skills and behavior is a great teacher. Primary traits
teaches us focus, clarity, endurance, emotional and
physical balance, and spiritual understanding.

The writing, symbols, and colors that I have
painted on one side of your face explains that your
spirit is the wolverine and invites you to complete
the other side of your face by adopting those same

wolverine traits." Great Aunt Sara rested.

"I thank you, Great Aunt Sara for the explanation and yes I will keep quiet concerning the information you have shared with me; and I am happy to have found my Spirit Animal and now I will continue to be known as Elayne Christofaro." Proclaimed Elayne.

"And what about me?" questioned Cory.

"You, Kineu, you know you are from one of the top five clans, Uj-e-jauk, the Crane. It is the Crane that possesses a loud ringing voice. The Crane is Chief over all the other Clans, so you must act as a Chief, and take charge."

"I thought I needed to search and hunt and find my spirit." Stated Cory.

"No" answered Great Aunt Sara.

"You need do no hunting or searching because you were born a Crane and that is your Spirit Animal. You must accept that that is what you are and representative of what you want to be, so choose the Crane just as the Crane has chosen you." Great Aunt Sara paused, drank some tea and continued.

"As I had predicted and yelled out many times over the years I said you must seek out the spirit and befriend him; and now you have another spirit beside you, the wolverine, to help you, and to guard the secret, and you must take possession of what you rightfully own, as Chief of our tribe.

And you must go out and seek the Ant and the Armadillo, the Bear and the Beaver, the Buffalo and the Butterfly, because you will need them all. And the Coyote and the Dog, the Eagle and the Elk, the Falcon and Fox, the Horse and Hummingbird, as well the Lizard and Lynx, the Moose and Otter, the Owl and Panther; and the Rabbit and Raven, and the Skunk and Serpent, as well the Spider and Squirrel and Turkey, Turtle and Weasel.

You will need them all.

Zaagi'idiwin-Love them all; Minaadendamowin-Respect them all; Gwayakwaadiziwin-Be honest towards them all; and be humble-Dabaadeniziwin, and bekaadiziwin-have patience and be calm and gentle and you will truly prosper."

"Thank you Great Aunt Sara" Cory exclaimed

Forty-Two

Homer Webb finds another body on Ghost Road also headless . Homer was questioned by the police about the headless remains. He denied having anything to do with it; and after several hours of interrogation he signed a statement. Regional Police Detective Roger Mitchell notices Homer signs the statement with his left hand but Mitchell says nothing.

The Police fear the body may be one of the missing students and urge the coroner to hurry up with forensic examination. The coroner comes out with his report.

"Mayor Kay. The coroner has come out with his report." states the police chief.

"So What does it say?"

"The first body is not that of a missing student but is that of a construction worker from the previous crew ten years ago when work stopped on the Blue Heron Casino; and this second body is also not that of a student but is unknown ".

"Oh! Well what do you know about that !".

Antonio Briganti was told about the bodies and his construction crew leave the half completed Blue Heron en masse and refuse to ever cross past Ghost Road.

Jenny Munro arrives with the CNN crew and sets up at the Library where the Mayor is holding a press conference in front of about fifty residents and parents.

"Now everyone remain calm. There is no need to panic. The body found on Ghost Road was that of a construction worker killed ten years ago. The second body is not a students. There is no reason to believe any harm has come to the two film students from Niagara College. Police are still investigating".

"Well we demand that the search be expanded and additional Police be brought in" stated Judy Ebert , Marcy's mother. "Yeh, expand the search "the crowd demanded.

"Why didn't you expand the search before" asked Jenny Munro of CNN. "Tell our listeners across the U.S. and Canada why you waited so long? What are you afraid of? What are you waiting for? And what's going on with this Ghost Rider?" The crowd started pushing forward. Some one in the front fell. Police try to push the surging crowd back. The crowd continues to push forward. Glass breaks. The police fire two shots in the air. Port Perry has never seen anything like this. Jenny Munro of CNN dubs Ghost Road another *Bermuda Triangle*. Two film students have disappeared without a trace for the past seven days and cannot be located. Mayor Kay Aldred is extremely upset.

Cory Littlehorn aka Kineu – War Eagle had to do something. The half finished Blue Heron could not sit through another winter open to the elements.

Antonio Briganti's construction crew would not finish the job A Ghost scared them away..

Cory had to appeal to his people. He went to the sweat lodge.

"I am Uj-e-jauk , the Crane . Call able-bodied men from all the totems. Call the man-um-aig, the mong, the Muk-wah, and the waub-ish-ash-e. Call the Addick, the Mah-een-gun and the Ne-baun-aub-ay. Get men from the Be-sheu, the Me-gizzee and the Che-shepgwa. Don't leave out anyone. Call every badge that is known among the Ojibways and ask every Chief amongst them to send their young able-bodied men to help. Let them remember our ancestors and Tug-waug-aun-ay the head chief and tell them that 'The Great Spirit once made a bird , and he sent it from the skies to make its abode on earth. The bird came and it sent forth a loud and far sounding cry , which was heard by all and when that bird chose its resting place it sent forth its loud but solitary cry and all the clans followed and gathered at its call; and now we of the Crane need the clans to come forward and heed our call for help. "

Native Indian workers from all the clans came to finish the Blue Heron .

Meanwhile the police were checking house to

house on Island Road, on Ghost Road and surrounding areas. They went to every house on the Island and discovered the two film students alive and well in the basement of Homer Webb's farmhouse.

They were tied up , hungry but unharmed. Homer Webb confessed to kidnapping but not murder of a construction worker or anyone else.

"I did kidnap those film students to try to stop the casino but I never murdered anyone"

"Then who murdered that construction worker ten years ago? And who murdered and mutilated that body you just found ? I know your left handed and the construction worker was killed by someone left-handed." questioned Police Officer Roger Mitchell.

After five hours of interrogation Homer broke down.

"OK all right. Raeburn Shaw had a partner when he first came to Port Perry ten years ago. Albert Marksted. We were out in the field near Ghost Road surveying and drinking. Shaw was with us and had an argument with Albert. Shaw struck Albert with a rock five or six times to the head , but Albert was not dead, although he was probably almost mortally wounded, so I killed him with a few more blows. Shaw decapitated Albert to make it look like the Ghost Rider and we buried the body and the head. Shaw promised me free rent forever but threatened me that if I told anyone he would say I killed Albert and I would go to jail."

Officer Roger Mitchell then went over to Raeburn Shaw's mansion and in questioning Raeburn Shaw he entrapped him into confessing that he killed Albert Markstead, arrested him and Homer for the killing of the construction worker.

Forty-Three

Jenny Munroe could swear she saw a familiar figure walking down Main Street and as it came closer she recognized Elayne Christofaro, the same Elayne from Boston and the Cape, the same Elayne from Hawaii and *Chocolate Gold.*

" Elayne is that really you? What are you doing in this small town?, many miles from nowhere''
Elayne thought she was hearing things-a voice from the past but a face that had remained the same-yes it was Jenny-her old friend Jenny who had gone off to be a journalist. Elayne spotted the CNN badge with J. Munroe etched in bronze, which confirmed this person in front of hear was Jenny, her former roommate , confidante, marathon runners mate, and all around buddy.

A quick and robust hug and Elayne confirmed to Jenny that, yes, this was her small town. This was where she had grown up, and this was where her roots and future would be.

"Jenny, do you know someone who can solve this Ghost Road Legend?" Elayne asked.

"Yes Elayne, in fact the Para-Researchers that I know could analyze and study the Ghost light, and then make a report and conclusion that might solve the Legend once and for all". Jenny responded.

"Well then get them up here, let's solve this dilemma!"

"OK Elayne, I'll make some phone calls." promised Jenny.

Jenny made some phone calls and four Para-researchers showed up within three days.

Elayne briefed them" The legend goes that in or around 1968 a young man was testing the limits of a motorcycle on an old concession road on Scugog Island. He was on a straightaway pushing the engine as fast as he could. The road is not too long and he soon realized he was running out of road and heading far too fast for the spot where the road meets with the ninth concession. About 100 meters from the South end near a large tree, he lost control, plowed into a field, caught himself on an old rusty barbed wire fence and was decapitated.

Of course we've also heard that he simply banged his head on a rock still located on the road and met his end that way. It is this story that goes along with the report of the large round white light heading down the road that when it passes you, turns into a small red light. There are also occasional reports of the sounds of a motorcycle to accompany the light.

Actually does exist but does not, as reported , travel down the road. It appears above the road and only if facing south. The image has been caught on film but the pictures confirm the fact that the light isn't much to look at. It appears as if it was a small plane some miles in the distance but hovering like a UFO. Some say it is an alien spacecraft that is hovering around and the aliens are so super intelligent and so advanced that they treat humans like we treat ants, so they don't bother communicating with us, and anyway they don't speak our language. Elayne rested for a moment.

"Go on, Elayne. Tell them everything so they can be up to speed and then do their work. They are the best and will solve this, I guarantee it." Stated Jenny.

Elayne continued "Well, even more interesting is that several people who have investigated the haunting have not been able to find any reports of the death of the motorcyclist in any of the local newspapers at the approximate time of the accident. The individuals who were investigating were threatened by a person who stated that he was related to this possibly non-existent motorcyclist and threatened his return to haunt the investigators looking into the lights on ghost road should they not stop their investigation. Luckily this threat went without any serious harm to anyone and the investigators completed some excellent work.

The image of the 'ghost light' will be studied by yourselves and hopefully you will be able to discover it's origin, and for all intents and purposes uncover whether it is a Hoax or real." Elayne concluded.

"We will investigate and present a thorough and conclusive report, stated Dr.Honny Josefson, Manager Para Researchers Inc., a team sponsored by several Universities..

Dr. Honny and her team started the next day, crisscrossed the area, the lakeshore on both sides of the lake, up and down Island road, both at night and during the day, early morning before sunrise, and at end of day; mid-day and mid-night, and after several weeks they were ready with their report.

Mayor Kay Aldred, Baxter Smith, and twenty other interested souls gathered in the library, along with Elayne, Jennie, Cory, and Dr. Honny who presented their report entitled *"Ghost Road a Legend- A Thorough Investigation and Conclusion.*

Dr. Honny read aloud the report" This report is a summary of our observations and research in regards to the ghost light and various other strange phenomena occurring on Scugog Island between the period of October thru December of each year. It also contains our conclusions in regards to the same. Please note that the use of the terms 'spook light', ghost light, 'lights' throughout denote the same phenomena. This report is lengthy so please have patience as it will take some time to dictate.

The light displays witnessed by us include amber, white and red lights. They appear spherical in shape, and the larger amber and white lights are approximately the size of a basketball at approximately one mile distance from the field. The smaller red light, referred to in the legend of Ghost Road as the tail light appears as the size of the larger lights at the same distance."

"We didn't see any red or amber lights" Mayor Kay put in her words.

"Let me continue. From the ½ mile and ¼ mile points on Ghost Road the ghost light appears as one solid light with the naked eye as well as through optical devices such as telescopes, binoculars, etc. Occasionally it appears as if more than one light is merging together to result in a larger light that pulses. The luminosity, frequency of, and duration of the lights vary considerably between each separate observation."

"We need some coffee. Elayne could you get some coffee made?" Asked Mayor Kay.

"Sure no problem" answered Elayne.

Dr. Honny continued" Location and apparent path of the lights seem to follow a set pattern with the occasional variance, such as the light traveling further, and making an erratic movement, not normally sighted. The red light usually follows directly behind the larger white and amber lights and has been observed on several occasions independent of those other lights. We have observed the light phenomena during different weather and visibility conditions such as fog, snowstorms, rain, severe thunderstorms, cloudy and clear sky conditions without any apparent bearing on the display of lights.

With the possible exception to the previous statement being the increase and frequency of light displays during intense electrical activity overhead and increased humidity. We have observed a light exit the field, race up the road, in an apparent attraction to the location of an impending lightning strike."

"Sounds an awful like alien spaceships moving around" stated Elayne.

"Well, these observations were made with both the naked eye and while using binoculars. We have deemed this a separate event from the 'ghost light' and speculate that this may have in fact been ball lightning. Different phases of the moon do not have an effect on the appearance, behavior of the lights either. We have observed both a slow fading out of, and a quick wink out with the eventual disappearance of the lights. The light phenomenon has been observed from the one mile mark on Ghost

Road and the two mile mark. Attempts to view the light from the crossroads of Pine Point and Ghost road have been unsuccessful.

No sounds are connected with the display of lights. We feel that sounds such as a motorcycle revving, native drumbeats, etc. occasionally mentioned by other witnesses are the simple, and wholly understandable misidentification of the natural sound made by pheasants, which we have heard frequently during our observations on 'Ghost Road'. The sound of horses galloping within nearby fields may also result in this type of misidentification.

Observations in an attempt to gauge a pet dog's reaction to the ghost light and location in general remain inconclusive."

"So, you're saying dogs don't notice the light." Jenny said.

"Right".

"Now the time frame for the first appearance of the light phenomena varies considerably depending on the source of information. The earliest date recorded so far comes from a notation contained within the diary of an early resident of Scugog Island, which refers to ghost lights occurring on Devil's Light Island, which dates to the late 1800's."

"Doesn't that rule out light coming from a headless motorcycle driver, who supposedly died in the 1950s?" Elayne asked.

That reference to ghost lights implies a possible connection to some of the light phenomena reported at the Ghost Road location, however our efforts to find any supporting documents, which contain similar references from the same time period did not yield any corroborating information.

This in conjunction with the fact that there would be no living witnesses from that time period leaves the possibility of 'ghost lights' occurring on the island during the 19th century as speculative only.

The latest possible date in regards to first reports of the light phenomena is 1979. This date was obtained by a newspaper clipping of an article featured in the Port Perry Star on the mystery lights that we were able to locate at the Port Perry Public Library."

"Doesn't that correspond with the time they say the careless motorcycle driver got beheaded?" asked Jenny.

"Well maybe but we feel that the legend surrounding the ghost lights on Ghost Road is simply that, an urban legend. Similar stories accompany the display of spook lights worldwide and suggest a common folklore/myth."

"What about Alien spacecraft" Elayne inquired."Maybe the same aircraft are making the same lights appear at different places all over the world."

"Possibly" responded Dr.Honny."We are however not concerned with what has happened in other parts of the world, even if events are similar, we have analyzed what has transpired here, and this is our detailed Scientific Analysis as to what we think has happened here in Port Perry.

We also learned that the area long before becoming an Island was the scene of tribal warfare between the Mohawks and Ojibwa tribes. It was also the location of a well-travelled Native foot path. There have been many artefacts, including Native remains unearthed in the immediate region. Recent visits to the location in the company of two 'sensitives' of Native ancestry , whom we work with and consult with often, suggest that this may have some bearing on the reports of possible paranormal events other than the 'ghost light'."

"What? Now we're getting possible paranormal stuff mixed in here!" Cory questioned.

"We check everything. Every possibility. Every happening. That's what we do. That's why people and organizations hire us. We are very thorough, and we report on every possibility, and rule out some, and except others, and question some, and don't understand others. Anyway let me continue." Dr. Honny went on with her report.

"As Jenny brought it up, let's talk about the timing as to when the ghost light started to be noticed. In July 1983 Cathy Robb, a journalist with the Port Perry Star, interviewed retired Police Officer Harold Hockins who had policed Scugog Island since 1954. He was able to confirm with her that no motorcycle accidents or otherwise that resulted in a fatality had occurred in the vicinity of Ghost Road during that time period. There are no police records, hospital records, obituaries , nor news clippings that would support the legend as an actual historical event.

Now let's review the possibility of reflecting car headlights. We had been informed that a well watched television news program ran an episode on the light phenomena of Ghost Road several years ago and that one theory suggested by the program as a possible explanation for the phenomena was reflecting car headlights from Shirley Road and the West Quarter Line. This proved to be false as we contacted the program producers and they denied that they had ever produced such a report and stated there was never any filming done nor any report ever aired.

We have conducted various experiments involving car headlights, from the highest elevation of the W. Quarter Line , 4 miles to the south, and Ma Browns Road, located 2 miles to the south. These experiments involving both high and low beams, and brake lights failed to reproduce the light phenomena seen from Ghost Road during all attempts, with the exception of our last experiment."

"Oh Tell us what happened. This might tell us the answer we at waiting for!" Elayne declared.

"Well the monitoring of traffic on these roads by us also proved inconclusive, but is irrelevant at this time." Dr. Honny stated. "We feel that this unsupported (by our experiments) hypothesis may be relevant to reports of light phenomena other than the consistent 'ghost light' due to Scugog Island's close proximity to an active geological fault line and geophysical makeup."

"I'm getting dizzy with all this hypothesis stuff!" Mayor Kay said, a little impatient with this report.

"Ok let's discuss the fact that we have seen hoaxes attempted on Ghost Road and within the field on two separate occasions involving the use of flashlights". Dr. Honny pointed out. "These along with our own flashlight failed to reproduce the light display. However, this could potentially account for some reports made by those who make one time visits to the road and are unsure of exactly what the 'ghost light' appears like."

"I'll bet you it's Homer Webb, being directed By Raeburn Shaw, who has been trying to stop construction of our casino all these years. Homer is crazy, and I wouldn't put it past him to be using flashlights, or any type of light to imitate the Ghost Light so he can scare the Heebe-jeebies out of people, and any construction workers that we hire." Cory pointed out.

"Some other strange happenings have been uncovered that occurred on Ghost Road." Dr. Honny started up again." Cars being pulled backwards and forwards have been reported on Ghost Road and Compass readings and the use of an EMF detector taken at various locations on the road and the edge of the field including underneath the Poltergeist Tree have shown nothing out of the norm.

However."

"Oh Oh. There's a however!" Elayne remarked.

"However, the vicinity of most of these occurrences was identified as a 'ley line' by our colleagues who are 'sensitives' and whom were not privy to this information beforehand. A sighting of a possible 'being' of some sorts on Ghost Road' was made by one of our members, which defies a proper explanation at this point in time."

"I knew it. I knew it. The Ghost Rider is there. He's really there!" yelled out Cory with conviction.

Dr. Honny explained further." Our member was the sole witness and factors of misidentification, heightened anxiety due to the circumstances cannot be ruled out. However, it is interesting to note that a young women, whom we interviewed on the road a couple of weeks later, was able to corroborate many of the details of our member's sightings without prior knowledge of the event."

Cory interrupted. "See. I knew it. He's there! I will share with you a little secret- Elayne and I have been on Ghost Road ourselves and had an encounter with the Ghost Rider".

"Let me tell you about a large infamous rock located on the southeast corner of the road" Dr. Honny continued. "A part of the legend of 'Ghost Road' involves that rock and legend states that if you sit on the rock, you will be thrown off by unseen hands and/or become violently ill. We have personally tested this out on numerous occasions without incident. Our two 'sensitives' also stated they received no 'feelings' from the rock either-and further stated they felt "it's just a rock".

"Elayne, it's time for some more coffee, and how about bringing in those muffins, I'm starving, what with all this Ghost talk, sensitives, sightings, a possible being, and other strange happenings all on Ghost Road!" stated Baxter Smith, who had been , not normal for him, quiet all this time during the reporting."Frankly, I don't believe any of this!"

"I'll get more coffee." Elayne responded, and excited quickly.

"Mr. Smith, please accept the fact that my colleagues and I have spent weeks investigating and looking under every rock and crevice to attempt to find the answer everyone is anxious to find, and we are just pointing out each and every possibility so that we as human beings, and some of us Scientists, can be logical and decide, from the evidence before us, who or what is making those god darn lights move and grove. So please refrain from making those comments and listen to our conclusion. Thank you." Dr. Honny seemed annoyed , exhausted , and perhaps with all the research did not find a logical answer, and was upset with Rev. Baxter Smith, who might be right on the money after all.

Dr. Honny sipped some fresh coffee, took a bite out of a chocolate-chip , banana/ mango muffin, and gave her conclusion. " We have researched and observed the ghost lights of Ghost Road and other various strange reports for a period of several weeks, and others before us viewed strange happenings over a period of fifteen months and reported to us , and all the reports are as of today.

Our failure to reproduce the 'spook light's during controlled experiments on all, but our last visit had led us to believe that factors other than reflecting car headlights were in fact the true origin of the 'mystery lights'. We also had believed that all credible reports of anomalous light phenomena shared the same origin and cause with the consistent reports of 'ghost lights' and that other phenomena would also be associated. Similar unusual experiences are associated with occurrences of 'ghost lights' and their various names throughout the world. This is not the case and these should have been treated separately.

However our experiments conducted recently and detailed here prove that the 'ghost light' enigma is indeed solvable if not the other more unusual reports at this time. Vehicle lights travelling downhill at a specific location on the W. Quarter line and refracting over the moist air above Lake Scugog are viewed as the 'ghost lights' from the ¼ mile and ½ mile marks on 'Ghost Road'.

Differing traffic conditions at this specific location of the W. Q line and weather conditions contribute to the differences in appearance of the 'ghost lights'. Example is High Beams would be used more often on the W. Q line during storm conditions. Any reports received of 'ghost lights' witnessed at the intersection of Mississauga's and Pine Point or physically on the 'Ghost Road' itself are not attributed to the previous explanation and therefore should be treated as separate events as already explained previously."

"I'm really mixed up and dizzy. This is making me sick." Mayor Kay remarked.

"You're not the only one" repeated Baxter Smith.

Dr. H continued , despite the remarks. "We have received many reports of possible paranormal activity on the 'Ghost Road' including those made by our own team. The location is famed for it's known party atmosphere, and coupled with the increased anxiety of individuals on the road due to the popular legend, we believe a large percentage of these reports occur due to these and other natural reasons. It is also our opinion that a small percentage may in fact have a genuine preternatural origin, but for obvious reasoning this is pure speculation on our part."

"Well Elayne and I went there , and there was no partying. In fact Elayne didn't even let me put my arm around her!" Cory pointed out.

"Let me finish by telling you the following" Dr. H continued." One of the strangest, and to date unexplained stories that our team uncovered when interviewing an Island resident was her telling us about her Great Great grandmother who was born on Scugog Island. Her Great Great Grandmother was born on December 7, 1858 and lived next to Thompson's Farm which was near the so called haunted field. The interview was early in our mandate and we took little notice until we completed our investigation.

It's possible the haunting was noted in the 1850's, then a motorcycle, may be another part of the legend, now it only takes a complete research to find out just how long the haunting has been around.

The resident we interviewed told us that she had a direct ancestor who was born on Scugog Island, her Great Great Grandmother, and now get this, there was a note left by her Great Great Grandmother that no one could explain; and I say until now."

Everyone was listening very carefully. Elayne and Cory starred at Dr. H. Mayor Kay and Baxter Smith leaned forward in their chairs and studied Dr. H's lips, in case their elderly hearing failed them. The other twenty or so persons in the library sucked in their breath and no one moved.

"What the Island resident told us was, as we know, her Great Great Grandmother was born in the 1850's, and her ancestor left a handwritten notation with the family papers, that she was born on......
The island of the "devil" lights. No other mention was ever made, nor has any ever been found as to who made the notation or when the original notation was made, possibly in the late 1800's?"

Dr. H continued. " This was our first group investigation and a valuable learning experience for all of us. We would like to give a special thank you to all of those who have contacted us and who talked to us on Ghost Road and shared their experiences. We also wish to thank those fellow investigators who shared their expertise with us, and those friends who accompanied us to the location; and perhaps most importantly the town of Port Perry and residents of Scugog Island."

Dr. Honny Josefson sat down, exhausted after completing her extensive report, which explained a lot, detailed a lot, but left a lot unexplained. Cory thought how is it that the mysterious moving light could be seen over 150 years ago, yet described as being attributed to a motorcycle rider, beheaded maybe 50 years ago. The audience clapped their approval of the hard work and research done by Dr. H and her associates. Mayor Kay thanked Dr. H for her extensive and detailed work and report. Rev. Baxter Smith muttered "hogwash" as he walked out of the library.

Elayne and Cory held hands as they went out the back door of the library and down to the beach beside Lake Scugog. Jenny followed but respected their wanting to be together and alone, and keep a distance behind, sitting on a park bench before entering the beach. Nightfall was approaching, and Jenny could see the mirror image of the sun setting in the west just over and past the town of Port Perry, reflected in Lake Scugog, with golden streaks of light crossing the lake connecting the image of the sun with the opposite shore. Two large Canadian Geese were flying together , rising up from the bulrushes on the far shore, as if they were husband and wife, travelling together to some far away land.

Forty-Four

Great Aunt Sara was the first to sense what happened and she woke up screaming, and yelled out in sadness.

"Oh No! Gitchie Manitou has taken him, but he has not died-he is only changing his world."

It was early morning and as she ran out of her house, out onto the main street ,dogs were running playfully around her, and the fog was still sitting like a slight mist just clinging to the bulrushes along the shore of Lake Scugog. She knocked on the Chief's door even though she knew there would be no answer. She ran down to the community centre , pushed open the screen door, and pushed open the door with a glass window that had a crack running diagonally across it. She grabbed the old black phone and dialed Cory's number.

Ring, Ring, Ring. Cory woke up from a deep sleep and reached for the phone. He thought who would be calling this early in the morning.

Great Aunt Sara was in tears. "Cory, your Grandfather has changed worlds. His earthly body has ceased to be. I hope the Heavenly Father ,who looks down upon us, will give us all his blessing, and that he will take care of your Grandfather, our former Chief, and that he will bless you, our new

Chief."

"Great Aunt, how do you know this?" Cory asked, wiping the sleep from his eyes.

"I know. A Spirit came to me in the night, A bird swopped down from its' resting place and sat outside my cabin and spat out the news. I checked your Grandfathers' house and he did not answer." Replied Great Aunt Sara.

"Great Aunt stay where you are. I will check myself, and after come to see you." Cory stated.

Cory , already up got dressed, splashed some water on his face, grabbed some juice, and ran out the door down to his Grandfather's place.

He couldn't open the door, and after knocking and banging on the door, without success he had no choice but to smash the door handle with a rock that was handy, and twist the handle and enter.

Darkness flooded the room. Blankets covered the three windows as Cory carefully worked his way over to the wall and pulled one blanket off the window which immediately let enough daylight in so that Cory could then make out the furniture , couch, and table scattered around the room. He made his way to the rear bedroom, pushed aside the blanket acting as a door, and starred at the small bed nestled in a corner at the back of the small room. A room big enough only to be able to contain one single bed, a small dresser, and a rocking chair sitting still against a window. A small television sat on the dresser resembling a small box sitting on a larger box, encased in a box sized room.

Cory approached the wrapped up figure perched on the bed, and immediately could see his Grandfather with the bedding tight up to his neck and lying on his back with his face upward and eyes closed.

Cory leaned over and put his face close and did not see any breath or his Grandfather moving and appeared not to be breathing. Cory put his hand on his Grandfather's mouth and could feel no breath.

Tears began to trickle down Cory's cheeks as he retreated first from the bedroom, and then from the cabin. The full emotional hit had not overcome him yet. He ran down to the community centre where he guessed Great Aunt Sara was, as that was the only place around with a phone. He entered the centre and viewed Great Aunt Sara lying on a bench apparently sleeping. He reached for the phone and called for the ambulance.

It was verified that the Chief had passed away, probably in his sleep, and a Native Indian funeral was scheduled for four days after. The women cleaned the body and dressed it in special clothing.

Put deerskin moccasins on the feet. The body was wrapped in birch bark to protect it from harm. Food and water were being prepared to be with the body to help the soul travel to the afterlife. The tribe believed that the soul embarks on a four-day journey to a special place after dying. There will be prayers and singing by the living during the four-day time period. Great Aunt Sara knew all the traditions.

"Cory, a spirit may not want to journey to the afterlife alone. You are his family so make a paper snake of birch and hang it by the front door of his cabin. We believe that spirits are fearful of snakes and by displaying this symbol we will let them know they can journey alone. A spirit may also communicate with family through dreams. If they ask for supplies in the dream, then you must honor that request. If they ask for someone living to come with them, it is acceptable to say no."

The funeral was held on open ground beside the community centre. Everyone in the community attended. Mayor Kay Aldred, Rev. Baxter Smith, Raeburn Shaw, out on bail, also were in attendance. Cory sat in the front row dressed in traditional Ojibway ceremonial costume, with Elayne at his side, rubbing his shoulders and comforting him. Jenny and a few reporters sat a few rows back.

The body, which had rested near the cabin for four days to allow the spirits to leave, was transported in a wagon pulled by a black horse. Horses were revered by the people, respected and loved. The black horse, named Blackie was loved by the Chief, and Blackie, in turn , was showing his love for the Chief by bringing him to the body's resting place.

Ceremonial drums were being beaten to make contact with the Creator and send the deceased to the spirit world. Tobacco pipes were lit and passed around as an offer to the spirits to request special care for this community member travelling to the spirit world.

"Cory, some of the communities children are here in respect for your Grandfather, The Chief." Great Aunt Sara explained. "Of course their foreheads are painted black to signal the spirits they will not go with them to the afterlife. They are told to avoid eye contact with people in case the spirit tries to speak to them through someone else."

Cory could hear his Great Aunt but he was really not paying attention. His head was bowed, and he was full of sorrow. His Grandfather had been everything to him since he was five years old. A Father, a Mother, a Grandfather. A teacher, a friend, a confidant. Tough as a General yes, but also compassionate, and a teacher of the Native ways.

Great Aunt Sara read the Ojibway Prayer written on a birchbark scroll.

"Great Spirit, whose voice I hear in the winds,
and whose breath gives life to everyone, Hear me
for my brother comes to you as one of your many
children, and he is weak and small and needs your
wisdom and your strength. Let him walk in beauty,

and make his eyes ever behold the red and purple sunsets. Let his hands respect the things you have made, and make his ears sharp so he may hear your voice. Make him wise, so he may understand what you have taught to our people and the lesson you have hidden in each leaf and each rock. He asks for wisdom and strength, not to be superior to his brothers, but be able to fight his greatest enemy, himself. Make him ever ready to come before you with clean hands and a straight eye.

So as life fades away like the fading sunset so may his spirit come to you without shame."

The food that had been brought by all community members was shared by the attendees. Fish, wild rice, venison, macaroni, and was offered to the spirit as a way of the mourners sharing a meal with the spirit. The community leaders carried the coffin out the back of the building and laid the coffin to rest in the spirit house built by the family to honor the deceased. One opening faced west, and offerings were left near the opening. One opening faced East with offerings left near the door, which was cigarettes that the Chief had enjoyed during his stay on earth. A traditional travelling song was being sung by four of the community.

Cory thanked everyone who attended. Shook Raeburn Shaws' hand, and patted Mayor Kay's shoulder. He expressed his thanks to Jenny, and with Elayne at his side, helped Great Aunt Sara walk back to her house. After she was safely in he moved slowly to his own shack and said to Elayne " I don't think I can be alone thru the night tonight. I fear Ghosts and Spirits and such demons will come to me and I will be afraid."

"Cory, I will stay with you tonight. I will be with you and I will comfort you. You are my spirit, and I am yours. We both were hunting for our spirit most of our lives, and it appears we have both found our spirits." Elayne spoke softly with emotion." Cory look at the sunset over the lake, how beautiful it is, and be thankful for this day, and for the day tomorrow, for the Sun will rise again tomorrow and there will be a new day, with new experiences."

Cory opened the door, and as they both entered the shack he felt warmth and love emanating from Elayne's body next to his. He indeed had high hopes for tomorrow and the coming tomorrows.

Forty-Five

The Great Blue Heron Charity Casino was set for its' official opening the next day and Jenny was deep in thought as to what and how she was going to report, live on CNN about the opening. The night was brisk but she was exhausted and fell asleep on the bench; only to wake up at dawn the next morning.

"This is Jenny Munroe of CNN covering the grand opening of a Charity Casino. The Casino is officially called The Great Blue Heron Casino and will benefit The Mississauga of Scugog Island. Mayor Kay Aldred of nearby Port Perry says that her town might enjoy some spinoff business and if it goes well they might get a new hotel out of it and she expects the majority of casino business will be from out- of- towners. Mississauga Band Chief says the project will have economic benefits for the entire region. It will create more than 200 jobs. This past week workers have been busy installing the multi colored dome roof over the bingo hall and casino areas."

"Reverend Baxter Smith. Do you have a blessing for the new casino?"

"Yes, We are very excited about this project. The casino will generate tremendous interest and provide benefits not only for the First Nation, but for the entire community. If the casino is successful then the entire community will benefit. They will return to be masters of their own fate and will once again control their destiny and they will truly be the First Nation."

Jenny Munroe asks Great Aunt Sara " Do you have a blessing or a message that you would like to share with us today?"

"Miss Munroe, Big Thunder (Bedagi) who was Wabanaki Algonquin, in the late 19th Century cried out to the Spirits as follows:

"THE GREAT SPIRIT IS IN ALL THINGS;
HE IS IN THE AIR WE BREATHE. THE GREAT SPIRIT IS OUR FATHER, BUT THE EARTH IS OUR MOTHER. SHE NOURISHES US, THAT WHICH WE PUT INTO THE GROUND SHE RETURNS TO US"....and then Great Aunt Sara added "Go Out and treat each other like brothers and sisters of one father and one mother, with the sky above us and one country around us, and we will have no more wars."

William Wolfe

One Year Later

The headline in the Port Perry Star read
'Modern Icabod Crane Hoax'.

The Great Blue Heron Casino has been open almost
a year and players were gathered in the casino. The
first snow had fallen in October and Halloween was
here again. Port Perry was quiet. A wolf 's howl
could be heard from somewhere out in the woods.
Crickets' noise could be distinguished from any
other noise as dusk was approaching.

Cory and Elayne were sitting in Cory's
Honda on   Ghost Road.

The Ghost light appears, coming closer and closer.
A motorcycle's loud engine sound appears.
The bright Ghost light engulfs everything!

The End

Star reporter off to find the ghost

by Cathy Robb

Oh yah, fer sure, hey I'm no dummy. Ghosts, eh John? Been working too hard now that Pete's on vacation?

Shucks no, sez John B. McClelland, editor and full-time cynic at the Star office. John's so cynical that he hates cats, doesn't believe in vitamins and thinks Santa Claus was invented by Revenue Canada. Stems from too many Regional Council meetings.

But here he is, grinning behind his glasses about some mysterious light on Scugog Island. Supposed to be the ghost of a kid killed on a motorbike.

"I think I've seen it," he says carefully. "Or something".

Folks claim there was a bad accident on the island 12 or maybe 17 years ago (nobody's exactly sure) on a lonely stretch of road running north-south between the ninth and tenth Concessions. There are no houses on it, no lights, a great spot for the romantically inclined to park and watch the stars or for a young man with a yen for speed to push his motorcycle to the limit.

Legend has it he was a youngish man with the initial R, probably between 18 and 22. His biggest downfall was being out of town and not knowing the local road well enough to travel as fast as he did that night. Speed, you

(Turn to page 6)

Officer hired

Gerald Gervais, 39, has been hired by Durham Region as commissioner for economic development at an an-

He will be in charge of a department which now has two development officers and one secretary, and his job will be to pro-

Building permi

Reporter on trail of the island ghost

(From page 1)

...ter, was his weakness. The faster this boy could go, the better.

One night, sometime between dusk and midnight, the boy was killed in a crash. Psychics say he was southbound down the deserted road, relaxed in spite of the high speed, enjoying the darkness. Too relaxed, he didn't see that the road ended at the ninth Concession. Too late, he tried swerving to avoid the fence dividing the road from a neighbour's corn field.

Without slowing he struck the fence and was instantly decapitated.

And now his ghost rides the road on which he was killed, every night, still loving his bike and the sensation of speed.

At least that's the story. What people claim to see is a bright, white light that appears in the cornfield and travels north along the road to a certain point where it disappears and is replaced by a red light which seems to return whence it came.

The white light is supposed to resemble the single beam of an old-fashioned motorcycle headlamp. The red light has been described as a motorcycle tail-light.

"I'm not afraid of the white light but I don't like the red light because you never know

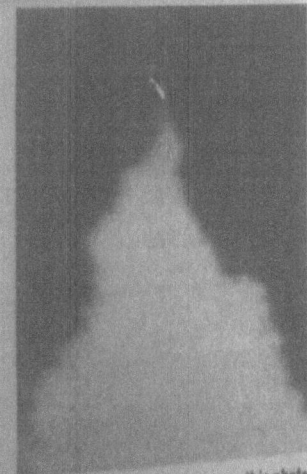

For those sceptics among us, this photo proves once and for all that there is a mysterious light on Scugog Island. This is an ...retouched photograph of the road

appears under the shade of a large tree close to the ninth Concession. It's the spot where the biker supposedly first realized the sideroad was ending. However, the red light doesn't confine itself to one spot. It has also been known to appear further north, often directly in front of the cars that park along the road.

On some nights, the stretch of road has been crammed with motorists from all over who come to catch the glimpse of the ghost light. Mrs. Kane says she has seen as many as 17 cars, overflowing with party-goers looking for a cheap thrill.

She claims the red light has chased more than one car from one end of the road to the other, terrifying the people inside. After all, there's no noise attached to these lights. No shapes. No white sheets.

here?"

"Don't talk about ghosts," I said quickly, childishly. It was a bright, clear night with a moon that was nearly full, throwing long black shadows across the empty fields. Even though we were there to see a ghost, I didn't want to talk about it. Paul sensed my apprehension and gave me a hug.

Feeling reassured, I sat up and looked out the window. And screamed.

A single white light was shining from down near the end of the road. It lasted a second and then disappeared.

"Did you see that!" I shrieked, pointing wildly down the road.

"See what?"

"The light! It was there! It was..."

Without warning the light appeared again, brighter than before, seemingly closer to our car. Silently I began...

struck the fence and was instantly decapitated.

And now his ghost rides the road on which he was killed, every night, still loving his bike and the sensation of speed.

At least that's the story. What people claim to see is a bright, white light that appears in the cornfield and travels north along the road to a certain point where it disappears and is replaced by a red light which seems to return whence it came.

The white light is supposed to resemble the single beam of an old-fashioned motor-cycle headlamp. The red light has been des-cribed as a motorcycle tail-light.

"I'm not afraid of the white light but I don't like the red light because you never know where it's going to show up," says Island resident Allene Kane, a woman who has report-edly seen the light many times over the years.

Most often, she explains, the red light

the ninth Concession. It's the spot where the biker supposedly first realized the sideroad was ending. However, the red light doesn't confine itself to one spot. It has also been known to appear further north, often directly in front of the cars that park along the road.

On some nights, the stretch of road has been crammed with motor-ists from all over who come to catch the glimpse of the ghost light. Mrs. Kane says she has seen as many as 17 cars, overflowing with party-goers looking for a cheap thrill.

She claims the red light has chased more than one car from one end of the road to the other, terrifying the people inside. After all, there's no noise attach-ed to these lights. No shapes. No white sheets. Just the lights which come and go on an irregular basis.

"It's scared the devil out of me, the first time I saw it," Mrs. Kane recalls. "I went there specifically but I didn't know what I was looking for other than a light."

ghost," I said childishly. It bright, clear a a moon that wa hill, throwing in shadows acr empty fields, though we were see a ghost, want to talk Paul sensed my hension and ga hug.

Feeling reas sat up and looke window. And so

A single whi was shining fro near the end of It lasted a sec then disappeare

"Did you see shrieked, point ly down the roa

"See what?"

"The light there! It was...

Without war light appeare brighter than seemingly clos car. Silently God or some there to stop from coming c

"See? See?"

Wide-eyed, P

I couldn't tell long we wait light. It could five seconds, more, maybe abruptly the w

GHOST STORY

-Cathy Robb, Port Perry Star, Tuesday, July 28, 1983

"Oh yah, fer sure, hey I'm no dummy. Ghosts, eh John? Been working too hard now that Pete's on vacation?" "Shucks no," sez John B. McClelland, editor and half-time cynic at The Star office. Here he is behind his glasses about some mysterious light on Scugog Island. Supposed to be the ghost of a kid killed on a motorbike. "I think I've seen it" he says carefully" or something". But what he can't explain is the white light. He admits it was not, could not possibly be a car going by, or swamp gas or anything else. "But it's not a ghost" he says flatly."Since 'our sighting' I've been trying to develop some satisfactory explanations for the light. Swamp gas? Reflections? Pranks? Or a real live (or should I say dead) honest-to-goodness ghost? If you've got any ideas, give John a call.

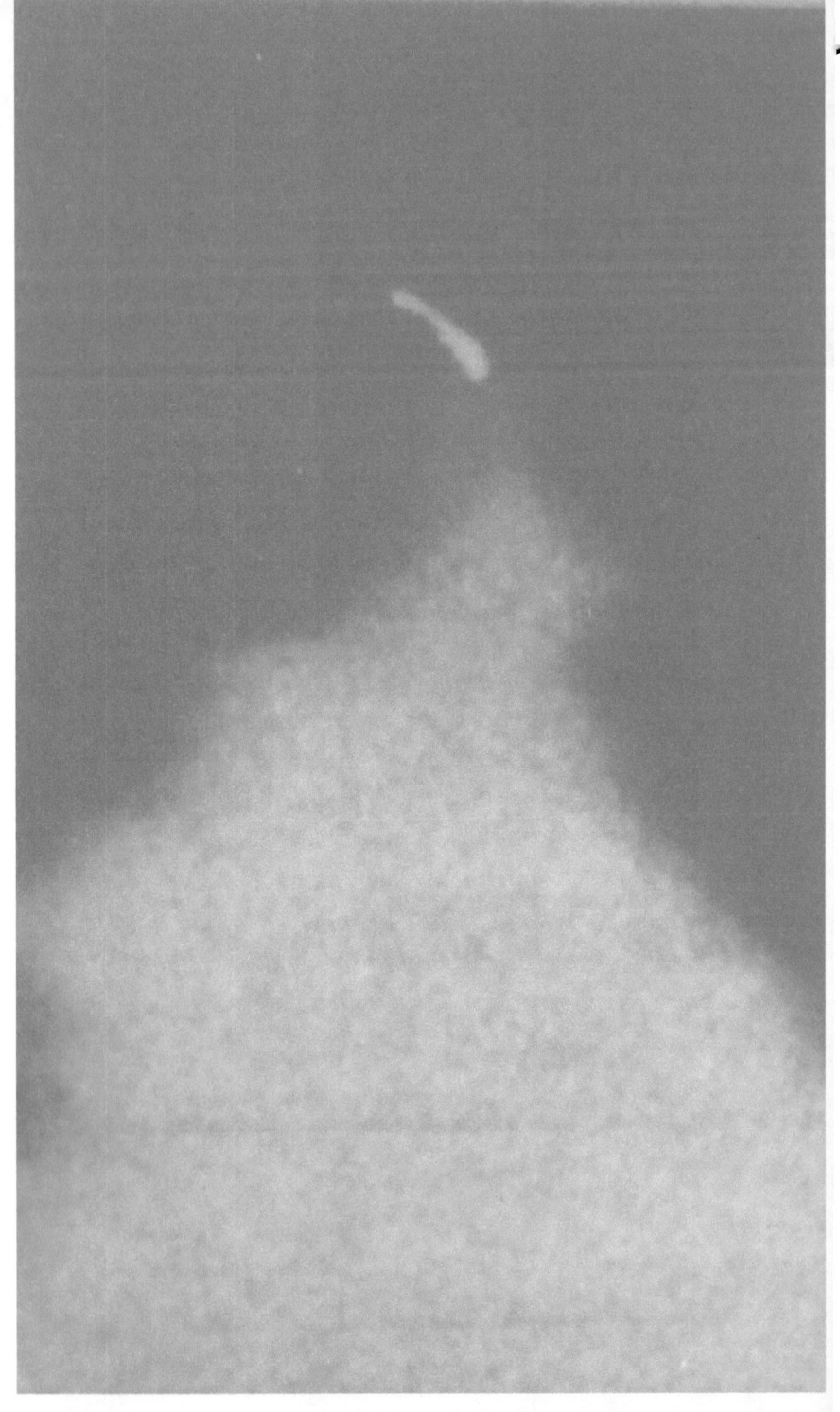

"For those sceptics among us, this photo opposite page proves once and for all that there is a mysterious light on Scugog Island. This is an actual, unretouched photograph of the road that joins the ninth and tenth concessions. Taken at approximately 10 P.M. on a Sunday night, with a hand-held camera (film exposed approximately three seconds), the black is the trees and sky, the grey is the moonlit road and the small white streak at the top is the so-called ghost rider (ooh, scarey, kids).

EPILOGUE

In this work of fiction, the characters, places and events are either the product of the author's imagination or they are entirely fictitious or they are based on true events but altered to be presented in a fashion that can be told in a manner that the reader can understand, enjoy, and absorb.

The *Great Blue Heron Casino* was built, and the Mississauga to this day are enjoying the fruits of their labor. Some of the passages in this novel were taken from outside sources, with names or events altered, and the Author thanks those sources which proved useful in the eventual telling of the complete story.

Each Author has a unique perspective and a different way of putting a story down on paper which we seek, by our way of looking at the world, and the events around us, to communicate to the interested reader who we hope will be enriched by the work and be able to travel to other parts of the world through the vivid descriptions of the Author, and in using Author's license the reader, who is the ultimate critic, can thoroughly enjoy the work from page one through to the end, and say" Wow, that was a great read!".

Every effort has been made to trace original authors of some works and obtain permission to allow the reprint of extracts and some are in the public domain. Excerpts and references were taken from the following:

Frommer's Hawaii
Internet reports on Trial of Murder in Michigan
Alexis Sclamberg's Blog on Hawaiian Sunset
Blessings For a Marriage by James Dillet Freeman
Miss Me But Let Me Go from Mana'olana Pink Paddlers
Para-Researchers of Ontario Ghost Road Report
Ghost Storey by Cathy Robb-Port Perry Star

William Wolfe

William Wolfe is the *Nom de Plume* of Michael W. Ostroff who studied at Montreal Museum of Fine Arts Art School when Arthur Lismer of the Group of Seven was Principal and one of his teachers. Michael always had a love of storytelling and *The Spirit Hunter* is his first novel, although the outline was put on paper more than seven years ago.

Michael W. Ostroff lives with his wife in Toronto, Canada, enjoys his three children, their spouses, and his six grandchildren; is busy at work on his 2nd novel, and has outlines for many more.

As William Wolfe he can be found on the web at www.williamwolfeauthor.com

William Wolfe